EVERYMAN, I will go with thee,

and be thy guide,

In thy most need to go by thy side

EDMUND SPENSER

Born about 1552 in East Smithfield, London.
M.A. Cambridge in 1576. Obtained place in
Leicester's household. Went to Ireland with
Lord Grey de Wilton, 1580, and lived there
until 1598. Died in Westminster in 1599, and
buried in Westminster Abbey.

EDMUND SPENSER

The Shepherd's Calendar and Other Poems

EDITED WITH AN INTRODUCTION BY
PHILIP HENDERSON

DENT: LONDON
EVERYMAN'S LIBRARY
DUTTON: NEW YORK

*All rights reserved
Printed in Great Britain by
Biddles Ltd, Guildford, Surrey
and bound at the
Aldine Press · Letchworth · Herts
for*
J. M. DENT & SONS LTD
*Aldine House · Albemarle Street · London
This edition was first published in
Everyman's Library in 1932
Last reprinted 1975*

*Published in the U.S.A. by arrangement
with J. M. Dent & Sons Ltd*

No. 879 Hardback ISBN 0 460 00879 X

INTRODUCTION

I

THE existing portraits of Spenser represent him as a man whose noble height of brow and resolute nose are somewhat contradicted by an irritable and discontented mouth. The eyes regard the world with cold disapproval.

Indeed, Spenser was ever a disdainful critic of men and affairs, and there is no doubt that he considered himself ill requited. One of the great men of his age, he raised England poetically from the almost insignificant position into which she had fallen since the death of Chaucer to that of a major power among the nations. For this, his reward was virtual exile to Ireland, and a small pension that, according to some accounts, was not regularly paid. Certainly he was recognized as The Prince of Poets in his Time, but then praise tends to take on a hollow note when unaccompanied by more substantial rewards.

It may be that Elizabeth I. herself, while recognizing his qualities, did not altogether like this "little man with little bands and little cuffs," for all his fantastic flattery of her. After all, Spenser was quite a sharp critic of her reign, and although his grievances were spoken covertly by shepherds, or public ills pointed to in the allegorical doings of foxes and apes, it did not need very much perspicacity to unravel such parables. And he had already made an enemy of Burghley by his satire, *Mother Hubbard's Tale*, where there was little chance of that minister mistaking the intended identity of the fox. But in the *Prothalamion* he no longer makes any attempt to hide his feelings under parables. He writes of himself as:

> When I (whom sullen care,
> Through discontent of my long fruitless stay
> In prince's court, and expectation vain
> Of idle hopes, which still do fly away,
> Like empty shadows, did afflict my brain),
> Walked forth to ease my pain
> Along the shore of silver-streaming Thames. . . .

vi   INTRODUCTION

And this was upon his second return from Ireland in 1595, even after the publication of the second three books of the *Faery Queen*, and within four years of his death.

It is evident that Spenser had hoped for some high position at court suitable to his merits; or he may have seen himself as a man of action and sometimes dreamed of performing deeds upon the high seas like Essex and Ralegh; or imagined himself marching beneath the banner of Sidney, that "parfit knight," in the Lowlands, though the thought of the poet engaged in any of these activities is incongruous. His nature was as delicately balanced, his temperament as finely spun, as his verse; he was idealistic in the extreme; and neither in a court where the precepts of Machiavelli were as assiduously followed as those of Castiglione, nor upon the seas, of which he was terrified, would Spenser have attained such a full and perfect self-expression as he did in poetry. But that he had proved himself efficient in practical life we know, for upon his being recommended by Elizabeth as a prospective Sheriff of Cork in 1595, we find him described in the royal letters as "a gentleman so well known unto you for all his good and commendable parts . . . and not unskilful or without experience in the wars."

Nevertheless, one feels that the real world for Spenser was that of his poetry, the poetry of the *Faery Queen*, the *Epithalamion*, and the Platonic *Hymns*, rather than of the satires where, not being able to see the external world in the terms of his ideality, he rebelled against it, became bitter and discontented. Knowing, and having known, the essence of life, to concentrate upon the mechanism of material cause and effect must have seemed to him as tedious as a twice-told tale. But that is a malady common to poets. The world is there, and must be dealt with if we are to live in it. And if Spenser never really succeeded in living in the world of men as Shakespeare did, he compromised by embracing the Neoplatonism then fashionable in Europe, and that enabled him to regard all sensual beauty, and especially the beauty of women, as an aspect of virtue and therefore divine. This belief is most sweetly and succinctly expressed in the following stanza from the *Hymn in Honour of Beauty*:

> So every spirit, as it is most pure,
> And hath in it the more of heavenly light,
> So it the fairer body doth procure
> To habit in, and it more fairly dight

> With cheerful grace and amiable sight.
> For of the soul the body form doth take:
> For soul is form, and doth the body make.

In this way Spenser was able to satisfy both the longings of his blood and of his spirit, by elevating the one to the sphere of the other. With him, as Professor Legouis has remarked,[1] making love to a beautiful woman thus became a delightful way of honouring God. And certainly in this hymn he has given us the purest and noblest expression of the Platonic ideal of love in our poetry. It is just this admixture of the sensuous artist and the celestial idealist in him that produced that quality in his poetry which is the most truly Spenserian, a quality that being the inevitable expression of his nature as a poet is his alone, and one that not a single imitator of him has ever been able to reproduce.

It is as the moralist, distinct from the idealist, that Spenser is least interesting; and although there can be no doubt as to the moral basis of his work, his sentiments in this respect, as W. B. Yeats has suggested,[2] always seem more of an official attitude than a truly personal one. Thus we have the rather priggish remarks of Piers, the Puritan moralist, in the fifth eclogue of the *Shepherd's Calendar*, censuring the May-day festivities:

> For younkers, Palinode, such follies fit,
> But we tway bene men of elder wit.

But Spenser himself, in the person of Palinode, can only dwell in delighted imagination on the sports:

> O that I were there
> To helpen the ladies their maybush bear!

The *Faery Queen*, structurally at any rate, is a moral allegory, but then even there the moralic acid has not bitten very deeply into the poet's nature, and the sombre colours left upon his epic by its stains only threw the brightness of the Gardens of Acrasia, by contrast, into a more dazzling splendour, just as the presence of the Palmer with Sir Guyon heightens the dramatic interest of that whole episode. Indeed, Spenser's attitude to morality had ever more in it of the dainty epicure than of the true philosopher. Had it been otherwise he would have been less pure as an artist.

---

[1] *Edmund Spenser*, by Émile Legouis.
[2] *The Cutting of an Agate*, by W. B. Yeats.

II

When Spenser began to write he was faced with the problem of remaking the English language for the purposes of poetry. Since Chaucer pronunciation had changed to such an extent, and accents had become so fluid, that any precise and disciplined writing of verse was impossible. The fifteenth century had produced one or two anonymous poems that compare with the best work of any succeeding age, and early in the sixteenth century there is the isolated figure of John Skelton, who, far from following any tradition, struck out with a brilliant syncopated verse of his own, very cleverly taking full advantage of the uncertain state of the language. But neither he, with his "ragged rhyme," nor his contemporaries, the painstaking though clumsy Barclay and Hawes, brought anything to the technical development of poetry. The secret of Chaucer's melody had been lost through the disuse of the final accented *e*, and with the Renaissance English prosody was simply a welter of unresolved Italian, classical, and medieval influences.

Spenser set himself to introduce into English poetry an elegance and precision combined with a richness of diction and a variety of tonal values such as it had never known. He set out to show the world that modern England was capable of as great a poetry as any age or country.[1] To do this meant rivalling all the poets most admired at the time of the Renaissance—Virgil and Ovid, Petrarch and Ariosto, Marot and Ronsard. Yet with all these foreign models he was still jealous of his national inheritance in Chaucer, "the well of English undefiled," and was anxious lest, through too close an imitation of all that was then considered finest in poetry, the English genius should be lost to the tongue. He is careful, therefore, to acknowledge his debt to Chaucer, whom he calls the English Tityrus, just as Virgil was the Roman Tityrus, and in his first book he reconciles their two very different principles in his verse.

On a basis of carefully reasoned critical theory, then, and not without hard training and self-discipline in the art of poesy, were published the eclogues that form the *Shepherd's Calendar* in 1579. This book was the first flowering of the English

[1] *Edmund Spenser*, by W. L. Renwick.

INTRODUCTION ix

Renaissance spirit in verse, and at once won for its author the position of first poet of the day, which he held undisputed till his death.

Not the least remarkable thing about the *Shepherd's Calendar* is the diversity of its metres. There are thirteen different metres in the book, ranging from the elaborate artificiality of the sestine in the eighth eclogue to the jigging couplets of the second, fifth, and ninth, in which Spenser was using Chaucer's line as it was read by his contemporaries. It is only necessary to compare these poems with Barclay's *Eclogues*, written at the end of the preceding century, to appreciate Spenser's triumph. In the *Shepherd's Calendar* poetry left once and for all the dull fallow fields through which those earlier writers had so patiently yet so barrenly ploughed their way, left them for a new land of spring where a silvery music plays in the wind, where poet-shepherds converse all day on the hillside, the lull of their solitude invaded only by the falling of streams and the jocund voices of birds. Here they converse, delightfully far away from reality, till they seem figures in the minute world of an illuminated manuscript. Their sorrows and their joys have this remoteness too; they do not trouble us, even when in *Daphnaïda* the little lamenting figure, with his graven face of woe and dull pilgrim's dress, lifts wide arms in an universal imprecation: for though we clearly hear his voice, he is far away, set in the flawless crystal of Spenser's art.

But *Daphnaïda* and the *Complaints* are "minor" poetry in a sense that the *Shepherd's Calendar* is not. The *Complaints* were published in 1591, a year after the first three books of the *Faery Queen*, and may be regarded as a medley collection of mostly early pieces revised and hastily put together and left in the hands of the printer upon the author's second going into Ireland. Yet, as they finally appeared, none of them are so early as not to have something of that transfiguring grace of the poet's mature spiritualized diction. Along with the translations of Petrarch and Du Bellay, and the *Ruins of Time* and the *Visions of the World's Vanity* written in imitation of these authors, and a very much expanded version of Virgil's mock-heroic *Culex*, the volume contained Spenser's bitterest political satire, *Mother Hubbard's Tale*, and the rather insincerely protracted *Tears of the Muses*. The first of these last, with its vivid picture of the pitifully humiliating state of the suitor, was partly the outcome of Spenser's disappointed hopes at court, and the second the result of the discovery that his prestige as a poet would not carry him very far in the world of affairs.[1]

Mother Hubbard's Tale reveals the poet in a Chaucerian mood. It is the most worldly of his poems, the most vigorous and plain in style. As already indicated, the fox of the parable is intended for Burghley, while the ape represents the joint persons of Alençon and Simier at a time when the former was pushing his suit in person and there was a danger of him "stealing the lion's skin." The designation of the Frenchmen was the more unmistakable, as the queen had actually nicknamed Simier her "petit singe." Indeed, the satire was dangerously outspoken, and Spenser paid for it with Burghley's displeasure. *Muiopotmos* is a later poem. Written in 1590, it seems to have been printed separately and then added to the *Complaints*. Unlike the general tenor of that volume, it is not "a meditation of the world's vanity, very grave and profitable," but a poem, like *Virgil's Gnat*, in which the poet is content to be

> Tuning our song unto a tender Muse,
> And like a cobweb weaving slenderly.

Its texture is as light as summer air and glittering with the turn and flash of small insect wings. It inhabits that rare non-human realm in which Spenser delighted, far from the intrigues and passions of men. *Daphnaïda*, written about the same time and published in 1591, is no return to the human realm, being a piece in which the theme of despair is treated with the most exquisite and artificial lyricism.

Colin Clout's Come Home Again (published in 1595) was probably written on his return to Ireland at this time, and recounts in pastoral form his visit to England. Beginning with the visit of Ralegh to Kilcolman and their voyage across the Irish Sea, it takes us into the midst of the court where, once again thrown into contact with the outside world, the satirist in Spenser makes itself felt. Though at first intoxicated with the fine luxury of the court and the reception

---

[1] At the time of the publication of this lament on the degeneracy of the arts, Shakespeare had written his early plays, Marlowe was already threatening the world with high astounding terms, and a whole body of drama from such minor wits as Lyly, Greene, Peele, and Nash had been launched across the boards. It is possible, of course, that Spenser's more maidenly muse found all this work horrifying.

INTRODUCTION

accorded to him, being soon neglected he begins to realize the vanity of such a life and the corruption beneath the fair outward show. But, as usual, the queen is an exception:

> Her power, her mercy, and her wisdom, none
> Can deem, but who the Godhead can define.

To this period also belong *Astrophel* and its companion elegy, the *Lay of Clorinda*. But only those poems which Spenser wrote himself for the volume of verses commemorative of Sidney's death have been included in this edition.

Not long after his return to Ireland Spenser fell in love with Elizabeth Boyle, and after a courtship of rather more than twelve months, of which the *Amoretti* are an idealized account, he married her on 11th June, 1594. Their marriage is celebrated in the *Epithalamion*, one of the miracles of poetry and the very essence and culmination of Spenser's art. It is the product of the most ecstatic passion, in which medieval superstition, classic myth, and a lover's impatient desire, are blended in an icy silvery grace. The *Prothalamion*, which followed it in 1596, is almost as beautiful metrically as his own marriage ode, but it lacks the perfect synthesis of the greater poem, and the passion. Of the *Four Hymns*, published at this time, the first two, as already mentioned, give expression to his Platonic conception of Love and Beauty and were written in "the greener times of his youth," while the last two were added to embody the central ideas of Christianity. Nevertheless, Love and Beauty in themselves were celestial things to Spenser, so the principles involved by the four poems are radically the same.

Spenser is still the touchstone of English poetic sensibility; the English tradition is rooted in him, and poets who have regarded their art as a profession have striven to acquire it through him. It is for this reason that Charles Lamb called him "the poets' poet."

To Spenser the idea that "the style is the man" would have been meaningless; to him there were as many styles in poetry as there were kinds. He could well distinguish between the personal and the impersonal style in a poet's work, and realizing this impersonal element in great poetry he deliberately set himself to acquire it, as Milton, Pope, Keats, Shelley, and Bridges did after him, and, as suggested, largely through him.

Spenser is not a popular poet: that is because he is too

purely and exclusively a poet and concerned with creating abstract æsthetic beauty rather than with telling a story or conveying human emotion, and it is the poets who tell stories or convey human emotion that are the most popular with that small section of the public that is interested in poetry.

It only remains to be said that in the modernization of some of the spelling in this edition special care has been taken not to interfere with Spenser's use of archaic words, nor with his peculiar metamorphoses of familiar words for the sake of rhyme; nor have words whose vowel sounds are an integral part of the texture of a line or passage been tampered with. The aim throughout has been to facilitate the reading of the poems for those who are not familiar with archaic spelling. In doing this a certain superficial charm has necessarily been sacrificed to plainness. But it is to be hoped that nobody's susceptibilities will be seriously offended, on turning to the *Shepherd's Calendar*, by finding "myrrhour" changed according to modern usage into "mirror," or "music" spelt without the picturesque terminal *k*. The text is based on that of Dr. R. Morris, which is substantially that of the first editions, by permission of Messrs. Macmillan and Co.

PHILIP HENDERSON.

SELECT BIBLIOGRAPHY

WORKS. *The Shepheardes Calender*, 1579; *The Faerie Queene*, Books I to III, 1590; *Daphnaida*, 1591; *Complaints*, 1591; *Amoretti* and *Epithalamion*, 1595; *Colin Clouts Come Home Againe* and *Astrophel*, 1595; *The Faerie Queene*, Books I to V inclusive, 1596; *Fowre Hymnes*, 1596; *Prothalamion*, 1596; *A Vewe of the present state of Irelande*, 1598; first folio edn of *The Faerie Queene*, including for the first time the *Two Cantos of Mutabilitie*, 1609.

EDITIONS. J. C. Smith (ed.), *Spenser's Faerie Queene*, 2 vols, 1909; E. de Selincourt (ed.), *Spenser's Minor Poems*, 1910; E. A. Greenlaw, F. M. Padelford, C. G. Osgood, et al. (eds), *The Works of Edmund Spenser: A Variorum Edition*, 10 vols, 1932-49.

FURTHER READING. Invaluable background material will be found in: the works of Plato; Vergil's *Aeneid*; Ovid's *Metamorphoses*; the Bible, especially Genesis, The Song of Solomon, Isaiah, and Revelation; and Geoffrey of Monmouth's *History of the Kings of Britain*. Edgar Wind's *Pagan Mysteries in the Renaissance*, 1958, is most helpful for Spenser's neo-Platonism and mythology.

SUGGESTED CRITICAL READING. Paul Alpers, *The Poetry of 'The Faerie Queene'*, 1967; Alpers has also edited the useful *Edmund Spenser: A Critical Anthology*, 1969; J. W. Bennett, *The Evolution of 'The Faerie Queene'*, 1942; Harry Berger Jr, *The Allegorical Temper*, 1957; Patrick Cullen, *Spenser, Marvell and Renaissance Pastoral*, 1970; Robert Ellrodt, *Neoplatonism in the Poetry of Spenser*, 1960; A. D. S. Fowler, *Spenser and the Numbers of Time*, 1964; Rosemary Freeman, *The Faerie Queene: A Companion for Readers* 1970; A. C. Hamilton, *The Structure of Allegory in 'The Faerie Queene'*, 1961; J. E. Hankins, *Source and Meaning in Spenser's Allegory: A Study of 'The Faerie Queene'*, 1971; Graham Hough, *A Preface to 'The Faerie Queene'*, 1962; H. S. V. Jones, *A Spenser Handbook*, 1930 (out of date but still indispensable); A. C. Judson, *The Life of Edmund Spenser*, 1945; J. M. Kennedy and J. A. Reither (eds), *A Theatre for Spenserians*, 1973; C. S. Lewis, *The Allegory of Love*, 1936, *English Literature in the Sixteenth Century*, 1954, and *Spenser's Images of Life* (ed. Fowler), 1967; P. E. McLane, *Spenser's 'Shepheardes Calender': A Study in Elizabethan Allegory*; 1968; W. Nelson (ed.), *Form and Convention in the Poetry of Edmund Spenser*, 1961, and *The Poetry of Edmund Spenser*, 1963 (an excellent introduction); W. L. Renwick, *Edmund Spenser*, 1925; T. P. Roche Jr, *The Kindly Flame*, 1964; Roger Sale, *Reading Spenser: An Introduction to 'The Faerie Queene'*, 1968; Hallett Smith, *Elizabethan Poetry: A Study in Conventions Meaning and Expression*, 1952; Kathleen Williams, *Spenser's 'Faerie Queene'*, 1966.

CONTENTS

	PAGE
INTRODUCTION by Philip Henderson	v
TO HIS BOOK	2
DEDICATION	3
THE GENERAL ARGUMENT OF THE WHOLE BOOK	9
THE SHEPHERD'S CALENDAR	13
THE RUINS OF TIME	105
THE TEARS OF THE MUSES	124
VIRGIL'S GNAT	141
PROSOPOPOIA: OR MOTHER HUBBARD'S TALE	159
THE RUINS OF ROME	192
MUIOPOTMOS: OR THE FATE OF THE BUTTERFLY	205
VISIONS OF THE WORLD'S VANITY	217
THE VISIONS OF BELLAY	222
THE VISIONS OF PETRARCH	228
DAPHNAÏDA	231
COLIN CLOUT'S COME HOME AGAIN	247
ASTROPHEL	270
THE DOLEFUL LAY OF CLORINDA	277
AMORETTI AND EPITHALAMION	280
Madrigals	314
EPITHALAMION	317
FOUR HYMNS:	
An Hymn in Honour of Love	328
An Hymn in Honour of Beauty	337
An Hymn of Heavenly Love	344
An Hymn of Heavenly Beauty	352
PROTHALAMION, OR A SPOUSAL VERSE	361
SONNETS	366
GLOSSARY	369

THE SHEPHERD'S CALENDAR

CONTAINING TWELVE ÆGLOGUES
PROPORTIONABLE TO THE TWELVE MONTHS

ENTITLED

To the noble and virtuous Gentleman, most worthy of
all titles both of learning and chivalry

MASTER PHILIP SIDNEY

TO HIS BOOK

Go, little book! thyself present,
As child whose parent is unkent,
To him that is the president
Of noblesse and of chivalree:
And if that Envy bark at thee,
As sure it will, for succour flee
Under the shadow of his wing;
And askéd who thee forth did bring,
A shepherd's swain, say, did thee sing
All as his straying flock he fed:
And, when his honour has thee read,
Crave pardon for my hardihead.
But, if that any ask thy name,
Say, thou wert base-begot with blame;
For-thy thereof thou takest shame,
And, when thou art past jeopardee,
Come tell me what was said of me,
And I will send more after thee.

IMMERITÔ.

TO THE MOST EXCELLENT AND LEARNED BOTH ORATOR AND POET

MASTER GABRIEL HARVEY

HIS VERY SPECIAL AND SINGULAR GOOD FRIEND E. K. COMMENDETH THE GOOD LIKING OF THIS HIS LABOUR, AND THE PATRONAGE OF THE NEW POET

Uncouth, unkist, said the old famous poet Chaucer: whom for his excellency and wonderful skill in making, his scholar Lydgate, a worthy scholar of so excellent a master, calleth the loadstar of our language: and whom our Colin Clout in his æglogue calleth Tityrus the god of shepherds, comparing him to the worthiness of the Roman Tityrus, Virgil. Which proverb, mine own good friend Ma. Harvey, as in that good old poet it served well Pandar's purpose for the bolstering of his bawdy brocage, so very well taketh place in this our new poet, who for that he is uncouth (as said Chaucer) is unkist, and unknown to most men, is regarded but of few. But I doubt not, so soon as his name shall come into the knowledge of men, and his worthiness be sounded in the trump of fame, but that he shall be not only kist, but also beloved of all, embraced of the most, and wondered at of the best. No less, I think, deserveth his wittiness in devising, his pithiness in uttering, his complaints of love so lovely, his discourses of pleasure so pleasantly, his pastoral rudeness, his moral wiseness, his due observing of decorum everywhere, in personages, in seasons, in matter, in speech; and generally, in all seemly simplicity of handling his matter, and framing his words: the which of many things which in him be strange, I know will seem the strangest, the words themselves being so ancient, the knitting of them so short and intricate, and the whole period and compass of speech so delightsome for the roundness, and so grave for the strangeness. And first of the words to speak, I grant they be something hard, and of most men unused, yet both English, and also used of most excellent authors, and most famous poets. In whom, whenas this our poet hath been much travailed and thoroughly read, how could it be, (as that worthy orator said) but that walking in the sun, although for other cause he walked, yet needs he mought be sunburnt; and, having the sound of those ancient poets still ringing in his ears, he mought needs, in singing, hit out some of their tunes. But whether he useth them by such casualty and custom, or of set purpose and choice, as thinking them fittest for such rustical rudeness of shepherds, either for that their rough sound would make his rhymes more ragged and rustical, or else because such old and obsolete words are most used of country folk, sure I think, and think I think not amiss, that they bring great grace, and, as one would say, authority to the verse. For albe, amongst many other faults, it specially be objected of Valla against Livy, and of other against Sallust, that with overmuch study they affect antiquity, as coveting thereby credence and honour of elder years, yet I am of opinion, and eke the best learned are of the like, that those ancient solemn words are a great ornament, both in the one, and in the other; the one labouring to set forth in his work an eternal image of antiquity, and the other carefully discoursing matters of gravity and importance. For, if my memory fail not, Tully, in that book wherein he endeavoureth to set forth the pattern of a perfect orator, saith that oft-times an ancient word maketh the style seem grave, and as it were reverend, no otherwise than we honour and reverence gray hairs, for a certain religious regard, which we have of old age. Yet neither everywhere must old words be stuffed in, nor the common dialect and manner of speaking so corrupted thereby, that, as in old buildings, it seem disorderly and ruinous. But all as in most exquisite pictures they use to blaze and portraict not only the dainty lineaments of beauty, but also round about it to shadow the rude thickets and craggy cliffs, that, by the baseness of such parts, more excellency may accrue to the principal; for oft-times we find ourselves, I know not how, singularly delighted with the shew of such natural rudeness, and take great pleasure in that disorderly order. Even so do those rough and harsh terms illumine, and make more clearly to appear, the brightness of brave and glorious words. So oftentimes a discord in music maketh a comely concordance: so great delight took the worthy poet Alcæus to behold a blemish in the joint of a well-shaped body. But, if any will rashly blame such his purpose in choice of old and unwonted words, him may I more justly blame and condemn, or of witless headiness in judging, or of heedless hardiness in condemning; for, not marking the compass of his bent, he will judge of the length of his cast: for in my opinion it is one special praise of many, which are due to this poet, that he hath laboured to restore, as to their rightful heritage, such good and natural English words, as have been long time out of use, and almost clean disherited. Which is the only cause, that our mother tongue, which truly of itself is both full enough for prose, and stately enough for verse, hath long time been counted most bare and barren of both. Which default whenas some endeavoured to salve and recure, they patched up the holes with pieces and rags of other languages, borrowing here of the French, there of the Italian, everywhere of the Latin; not weighing how ill those tongues accord with themselves, but much worse with ours: so now they have made our English tongue a gallimaufry, or hodgepodge of all other speeches. Other some, not so well seen in the English tongue as perhaps in other languages, if they happen to hear an old word, albeit very natural and significant, cry out straightway, that we speak no English, but gibberish, or rather such as in old time Evander's mother spake: whose first shame is, that they are not ashamed, in their own mother tongue, to be counted strangers and aliens. The second shame no less then the first, that whatso they understand not, they straightway deem to be senseless, and not at all to be understood. Much like to the mole in Æsop's fable, that, being blind herself, would in no wise be persuaded that any beast could see. The last, more shameful than both, that of their own country and natural speech, which together with their nurses' milk they sucked, they have so base regard and bastard judgement, that they will not only themselves not labour to garnish and beautify it, but also repine, that of other it should be embellished. Like to the dog in the manger, that himself can eat no hay, and yet barketh at the hungry bullock, that so fain would feed; whose currish kind, though it cannot be kept from barking, yet can I them thank that they refrain from biting.

Now, for the knitting of sentences, which they call the joints and members thereof, and for all the compass of the speech, it is round without roughness, and learned without hardness, such indeed as may be perceived of the least, understood of the most, but judged only of the learned. For what in most English writers useth to be loose, and as it were ungirt, in this author is well grounded, finely framed, and strongly trussed up together. In regard whereof, I scorn and spue out the rascally rout of our ragged rhymers (for so themselves use to hunt the letter) which without learning boast, without judgement jangle, without reason rage and foam, as if some instinct of poetical spirit had newly ravished them above the meanness of common capacity. And being, in the midst of all their bravery, suddenly, either for want of matter, or of rhyme, or having forgotten their former conceit, they seem to be so pained and travailed in their remembrance, as it were a woman in childbirth, *or as that same Pythia, when the trance came upon her:* "Os rabidum fera corda domans, &c."

Natheless, let them a' God's name feed on their own folly, so they seek not to darken the beams of others' glory. As for Colin, under whose person the author's self is shadowed, how far he is from such vaunted titles and glorious shows, both himself sheweth, where he saith,

> Of Muses, Hobbinol, I con no skill.

And

> Enough is me to paint out my unrest, &c.

And also appeareth by the baseness of the name, wherein it seemeth he chose rather to unfold great matter of argument covertly than, professing it, not suffice thereto accordingly. Which moved him rather in æglogues than otherwise to write, doubting perhaps his ability, which he little needed, or minding to furnish our tongue with this kind, wherein it faulteth; or following the example of the best and most ancient poets, which devised this kind of writing, being both so base for the matter, and homely for the manner, at the first to try their abilities; and as young birds, that be newly crept out of the nest, by little first to prove their tender wings, before they make a greater flight. So flew Theocritus, as you may perceive he was already full fledged. So flew Virgil, as not yet well feeling his wings. So flew Mantuan, as not being full summed. So Petrarch. So Boccace. So Marot, Sannazarus, and also divers other excellent both Italian and French poets, whose footing this author everywhere followeth; yet so as few, but they be well scented, can trace him out. So finally flieth this our new poet as a bird whose principals be scarce grown out, but yet as one that in time shall be able to keep wing with the best.

Now, as touching the general drift and purpose of his æglogues, I mind not to say much, himself labouring to conceal it. Only this appeareth, that his unstayed youth had long wandered in the common labyrinth of love, in which time to mitigate and allay the heat of his passion, or else to warn (as he saith) the young shepherds, s. his equals and companions, of his unfortunate folly, he compiled these xij æglogues, which, for that they be proportioned to the state of the xij months, he termeth the Shepherd's Calendar, applying an old name to a new work. Hereunto have I added a certain gloss, or scholion, for the exposition of old words, and harder phrases; which manner of glosing and commenting, well I wot, will seem strange and rare in our tongue: yet, for so much as I knew many excellent and proper devices, both in words and matter, would pass in the speedy course of reading, either as unknown, or as not marked, and that in this kind, as in other, we might be equal to the learned of other nations, I thought good to take the pains upon me, the rather for that by means of some familiar acquaintance I was made privy to his counsel and secret meaning in them, as also in sundry other works of his, which albeit I know he nothing so much hateth as to promulgate, yet thus much have I adventured upon his friendship, himself being for long time far estranged, hoping that this will the rather occasion him to put forth divers other excellent works of his, which sleep in silence; as his Dreams, *his* Legends, *his* Court of Cupid, *and sundry others, whose commendations to set out were very vain, the things though worthy of many, yet being known to few. These my present pains, if to any they be pleasurable or profitable, be you judge, mine own good Master Harvey, to whom I have, both in respect of your worthiness generally, and otherwise upon some particular and special considerations, vowed this my labour, and the maidenhead of this our common friend's poetry; himself having already in the beginning dedicated it to the noble and worthy gentleman, the right worshipful Ma. Phi. Sidney, a special favourer and maintainer of all kind of learning. Whose cause, I pray you, sir, if envy shall stir up any wrongful accusation, defend with your mighty rhetoric and other your rare gifts of learning, as you can, and shield with your good will, as you ought, against the malice and outrage of so many enemies, as I know will be set on fire with the sparks of his kindled glory. And thus recommending the author unto you, as unto his most special good friend, and myself unto you both, as one making singular account of two so very good and so choice friends, I bid you both most heartily farewell, and commit you and your commendable studies to the tuition of the Greatest.*

Your own assuredly to be commanded,

E. K.

Post scr.

Now I trust, M. Harvey, that upon sight of your special friend's and fellow poet's doings, or else for envy of so many unworthy quidams, which catch at the garland which to you alone is due, you will be persuaded to pluck out of the hateful darkness those so many excellent English poems of yours which lie hid, and bring them forth to eternal light. Trust me, you do both them great wrong, in depriving them of the desired sun; and also yourself, in smothering your deserved praises; and all men generally, in withholding from them so divine pleasures, which they might conceive of your gallant English verses, as they have already done of your Latin poems, which, in my opinion, both for invention and elocution are very delicate and superexcellent. And thus again I take my leave of my good Master Harvey: from my lodging at London this 10th *of April,* 1579.

THE GENERAL ARGUMENT OF THE WHOLE BOOK

LITTLE, I hope, needeth me at large to discourse the first original of æglogues, having already touched the same. But, for the word æglogues, I know, is unknown to most, and also mistaken of some of the best learned (as they think,) I will say somewhat thereof, being not at all impertinent to my present purpose.

They were first of the Greeks, the inventours of them, called *Æglogai*, as it were αἰγῶν, or αἰγονόμων λόγοι, that is, goatherds' tales. For although in Virgil and others the speakers be more shepherds than goatherds, yet Theocritus, in whom is more ground of authority than in Virgil, this specially from that deriving, as from the first head and wellspring, the whole invention of these æglogues, maketh goatherds the persons and authors of his tales. This being, who seeth not the grossness of such as by colour of learning would make us believe that they are more rightly termed *eclogai*, as they would say, extraordinary discourses of unnecessary matter: which definition albe in substance and meaning it agree with the nature of the thing, yet no whit answereth with the ἀνάλυσις and interpretation of the word For they be not termed *eclogues*, but *æglogues*; which sentence this author very well observing, upon good judgement, though indeed few goatherds have to do herein, natheless doubteth not to call them by the used and best known name. Other curious discourses hereof I reserve to greater occasion.

These xij æglogues, everywhere answering to the seasons of the twelve months, may be well divided into three forms or ranks. For either they be plaintive, as the first, the sixth, the eleventh, and the twelfth; or recreative, such as all those be, which contain matter of love, or commendation of special personages; or moral, which for the most part be mixed with some satirical bitterness; namely, the second, of reverence due to old age; the fifth, of coloured deceit; the seventh and ninth, of dissolute shepherds and pastors; the tenth, of contempt of poetry and pleasant wits. And to this division may everything herein be reasonably applied: a few only except, whose special purpose and meaning I am not privy to. And thus much generally of these xij æglogues. Now will we speak particularly of all, and first of the first, which he calleth by the first month's name, January: wherein to some he may seem foully to have faulted, in that he erroneously beginneth with that month, which beginneth not the year. For it is well known, and stoutly maintained with strong reasons of the learned, that the year beginneth in March; for then the sun reneweth his finished course, and the seasonable spring refresheth the earth, and the pleasance thereof, being buried in the sadness of the dead winter now worn away, reliveth.

This opinion maintain the old astrologers and philosophers, namely, the reverend Andalo, and Macrobius in his *Holidays of Saturn*; which account also was generally observed both of Grecians and Romans. But, saving the leave of such learned heads, we maintain a custom of counting the seasons from the month January, upon a more special cause than the heathen philosophers ever could conceive, that is, for the incarnation of our mighty Saviour, and eternal redeemer the L. Christ, who, as then renewing the state of the decayed world, and returning the compass of expired years to their former date and first commencement, left to us his heirs a memorial of his birth in the end of the last year and beginning of the next. Which reckoning, beside that eternal monument of our salvation, leaneth also upon good proof of special judgement.

For albeit that in elder times, when as yet the compt of the year was not perfected, as afterward it was by Julius Cæsar, they began to tell the months from March's beginning, and according to the same God (as is said in Scripture) commanded the people of the Jews, to count the month Abib, that which we call March, for the first month, in remembrance that in that month he brought them out of the land of Egypt: yet, according to tradition of later times, it hath been otherwise observed, both in government of the Church and rule of mightiest realms. For from Julius Cæsar who first observed the leap year, which he called *bissextilem annum*, and brought into a more certain course the odd wandering days which of the Greeks were called ὑπερβαίνοντες, of the Romans *intercalares*, (for in such matter of learning I am forced to use the terms of the learned,) the months have been numbered xij, which in the first ordinance of Romulus were but ten, counting but ccciiij days in every year, and beginning with March. But Numa Pompilius, who was the father of all the Roman ceremonies and religion, seeing that reckoning to agree neither with the course of the sun nor of the moon, thereunto added two months, January and February; wherein it seemeth, that wise king minded, upon good reason, to begin the year at January, of him therefore so called *tanquam Janua anni*, the gate and entrance of the year; or of the name of the god *Janus*, to which god for that the old Paynims attributed the birth and beginning of all creatures new coming into the world, it seemeth that he therefore to him assigned the beginning and first entrance of the year. Which account for the most part hath hitherto continued: notwithstanding that the Egyptians begin their year at September; for that, according to the opinion of the best Rabbins and very purpose of the Scripture itself, God made the world in that month, that is called of them *Tisri*. And therefore he commanded them to keep the feast of Pavilions in the end of the year, in the 15th day of the seventh month, which before that time was the first.

But our author respecting neither the subtilty of the one part, nor the antiquity of the other, thinketh it fittest, according to the simplicity of common understanding, to begin with January; weening it perhaps no decorum that shepherds should be seen in matter of so deep insight, or canvass a case of so doubtful judgement. So therefore beginneth he, and so continueth he throughout.

THE SHEPHERD'S CALENDAR

JANUARY

ÆGLOGA PRIMA. ARGUMENT

IN *this first æglogue Colin Clout, a shepherd's boy, complaineth him of his unfortunate love, being but newly (as seemeth) enamoured of a country lass called Rosalind: with which strong affection being very sore travailed, he compareth his careful case to the sad season of the year, to the frosty ground, to the frozen trees, and to his own winter-beaten flock. And, lastly, finding himself robbed of all former pleasance and delights, he breaketh his pipe in pieces, and casteth himself to the ground.*

COLIN CLOUT

A SHEPHERD's boy (no better do him call)
When winter's wasteful spite was almost spent,
All in a sunshine day, as did befall,
Led forth his flock, that had been long ypent:
   So faint they wox, and feeble in the fold,
   That now unnethes their feet could them uphold.

All as the sheep, such was the shepherd's look,
For pale and wan he was, (alas the while!)
May seem he loved, or else some care he took:
Well couth he tune his pipe and frame his style.
   Then to a hill his fainting flock he led,
   And thus him plained, the while his sheep there fed.

"Ye gods of love, that pity lovers' pain,
(If any gods the pain of lovers pity:)
Look from above, where you in joys remain,
And bow your ears unto my doleful ditty.
   And Pan thou shepherd's god, that once didst love,
   Pity the pains that thou thyself didst prove.

"Thou barren ground, whom winter's wrath hath wasted,
Art made a mirror to behold my plight:
Whilom thy fresh spring flowered, and after hasted
Thy summer proud, with daffadillies dight.

And now is come thy winter's stormy state,
Thy mantle marred, wherein thou maskedst late.

"Such rage as winter's reigneth in my heart,
My life-blood freezing with unkindly cold;
Such stormy stours do breed my baleful smart,
As if my year were waste and woxen old.
    And yet, alas, but now my spring begun,
    And yet, alas, it is already done.

"You naked trees, whose shady leaves are lost,
Wherein the birds were wont to build their bower,
And now are clothed with moss and hoary frost,
Instead of bloosmes, wherewith your buds did flower:
    I see your tears that from your boughs do rain,
    Whose drops in dreary icicles remain.

"All so my lustful leaf is dry and sere,
My timely buds with wailing all are wasted;
The blossom which my branch of youth did bear
With breathéd sighs is blown away and blasted;
    And from mine eyes the drizzling tears descend,
    As on your boughs the icicles depend.

"Thou feeble flock, whose fleece is rough and rent,
Whose knees are weak through fast and evil fare,
May'st witness well, by thy ill government,
Thy master's mind is overcome with care:
    Thou weak, I wan; thou lean, I quite forlorn:
    With mourning pine I; you with pining mourn.

"A thousand sithes I curse that careful hour
Wherein I longed the neighbour town to see,
And eke ten thousand sithes I bless the stour
Wherein I saw so fair a sight as she:
    Yet all for naught: such sight hath bred my bane.
    Ah God! that love should breed both joy and pain.

"It is not Hobbinol wherefore I plain,
Albe my love he seek with daily suit;
His clownish gifts and court'sies I disdain,
His kids, his cracknels, and his early fruit.
    Ah, foolish Hobbinol! thy gifts bene vain:
    Colin them gives to Rosalind again.

JANUARY

"I love thilk lass (alas, why do I love?)
And am forlorn (alas, why am I lorn?)
She deigns not my good will, but doth reprove,
And of my rural music holdeth scorn.
   Shepherd's device she hateth as the snake,
   And laughs the songs that Colin Clout doth make.

"Wherefore, my pipe, albe rude Pan thou please,
Yet for thou pleasest not where most I would:
And thou, unlucky Muse, that wont'st to ease
My musing mind, yet canst not when thou should:
   Both pipe and Muse shall sore the while abie."
   So broke his oaten pipe, and down did lie.

By that, the welkéd Phœbus gan avail
His weary wain, and now the frosty night
Her mantle black through heaven gan overhail:
Which seen, the pensive boy, half in despight,
   Arose, and homeward drove his sunnéd sheep,
   Whose hanging heads did seem his careful case to weep.

COLIN'S EMBLEM

Anchôra speme.

GLOSS

Colin Clout is a name not greatly used, and yet have I seen a poesy of M. Skelton's under that title. But indeed the word Colin is French, and used of the French poet Marot (if he be worthy of the name of a poet) in a certain æglogue. Under which name this poet secretly shadoweth himself, as sometimes did Virgil under the name of Tityrus, thinking it much fitter than such Latin names, for the great unlikelihood of the language.

Unnethes, scarcely.

Couth cometh of the verb *con*, that is, to know, or to have skill. As well interpreteth the same, the worthy Sir Tho. Smith, in his book of government: wherof I have a perfect copy in writing, lent me by his kinsman, and my very singular good frend, M. Gabriel Harvey: as also of some other his most grave and excellent writings.

Sithe, time.

Neighbour town, the next town: expressing the Latin *Vicina*.

Stour, a fit.

Sere, withered.

His clownish gifts, imitateth Virgil's verse:

   "Rusticus es, Corydon, nec munera curat Alexis."

Hobbinol is a feigned country name, whereby, it being so common and usual, seemeth to be hidden the person of some his very special and most familiar friend, whom he entirely and extraordinarily beloved, as peradventure shall be more largely declared hereafter. In this place seemeth to be some savour of disorderly love, which the learned call *pæderastice*; but it is gathered beside his meaning. For who that hath read Plato his dialogue called *Alcibiades*, Xenophon, and Maximus Tyrius, of Socrates' opinions, may easily perceive, that such love is much to be allowed and liked of, specially so meant, as Socrates used it: who saith, that indeed he loved Alcibiades extremely, yet not Alcibiades' person, but his soul, which is Alcibiades' own self. And so is *pæderastice* much to be preferred before *gynerastice*, that is, the love which enflameth men with lust toward womankind. But yet let no man think, that herein I stand with Lucian, or his devilish disciple Unico Aretino, in defence of execrable and horrible sins of forbidden and unlawful fleshliness. Whose abominable error is fully confuted of Perionius, and others.

I love, a pretty epanorthosis in these two verses; and withal a paronomasia or playing with the word, where he saith *I love thilk lass alas*, &c.

Rosalind is also a feigned name, which, being well ordered, will bewray the very name of his love and mistress, whom by that name he coloureth. So as Ovid shadoweth his love under the name of Corinna, which of some is supposed to be Julia, the emperor Augustus his daughter, and wife to Agrippa. So doth Aruntius Stella every where call his Lady Asteris and Ianthis, albe it is well known that her right name was Violantilla: as witnesseth Statius in his *Epithalamium*. And so the famous paragon of Italy, Madonna Cœlia, in her letters envelopeth herself under the name of Zima: and Petrona under the name of Bellochia. And this generally hath been a common custom of counterfeiting the names of secret personages.

Avail, bring down.

Overhail, draw over.

EMBLEM

His emblem or *poesy* is hereunder added in Italian, *Anchóra speme*: the meaning whereof is, that notwithstanding his extreme passion and luckless love, yet, leaning on hope, he is somewhat recomforted.

FEBRUARY

FEBRUARY

ÆGLOGA SECUNDA. ARGUMENT

THIS *æglogue is rather moral and general, than bent to any secret or particular purpose. It specially containeth a discourse of old age, in the person of Thenot, an old shepherd, who for his crookedness and unlustiness is scorned of Cuddie, an unhappy herdman's boy. The matter very well accordeth with the season of the month, the year now drooping, and as it were drawing to his last age. For as in this time of year, so then in our bodies, there is a dry and withering cold, which congealeth the cruddled blood, and freezeth the weatherbeaten flesh with storms of Fortune, and hoar frosts of Care. To which purpose the old man telleth a tale of the oak and the briar, so lively, and so feelingly, as, if the thing were set forth in some picture before our eyes, more plainly could not appear.*

CUDDIE. THENOT

Cuddie. Ah for pity! will rank winter's rage
  These bitter blasts never gin t' assuage?
  The kene cold blows through my beaten hide,
  All as I were through the body gride.
  My ragged ronts all shiver and shake,
  As doen high towers in an earthquake:
  They wont in the wind wag their wrigle tails,
  Perk as a peacock; but now it avails.
Thenot. Lewdly complainest thou, lazy lad,
  Of winter's wrack for making thee sad.
  Must not the world wend in his common course,
  From good to bad, and from bad to worse,
  From worse unto that is worst of all,
  And then return to his former fall?
  Who will not suffer the stormy time,
  Where will he live till the lusty prime?
  Self have I worn out thrice thirty years,
  Some in much joy, many in many tears,
  Yet never complained of cold nor heat,
  Of summer's flame, nor of winter's threat,
  Ne ever was to Fortune foeman,
  But gently took that ungently came;
  And ever my flock was my chief care,
  Winter or summer they mought well fare.
Cuddie. No marvel, Thenot, if thou can bear
  Cheerfully the winter's wrathful cheer;

> For age and winter accord full nigh,
> This chill, that cold: this crooked, that wry;
> And as the low'ring weather looks down,
> So seemest thou like Good Friday to frown.
> But my flow'ring youth is foe to frost,
> My ship unwont in storms to be tost.
>
> *Thenot.* The sovereign of seas he blames in vain,
> That, once sea-beat, will to sea again.
> So loit'ring live you little herdgrooms,
> Keeping your beasts in the budded brooms:
> And when the shining sun laugheth once,
> You deemen the spring is come atonce;
> Then gin you, fond flies, the cold to scorn,
> And crowing in pipes made of green corn,
> You thinken to be lords of the year.
> But eft, when ye count you freed from fear,
> Comes the breme winter with chamfred brows,
> Full of wrinkles and frosty furrows,
> Drearily shooting his stormy dart,
> Which cruddles the blood and pricks the heart.
> Then is your careless corage accoyed,
> Your careful herds with cold bene annoyed.
> Then pay you the price of your surquedry,
> With weeping, and wailing, and misery.
>
> *Cuddie.* Ah, foolish old man! I scorn thy skill,
> That wouldest me my springing youngth to spill:
> I deem thy brain emperished be
> Through rusty eld, that hath rotted thee:
> Or sicker thy head very tottie is,
> So on thy corbe shoulder it leans amiss.
> Now thyself hast lost both lop and top,
> Als my budding branch thou wouldest crop;
> But were thy years green, as now bene mine,
> To other delights they would incline:
> Then wouldest thou learn to carol of love,
> And hery with hymns thy lass's glove;
> Then wouldest thou pipe of Phyllis' praise;
> But Phyllis is mine for many days.
> I won her with a girdle of gelt,
> Embost with bugle about the belt.
> Such an one shepherds would make full fain;
> Such an one would make thee young again.
>
> *Thenot.* Thou art a fon of thy love to boast;

FEBRUARY

All that is lent to love will be lost.
Cuddie. Seest how brag yond bullock bears,
   So smirk, so smooth, his prickéd ears?
   His horns bene as broad as rainbow bent,
   His dewlap as lithe as lass of Kent:
   See how he venteth into the wind;
   Weenest of love is not his mind?
   Seemeth thy flock thy counsel can,
   So lustless bene they, so weak, so wan;
   Clothéd with cold, and hoary with frost,
   Thy flock's father his corage hath lost.
   Thy ewes, that wont to have blowen bags,
   Like wailful widows hangen their crags;
   The rather lambs bene starvéd with cold,
   All for their master is lustless and old.
Thenot. Cuddie, I wote thou kenn'st little good,
   So vainly t' advance thy headless hood;
   For youth is a bubble blown up with breath,
   Whose wit is weakness, whose wage is death,
   Whose way is wilderness, whose inn Penance,
   And stoop-gallant Age, the host of Grievance.
   But shall I tell thee a tale of truth,
   Which I conned of Tityrus in my youth,
   Keeping his sheep on the hills of Kent?
Cuddie. To nought more, Thenot, my mind is bent
   Than to hear novels of his devise;
   They bene so well-thewed, and so wise,
   Whatever that good old man bespake.
Thenot. Many meet tales of youth did he make,
   And some of love, and some of chivalry;
   But none fitter than this to apply.
   Now listen a while and hearken the end.

   There grew an aged tree on the green,
   A goodly oak sometime had it been,
   With arms full strong and largely displayed,
   But of their leaves they were disarrayed:
   The body big, and mightily pight,
   Throughly rooted, and of wonderous height;
   Whilom had been the king of the field,
   And mochell mast to the husband did yield,
   And with his nuts larded many swine:
   But now the gray moss marréd his rine;
   His baréd boughs were beaten with storms,

His top was bald, and wasted with worms,
His honour decayed, his branches sere.

   Hard by his side grew a bragging brere,
Which proudly thrust into th' element,
And seemed to threat the firmament:
It was embellisht with blossoms fair,
And thereto aye wonnéd to repair
The shepherds' daughters to gather flowers,
To paint their girlonds with his colours;
And in his small bushes used to shroud
The sweet nightingale singing so loud;
Which made this foolish brere wax so bold,
That on a time he cast him to scold
And sneb the good oak, for he was old.
"Why stand'st there (quoth he) thou brutish block?
Nor for fruit nor for shadow serves thy stock;
Seest how fresh my flowers bene spread,
Dyed in lily white and crimson red,
With leaves engrained in lusty green;
Colours meet to clothe a maiden queen?
Thy waste bigness but cumbers the ground,
And dirks the beauty of my blossoms round:
The mouldy moss, which thee accloyeth,
My cinnamon smell too much annoyeth:
Wherefore soon I rede thee hence remove,
Lest thou the price of my displeasure prove."
So spake this bold brere with great disdain:
Little him answered the oak again,
But yielded, with shame and grief adawed,
That of a weed he was overcrawed.

   It chancéd after upon a day,
The husbandman self to come that way,
Of custom for to surview his ground,
And his trees of state in compass round:
Him when the spiteful brere had espied,
Causeless complained, and loudly cried
Unto his lord, stirring up stern strife.

   "O, my liege lord! the god of my life!
Pleaseth you ponder your suppliant's plaint,
Causéd of wrong and cruel constraint,
Which I your poor vassal daily endure;
And, but your goodness the same recure,
Am like for desperate doole to die,

FEBRUARY

Through felonous force of mine enemy."
  Greatly aghast with this piteous plea,
Him rested the goodman on the lea,
And bade the brere in his plaint proceed.
With painted words then gan this proud weed
(As most usen ambitious folk:)
His coloured crime with craft to cloak.
  "Ah, my sovereign! Lord of creatures all,
Thou placer of plants both humble and tall,
Was not I planted of thine own hand,
To be the primrose of all thy land;
With flow'ring blossoms to furnish the prime,
And scarlet berries in summer time?
How falls it then that this faded oak,
Whose body is sere, whose branches broke,
Whose naked arms stretch unto the fire,
Unto such tyranny doth aspire;
Hindering with his shade my lovely light,
And robbing me of the sweet sun's sight?
So beat his old boughs my tender side,
That oft the blood springeth from wounds wide;
Untimely my flowers forced to fall,
That bene the honour of your coronal.
And oft he lets his canker-worms light
Upon my branches, to work me more spite;
And oft his hoary locks down doth cast,
Wherewith my fresh flowerets bene defaced:
For this, and many more such outrage,
Craving your goodlihead to assuage
The rancorous rigour of his might,
Nought ask I, but only to hold my right;
Submitting me to your good sufferance,
And praying to be guarded from grievance."
  To this the oak cast him to reply
Well as he couth; but his enemy
Had kindled such coals of displeasúre,
That the goodman nould stay his leisúre,
But home him hasted with furious heat,
Increasing his wrath with many a threat:
His harmful hatchet he hent in hand,
(Alas, that it so ready should stand!)
And to the field alone he speedeth,
(Ay little help to harm there needeth!)

Anger nould let him speak to the tree,
Enaunter his rage mought cooléd be;
But to the root bent his sturdy stroke,
And made many wounds in the waste oak.
The axe's edge did oft turn again,
As half unwilling to cut the grain;
Seemed, the senseless iron did fear,
Or to wrong holy eld did forbear.
For it had been an ancient tree,
Sacred with many a mystery,
And often crossed with the priestës crew,
And often hallowed with holy-water dew:
But sike fancies weren foolery,
And broughten this oak to this misery.
For nought mought they quitten him from decay,
For fiercely the goodman at him did lay.
The block oft groanéd under the blow,
And sighed to see his near overthrow.
In fine, the steel had pierced his pith,
Then down to the earth he fell forthwith.
His wonderous weight made the ground to quake,
Th' earth shrunk under him, and seemed to shake:
There lieth the oak, pitied of none!

   Now stands the brere like a lord alone,
Puffed up with pride and vain pleasance;
But all this glee had no continuance:
For eftsoons winter gan to approach;
The blustering Boreas did encroach,
And beat upon the solitary brere;
For now no succour was seen him near.
Now gan he repent his pride too late;
For naked left and disconsolate,
The biting frost nipt his stalk dead,
The watery wet weighed down his head,
And heapéd snow burd'ned him so sore,
That now upright he can stand no more;
And, being down, is trod in the dirt
Of cattle, and bruised, and sorely hurt.
Such was th' end of this ambitious brere,
For scorning eld—

Cuddie. Now I pray thee, shepherd, tell it not forth:
Here is a long tale, and little worth.
So long have I listenéd to thy speech,

FEBRUARY

That grafféd to the ground is my breech:
My heart-blood is well-nigh frorn, I feel,
And my galage grown fast to my heel:
But little ease of thy lewd tale I tasted.
Hie thee home, shepherd, the day is nigh wasted.

THENOT'S EMBLEM

*Iddio, perche è vecchio,
Fa suoi al suo essempio.*

CUDDIE'S EMBLEM

*Niuno vecchio
Spaventa Iddio.*

GLOSS

Kene, sharp.

Gride, pierced: an old word much used of Lydgate, but not found (that I know of) in Chaucer.

Ronts, young bullocks.

Wrack, ruin or violence, whence cometh shipwrack: and not *wreak*, that is vengeance or wrath.

Foeman, a foe.

Thenot, the name of a shepherd in Marot his Æglogues.

The sovereign of seas is Neptune the god of the seas. The saying is borrowed of Mimus Publianus, which used this proverb in a verse.

"Improbè Neptunum accusat, qui iterum naufragium facit."

Herdgrooms, Chaucer's verse almost whole.

Fond flies. He compareth careless sluggards, or ill husbandmen, to flies that, so soon as the sun shineth, or it wexeth anything warm, begin to fly abroad, when suddenly they be overtaken with cold.

But eft when, a very excellent and lively description of winter, so as may be indifferently taken, either for old age, or for winter season.

Breme, chill, bitter.

Chamfred, chapt, or wrinkled.

Accoyed, plucked down and daunted.

Surquedry, pride.

Eld, old age.

Sicker, sure.

Tottie, wavering.

Corbe, crooked.

Hery, worship.

Phyllis, the name of some maid unknown, whom Cuddie, whose person is secret, loved. The name is usual in Theocritus, Virgil, and Mantuan.

Belt, a girdle or waistband.

A fon, a fool.
Lithe, soft and gentle.
Venteth, snuffeth in the wind.
Thy flock's father, the ram.
Crags, necks.
Rather lambs, that be ewed early in the beginning of the year.
Youth is, a very moral and pithy allegory of youth, and the lusts thereof, compared to a weary wayfaring man.
Tityrus. I suppose he means Chaucer, whose praise for pleasant tales cannot die, so long as the memory of his name shall live, and the name of poetry shall endure.
Well-thewed, that is, *Bene moratæ*, full of moral wiseness.
There grew. This tale of the oak and the briar, he telleth as learned of Chaucer, but it is clean in another kind, and rather like to Æsop's fables. It is very excellent for pleasant descriptions, being altogether a certain icon, or hypotyposis, of disdainful younkers.
Embellisht, beautified and adorned.
Sneb, check.
Why stand'st. The speech is scornful and very presumptuous.
Engrained, dyed in grain.
Accloyeth, encumbereth.
Adawed, daunted and confounded.
Trees of state, taller trees, fit for timber wood.
Stern strife, said Chaucer, s. fell and sturdy.
O my liege, a manner of supplication, wherein is kindly coloured the affection and speech of ambitious men.
Coronal, garland.
Flowerets, young blossoms.
The primrose, the chief and worthiest.
Naked arms, metaphorically meant of the bare boughs, spoiled of leaves. This colourably he speaketh, as adjudging him to the fire.
The blood, spoken of a block, as it were of a living creature, figuratively, and (as they say) κατ' εἰκασμόν.
Hoary locks, metaphorically for withered leaves.
Hent, caught.
Nould, for would not.
Ay, evermore.
Wounds, gashes.
Enaunter, lest that.
The priestës crew, holy-water pot, wherewith the popish priest used to sprinkle and hallow the trees from mischance. Such blindness was in those times, which the poet supposeth to have been the final decay of this ancient oak.
The block oft groaned, a lively figure, which giveth sense and feeling to unsensible creatures, as Virgil also sayeth: "Saxa gemunt gravido," &c.
Boreas, the northern wind, that bringeth the most stormy weather.
Glee, cheer and jollity.
For scorning eld. And minding (as should seem) to have made rhyme to the former verse, he is cunningly cut off by Cuddie, as disdaining to hear any more.
Galage, a startup or clownish shoe.

FEBRUARY

EMBLEM

This emblem is spoken of Thenot, as a moral of his former tale: namely, that God, which is himself most aged, being before all ages, and without beginning, maketh those, whom he loveth, like to himself, in heaping years unto their days, and blessing them with long life. For the blessing of age is not given to all, but unto those whom God will so bless. And albeit that many evil men reach unto such fullness of years, and some also wax old in misery and thraldom, yet therefore is not age ever the less blessing. For even to such evil men such number of years is added, that they may in their last days repent, and come to their first home. So the old man checketh the rash-headed boy for despising his gray and frosty hairs.

Whom Cuddie doth counterbuff with a biting and bitter proverb, spoken indeed at the first in contempt of old age generally: for it was an old opinion, and yet is continued in some men's conceit, that men of years have no fear of God at all, or not so much as younger folk; for that being ripened with long experience, and having passed many bitter brunts and blasts of vengeance, they dread no storms of Fortune, nor wrath of God, nor danger of men, as being either by long and ripe wisdom armed against all mischances and adversity, or with much trouble hardened against all troublesome tides: like unto the ape, of which is said in Æsop's fables, that, oftentimes meeting the lion, he was at first sore aghast and dismayed at the grimness and austerity of his countenance, but at last, being acquainted with his looks, he was so far from fearing him, that he would familiarly gibe and jest with him. Such long experience breedeth in some men security. Although it please Erasmus, a great clerk, and good old father, more fatherly and favourably to construe it, in his *Adages*, for his own behoof, that by the proverb, "Nemo senex metuit Jovem," is not meant, that old men have no fear of God at all, but that they be far from superstition and idolatrous regard of false gods, as is Jupiter. But his great learning notwithstanding, it is too plain to be gainsaid, that old men are much more inclined to such fond fooleries than younger heads.

MARCH

ÆGLOGA TERTIA.   ARGUMENT

IN *this æglogue two shepherds' boys, taking occasion of the season, begin to make purpose of love, and other pleasance which to spring- time is most agreeable. The special meaning hereof is, to give certain marks and tokens to know Cupid, the poets' god of Love. But more particularly, I think, in the person of Thomalin is meant some secret friend, who scorned Love and his knights so long, till at length himself was entangled, and unawares wounded with the dart of some beautiful regard, which is Cupid's arrow.*

WILLY.   THOMALIN

Wil. Thomalin, why sitten we so,
   As weren overwent with woe,
     Upon so fair a morrow?
   The joyous time now nigheth fast,
   That shall alegge this bitter blast,
     And slake the winter's sorrow.
Tho. Sicker, Willy, thou warnest well;
   For winter's wrath begins to quell;
     And pleasant spring appeareth:
   The grass now gins to be refresht,
   The swallow peeps out of her nest,
     And cloudy welkin cleareth.
Wil. Seest not thilk same hawthorn stud,
   How bragly it begins to bud,
     And utter his tender head?
   Flora now calleth forth each flower,
   And bids make ready Maia's bower,
     That new is uprist from bed.
   Then shall we sporten in delight,
   And learn with Lettice to wex light,
     That scornfully looks askance;
   Then will we little Love awake,
   That now sleepeth in Lethe lake,
     And pray him leaden our dance.
Tho. Willy, I ween thou be assot;
   For lusty Love still sleepeth not,
     But is abroad at his game.
Wil. How kenn'st thou that he is awoke?
   Or hast thy self his slumber broke,
     Or made privy to the same?
Tho. No: but haply I him spied,

MARCH

Where in a bush he did him hide,
  With wings of purple and blue;
And, were not that my sheep would stray,
The privy marks I would bewray,
  Whereby by chance I him knew.

Wil. Thomalin, have no care for-thy;
  Myself will have a double eye,
    Ylike to my flock and thine;
  For als at home I have a sire,
  A stepdame eke, as hot as fire,
    That duly adays counts mine.

Tho. Nay, but thy seeing will not serve,
  My sheep for that may chance to swerve,
    And fall into some mischief:
  For sithens is but the third morrow
  That I chanced to fall asleep with sorrow
    And waked again with grief;
  The while thilk same unhappy ewe,
  Whose clouted leg her hurt doth shew,
    Fell headlong into a dell,
  And there unjointed both her bones:
  Mought her neck bene jointed attones,
    She should have need no more spell.
  Th' elf was so wanton and so wood,
  (But now I trow can better good)
    She mought ne gang on the green.

Wil. Let be, as may be, that is past:
  That is to come, let be forecast:
    Now tell us what thou hast seen.

Tho. It was upon a holiday,
  When shepherds' grooms han leave to play,
    I cast to go a shooting.
  Long wand'ring up and down the land,
  With bow and bolts in either hand,
    For birds in bushes tooting,
  At length within an ivy tod
  (There shrouded was the little god)
    I heard a busy bustling.
  I bent my bolt against the bush,
  Listening if anything did rush,
    But then heard no more rustling.
  Then, peeping close into the thick,
  Might see the moving of some quick,

    Whose shape appearéd not:
But were it faery, fiend, or snake,
My courage yearned it to awake,
    And manfully thereat shot.
With that sprang forth a naked swain
With spotted wings, like peacock's train,
    And laughing lope to a tree;
His gilden quiver at his back,
And silver bow, which was but slack,
    Which lightly be bent at me.
That seeing, I levelléd again
And shot at him with might and main,
    As thick as it had hailed.
So long I shot, that all was spent;
Then pumice stones I hastly hent
    And threw; but nought availed:
He was so wimble and so wight,
From bough to bough he leppéd light,
    And oft the pumice latched.
Therewith affrayed, I ran away;
But he, that erst seemed but to play,
    A shaft in earnest snatched,
And hit me running in the heel:
For then I little smart did feel,
    But soon it sore increaséd;
And now it rankleth more and more,
And inwardly it fest'reth sore,
    Ne wot I how to cease it.

Wil. Thomalin, I pity thy plight,
Perdie with Love thou diddest fight;
    I know him by a token;
For once I heard my father say,
How he him caught upon a day,
    (Whereof he will be wroken)
Entangled in a fowling net,
Which he for carrion crows had set
    That in our pear-tree haunted:
Then said, he was a wingéd lad,
But bow and shafts as then none had,
    Else had he sore been daunted.
But see, the welkin thicks apace,
And stooping Phœbus steeps his face:
    It's time to haste us homeward.

WILLY'S EMBLEM
To be wise, and eke to love,
Is granted scarce to gods above.

THOMALIN'S EMBLEM
Of honey and of gall in love there is store;
The honey is much, but the gall is more.

GLOSS

This æglogue seemeth somewhat to resemble that same of Theocritus, wherein the boy likewise telling the old man, that he had shot at a winged boy in a tree, was by him warned to beware of mischief to come.

Overwent, overgone.

Alegge, to lessen or assuage.

To quell, to abate.

Welkin, the sky.

The swallow, which bird useth to be counted the messenger, and as it were, the forerunner, of spring.

Flora, the goddess of flowers, but indeed (as saith Tacitus) a famous harlot, which, with the abuse of her body having gotten great riches, made the people of Rome her heir: who, in remembrance of so great beneficence, appointed a yearly feast for the memorial of her, calling her, not as she was, nor as some do think, *Andronica*, but *Flora*; making her the goddess of flowers, and doing yearly to her solemn sacrifice.

Maia's bower, that is, the pleasant field, or rather the May bushes. Maia is a goddess, and the mother of Mercury, in honour of whom the month of May is of her name so called, as saith Macrobius.

Lettice, the name of some country lass.

Askance, askew, or asquint.

For-thy, therefore.

Lethe is a lake in hell, which the poets call the lake of forgetfulness. For *Lethe* signifieth forgetfulness. Wherein the souls being dipped did forget the cares of their former life. So that by love sleeping in *Lethe* lake, he meaneth he was almost forgotten, and out of knowledge, by reason of winter's hardness, when all pleasures, as it were, sleep and were out of mind.

Assot, to dote.

His slumber. To break Love's slumber is to exercise the delights of love, and wanton pleasures.

Wings of purple, so is he feigned of the poets.

For als, he imitateth Virgil's verse:

"Est mihi namque domi pater, est injusta noverca, &c."

A dell, a hole in the ground.

Spell is a kind of verse or charm, that in elder times they used often to say over every thing that they would have preserved, as the nightspell for thieves, and the woodspell. And herehence, I think, is named the gospel, as it were God's spell, or word. And so saith Chaucer: "Listeneth lordings to my spell."

Gang, go.

An ivy tod, a thick bush.

Swain, a boy. For so is he described of the poets to be a boy, s. always fresh and lusty: blindfolded, because he maketh no difference of personages: with divers coloured wings, s. full of flying fancies: with bow and arrow, that is, with glance of beauty, which pricketh as a forked arrow. He is said also to have shafts, some leaden, some golden: that is, both pleasure for the gracious and loved, and sorrow for the lover that is disdained or forsaken. But who list more at large to behold Cupid's colours and furniture, let him read either Propertius, or Moschus his Idyllion of *Winged Love*, being now most excellently translated into Latin, by the singular learned man Angelus Politianus: which work I have seen, amongst other of this poet's doings, very well translated also into English rhymes.

Wimble and wight, quick and deliver.

In the heel, is very poetically spoken, and not without special judgement. For I remember that in Homer it is said of Thetis, that she took her young babe Achilles, being newly born, and, holding him by the heel, dipped him in the River of Styx. The virtue whereof is, to defend and keep the bodies washed therein from any mortal wound. So Achilles being washed all over, save only his heel, by which his mother held, was in the rest invulnerable; therefore by Paris was feigned to be shot with a poisoned arrow in the heel, whiles he was busy about the marrying of Polyxena in the Temple of Apollo: which mystical fable Eustathius unfolding saith: that by wounding in the heel is meant lustful love. For from the heel (as say the best physicians) to the privy parts there pass certain veins and slender sinews, as also the like come from the head, and are carried like little pipes behind the ears: so that (as saith Hippocrates) if those veins there be cut asunder, the part straight becometh cold and unfruitful. Which reason our poet well weighing, maketh this shepherd's boy of purpose to be wounded by Love in the heel.

Latched, caught.

Wroken, revenged.

For once. In this tale is set out the simplicity of shepherds' opinion of Love.

Stooping Phœbus, is a periphrasis of the sun setting.

EMBLEM

Hereby is meant, that all the delights of love wherein wanton youth walloweth, be but folly mixt with bitterness, and sorrow sauced with repentance. For besides that the very affection of love itself, tormenteth the mind, and vexeth the body many ways, with unrestfulness all night, and weariness all day, seeking for that we cannot have, and finding that we would not have: even the self things which best before us liked, in course of time, and change of riper years, which also therewithal changeth our wonted liking and former fantasies, will then seem loathsome, and breed us annoyance, when youth's flower is withered, and we find our bodies and wits answer not to such vain jollity and lustful pleasance.

APRIL

ÆGLOGA QUARTA. ARGUMENT

THIS *æglogue* is purposely intended to the honour and praise of our most gracious sovereign, Queen Elizabeth. The speakers herein be Hobbinol and Thenot, two shepherds: the which Hobbinol, being before mentioned greatly to have loved Colin, is here set forth more largely, complaining him of that boy's great misadventure in love: whereby his mind was alienate and withdrawn not only from him, who most loved him, but also from all former delights and studies, as well in pleasant piping, as conning rhyming and singing, and other his laudable exercises. Whereby he taketh occasion, for proof of his more excellency and skill in poetry, to record a song, which the said Colin sometime made in honour of her Majesty, whom abruptly he termeth Elisa.

THENOT. HOBBINOL

The. Tell me, good Hobbinol, what gars thee greet?
 What? hath some wolf thy tender lambs ytorn?
Or is thy bagpipe broke, that sounds so sweet?
 Or art thou of thy lovéd lass forlorn?

Or bene thine eyes attemp'red to the year,
 Quenching the gasping furrows' thirst with rain?
Like April shower so streams the trickling tears
 Adown thy cheek, to quench thy thirsty pain.

Hob. Nor this, nor that, so much doth make me mourn,
 But for the lad, whom long I loved so dear,
Now loves a lass that all his love doth scorn:
 He plunged in pain, his tresséd locks doth tear.

Shepherds' delights he doth them all forswear;
 His pleasant pipe, which made us merriment,
He wilfully hath broke, and doth forbear
 His wonted songs, wherein he all outwent.

The. What is he for a lad, you so lament?
 Is love such pinching pain to them that prove?
And hath he skill to make so excellent,
 Yet hath so little skill to bridle love?

Hob. Colin thou kenn'st, the southern shepherd's boy;
 Him Love hath wounded with a deadly dart:
Whilom on him was all my care and joy,
 Forcing with gifts to win his wanton heart.

But now from me his madding mind is start,
    And woos the widow's daughter of the glen;
So now fair Rosalind hath bred his smart,
    So now his friend is changéd for a fren.

The. But if his ditties bene so trimly dight,
    I pray thee, Hobbinoll, record some one,
The whiles our flocks do graze about in sight,
    And we close shrouded in this shade alone.

Hob. Contented I: then will I sing his lay
    Of fair Elisa, queen of shepherds all,
Which once he made as by a spring he lay,
    And tunéd it unto the water's fall.

"Ye dainty nymphs, that in this blessed brook
    Do bathe your breast,
Forsake your wat'ry bowers, and hither look,
    At my request:
And eke you virgins, that on Parnasse dwell,
Whence floweth Helicon, the learned well,
    Help me to blaze
    Her worthy praise,
Which in her sex doth all excel.

"Of fair Elisa be your silver song,
    That blessed wight,
The flower of virgins: may she flourish long
    In princely plight!
For she is Syrinx' daughter without spot,
Which Pan, the shepherds' god, of her begot:
    So sprong her grace
    Of heavenly race,
No mortal blemish may her blot.

"See, where she sits upon the grassy green,
    (O seemly sight!)
Yclad in scarlet, like a maiden queen,
    And ermines white:
Upon her head a cremosin coronet,
With damask roses and daffadillies set:
    Bay leaves between,
    And primroses green,
Embellish the sweet violet.

APRIL

"Tell me, have ye seen her angelic face,
   Like Phœbe fair?
Her heavenly 'haviour, her princely grace,
   Can you well compare?
The red rose medled with the white yfere,
In either cheek depeincten lively cheer:
   Her modest eye,
   Her majesty,
Where have you seen the like but there?

"I saw Phœbus thrust out his golden head,
   Upon her to gaze:
But, when he saw how broad her beams did spread,
   It did him amaze.
He blushed to see another sun below,
Ne durst again his fiery face out show:
   Let him, if he dare,
   His brightness compare
With hers, to have the overthrow.

"Shew thyself, Cynthia, with thy silver rays,
   And be not abasht;
When she the beams of her beauty displays,
   O, how art thou dasht!
But I will not match her with Latona's seed,
Such folly great sorrow to Niobe did breed:
   Now she is a stone,
   And makes daily moan,
Warning all other to take heed.

"Pan may be proud that ever he begot
   Such a bellibone;
And Syrinx rejoice that ever was her lot
   To bear such an one.
Soon as my younglings crien for the dam
To her will I offer a milkwhite lamb:
   She is my goddess plain,
   And I her shepherd's swain,
Albe forswonk and forswat I am.

"I see Calliope speed her to the place,
   Where my goddess shines;
And after her the other Muses trace,
   With their violines.

Bene they not bay branches which they do bear,
All for Elisa in her hand to wear?
  So sweetly they play,
  And sing all the way,
That it a heaven is to hear.

"Lo! how finely the Graces can it foot
  To the instrument:
They dancen deffly, and singen soot,
  In their merriment.
Wants not a fourth Grace, to make the dance even?
Let that room to my lady be yeven:
  She shall be a Grace,
  To fill the fourth place,
And reign with the rest in heaven.

"And whither runs this bevy of ladies bright,
  Ranged in a row?
They bene all Ladies of the Lake behight,
  That unto her go.
Chloris, that is the chiefest nymph of all,
Of olive branches bears a coronal:
  Olives bene for peace,
  When wars do surcease:
Such for a princess bene principal.

"Ye shepherds' daughters, that dwell on the green,
  Hie you there apace:
Let none come there but that virgins bene,
  To adorn her grace:
And when you come, whereas she is in place,
See that your rudeness do not you disgrace:
  Bind your fillets fast,
  And gird in your waist,
For more fineness, with a tawdry lace.

"Bring hither the pink and purple columbine,
  With gillyflowers;
Bring coronations, and sops in wine,
  Worn of paramours:
Strow me the ground with daffadowndillies,
And cowslips, and kingcups, and lovéd lilies:

APRIL

    The pretty paunce,
      And the chevisaunce,
Shall match with the fair flower-de-lis.

"Now rise up, Elisa, deckéd as thou art
    In royal array;
And now ye dainty damsels may depart
    Each one her way.
I fear I have troubléd your troops too long:
Let dame Elisa thank you for her song:
    And if you come hether
    When damsons I gether,
I will part them all you among."

The. And was thilk same song of Colin's own making?
    Ah, foolish boy! that is with love yblent:
Great pity is, he be in such taking,
    For naught caren, that bene so lewdly bent.

Hob. Sicker I hold him for a greater fon,
    That loves the thing he cannot purcháse.
But let us homeward, for night draweth on,
    And twinkling stars the daylight hence chase.

THENOT'S EMBLEM
O quam te memorem Virgo!

HOBBINOL'S EMBLEM
O dea certe!

GLOSS

Gars thee greet, causeth thee weep and complain.
Forlorn, left and forsaken.
Attemp'red to the year, agreeable to the season of the year, that is April, which month is most bent to showers and seasonable rain: to quench, that is, to delay the drought, caused through dryness of March winds.
The Lad, Colin Clout.
The Lass, Rosalinda.
Tresséd locks, wreathed and curled.
Is he for a lad? a strange manner of speaking, s. what manner of lad is he?
To make, to rhyme and versify. For in this word, *making,* our old English poets were wont to comprehend all the skill of poetry,

according to the Greek word ποιεῖν, to make, whence cometh the name of poets.

Colin thou kenn'st, knowest. Seemeth hereby that Colin pertaineth to some southern nobleman, and perhaps in Surrey or Kent, the rather because he so often nameth the Kentish downs, and before, *As lithe as lass of Kent*.

The widow's. He calleth Rosalind the widow's daughter of the glen, that is, of a country hamlet or borough, which I think is rather said to colour and conceal the person, than simply spoken. For it is well known, even in spite of Colin and Hobbinol, that she is a gentle woman of no mean house, nor endued with any vulgar and common gifts, both of nature and manners: but such indeed, as need neither Colin be ashamed to have her made known by his verses, nor Hobbinol be grieved, that so she should be commended to immortality for her rare and singular virtues: specially deserving it no less, than either Myrto the most excellent poet Theocritus his darling, or Lauretta the divine Petrarch's goddess, or Himera the worthy poet Stesichorus his idol; upon whom he is said so much to have doted, that, in regard of her excellency, he scorned and wrote against the beauty of Helena. For which his presumptuous and unheedy hardiness, he is said by vengeance of the gods, thereat being offended, to have lost both his eyes.

Fren, a stranger. The word, I think, was first poetically put, and afterward used in common custom of speech for foreign.

Dight, adorned.

Lay, a song, as roundelays and virelays.

In all this song is not to be respected, what the worthiness of her Majesty deserveth, nor what to the highness of a prince is agreeable, but what is most comely for the meanness of a shepherd wit, or to conceive, or to utter. And therefore he calleth her Elisa, as through rudeness tripping in her name; and a shepherd's daughter, it being very unfit, that a shepherd's boy, brought up in the sheepfold, should know, or ever seem to have heard of, a queen's royalty.

Ye dainty, is, as it were, an exordium *ad preparandos animos*.

Virgins, the nine Muses, daughters of Apollo and Memory, whose abode the poets feign to be on Parnassus, a hill in Greece, for that in that country specially flourished the honour of all excellent studies.

Helicon is both the name of a fountain at the foot of Parnassus, and also of a mountain in Bœotia, out of which floweth the famous spring Castalius, dedicate also to the Muses: of which spring it is said, that, when Pegasus the winged horse of Perseus (whereby is meant fame and flying renown) struck the ground with his hoof, suddenly thereout sprang a well of most clear and pleasant water, which from thenceforth was consecrate to the Muses and Ladies of learning.

Your silver song seemeth to imitate the like in Hesiodus, ἀργύριον μέλος.

Syrinx is the name of a nymph of Arcady, whom when Pan being in love pursued, she, flying from him, of the gods was turned into a reed. So that Pan catching at the reeds, instead of the damsel, and puffing hard (for he was almost out of wind) with his breath made the reeds to pipe; which he seeing, took of them, and, in

APRIL

remembrance of his lost love, made him a pipe thereof. But here by Pan and Syrinx is not to be thought, that the shepherd simply meant those poetical gods: but rather supposing (as seemeth) her grace's progeny to be divine and immortal (so as the Paynims were wont to judge of all kings and princes, according to Homer's saying,

Θυμὸς δὲ μέγας ἐστι διοτρεφέος βασιλῆος,
Τιμὴ δ' ἐκ Διός ἐστι, φιλεῖ δέ ἑ μητίετα Ζεύς,)

could devise no parents in his judgement so worthy for her, as Pan the shepherds' god, and his best beloved Syrinx. So that by Pan is here meant the most famous and victorious king, her highness' father, late of worthy memory, K. Henry the Eighth. And by that name, oft-times (as hereafter appeareth) be noted kings and mighty potentates: and in some place Christ himself, who is the very Pan and god of shepherds.

Cremosin coronet. He deviseth her crown to be of the finest and most delicate flowers, instead of pearls and precious stones, wherewith princes' diadems use to be adorned and embossed.

Embellish, beautify and set out.

Phœbe, the moon, whom the poets feign to be sister unto Phœbus, that is, the sun.

Medled, mingled.

Yfere, together. By the mingling of the red rose and the white is meant the uniting of the two principal houses of Lancaster and York: by whose long discord and deadly debate this realm many years was sore travailed, and almost clean decayed. Till the famous Henry the Seventh, of the line of Lancaster, taking to wife the most virtuous Princess Elizabeth, daughter to the fourth Edward of the house of York, begat the most royal Henry the Eighth aforesaid in whom was the first union of the white rose and the red.

Calliope, one of the nine Muses: to whom they assign the honour of all poetical invention, and the first glory of the heroical verse. Others say, that she is the goddess of rhetoric; but by Virgil it is manifest, that they mistake the thing. For there, in his Epigrams, that art seemeth to be attributed to Polymnia, saying,

"Signat cuncta manu, loquiturque Polymnia gestu."

Which seemeth specially to be meant of action, and elocution, both special parts of rhetoric: beside that her name, which (as some construe it) importeth great remembrance, containeth another part: but I hold rather with them, which call her Polymnia, or Polyhymnia, of her good singing.

Bay branches be the sign of honour and victory, and therefore of mighty conquerors worn in their triumphs, and eke of famous poets, as saith Petrarch in his Sonnets,

"Arbor vittoriosa triomphale,
  Honor d' Imperadori et di Poeti," &c.

The Graces be three sisters, the daughters of Jupiter, (whose names are Aglaia, Thalia, Euphrosyne; and Homer only added a fourth, s. Pasithea) otherwise called Charites, that is, thanks: whom the poets feigned to be the goddesses of all bounty and comeliness, which therefore (as saith Theodontius) they make three, to wit, that men first ought to be gracious and bountiful to other freely; then to receive benefits at other men's hands courteously; and thirdly, to requite them thankfully; which are three sundry actions in liberality. And Boccace saith, that they be painted naked (as they were indeed on the tomb of C. Julius Cæsar) the one having her back toward us, and her face fromward, as proceeding from us; the other two toward us, noting double thank to be due to us for the benefit we have done.

Deffly, finely and nimbly.

Soot, sweet.

Merriment, mirth.

Bevy. A bevy of ladies is spoken figuratively for a company, or troop: the term is taken of larks. For they say a bevy of larks, even as a covey of partridge, or an eye of pheasants.

Ladies of the Lake be nymphs. For it was an old opinion amongst the ancient heathen, that every spring and fountain was a goddess the sovereign. Which opinion stuck in the minds of men not many years sithence, by means of certain fine fablers, and loud liars, such as were the authors of *King Arthur the Great*, and such-like, who tell many an unlawful leasing of the Ladies of the Lake, that is, the nymphs. For the word nymph in Greek, signifieth well-water, or otherwise, a spouse or bride.

Behight, called or named.

Chloris, the name of a nymph, and signifieth greenness; of whom is said, that Zephyrus, the western wind, being in love with her, and coveting her to wife, gave her for a dowry the chiefdom and sovereignty of all flowers and green herbs growing on earth.

Olives bene. The olive was wont to be the ensign of peace and quietness, either for that it cannot be planted and pruned, and so carefully looked to as it ought, but in time of peace; or else for that the olive tree, they say, will not grow near the fir tree, which is dedicate to Mars the god of battle, and used most for spears, and other instruments of war. Whereupon is finely feigned, that when Neptune and Minerva strove for the naming of the city of Athens, Neptune striking the ground with his mace caused a horse to come forth, that importeth war, but at Minerva's stroke sprung out an olive, to note that it should be a nurse of learning, and such peaceable studies.

Bind your, spoken rudely, and according to shepherds' simplicity.

Bring. All these be names of flowers. *Sops in wine*, a flower in colour much like to a coronation, but differing in smell and quantity.

Flower-de-lis, that which they use to misterm flower deluce, being in Latin called *Flos deliciarum*.

A Bellibone, or a bonibell, homely spoken for a fair maid, or bonilass.

Forswonk and forswat, overlaboured and sunburnt.

I saw Phœbus, the sun. A sensible narration, and present view of the thing mentioned, which they call παρουσία.

Cynthia, the moon, so called of *Cynthus* a hill, where she was honoured.

Latona's seed was Apollo and Diana. Whom, whenas Niobe the wife of Amphion scorned, in respect of the noble fruit of her womb, namely her seven sons, and so many daughters, Latona, being there-

APRIL

with displeased, commanded her son Phœbus to slay all the sons, and Diana all the daughters: whereat the unfortunate Niobe being sore dismayed, and lamenting out of measure, was feigned of the poets to be turned into a stone, upon the sepulchre of her children: for which cause the shepherd saith, he will not compare her to them, for fear of like misfortune.

Now rise, is the conclusion. For, having so decked her with praises and comparisons, he returneth all the thank of his labour to the excellency of her Majesty.

When damsons, a base reward of a clownish giver.

Yblent. Y is a poetical addition; *blent*, blinded.

EMBLEM

This poesy is taken out of Virgil, and there of him used in the person of Æneas to his mother Venus, appearing to him in likeness of one of Diana's damosels: being there most divinely set forth. To which similitude of divinity Hobbinol, comparing the excellency of Elisa, and being, through the worthiness of Colin's song, as it were, overcome with the hugeness of his imagination, bursteth out in great admiration, (*O quam te memorem virgo!*) being otherwise unable, than by sudden silence, to express the worthiness of his conceit. Whom Thenot answereth with another part of the like verse, as confirming by his grant and approvance, that Elisa is no whit inferior to the majesty of her, of whom that poet so boldly pronounced *O dea certe*.

MAY

ÆGLOGA QUINTA. ARGUMENT

IN *this fifth æglogue, under the persons of two shepherds, Piers and Palinode, be represented two forms of pastors or ministers, or the Protestant and the Catholic: whose chief talk standeth in reasoning, whether the life of the one must be like the other: with whom having shewed, that it is dangerous to maintain any fellowship, or give too much credit to their colourable and feigned good will, he telleth him a tale of the fox, that, by such a counterpoint of craftiness, deceived and devoured the credulous kid.*

PALINODE. PIERS

Palinode. Is not thilk the merry month of May,
  When love-lads masken in fresh array?
  How falls it, then, we no merrier bene,
  Ylike as others, girt in gaudy green?
  Our bloncket liveries bene all too sad
  For thilk same season, when all is yclad

With pleasance: the ground with grass, the woods
With green leaves, the bushes with bloosming buds.
Youngthes folk now flocken in everywhere,
To gather May buskets and smelling brere:
And home they hasten the posts to dight,
And all the kirk pillars ere daylight,
With hawthorn buds, and sweet eglantine,
And girlonds of roses, and sops in wine.
Such merrymake holy saints doth queme,
But we here sitten as drowned in a dream.

Piers. For younkers, Palinode, such follies fit,
But we tway bene men of elder wit.

Pal. Sicker this morrow, no longer ago,
I saw a shoal of shepherds outgo
With singing, and shouting, and jolly cheer:
Before them yode a lusty tabrere,
That to the many a horn-pipe played,
Whereto they dancen, each one with his maid.
To see those folks make such jouissance,
Made my heart after the pipe to dance:
Then to the green wood they speeden hem all,
To fetchen home May with their musicall:
And home they bringen in a royal throne,
Crownéd as king: and his queen attone
Was Lady Flora, on whom did attend
A fair flock of faeries, and a fresh bend
Of lovely nymphs. (O that I were there,
To helpen the ladies their maybush bear!)
Ah! Piers, bene not thy teeth on edge, to think
How great sport they gainen with little swink?

Piers. Perdie, so far am I from envy,
That their fondness inly I pity:
Those faitours little regarden their charge,
While they, letting their sheep run at large,
Passen their time, that should be sparely spent,
In lustihead and wanton merriment.
Thilk same bene shepherds for the devil's stead,
That playen while their flocks be unfed:
Well is it seen their sheep bene not their own,
That letten them run at random alone:
But they bene hiréd for little pay
Of other, that caren as little as they
What fallen the flock, so they han the fleece,

MAY

And get all the gain, paying but a piece.
I muse, what account both these will make,
The one for the hire, which he doth take,
And th' other for leaving his lord's task,
When great Pan account of shepherds shall **ask**.

Pal. Sicker, now I see thou speakest of spite,
All for thou lackest somedeal their delight.
I (as I am) had rather be envied,
All were it of my foe, then fonly pitied:
And yet, if need were, pitied would be,
Rather than other should scorn at me:
For pitied is mishap that nas remedy,
But scorned bene deeds of fond foolery.
What shoulden shepherds other things tend,
Than sith their god his good does them send,
Reapen the fruit thereof, that is pleasure,
The while they here liven at ease and leisure?
For, when they bene dead, their good is ygo,
They sleepen in rest, well as other mo.
Tho with them wends what they spent in cost,
But what they left behind them is lost.
Good is no good, but if it be spend;
God giveth good for none other end.

Piers. Ah, Palinode, thou art a world's child:
Who touches pitch, mought needs be defiled;
But shepherds (as Algrind used to say)
Mought not live ylike as men of the lay.
With them it sits to care for their heir,
Enaunter their heritage do impair.
They must provide for means of maintenance,
And to continue their wont countenance.
But shepherd must walk another way,
Sike worldly sovenance he must forsay.
The son of his loins why should he regard
To leave enrichéd with that he hath spared?
Should not thilk God, that gave him that good,
Eke cherish his child, if in his ways he stood?
For if he mislive in lewdness and lust,
Little boots all the wealth and the trust
That his father left by inheritance;
All will be soon wasted with misgovernance;
But through this, and other their miscreance,
They maken many a wrong chevisance,

Heaping up waves of wealth and woe,
The floods whereof shall them overflow.
Sike men's folly I cannot compare
Better than to the ape's foolish care,
That is so enamouréd of her young one,
(And yet, God wot, such cause hath she none)
That with her hard hold, and strait embracing,
She stoppeth the breath of her youngling.
So oftentimes, whenas good is meant,
Evil ensueth of wrong intent.

 The time was once, and may again retorn,
(For aught may happen, that hath been beforn)
When shepherds had none inheritánce,
Ne of land, nor fee in sufferánce,
But what might arise of the bare sheep,
(Were it more or less) which they did keep.
Well ywis was it with shepherds tho:
Nought having, nought feared they to forgo;
For Pan himself was their inheritance,
And little them served for their maintenance.
The shepherds' god so well them guided,
That of nought they were unprovided;
Butter enough, honey, milk, and whey,
And their flocks' fleeces them to array:
But tract of time, and long prosperity,
That nurse of vice, this of insolency,
Lulled the shepherds in such security,
That, not content with loyal obeisance,
Some gan to gape for greedy governance,
And match themself with mighty potentates,
Lovers of lordship, and troublers of states.
Then gan shepherds' swains to look aloft,
And leave to live hard, and learn to lie soft:
Then, under colour of shepherds, somewhile
There crept in wolves, full of fraud, and guile,
That often devouréd their own sheep,
And often the shepherds that did hem keep:
This was the first source of shepherds' sorrow,
That now nill be quit with bail nor borrow.

Pal. Three things to bear bene very burdenous,
But the fourth to forbear is outragéous:
Women, that of love's longing once lust,
Hardly forbearen, but have it they must:

MAY

So when choler is inflaméd with rage,
Wanting revenge, is hard to assuage:
And who can counsel a thirsty soul,
With patience to forbear the off'red bowl?
But of all burdens, that a man can bear,
Most is a fool's talk to bear and to hear.
I ween the giant has not such a weight,
That bears on his shoulders the heavens' height.
Thou findest fault where nis to be found,
And buildest strong wark upon a weak ground:
Thou railest on, right withouten reason,
And blamest hem much for small encheason.
How shoulden shepherds live, if not so?
What! should they pinen in pain and woe?
Nay, say I thereto, by my dear borrow,
If I may rest, I nill live in sorrow.

   Sorrow ne need be hastened on,
For he will come, without calling, anon.
While times enduren of tranquillity,
Usen we freely our felicity;
For, when approachen the stormy stours,
We mought with our shoulders bear of the sharp
    showers;
And, sooth to sayn, nought seemeth sike strife,
That shepherds so witen each other's life,
And layen her faults the world beforn,
The while their foes done each of hem scorn.
Let none mislike of that may not be mended:
So conteck soon by concord mought be ended.

Piers. Shepherd, I list none accordance make
With shepherd that does the right way forsake:
And of the twain, if choice were to me,
Had lever my foe than my friend he be.
For what concord han light and dark sam?
Or what peace has the lion with the lamb?
Such faitours, when their false hearts bene hid,
Will do as did the fox by the kid.

Pal. Now, Piers, of fellowship, tell us that saying:
For the lad can keep both our flocks from straying.

Piers. Thilk same kid (as I can well devise)
Was too very foolish and unwise;
For on a time, in summer season,
The gate her dam, that had good reason,

Yode forth abroad unto the green wood,
To browse, or play, or what she thought good:
But, for she had a motherly care
Of her young son, and wit to beware,
She set her youngling before her knee,
That was both fresh and lovely to see,
And full of favour as kid mought be.
His velvet head began to shoot out,
And his wreathed horns gan newly sprout:
The bloosmes of lust to bud did begin,
And spring forth rankly under his chin.
"My son," (quoth she and with that gan weep,
For careful thoughts in her heart did creep)
"God bless thee, poor orphan! as He mought me,
And send thee joy of thy jollity.
Thy father" (that word she spake with pain,
For a sigh had nigh rent her heart in twain)—
"Thy father, had he lived this day,
To see the branch of his body display,
How would he have joyéd at this sweet sight!
But ah! false Fortune such joy did him spite,
And cut off his days with untimely woe,
Betraying him into the trains of his foe.
Now I, a wailful widow behight,
Of my old age have this one delight,
To see thee succeed in thy father's stead,
And flourish in flowers of lustihead:
For even so thy father his head upheld,
And so his haughty horns did he weld."
   Then marking him with melting eyes,
A thrilling throb from her heart did arise,
And interrupted all her other speech
With some old sorrow that made a new breach:
Seemed she saw in the youngling's face
The old lineaments of his father's grace.
At last her solein silence she broke,
And gan his new-budded beard to stroke.
"Kiddie," (quoth she) "thou kenn'st the great care
I have of thy health and thy welfare,
Which many wild beasts liggen in wait
For to entrap in thy tender state:
But most the fox, master of collusion:
For he has vowed thy last confusion.

MAY

For-thy, my Kiddie, be ruled by me,
And never give trust to his treachery:
And, if he chance come when I am abroad,
Sperre the yate fast for fear of fraud:
Ne for all his worst, nor for his best,
Open the door at his request."

So schooled the gate her wanton son,
That answered his mother, all should be done.
Then went the pensive dam out of door,
And chanced to stumble at the threshold floor:
Her stumbling step somewhat her amazed,
(For such, as signs of ill luck, bene dispraised)
Yet forth she yode, thereat half aghast:
And Kiddie the door sperred after her fast.
It was not long, after she was gone,
But the false fox came to the door anon:
Not as a fox, for then he had be kenned,
But all as a poor pedlar he did wend,
Bearing a truss of trifles at his back,
As bells, and babes, and glasses, in his pack.
A biggen he had got about his brain,
For in his headpiece he felt a sore pain:
His hinder heel was wrapt in a clout,
For with great cold he had got the gout.
There at the door he cast me down his pack,
And laid him down, and groaned, "Alack! Alack!
Ah, dear Lord! and sweet Saint Charity!
That some good body would once pity me!"

Well heard Kiddie all this sore constraint,
And longed to know the cause of his complaint:
Then, creeping close behind the wicket's clink,
Privily he peeped out through a chink,
Yet not so privily but the fox him spied;
For deceitful meaning is double eyed.

"Ah, good young master!" (then gan he cry)
"Jesus bless that sweet face I espy,
And keep your corpse from the careful stounds
That in my carrion carcass abounds."

The kid, pitying his heaviness,
Asked the cause of his great distress,
And also who, and whence that he were?

Then he, that had well yconned his lere,
Thus medled his talk with many a tear:

"Sick, sick, alas! and little lack of dead,
But I be relieved by your beastlihead.
I am a poor sheep, albe my colour dun,
For with long travail I am burnt in the sun:
And, if that my grandsire me said be true,
Sicker, I am very sib to you:
So be your goodlihead do not disdain
The base kindred of so simple swain.
Of mercy and favour, then, I you pray
With your aid to forestall my near decay."

Then out of his pack a glass he took,
Wherein while Kiddie unwares did look,
He was so enamoured with the newel,
That nought he deeméd dear for the jewel:
Then opened he the door, and in came
The false fox, as he were stark lame:
His tail he clapt betwixt his legs twain,
Lest he should be descried by his train.

Being within, the kid made him good glee,
All for the love of the glass he did see.
After his cheer the pedlar gan chat,
And tell many leasings of this and that,
And how he could shew many a fine knack:
Then shewed his ware and opened his pack,
All save a bell, which he left behind
In the basket for the kid to find:
Which when the kid stooped down to catch,
He popt him in, and his basket did latch:
Ne stayed he once the door to make fast,
But ran away with him in all haste.

Home when the doubtful dam had her hied,
She mought see the door stand open wide.
All aghast, loudly she gan to call
Her kid; but he nould answer at all:
Then on the floor she saw the merchandise
Of which her son had set too dear a price.
What help? her kid she knew well was gone:
She weeped, and wailed, and made great moan.
Such end had the kid, for he nould warnéd be
Of craft, colouréd with simplicity:
And such end, perdie, does all hem remain,
That of such falsers' friendship bene fain.

Pal. Truly, Piers, thou art beside thy wit,

MAY

Furthest fro the mark, weening it to hit.
Now, I pray thee, let me thy tale borrow
For our Sir John, to say to-morrow
At the kirk, when it is holiday;
For well he means, but little can say.
But, and if foxes bene so crafty as so,
Much needeth all shepherds hem to know.
Piers. Of their falsehood more could I recount,
But now the bright sun ginneth to dismount,
And, for the dewy night now doth nye,
I hold it best for us home to hie.

PALINODE'S EMBLEM

Πᾶς μὲν ἄπιστος ἀπιστεῖ.

PIERS HIS EMBLEM

Τίς δ' ἄρα πίστις ἀπίστῳ;

GLOSS

Thilk, this same month. It is applied to the season of the month, when all men delight themselves with pleasance of fields, and gardens, and garments.

Blonket liveries, gray coats.

Yclad, arrayed. *Y* redoundeth, as before.

In everywhere, a strange, yet proper kind of speaking.

Buskets, a diminutive, s. little bushes of hawthorn.

Kirk, church.

Queme, please.

A shoal, a multitude, taken of fish, whereof some, going in great companies, are said to swim in a shoal.

Yode, went.

Jouissance, joy.

Swink, labour.

Inly, entirely.

Faitours, vagabonds.

Great Pan is Christ, the very God of all shepherds, which calleth himself the great, and good shepherd. The name is most rightly (methinks) applied to him; for Pan signifieth all, or omnipotent, which is only the Lord Jesus. And by that name (as I remember) he is called of Eusebius, in his fifth book *De Preparat. Evang.*, who thereof telleth a proper story to that purpose. Which story is first recorded of Plutarch, in his book of the ceasing of oracles: and of Lavatere translated, in his book of walking sprites; who saith, that about the same time that our Lord suffered his most bitter passion, for the redemption of man, certain passengers sailing from Italy to Cyprus, and passing by certain isles called Paxæ, heard a voice calling aloud Thamus, Thamus! (now Thamus was the name of an Egyptian, which was pilot of the ship) who, giving ear to the cry, was bidden, when he came to Palodes, to tell that the great Pan was dead: which he doubting to do, yet for that when he came to Palodes, there suddenly was such a calm of wind, that the ship stood still in the sea unmoved, he was forced to cry aloud, that Pan was dead: wherewithal there was heard such piteous outcries, and dreadful shriekings, as hath not been the like. By which Pan, though of some be understood the great Satanas, whose kingdom at that time was by Christ conquered, the gates of hell broken up, and death by death delivered to eternal death, (for at that time, as he saith, all oracles surceased, and enchanted spirits, that were wont to delude the people, thenceforth held their peace:) and also at the demand of the Emperor Tiberius, who that Pan should be, answer was made him by the wisest and best learned, that it was the son of Mercury and Penelope: yet I think it more properly meant of the death of Christ, the only and very Pan, then suffering for his flock.

I as I am, seemeth to imitate the common proverb, *Malim invidere mihi omnes, quam miserescere.*

Nas is a syncope, for *ne has,* or *has not*: as *nould* for *would not.*

Tho with them doth imitate the epitaph of the riotous King Sardanapalus, which he caused to be written on his tomb in Greek; which verses be thus translated by Tully:

> "Hæc habui quæ edi, quæque exsaturata libido
> Hausit, at illa manent multa ac præclara relicta."

Which may thus be turned into English:

> "All that I eat did I joy, and all that I greedily gorged:
> As for those many goodly matters left I for others."

Much like the epitaph of a good old Earl of Devonshire, which though much more wisdom bewrayeth than Sardanapalus, yet hath a smack of his sensual delights and beastliness: the rhymes be these:

> "Ho, ho! who lies here?
> I the good Earl of Devonshere,
> And Maulde my wife that was full dear:
> We lived together lv. year.
>
> That we spent, we had:
> That we gave, we have:
> That we left, we lost."

Algrind, the name of a shepherd.

Men of the lay, laymen.

Enaunter, lest that.

Sovenance, remembrance.

Miscreance, despair, or misbelief.

Chevisance, sometime of Chaucer used for gain: sometime of other for spoil, or booty, or enterprise, and sometime for chiefdom.

Pan himself, God: according as is said in Deuteronomy, that, in division of the land of Canaan, to the tribe of Levi no portion of heritage should be allotted, for God himself was their inheritance.

Some gan, meant of the Pope, and his antichristian prelates, which usurp a tyrannical dominion in the Church, and with Peter's

MAY

counterfeit keys open a wide gate to all wickedness and insolent government. Nought here spoken, as of purpose to deny fatherly rule and governance (as some maliciously of late have done, to the great unrest and hindrance of the Church) but to display the pride and disorder of such, as, instead of feeding their sheep, indeed feed of their sheep.

Source, wellspring and original.

Borrow, pledge or surety.

The giant is the great Atlas, whom the poets feign to be a huge giant, that beareth heaven on his shoulders: being indeed a marvellous high mountain in Mauritania, that now is Barbary, which, to man's seeming, pierceth the clouds, and seemeth to touch the heavens. Other think, and they not amiss, that this fable was meant of one Atlas king of the same country, (of whom may be, that that hill had his denomination) brother to Prometheus, who (as the Greeks say) did first find out the hidden courses of the stars, by an excellent imagination: wherefore the poets feigned, that he sustained the firmament on his shoulders. Many other conjectures needless be told hereof.

Wark, work.

Encheason, cause, occasion.

Dear borrow, that is our Saviour, the common pledge of all men's debts to death.

Witen, blame.

Nought seemeth, is unseemly.

Conteck, strife, contention.

Her, their, as useth Chaucer.

Han, for have.

Sam, together.

This tale is much like to that in Æsop's fables, but the catastrophe and end is far different. By the kid may be understood the simple sort of the faithful and true Christians. By his dam Christ, that hath already with careful watchwords (as here doth the goat) warned her little ones, to beware of such doubling deceit. By the fox, the false and faithless Papists, to whom is no credit to be given, nor fellowship to be used.

The gate, the goat: northernly spoken, to turn O into A.

Yode, went: aforesaid.

She set, a figure called *Fictio*, which useth to attribute reasonable actions and speeches to unreasonable creatures.

The bloosmes of lust be the young and mossy hairs, which then begin to sprout and shoot forth, when lustful heat beginneth to kindle.

And with, a very poetical πάθος.

Orphan, a youngling or pupil, that needeth a tutor and governor.

That word, a pathetical parenthesis, to increase a careful hyperbaton.

The branch, of the father's body, is the child.

For even so, alluded to the saying of Andromache to Ascanius in Virgil:

"Sic oculos, sic ille manus, sic ora ferebat."

A thrilling throb, a piercing sigh.

Liggen, lie.

Master of collusion, s. coloured guile, because the fox of all beasts, is most wily and crafty.

Sperre the yate, shut the door.

For such. The goat's stumbling is here noted as an evil sign. The like to be marked in all histories: and that not the least of the Lord Hastings in King Richard the Third his days. For, beside his dangerous dream (which was a shrewd prophecy of his mishap that followed) it is said, that in the morning, riding toward the Tower of London, there to sit upon matters of counsel, his horse stumbled twice or thrice by the way: which, of some, that riding with him in his company were privy to his near destiny, was secretly marked, and afterward noted for memory of his great mishap that ensued. For being then as merry as man might be, and least doubting any mortal danger, he was, within two hours after, of the tyrant put to a shameful death.

As bells. By such trifles are noted the relics and rags of popish superstition, which put no small religion in bells, and babies, s. idols, and glasses, s. paxes, and such-like trumperies.

Great cold, for they boast much of their outward patience, and voluntary sufferance, as a work of merit and holy humbleness.

Sweet S. Charity, the Catholics' common oath, and only speech, to have charity always in their mouth, and sometime in their outward actions, but never inwardly in faith and godly zeal.

Clink, a keyhole. Whose diminutive is clicket, used of Chaucer for a key.

Stounds, fits: aforesaid.

His lere, his lesson.

Medled, mingled.

Beastlihead, agreeing to the person of a beast.

Sib, of kin.

Newel, a new thing.

To forestall, to prevent.

Glee, cheer: aforesaid.

Dear a price, his life which he lost for those toys.

Such end is an epiphonema, or rather the moral of the whole tale, whose purpose is to warn the Protestant beware, how he giveth credit to the unfaithful Catholic; wherof we have daily proofs sufficient, but one most famous of all practised of late years in France, by Charles the Ninth.

Fain, glad or desirous.

Our Sir John, a Popish priest. A saying fit for the grossness of a shepherd, but spoken to taunt unlearned priests.

Dismount, descend or set.

Nye, draweth near.

EMBLEM

Both these emblems make one whole hexameter. The first, spoken of Palinode, as in reproach of them that be distrustful, is a piece of Theognis' verse, intending, that who doth most mistrust is most false. For such experience in falsehood breedeth mistrust in the mind, thinking no less guile to lurk in others than in himself.

JUNE

But Piers thereto strongly replieth with another piece of the same verse, saying, as in his former fable, what faith then is there in the faithless? For if faith be the ground of religion, which faith they daily false, what hold is then there of their religion? And this is all that they say.

JUNE

ÆGLOGA SEXTA.   ARGUMENT

THIS *æglogue is wholly vowed to the complaining of Colin's ill success in his love. For being (as is aforesaid) enamoured of a country lass, Rosalind, and having (as seemeth) found place in her heart, he lamenteth to his dear friend Hobbinol, that he is now forsaken unfaithfully, and in his stead Menalcas, another shepherd, received disloyally. And this is the whole argument of this æglogue.*

HOBBINOL.   COLIN CLOUT

Hob. Lo, Colin, here the place whose pleasant site
   From other shades hath weaned my wand'ring mind:
   Tell me, what wants me here to work delight?
   The simple air, the gentle warbling wind,
   So calm, so cool, as nowhere else I find:
   The grassy ground with dainty daisies dight,
   The bramble bush, where birds of every kind
   To the waters' fall their tunes attemper right.

Col. O happy Hobbinol! I bless thy state,
   That Paradise hast found which Adam lost:
   Here wander may thy flock, early or late,
   Withouten dread of wolves to bene ytost:
   Thy lovely lays here may'st thou freely boast.
   But I, unhappy man, whom cruel fate
   And angry gods pursue from coast to coast,
   Can nowhere find to shroud my luckless pate.

Hob. Then, if by me thou list advisèd be,
   Forsake the soil that so doth thee bewitch:
   Leave me those hills where harbour nis to see,
   Nor holly-bush, nor briar, nor winding witch:
   And to the dales resort, where shepherds rich,
   And fruitful flocks, bene everywhere to see:
   Here no night-ravens lodge, more black than pitch,
   For elvish ghosts, nor ghastly owls do flee.

   But friendly faeries, met with many Graces,
   And lightfoot nymphs, can chase the ling'ring night

With heydeguies, and trimly trodden traces,
Whilst sisters nine, which dwell on Parnasse height,
Do make them music for their more delight:
And Pan himself, to kiss their crystal faces,
Will pipe and dance when Phœbe shineth bright:
Such peerless pleasures have we in these places.

Col. And I, whilst youth and course of careless years,
    Did let me walk withouten links of love,
In such delights did joy amongst my peers:
But riper age such pleasures doth reprove:
My fancy eke from former follies move
To stayéd steps: for time in passing wears,
(As garments doen, which wexen old above)
And draweth new delights with hoary hairs.

Then couth I sing of love, and tune my pipe
Unto my plaintive pleas in verses made:
Then would I seek for queen-apples unripe,
To give my Rosalind; and in summer shade
Dight gaudy girlonds, was my common trade,
To crown her golden locks: but years more ripe,
And loss of her, whose love as life I weighed,
Those weary wanton toys away did wipe.

Hob. Colin, to hear thy rhymes and roundelays,
    Which thou were wont on wasteful hills to sing,
I more delight than lark in summer days:
Whose echo made the neighbour groves to ring,
And taught the birds, which in the lower spring
Did shroud in shady leaves from sunny rays,
Frame to thy song their cheerful cheriping,
Or hold their peace, for shame of thy sweet lays.

I saw Calliope with Muses mo,
Soon as thy oaten pipe began to sound,
Their ivory lutes and tamburines forgo,
And from the fountain, where they sat around,
Run after hastily thy silver sound;
But, when they came where thou thy skill didst show,
They drew aback, as half with shame confound
Shepherd to see them in their art outgo.

JUNE

Col. Of Muses, Hobbinol, I con no skill,
    For they bene daughters of the highest Jove,
    And holden scorn of homely shepherds' quill:
    For sith I heard that Pan with Phœbus strove,
    Which him to much rebuke and danger drove,
    I never list presume to Parnasse hill,
    But piping low in shade of lowly grove,
    I play to please myself, albeit ill.

Nought weigh I who my song doth praise or blame,
    Ne strive to win renown, or pass the rest:
    With shepherd sits not follow flying fame,
    But feed his flock in fields where falls hem best.
    I wot my rhymes bene rough, and rudely drest;
    The fitter they my careful case to frame:
    Enough is me to paint out my unrest,
    And pour my piteous plaints out in the same.

The god of shepherds, Tityrus, is dead,
    Who taught me homely, as I can, to make;
    He, whilst he livéd, was the sovereign head
    Of shepherds all that bene with love ytake:
    Well couth he wail his woes, and lightly slake
    The flames which love within his heart had bred,
    And tell us merry tales to keep us 'wake,
    The while our sheep about us safely fed.

Now dead he is, and lieth wrapt in lead,
    (Oh, why should Death on him such outrage show?)
    And all his passing skill with him is fled,
    The fame whereof doth daily greater grow.
    But, if on me some little drops would flow
    Of that the spring was in his learned head,
    I soon would learn these woods to wail my woe,
    And teach the trees their trickling tears to shed.

Then should my plaints, caused of discourtesy,
    As messengers of this my painful plight,
    Fly to my love, wherever that she be,
    And pierce her heart with point of worthy wite,
    As she deserves that wrought so deadly spite.
    And thou, Menalcas, that by treachery
    Didst underfong my lass to wex so light,
    Shouldst well be known for such thy villainy

But since I am not as I wish I were,
Ye gentle shepherds, which your flocks do feed,
Whether on hills, or dales, or otherwhere,
Bear witness all of this so wicked deed:
And tell the lass, whose flower is wox a weed,
And faultless faith is turned to faithless fear,
That she the truest shepherd's heart made bleed,
That lives on earth, and lovéd her most dear.

Hob. Oh, careful Colin! I lament thy case;
Thy tears would make the hardest flint to flow!
Ah, faithless Rosalind and void of grace,
That art the root of all this ruthful woe!
But now is time, I guess, homeward to go:
Then rise, ye blessed flocks, and home apace,
Lest night with stealing steps do you forslow,
And wet your tender lambs that by you trace.

COLIN'S EMBLEM

Gia speme spenta.

GLOSS

Site, situation and place.
Paradise. A paradise in Greek, signifieth a garden of pleasure, or place of delights. So he compareth the soil, wherein Hobbinol made his abode, to that earthly Paradise, in Scripture called Eden, wherein Adam in his first creation was placed: which of the most learned is thought to be in Mesopotamia, the most fertile pleasant country in the world (as may appear by Diodorus Siculus' description of it, in the history of Alexander's conquest thereof,) lying between the two famous rivers, (which are said in Scripture to flow out of Paradise) Tigris and Euphrates, whereof it is so denominate.
Forsake the soil. This is no poetical fiction, but unfeignedly spoken of the poet self, who for special occasion of private affairs, (as I have bene partly of himself informed) and for his more preferment, removing out of the north parts, came into the south, as Hobbinol indeed advised him privately.
Those hills, that is in the north country, where he dwelt.
Nis, is not.
The dales, the south parts, where he now abideth, which though they be full of hills and woods (for Kent is very hilly and woody; and therefore so called, for *Kantsh* in the Saxons' tongue signifieth woody,) yet in respect of the north parts they be called dales. For indeed the north is counted the higher country.

Night ravens, &c. By such hateful birds, he meaneth all misfortunes (whereof they be tokens) flying everywhere.

Friendly faeries. The opinion of faeries and elves is very old, and yet sticketh very religiously in the minds of some. But to root that rank opinion of elves out of men's hearts, the truth is, that there be no such things, nor yet the shadows of the things, but only by a sort of bald friars and knavish shavelings so feigned; which as in all other things, so in that, sought to nurse the common people in ignorance, lest, being once acquainted with the truth of things, they would in time smell out the untruth of their packed pelf, and masspenny religion. But the sooth is, that when all Italy was distracted into the factions of the Guelfs and the Gibelines, being two famous houses in Florence, the name began through their great mischiefs and many outrages, to be so odious, or rather dreadful, in the peoples' ears, that, if their children at any time were froward and wanton, they would say to them that the Guelf or the Gibeline came. Which words now from them (as many things else) be come into our usage, and, for Guelfs and Gibelines, we say elfs and goblins. No otherwise than the Frenchmen used to say of that valiant captain, the very scourge of France, the Lord Talbot, afterward Earl of Shrewsbury, whose noblesse bred such a terror in the hearts of the French, that oft-times even great armies were defeated and put to flight at the only hearing of his name. Insomuch that the French women, to affray their children, would tell them that the Talbot cometh.

Many Graces. Though there be indeed but three Graces or Charities (as afore is said) or at the utmost but four, yet, in respect of many gifts of bounty there may be said more. And so Musæus saith, that in Hero's either eye there sat a hundred Graces. And, by that authority, this same poet, in his Pageants, saith, "An hundred Graces on her eyelid sate," &c.

Heydeguies, a country dance or round. The conceit is, that the Graces and nymphs do dance unto the Muses and Pan his music all night by moonlight. To signify the pleasantness of the soil.

Peers, equals, and fellow shepherds.

Queen-apples unripe, imitating Virgil's verse:

"Ipse ego cana legam tenera lanugine mala."

Neighbour groves, a strange phrase in English, but word for word expressing the Latin *vicina nemora*.

Spring, not of water, but of young trees springing.

Calliope, aforesaid. This staff is full of very poetical invention.

Tamburines, an old kind of instrument, which of some is supposed to be the clarion.

Pan with Phœbus. The tale is well known, how that Pan and Apollo, striving for excellency in music, chose Midas for their judge. Who, being corrupted with partial affection, gave the victory to Pan undeserved: for which Phœbus set a pair of ass's ears upon his head, &c.

Tityrus. That by Tityrus is meant Chaucer, hath been already sufficiently said; and by this more plain appeareth, that he saith, he told merry tales, such as be his *Canterbury Tales*, whom he *calleth* the god of poets for his excellency; so as Tully calleth Lentulus, *deum vitæ suæ,* s. the god of his life.

To make, to versify.

O why, a pretty epanorthosis, or correction.

Discourtesy. He meaneth the falseness of his lover Rosalind, who forsaking him had chosen another.

Point of worthy wite, the prick of deserved blame.

Menalcas, the name of a shepherd in Virgil; but here is meant a person unknown and secret, against whom he often bitterly inveigheth.

Underfong, undermine, and deceive by false suggestion.

EMBLEM

You remember that in the first æglogue Colin's poesy was *Anchôra speme*: for that as then there was hope of favour to be found in time. But now being clean forlorn and rejected of her, as whose hope, that was, is clean extinguished and turned into despair, he renounceth all comfort, and hope of goodness to come: which is all the meaning of this emblem.

JULY

ÆGLOGA SEPTIMA. ARGUMENT

THIS *æglogue is made in the honour and commendation of good shepeherds, and to the shame and dispraise of proud and ambitious pastors, such as Morrel is here imagined to be.*

THOMALIN. MORREL

Thom. Is not thilk same a goatherd proud,
  That sits on yonder bank,
Whose straying herd themself doth shroud
  Among the bushes rank?
Mor. What ho! thou jolly shepherd's swain,
  Come up the hill to me;
Better is than the lowly plain,
  Als for thy flock and thee.
Thom. Ah, God shield, man, that I should climb,
  And learn to look aloft;
This rede is rife, that oftentime
  Great climbers fall unsoft.
In humble dales is footing fast,
  The trode is not so tickle:
And though one fall through heedless haste,
  Yet is his miss not mickle.
And now the sun hath rearéd up

JULY

    His fiery-footed team,
Making his way between the Cup
    And golden Diademe:
The rampant Lion hunts he fast,
    With Dogs of noisome breath,
Whose baleful barking brings in haste
    Pain, plagues, and dreary death.
Against his cruel scorching heat,
    Where hast thou coverture?
The wasteful hills unto his threat
    Is a plain overture.
But, if thee lust to holden chat
    With silly shepherds' swain,
Come down, and learn the little what,
    That Thomalin can sayn.
Mor. Sicker, thou's but a lazy loord,
    And recks much of thy swink,
That with fond terms, and weetless words,
    To blear mine eyes dóst think.
In evil hour thou hentest in hond
    Thus holy hills to blame,
For sacred unto saints they stond,
    And of them han their name.
St. Michael's Mount who does not know,
    That wards the western coast?
And of St. Bridget's Bower, I trow,
    All Kent can rightly boast:
And they that con of Muses' skill
    Sayn most-what, that they dwell
(As goatherds wont) upon a hill,
    Beside a learned well.
And wonnéd not the great God Pan
    Upon Mount Olivet,
Feeding the blessed flock of Dan,
    Which did himself beget?
Thom. O blessed sheep! O shepherd great!
    That bought his flock so dear,
And them did save with bloody sweat
    From wolves that would them tear.
Mor. Beside, as holy fathers sayn,
    There is a hilly place,
Where Titan riseth from the main
    To run his daily race,

Upon whose top the stars bene stayed,
    And all the sky doth lean;
There is the cave where Phœbe laid
    The shepherd long to dream.
Whilom there uséd shepherds all
    To feed their flocks at will,
Till by his folly one did fall,
    That all the rest did spill.
And, sithens shepherds bene forsaid
    From places of delight:
For-thy I ween thou be afraid
    To climb this hillës height.
Of Synah can I tell thee more,
    And of Our Lady's Bower;
But little needs to strow my store,
    Suffice this hill of our.
Here han the holy fauns recourse,
    And sylvans haunten rathe;
Here has the salt Medway his source,
    Wherein the nymphs do bathe;
The salt Medway, that trickling stremis
    Adown the dales of Kent,
Till with his elder brother Themis
    His brackish waves be meynt.
Here grows melampode everywhere,
    And terebinth, good for goats:
The one my madding kids to smear,
    The next to heal their throats.
Hereto, the hills bene nigher heaven,
    And thence the passage eath;
As well can prove the piercing levin,
    That seldom falls beneath.

Thom. Sicker, thou speaks like a lewd lorrel,
    Of Heaven to deemen so;
How be I am but rude and borrel,
    Yet nearer ways I know.
To kirk the nar, from God more far,
    Has been an old-said saw,
And he, that strives to touch a star,
    Oft stumbles at a straw.
Alsoon may shepherd climb to sky
    That leads in lowly dales,
As goatherd proud, that, sitting high,

JULY

    Upon the mountain sails.
My silly sheep like well below,
    They need not melampode:
For they bene hale enough, I trow,
    And liken their abode;
But, if they with thy goats should yede,
    They soon might be corrupted,
Or like not of the frowy feed,
    Or with the weeds be glutted.
The hills where dwelléd holy saints
    I reverence and adore:
Not for themself, but for the saints
    Which han be dead of yore.
And now they bene to heaven forewent,
    Their good is with them go:
Their sample only to us lent,
    That als we mought do so.
Shepherds they weren of the best,
    And lived in lowly leas:
And, sith their souls bene now at rest,
    Why done we them disease?
Such one he was (as I have heard
    Old Algrind often sayn)
That whilom was the first shepherd,
    And lived with little gain:
And meek he was, as meek mought be,
    Simple as simple sheep;
Humble, and like in each degree
    The flock which he did keep.
Often he uséd of his keep
    A sacrifice to bring,
Now with a kid, now with a sheep,
    The altars hallowing.
So louted he unto his Lord,
    Such favour couth he find,
That sithens never was abhorred
    The simple shepherds' kind.
And such, I ween, the brethren were
    That came from Canaän:
The brethren twelve, that kept yfere
    The flocks of mighty Pan.
But nothing such thilk shepherd was,
    Whom Ida hill did bear,

That left his flock to fetch a lass,
  Whose love he bought too dear;
For he was proud, that ill was paid,
  (No such mought shepherds be)
And with lewd lust was overlaid:
  Tway things doen ill agree.
But shepherd mought be meek and mild,
  Well-eyed, as Argus was,
With fleshly follies undefiled,
  And stout as steed of brass.
Sike one (said Algrind) Moses was,
  That saw his Maker's face,
His face, more clear than crystal glass,
  And spake to him in place.
This had a brother (his name I knew)
  The first of all his cote,
A shepherd true, yet not so true
  As he that erst I hote.
Whilom all these were low and lief,
  And loved their flocks to feed;
They never stroven to be chief,
  And simple was their weed:
But now (thankéd be God therefore)
  The world is well amend,
Their weeds bene not so nighly wore;
  Such simplesse mought them shend:
They bene yclad in purple and pall,
  So hath their God them blist;
They reign and rulen over all,
  And lord it as they list:
Ygirt with belts of glitterand gold,
  (Mought they good shepherds bene?)
Their Pan their sheep to them has sold,
  I say as some have seen.
For Palinode (if thou him ken)
  Yode late on pilgrimage
To Rome, (if such be Rome) and then
  He saw thilk misusage;
For shepherds (said he) there doen lead,
  As lords done otherwhere;
Their sheep han crusts, and they the bread;
  The chips, and they the cheer:
They han the fleece, and eke the flesh,

JULY

(O silly sheep the while!)
The corn is theirs, let other thresh,
    Their hands they may not file.
They han great stores and thrifty stocks,
    Great friends and feeble foes:
What need hem caren for their flocks,
    Their boys can look to those.
These wizards welter in wealth's waves,
    Pamp'red in pleasures deep:
They han fat kerns, and leany knaves,
    Their fasting flocks to keep.
Sike mister men bene all misgone,
    They heapen hills of wrath;
Sike surly shepherds han we none,
    They keepen all the path.
Mor. Here is a great deal of good matter
    Lost for lack of telling:
Now, sicker, I see thou dost but clatter,
    Harm may come of melling.
Thou meddlest more than shall have thank,
    To witen shepherds' wealth:
When folk bene fat, and riches rank,
    It is a sign of health.
But say me, what is Algrind, he
    That is so oft bynempt?
Thom. He is a shepherd great in gree,
    But hath been long ypent.
One day he sat upon a hill,
    (As now thou wouldest me:
But I am taught, by Algrind's ill,
    To love the low degree);
For sitting so with baréd scalp,
    An eagle soaréd high,
That, weening his white head was chalk,
    A shell-fish down let fly:
She weened the shell-fish to have broke,
    But therewith bruised his brain;
So now, astonied with the stroke,
    He lies in ling'ring pain.
Mor. Ah, good Algrind! his hap was ill,
    But shall be better in time.
Now farewell, shepherd, sith this hill
    Thou hast such doubt to climb.

THOMALIN'S EMBLEM
In medio virtus.

MORREL'S EMBLEM
In summo fœlicitas.

GLOSS

A goatherd. By goats, in Scripture, be represented the wicked and reprobate, whose pastor also must needs be such.
Bank is the seat of honour.
Straying herd, which wander out of the way of truth.
Als, for also.
Climb, spoken of ambition.
Great climbers, according to Seneca his verse:
      "Decidunt celsa, graviore lapsus."
Mickle, much.
The sun. A reason why he refuseth to dwell on mountains, because there is no shelter against the scorching sun, according to the time of the year, which is the hottest month of all.
The Cup and Diadem be two signs in the firmament, through which the sun maketh his course in the month of July.
Lion. This is poetically spoken, as if the sun did hunt a lion with one dog. The meaning whereof is, that in July the sun is in Leo. At which time the dog-star, which is called Sirius, or Canicula, reigneth with immoderate heat, causing pestilence, drought, and many diseases.
Overture, an open place. The word is borrowed of the French, and used in good writers.
To holden chat, to talk and prate.
A loord was wont among the old Britons to signify a lord. And therefore the Danes, that long time usurped their tyranny here in Britain, were called, for more dread then dignity, Lurdanes, s. *Lord Danes.* At which time it is said, that the insolency and pride of that nation was so outrageous in this realm, that if it fortuned a Briton to be going over a bridge, and saw the Dane set foot upon the same, he must return back, till the Dane were clean over, or else abide the price of his displeasure, which was no less than present death. But being afterward expelled, that name of Lurdane became so odious unto the people, whom they had long oppressed, that even at this day they use, for more reproach, to call the quartan ague the fever lurdane.
Recks much of thy swink, counts much of thy pains.
Weetless, not understood.
S. Michael's Mount is a promontory in the west part of England.
A hill, Parnassus aforesaid.
Pan, Christ.
Dan. One tribe is put for the whole nation, *per synecdochen.*
Where Titan, the sun. Which story is to be read in Diodorus

Sic. of the hill Ida; from whence, he saith, all night time is to be seen a mighty fire, as if the sky burned, which toward morning beginneth to gather into a round form, and thereof riseth the sun, whom the poets call Titan.

The Shepherd is Endymion, whom the poets feign to have been so beloved of Phœbe, s. the moon, that he was by her kept asleep in a cave by the space of thirty years, for to enjoy his company.

There, that is, in Paradise, where, through error of the shepherd's understanding, he saith, that all shepherds did use to feed their flocks, till one (that is Adam) by his folly and disobedience, made all the rest of his offspring be debarred and shut out from thence.

Synah, a hill in Arabia, where God appeared.

Our Lady's Bower, a place of pleasure so called.

Fauns, or *Sylvans*, be of poets feigned to be gods of the wood.

Medway, the name of a river in Kent, which, running by Rochester, meeteth with Thames, whom he calleth his elder brother, both because he is greater, and also falleth sooner into the sea.

Meynt, mingled.

Melampode and terebinth be herbs good to cure diseased goats: of the one speaketh Mantuan, and of the other Theocritus:

$$\text{Τερμίνθου τράγων είκατον ἀκρέμονα.}$$

Nigher heaven. Note the shepherd's simpleness, which supposeth that from the hills is nearer way to heaven.

Levin, lightning, which he taketh for an argument to prove the nighness to heaven, because the lightning doth commonly light on high mountains, according to the saying of the poet:

"Feriuntque summos fulmina montes."

Lorrel, a losel.

A borrel, a plain fellow.

Nar, nearer.

Hale, for whole.

Yede, go.

Frowy, musty or mossy.

Of yore, long ago.

Forewent, gone afore.

The first shepherd was Abel the righteous, who (as Scripture saith) bent his mind to keeping of sheep, as did his brother Cain to tilling the ground.

His keep, his charge, s. his flock.

Louted, did honour and reverence.

The brethren, the twelve sons of Jacob, which were sheep-masters, and lived only thereupon.

Whom Ida, Paris, which being the son of Priamus King of Troy, for his mother Hecuba's dream, which, being with child of him, dreamed she brought forth a firebrand, that set all the tower of Ilium on fire, was cast forth on the hill Ida, where being fostered of shepherds, he eke in time became a shepherd, and lastly came to the knowledge of his parentage.

A lass. Helena, the wife of Menelaus king of Lacedemonia, was by Venus, for the golden apple to her given, then promised to Paris, who thereupon with a sort of lusty Troyans, stole her out of

Lacedemonia, and kept her in Troy, which was the cause of the ten years' war in Troy, and the most famous city of all Asia lamentably sacked and defaced.

Argus was of the poets devised to be full of eyes, and therefore to him was committed the keeping of the transformed cow, Io: so called, because that, in the print of a cow's foot, there is figured an I in the midst of an O.

His name. He meaneth Aaron, whose name, for more decorum, the shepherd saith he hath forgot, lest his remembrance and skill in antiquities of holy writ should seem to exceed the meanness of the person.

Not so true, for Aaron, in the absence of Moses, started aside, and committed idolatry.

In purple, spoken of the Popes and Cardinals, which use such tyrannical colours and pompous painting.

Belts, girdles.

Glitterand, glittering, a participle used sometime in Chaucer, but altogether in J. Gower.

Their Pan, that is, the Pope, whom they count their God and greatest shepherd.

Palinode, a shepherd, of whose report he seemeth to speak all this.

Wizards, great learned heads.

Welter, wallow.

Kern, a churl or farmer.

Sike mister men, such kind of men.

Surly, stately and proud.

Melling, meddling.

Bett, better.

Bynempt, named.

Gree, for degree.

Algrind, the name of a shepherd aforesaid, whose mishap he alludeth to the chance that happened to the poet Æschylus, that was brained with a shell-fish.

EMBLEM

By this poesy Thomalin confirmeth that, which in his former speech by sundry reasons he had proved; for being both himself sequestered from all ambition, and also abhorring it in others of his cote, he taketh occasion to praise the mean and lowly state, as that wherein is safety without fear, and quiet without danger; according to the saying of old philosophers, that virtue dwelleth in the midst, being environed with two contrary vices: whereto Morrel replieth with continuance of the same philosopher's opinion, that albeit all bounty dwelleth in mediocrity, yet perfect felicity dwelleth in supremacy: for they say, and most true it is, that happiness is placed in the highest degree, so as if anything be higher or better, then that straightway ceaseth to be perfect happiness. Much like to that which once I heard alleged in defence of humility, out of a great doctor, "Suorum Christus humillimus": which saying a gentleman in the company taking at the rebound, beat back again with a like saying of another doctor, as he said "Suorum Deus altissimus."

AUGUST

ÆGLOGA OCTAVA. ARGUMENT

In *this æglogue is set forth a delectable controversy, made in imitation of that in Theocritus: whereto also Virgil fashioned his third and seventh Æglogue. They choose for umpire of their strife, Cuddie, a neatherd's boy; who, having ended their cause, reciteth also himself a proper song, whereof Colin, he saith, was author.*

WILLY. PERIGOT. CUDDIE

Wil. Tell me, Perigot, what shall be the game,
    Wherefore with mine thou dare thy music match?
Or bene thy bagpipes run far out of frame?
    Or hath the cramp thy joints benumbed with ache?
Per. Ah, Willy, when the heart is ill assayed,
    How can bagpipe or joints be well apaid?
Wil. What the foul evil hath thee so bestad?
    Whilom thou was peregal to the best,
And wont to make the jolly shepherds glad
    With piping and dancing, didst pass the rest.
Per. Ah, Willy, now I have learned a new dance;
    My old music marred by a new mischance.
Wil. Mischief mought to that mischance befall,
    That so hath raft us of our merriment.
But rede me what pain doth thee so appal?
    Or lovest thou, or bene thy younglings miswent?
Per. Love hath misled both my younglings, and me:
    I pine for pain, and they my pain to see.
Wil. Perdie, and wellaway, ill may they thrive!
    Never knew I lover's sheep in good plight.
But, and if in rhymes with me thou dare strive,
    Such fond fantasies shall soon be put to flight.
Per. That shall I do, though mochell worse I fared:
    Never shall be said that Perigot was dared.
Wil. Then lo, Perigot, the pledge which I plight,
    A mazer ywrought of the maple war,
Wherein is enchased many a fair sight
    Of bears and tigers, that maken fierce war;
And over them spread a goodly wild vine,
Entrailed with a wanton ivy twine.

Thereby is a lamb in the wolvës jaws:
    But see, how fast runneth the shepherd swain

To save the innocent from the beastës paws:
  And here, with his sheep-hook hath him slain.
Tell me, such a cup hast thou ever seen?
Well mought it beseem any harvest queen.

Per. Thereto will I pawn yonder spotted lamb,
  Of all my flock there nis sike another,
For I brought him up without the dam:
  But Colin Clout raft me of his brother,
That he purchased of me in the plain field:
Sore against my will was I forced to yield.
Wil. Sicker, make like account of his brother.
  But who shall judge the wager won or lost?
Per. That shall yonder herdgroom, and none other,
  Which over the pousse hitherward doth post.
Wil. But, for the sunbeam so sore doth us beat,
  Were not better to shun the scorching heat?
Per. Well agreed, Willy: then sit thee down, swain:
  Sike a song never heardest thou but Colin sing.
Cud. Gin when ye list, ye jolly shepherds twain:
  Sike a judge as Cuddie were for a king.
Per. "It fell upon a holy eve,
Wil.   Hey, ho, holiday!
Per. When holy fathers wont to shrieve;
Wil.   Now ginneth this roundelay.
Per. Sitting upon a hill so high,
Wil.   Hey, ho, the high hill!
Per. The while my flock did feed thereby;
Wil.   The while the shepherd self did spill.
Per. I saw the bouncing bellibone,
Wil.   Hey, ho, bonibell!
Per. Tripping over the dale alone,
Wil.   She can trip it very well.
Per. Well deckéd in a frock of gray,
Wil.   Hey, ho, gray is greet!
Per. And in a kirtle of green say,
Wil.   The green is for maidens meet.
Per. A chaplet on her head she wore,
Wil.   Hey, ho, chapelet!
Per. Of sweet violets therein was store,
Wil.   She sweeter than the violet.
Per. My sheep did leave their wonted food,
Wil.   Hey, ho, silly sheep!

Per. And gaz'd on her as they were wood,
Wil. Wood as he that did them keep.
Per. As the bonilass passéd by,
Wil. Hey, ho, bonilass!
Per. She rov'd at me with glancing eye,
Wil. As clear as the crystal glass;
Per. All as the sunny beam so bright,
Wil. Hey, ho, the sunbeam!
Per. Glanceth from Phœbus' face forthright,
Wil. So love into thy heart did stream:
Per. Or as the thunder cleaves the clouds,
Wil. Hey, ho, the thunder!
Per. Wherein the lightsome levin shrouds,
Wil. So cleaves thy soul asunder:
Per. Or as Dame Cynthia's silver ray,
Wil. Hey, ho, the moonlight!
Per. Upon the glittering wave doth play,
Wil. Such play is a piteous plight.
Per. The glance into my heart did glide;
Wil. Hey, ho, the glider!
Per. Therewith my soul was sharply gride,
Wil. Such wounds soon wexen wider.
Per. Hasting to raunch the arrow out,
Wil. Hey, ho, Perigot!
Per. I left the head in my heart-root,
Wil. It was a desperate shot.
Per. There it rankleth, aye more and more,
Wil. Hey, ho, the arrow!
Per. Ne can I find salve for my sore:
Wil. Love is a cureless sorrow.
Per. And though my bale with death I bought,
Wil. Hey, ho, heavy cheer!
Per. Yet should thilk lass not from my thought,
Wil. So you may buy gold too dear.
Per. But whether in painful love I pine,
Wil. Hey, ho, pinching pain!
Per. Or thrive in wealth, she shall be mine,
Wil. But if thou can her obtain.
Per. And if for graceless grief I die,
Wil. Hey, ho, graceless grief!
Per. Witness she slew me with her eye,
Wil. Let thy folly be the prief.
Per. And you, that saw it, simple sheep,

Wil.   Hey, ho, the fair flock!
Per.   For prief thereof, my death shall weep,
Wil.   And moan with many a mock.
Per.   So learned I love on a holy eve,
Wil.   Hey, ho, holiday!
Per.   That ever since my heart did grieve,
Wil.   Now endeth our roundelay."
Cud. Sicker, sike a roundle never heard I none:
   Little lacketh Perigot of the best,
And Willy is not greatly overgone,
   So weren his under-songs well addrest.
Wil. Herdgroom, I fear me, thou have a squint eye:
Arede uprightly who has the victory.
Cud. Faith of my soul, I deem each have gained:
   For-thy let the lamb be Willy his own:
And for Perigot, so well hath him pained,
   To him be the wroughten mazer alone.
Per. Perigot is well pleaséd with the doom:
Ne can Willy wite the witeless herdgroom.
Wil. Never dempt more right of beauty, I ween,
The shepherd of Ida that judgéd Beauty's queen.
Cud. But tell me, shepherds, should it not yshend
   Your roundels fresh, to hear a doleful verse
Of Rosalind (who knows not Rosalind?)
   That Colin made? ylk can I you rehearse.
Per. Now say it, Cuddie, as thou art a lad:
With merry thing it's good to medle sad.
Wil. Faith of my soul, thou shalt ycrownéd be
   In Colin's stead, if thou this song arede;
For never thing on earth so pleaseth me
   As him to hear, or matter of his deed.
Cud. Then list'neth each unto my heavy lay,
And tune your pipes as ruthful as ye may.

"Ye wasteful woods! bear witness of my woe,
Wherein my plaints did oftentimes resound:
Ye careless birds are privy to my cries,
Which in your songs were wont to make a part:
Thou, pleasant spring, hast lulled me oft asleep,
Whose streams my trickling tears did oft augment.

"Resort of people doth my griefs augment,
The walléd towns do work my greater woe;

AUGUST

The forest wide is fitter to resound
The hollow echo of my careful cries:
I hate the house, since thence my love did part,
Whose wailful want debars mine eyes from sleep.

"Let streams of tears supply the place of sleep;
Let all, that sweet is, void: and all that may augment
My doole, draw near! More meet to wail my woe
Bene the wild woods, my sorrows to resound,
Than bed, or bower, both which I fill with cries.
When I them see so waste, and find no part

"Of pleasure past. Here will I dwell apart
In gastful grove therefore, till my last sleep
Do close mine eyes: so shall I not augment
With sight of such as change my restless woe:
Help me, ye baneful birds, whose shrieking sound
Is sign of dreary death, my deadly cries

"Most ruthfully to tune. And as my cries
(Which of my woe cannot bewray least part)
You hear all night, when nature craveth sleep,
Increase, so let your irksome yells augment.
Thus all the night in plaints, the day in woe,
I vowéd have to waste, till safe and sound

"She home return, whose voice's silver sound
To cheerful songs can change my cheerless cries.
Hence with the nightingale will I take part,
That blessed bird, that spends her time of sleep
In songs and plaintive pleas, the more t' augment
The memory of his misdeed that bred her woe.

  And you that feel no woe,
   Whenas the sound
  Of these my nightly cries
   Ye hear apart,
  Let break your sounder sleep,
   And pity augment."

Per. O Colin, Colin! the shepherds' joy,
 How I admire each turning of thy verse!
And Cuddie, fresh Cuddie, the liefest boy,
 How dolefully his doole thou didst rehearse!

 Cud. Then blow your pipes, shepherds, till you be at home;
  The night nigheth fast, it's time to be gone.

PERIGOT HIS EMBLEM
Vincenti gloria victi.

WILLY'S EMBLEM
Vinto non vitto.

CUDDIE'S EMBLEM
Felice chi puo.

GLOSS

Bestad, disposed, ordered.
Peregal, equal.
Whilom, once.
Raft, bereft, deprived.
Miswent, gone astray.
Ill may, according to Virgil:
   "Infelix o semper ovis pecus."
 A mazer. So also do Theocritus and Virgil feign pledges of their strife.
 Enchased, engraved. Such pretty descriptions everywhere useth Theocritus to bring in his Idyllia. For which special cause, indeed, he by that name termeth his Æglogues; for Idyllion in Greek signifieth the shape or picture of anything, whereof his book is full. And not, as I have heard some fondly guess, that they be called not Idyllia, but Hædilia, of the goatherds in them.
 Entrailed, wrought between.
 Harvest queen, the manner of country folk in harvest time.
 Pousse, pease.
 It fell upon. Perigot maketh all his song in praise of his love, to whom Willy answereth every underverse. By Perigot who is meant, I cannot uprightly say: but if it be who is supposed, his love, she deserveth no less praise than he giveth her.
 Greet, weeping and complaint.
 Chaplet, a kind of garland like a crown.
 Levin, lightning.
 Cynthia was said to be the moon.
 Gride, pierced.
 But if, not unless.
 Squint eye, partial judgement.
 Each have. So saith Virgil
   "Et vitula tu dignus, et hic," &c.
So by interchange of gifts Cuddie pleaseth both parts.

Doom, judgement.
Dempt, for deemed, judged.
Wite the witeless, blame the blameless.
The shepherd of Ida was said to be Paris.
Beauty's queen, Venus, to whom Paris adjudged the golden apple, as the price of her beauty.

EMBLEM

The meaning hereof is very ambiguous: for Perigot by his poesy claiming the conquest, and Willy not yielding, Cuddie the arbiter of their cause, and patron of his own, seemeth to challenge it, as his due, saying, that he is happy which can, so abruptly ending: but he meaneth either him, that can win the best, or moderate himself being best, and leave off with the best.

SEPTEMBER

ÆGLOGA NONA. ARGUMENT

HEREIN *Diggon Davy is devised to be a shepherd that, in hope of more gain, drove his sheep into a far country. The abuses whereof, and loose living of Popish prelates, by occasion of Hobbinol's demand, he discourseth at large.*

HOBBINOL. DIGGON DAVY

Hob. Diggon Davy! I bid her good day;
    Or Diggon her is, or I missay.
Dig. Her was her, while it was daylight,
    But now her is a most wretched wight:
    For day, that was, is wightly past,
    And now at erst the dark night doth hast.
Hob. Diggon, arede who has thee so dight?
    Never I wist thee in so poor a plight.
    Where is the fair flock thou was wont to lead?
    Or bene they chaffred, or at mischief dead?
Dig. Ah, for love of that is to thee most lief,
    Hobbinol, I pray thee, gall not my old grief:
    Sike question ripeth up cause of new woe,
    For one, opened, mote unfold many moe.
Hob. Nay, but sorrow close shrouded in heart,
    I know, to keep is a burdenous smart:
    Each thing imparted is more eath to bear:
    When the rain is fall'n, the clouds wexen clear.

      And now, sithence I saw thy head last,
      Thrice three moons bene fully spent and past;
      Since when thou hast measuréd much ground,
      And wand'red, I ween, about the world round,
      So as thou can many things relate;
      But tell me first of thy flock's estate.
Dig. My sheep bene wasted; (wae is me therefore!)
      The jolly shepherd that was of yore
      Is now nor jolly, nor shepherd more.
      In foreign coasts men said was plenty;
      And so there is, but all of misery:
      I dempt there much to have ekéd my store,
      But such eking hath made my heart sore.
      In tho countries, whereas I have been,
      No being for those that truly mean;
      But for such, as of guile maken gain,
      No such country as there to remain;
      They setten to sale their shops of shame,
      And maken a mart of their good name:
      The shepherds there robben one another,
      And layen baits to beguile her brother;
      Or they will buy his sheep out of the cote,
      Or they will carven the shepherd's throat.
      The shepherd's swain you cannot well ken,
      But it be by his pride, from other men:
      They looken big as bulls that bene bate,
      And bearen the crag so stiff and so state,
      As cock on his dunghill crowing crank.
Hob. Diggon, I am so stiff and so stank,
      That uneath may I stand any more:
      And now the western wind bloweth sore,
      That now is in his chief sovereignty,
      Beating the withered leaf from the tree.
      Sit we down here under the hill;
      Then may we talk and tellen our fill,
      And make a mock at the blust'ring blast.
      Now say on, Diggon, whatever thou hast.
Dig. Hobbin, ah Hobbin! I curse the stound
      That ever I cast to have lorn this ground:
      Wellaway the while I was so fond
      To leave the good, that I had in hond,
      In hope of better that was uncouth!
      So lost the dog the flesh in his mouth.

SEPTEMBER

My silly sheep (ah, silly sheep!)
That here by there I whilom used to keep,
All were they lusty as thou didst see,
Bene all stervéd with pine and penuree:
Hardly myself escapéd thilk pain,
Driven for need to come home again.

Hob. Ah fon! now by thy loss art taught,
That seldom change the better brought:
Content who lives with triéd state,
Need fear no change of frowning fate;
But who will seek for unknown gain,
Oft lives by loss, and leaves with pain.

Dig. I wot ne, Hobbin, how I was bewitcht
With vain desire and hope to be enricht;
But, sicker, so it is, as the bright star
Seemeth aye greater, when it is far:
I thought the soil would have made me rich,
But now I wot it is nothing sich;
For either the shepherds bene idle and still,
And led of their sheep what way they will,
Or they bene false, and full of covetise,
And casten to compass many wrong emprise:
But the more bene fraught with fraud and spite,
Ne in good nor goodness taken delight,
But kindle coals of conteck and ire,
Wherewith they set all the world on fire;
Which when they thinken again to quench,
With holy water they doen hem all drench.
They say they con to heaven the high-way,
But, by my soul, I dare undersay
They never set foot in that same troad,
But balk the right way, and strayen abroad.
They boast they han the devil at command,
But ask hem therefore what they han pawned:
Marry! that great Pan bought with dear borrow,
To quite it from the black bower of sorrow.
But they han sold thilk same long ago,
For-thy woulden draw with hem many mo.
But let hem gang alone a' God's name;
As they han brewed, so let hem bear blame.

Hob. Diggon, I pray thee, speak not so dirk;
Such mister saying me seemeth too mirk.

Dig. Then, plainly to speak of shepherds most-what,

Bad is the best (this English is flat).
Their ill haviour gars men missay
Both of their doctrine, and of their fay.
They sayn the world is much war than it wont,
All for her shepherds bene beastly and blont.
Other sayn, but how truly I note,
All for they holden shame of their cote:
Some stick not to say, (hot coal on her tongue!)
That sike mischief graseth hem among,
All for they casten too much of world's care,
To deck her dame, and enrich her heir;
For such encheason, if you go nigh,
Few chimneys reeking you shall espy:
The fat ox, that wont lig in the stall,
Is now fast stalled in her crumenall.
Thus chatten the people in their steads,
Ylike as a monster of many heads;
But they that shooten nearest the prick
Sayn, other the fat from their beards doen lick:
For big bulls of Basan brace hem about,
That with their horns butten the more stout:
But the lean souls treaden under foot,
And to seek redress mought little boot;
For liker bene they to pluck away more,
Than aught of the gotten good to restore:
For they bene like foul quagmires overgrast,
That, if thy galage once sticketh fast,
The more to wind it out thou dost swink,
Thou mought ay deeper and deeper sink.
Yet better leave off with a little loss,
Then by much wrestling to lose the gross.

Hob. Now, Diggon, I see thou speakest too plain;
Better it were a little to feign,
And cleanly cover that cannot be cured:
Such ill, as is forced, mought needs be endured.
But of sike pastors how done the flocks creep?

Dig. Sike as the shepherds, sike bene her sheep,
For they nill listen to the shepherd's voice,
But-if he call hem at their good choice;
They wander at will and stay at pleasure,
And to their folds yede at their own leisure.
But they had be better come at their call;
For many han into mischief fall,

SEPTEMBER

And bene of ravenous wolves yrent,
All for they nould be buxom and bent.
Hob. Fie on thee, Diggon, and all thy foul leasing!
Well is known that sith the Saxon king
Never was wolf seen, many nor some,
Nor in all Kent, nor in Christendom;
But the fewer wolves (the sooth to sayn)
The more bene the foxes that here remain.
Dig. Yes, but they gang in more secret wise,
And with sheep's clothing doen hem disguise.
They walk not widely as they were wont,
For fear of rangers and the great hunt,
But privily prowling to and fro,
Enaunter they mought be inly know.
Hob. Or privy or pert if any bene,
We han great bandogs will tear their skin.
Dig. Indeed, thy Ball is a bold big cur,
And could make a jolly hole in their fur:
But not good dogs hem needeth to chase,
But heedy shepherds to discern their face;
For all their craft is in their countenance,
They bene so grave and full of maintenance.
But shall I tell thee what myself know
Chancéd to Roffy not long ygo?
Hob. Say it out, Diggon, whatever it hight,
For not but well mought him betight:
He is so meek, wise, and merciable,
And with his word his work is convenable.
Colin Clout, I ween, be his self boy,
(Ah, for Colin, he whilom my joy!)
Shepherds sich, God mought us many send,
That doen so carefully their flocks tend.
Dig. Thilk same shepheard mought I well mark
He has a dog to bite or to bark;
Never had shepherd so keen a cur,
That waketh and if but a leaf stir.
Whilom there wonned a wicked wolf,
That with many a lamb had glutted his gulf,
And ever at night wont to repair
Unto the flock, when the welkin shone fair,
Yclad in clothing of silly sheep,
When the good old man used to sleep.
Then at midnight he would bark and bawl,

(For he had eft learned a cur's call,)
As if a wolf were among the sheep:
With that the shepherd would break his sleep,
And send out Lowder (for so his dog hote)
To range the fields with wide open throat.
Then, whenas Lowder was far away,
This wolvish sheep would catchen his pray,
A lamb, or a kid, or a weanel wast;
With that to the wood would he speed him fast.
Long time he used this slippery prank,
Ere Roffy could for his labour him thank.
At end, the shepherd his practice spied,
(For Roffy is wise, and as Argus eyed,)
And when at even he came to the flock,
Fast in their folds he did them lock,
And took out the wolf in his counterfeit coat,
And let out the sheep's blood at his throat.

Hob. Marry, Diggon, what should him affray
To take his own wherever it lay?
For, had his wesand been a little widder,
He would have devoured both hidder and shidder.

Dig. Mischief light on him, and God's great curse!
Too good for him had been a great deal worse;
For it was a perilous beast above all,
And eke had he conned the shepherd's call,
And oft in the night came to the sheep-cote,
And calléd Lowder, with a hollow throat,
As if it the old man self had been:
The dog his master's voice did it ween,
Yet half in doubt he opened the door,
And ran out as he was wont of yore.
No sooner was out, but, swifter than thought,
Fast by the hide the wolf Lowder caught;
And, had not Roffy run to the steven,
Lowder had be slain thilk same even.

Hob. God shield, man, he should so ill have thrive,
All for he did his devoir belive!
If sike bene wolves, as thou hast told,
How mought we, Diggon, hem behold?

Dig. How, but with heed and watchfulness,
Forstallen hem of their wiliness:
For-thy with shepherd sits not play,
Or sleep, as some doen, all the long day;

But ever liggen in watch and ward,
From sudden force their flocks for to guard.
Hob. Ah, Diggon! thilk same rule were too strait,
All the cold season to watch and wait;
We bene of flesh, men as other be,
Why should we be bound to such misery?
Whatever thing lacketh changeable rest,
Mought needs decay, when it is at best.
Dig. Ah! but, Hobbinol, all this long tale
Nought easeth the care that doth me forhail;
What shall I do? what way shall I wend,
My piteous plight and loss to amend?
Ah! good Hobbinol, mought I thee pray
Of aid or counsel in my decay.
Hob. Now, by my soul, Diggon, I lament
The hapless mischief that has thee hent;
Netheless thou seest my lowly sail,
That froward fortune doth ever avail:
But, were Hobbinol as God mought please,
Diggon should soon find favour and ease:
But if to my cottage thou wilt resort,
So as I can I will thee comfort;
There mayst thou lig in a vetchy bed,
Till fairer Fortune shew forth her head.
Dig. Ah, Hobbinol! God mought it thee requite;
Diggon on few such friends did ever 'light.

DIGGON'S EMBLEM
Inopem me copia fecit.

GLOSS

The dialect and phrase of speech, in this dialogue, seemeth somewhat to differ from the common. The cause whereof is supposed to be, by occasion of the party herein meant, who, being very friend to the author hereof, had been long in foreign countries, and there seen many disorders, which he here recounteth to Hobbinol.

Bid her, bid good morrow. For to bid is to pray, whereof cometh beads for prayers, and so they say, To bid his beads, s. to say his prayers.

Wightly, quickly, or suddenly.

Chaffred, sold.

Dead at mischief, an unusual speech, but much usurped of **Lydgate**, and sometime of Chaucer.

Lief, dear.
Eath, easy.
Thrice three moons, nine months.
Measured, for travelled.
Wae, woe, northernly.
Eked, increased.
Carven, cut.
Ken, know.
Crag, neck.
State, stoutly.
Stank, weary or faint.

And now. He applieth it to the time of the year, which is in the end of harvest, which they call the fall of the leaf; at which time the western wind beareth most sway.

A mock, imitating Horace, "*Debes ludibrium ventis.*"
Lorn, left.
Soot, sweet.
Uncouth, unknown.
Hereby there, here and there.
As the bright, translated out of Mantuan.
Emprise, for enterprise, *per syncopen*.
Conteck, strife.
Trode, path.

Marry that, that is, their souls, which by popish exorcisms and practices they damn to hell.

Black, hell.
Gang, go.
Mister, manner.
Mirk, obscure.
War, worse.
Crumenall, purse.
Brace, compass.
Encheson, occasion.
Overgrast, overgrown with grass.
Galage, shoe.
The gross, the whole.
Buxom and bent, meek and obedient.

Saxon king, King Edgar that reigned here in Britain in the year of our Lord [957-975], which king caused all the wolves, whereof then was store in this country, by a proper policy to be destroyed. So as never since that time there have been wolves here found, unless they were brought from other countries. And therefore Hobbinol rebuketh him of untruth, for saying that there be wolves in England.

Nor in Christendom. This saying seemeth to be strange and unreasonable; but indeed it was wont to be an old proverb and common phrase. The original whereof was, for that most part of England in the reign of King Ethelbert was christened, Kent only except, which remained long after in misbelief and unchristened: So that Kent was counted no part of Christendom.

Great hunt, executing of laws and justice.
Enaunter, lest that.
Inly, inwardly: aforesaid.

Prively or pert, openly, saith Chaucer.

Roffy, the name of a shepherd in Marot his æglogue of Robin and the King. Whom he here commendeth for great care and wise governance of his flock.

Colin Clout. Now I think no man doubteth but by Colin is meant the author self, whose especial good friend Hobbinol saith he is, or more rightly Master Gabriel Harvey: of whose special commendation, as well in poetry as rhetoric and other choice learning, we have lately had a sufficient trial in divers his works, but specially in his *Musarum Lachrymæ*, and his late *Gratulationum Valdinensium*, which book, in the progress at Audley in Essex, he dedicated in writing to her Majesty, afterward presenting the same in print to her Highness at the worshipful Master Capell's in Hertfordshire. Beside other his sundry most rare and very notable writings, partly under unknown titles, and partly under counterfeit names, as his *Tyrannomastix*, his *Ode Natalitia*, his *Rameidos*, and especially that part of *Philomusus*, his divine *Anticosmopolita*, and divers other of like importance. As also, by the name of other shepherds, he covereth the persons of divers other his familiar friends and best acquaintance.

This tale of Roffy seemeth to colour some particular action of his. But what, I certainly know not.

Wonned, haunted.

Welkin, sky: aforesaid.

A weanel wast, a weaned youngling.

Hidder and shidder, he and she, male and female.

Steven, noise.

Belive, quickly.

Whatever, Ovid's verse translated:

"Quod caret alterna requie durabile non est."

Forehail, draw or distress.

Vetchy, of pease straw.

EMBLEM

This is the saying of Narcissus in Ovid. For when the foolish boy, by beholding his face in the brook, fell in love with his own likeness, and not able to content himself with much looking thereon, he cried out, that plenty made him poor, meaning that much gazing had bereft him of sense. But our Diggon useth it to other purpose, as who that, by trial of many ways, had found the worst, and through great plenty was fallen into great penury. This poesy I know to have been much used of the author, and to such-like effect, as first Narcissus spake it.

OCTOBER

ÆGLOGA DECIMA.   ARGUMENT

IN *Cuddie is set out the perfect pattern of a poet, which, finding no maintenance of his state and studies, complaineth of the contempt of poetry, and the causes thereof: specially having been in all ages, and even amongst the most barbarous, always of singular account and honour, and being indeed so worthy and commendable an art; or rather no art, but a divine gift and heavenly instinct not to be gotten by labour and learning, but adorned with both; and poured into the wit by a certain* 'Ενθουσιασμὸς *and celestial inspiration, as the author hereof else where at large discourseth in his book called* The English Poet, *which book being lately come to my hands, I mind also by God's grace, upon further advisement, to publish.*

PIERS.   CUDDIE

Piers. Cuddie, for shame! hold up thy heavy head,
And let us cast with what delight to chase,
And weary this long ling'ring Phœbus' race.
Whilom thou wont the shepherds' lads to lead
In rhymes, in riddles, and in bidding base;
Now they in thee, and thou in sleep art dead.

Cud. Piers, I have pipéd erst so long with pain,
That all mine oaten reeds bene rent and wore,
And my poor Muse hath spent her sparéd store,
Yet little good hath got, and much less gain.
Such pleasance makes the grasshopper so poor,
And lig so layd, when winter doth her strain.

The dapper ditties, that I wont devise
To feed youth's fancy, and the flocking fry,
Delighten much; what I the bett for-thy?
They han the pleasure, I a slender price;
I beat the bush, the birds to them do fly:
What good thereof to Cuddie can arise?

Piers. Cuddie, the praise is better than the price,
The glory eke much greater than the gain:
O! what an honour is it, to restrain
The lust of lawless youth with good advice,
Or prick them forth with pleasance of thy vein,
Whereto thou list their trainéd wills entice.

OCTOBER

Soon as thou ginn'st to set thy notes in frame,
O, how the rural routs to thee do cleave!
Seemeth thou dost their soul of sense bereave:
All as the shepherd that did fetch his dame
From Pluto's baleful bower withouten leave,
His music's might the hellish hound did tame.

Cud. So praisen babes the peacock's spotted train,
And wond'ren at bright Argus' blazing eye;
But who rewards him e'er the more for-thy,
Or feeds him once the fuller by a grain?
Sike praise is smoke, that sheddeth in the sky;
Sike words bene wind, and wasten soon in vain.

Piers. Abandon, then, the base and viler clown;
Lift up thyself out of the lowly dust,
And sing of bloody Mars, of wars, of jousts;
Turn thee to those that wield the awful crown,
To 'doubted knights, whose woundless armour rusts,
And helms unbruiséd wexen daily brown.

There may thy Muse display her flutt'ring wing,
And stretch herself at large from east to west;
Whither thou list in fair Elisa rest,
Or, if thee please in bigger notes to sing,
Advance the worthy whom she loveth best,
That first the white bear to the stake did bring.

And, when the stubborn stroke of stronger stounds
Has somewhat slackt the tenor of thy string,
Of love and lustihead then may'st thou sing,
And carol loud, and lead the miller's round,
All were Elisa one of thilk same ring;
So mought our Cuddie's name to heaven sound.

Cud. Indeed the Romish Tityrus, I hear,
Through his Mæcenas left his oaten reed,
Whereon he erst had taught his flocks to feed,
And laboured lands to yield the timely ear,
And eft did sing of wars and deadly dreed,
So as the heavens did quake his verse to hear.

But ah! Mæcenas is yclad in clay,
And great Augustus long ago is dead,
And all the worthies liggen wrapt in lead,

That matter made for poets on to play:
For ever, who in derring-do were dread,
The lofty verse of hem was lovéd aye.

But after virtue gan for age to stoop,
And mighty manhood brought a bed of ease,
The vaunting poets found nought worth a pease
To put in press among the learned troop:
Then gan the streams of flowing wits to cease,
And sun-bright honour penned in shameful coop.

And if that any buds of poesy,
Yet of the old stock, gan to shoot again,
Or it men's follies mote be forced to feign,
And roll with rest in rhymes of ribaldry;
Or, as it sprang, it wither must again:
Tom Piper makes us better melody.

Piers. O peerless poesy! where is then thy place?
  If nor in prince's palace thou do sit,
  (And yet is prince's palace the most fit,)
  Ne breast of baser birth doth thee embrace:
  Then make thee wings of thine aspiring wit,
  And, whence thou cam'st, fly back to heaven apace.

Cud. Ah, Percy! it is all too weak and wan,
  So high to soar and make so large a flight;
  Her piecéd pinions bene not so in plight:
  For Colin fits such famous flight to scan;
  He, were he not with love so ill bedight,
  Would mount as high, and sing as soot as swan.

Piers. Ah, fon! for love does teach him climb so high,
  And lifts him up out of the loathsome mire:
  Such immortal mirror, as he doth admire,
  Would raise one's mind above the starry sky,
  And cause a caitiff corage to aspire;
  For lofty love doth loathe a lowly eye.

Cud. All otherwise the state of poet stands;
  For lordly love is such a tyrant fell,
  That where he rules all power he doth expel;
  The vaunted verse a vacant head demands,

Ne wont with crabbéd care the Muses dwell:
Unwisely weaves, that takes two webs in hand.

Who ever casts to compass weighty prize,
And thinks to throw out thund'ring words of threat,
Let pour in lavish cups and thrifty bits of meat,
For Bacchus' fruit is friend to Phœbus wise;
And, when with wine the brain begins to sweat,
The numbers flow as fast as spring doth rise.

Thou kenn'st not, Percy, how the rhyme should rage.
O! if my temples were distained with wine,
And girt in girlonds of wild ivy twine,
How I could rear the Muse on stately stage,
And teach her tread aloft in buskin fine,
With quaint Bellona in her equipage!

But ah! my corage cools ere it be warm:
For-thy content us in this humble shade,
Where no such troublóus tides han us assayed;
Here we our slender pipes may safely charm.

Piers. And when my goats shall han their bellies layed,
Cuddie shall have a kid to store his farm.

CUDDIE'S EMBLEM

Agitante calescimus illo, &c.

GLOSS

This æglogue is made in imitation of Theocritus his xvi. Idyllion, wherein he reproved the tyrant Hiero of Syracuse for his niggardise toward poets, in whom is the power to make men immortal for their good deeds, or shameful for their naughty life. And the like also is in Mantuan. The style hereof, as also that in Theocritus, is more lofty than the rest, and applied to the height of poetical wit.

Cuddie. I doubt whether by Cuddie be specified the author self, or some other. For in the eighth æglogue the same person was brought in, singing a cantion of Colin's making, as he saith. So that some doubt that the persons be different.

Whilom, sometime.

Oaten reeds, avena.

Lig so layd, lie so faint and unlusty.

Dapper, pretty.

Fry is a bold metaphor, forced from the spawning fishes; for the multitude of young fish be called the fry.

To restrain. This place seemeth to conspire with Plato, who in his first book *de Legibus* saith, that the first invention of poetry was of very virtuous intent. For at what time an infinite number of youth usually came to their great solemn feasts called Panegyrica, which they used every five year to hold, some learned man, being more able than the rest for special gifts of wit and music, would take upon him to sing fine verses to the people, in praise either of virtue or of victory, or of immortality, or such-like. At whose wonderful gift all men being astonied, and as it were ravished with delight, thinking (as it was indeed) that he was inspired from above, called him *vatem*: which kind of men afterward framing their verses to lighter music (as of music be many kinds, some sadder, some lighter, some martial, some heroical, and so diversely eke affect the minds of men,) found out lighter matter of poesy also, some playing with love, some scorning at men's fashions, some poured out in pleasures: and so were called poets or makers.

Sense bereave. What the secret working of music is in the minds of men, as well appeareth hereby, that some of the ancient philosophers, and those the most wise, as Plato and Pythagoras, held for opinion, that the mind was made of a certain harmony and musical numbers, for the great compassion, and likeness of affection in the one and in the other, as also by that memorable history of Alexander: to whom whenas Timotheus the great musician played the Phrygian melody, it is said, that he was distraught with such unwonted fury, that, straightway rising from the table in great rage, he caused himself to be armed, as ready to go to war (for that music is very warlike). And immediately whenas the musician changed his stroke into the Lydian and Ionic harmony, he was so far from warring, that he sat as still as if he had been in matters of counsel. Such might is in music: wherefore Plato and Aristotle forbid the Arcadian melody from children and youth. For that being altogether on the fifth and seventh tone, it is of great force to mollify and quench the kindly courage, which useth to burn in young breasts. So that it is not incredible which the poet here saith, that music can bereave the soul of sense.

The shepherd that, Orpheus: of whom is said, that by his excellent skill in music and poetry, he recovered his wife Eurydice from hell.

Argus' eyes. Of Argus is before said that Juno to whom committed her husband Jupiter his paragon Io, because he had an hundred eyes: but afterward Mercury, with his music lulling Argus asleep, slew him and brought Io away, whose eyes it is said that Juno, for his eternal memory, placed in her bird the peacock's tail; for those coloured spots indeed resemble eyes.

Woundless armour, unwounded in war, do rust through long peace.

Display, a poetical metaphor, whereof the meaning is, that if the poet list show his skill in matter of more dignity than is the homely æglogue, good occasion is him offered of higher vein and more heroical argument in the person of our most gracious sovereign, whom (as before) he calleth Elisa. Or if matter of knighthood and chivalry please him better, that there be many noble and valiant men, that are both worthy of his pain in their deserved praises, and also favourers of his skill and faculty.

The worthy. He meaneth (as I guess) the most honourable and renowned the Earl of Leicester, whom by his cognisance (although the same be also proper to other) rather than by his name he bewrayeth, being not likely that the names of worldly princes be known to country clown.

Slack, that is when thou changest thy verse from stately discourse, to matter of more pleasance and delight.

The miller's, a kind of dance.

Ring, company of dancers.

The Romish Tityrus, well known to be Virgil, who by Mæcenas' means was brought into the favour of the Emperor Augustus, and by him moved to write in loftier kind then he erst had done.

Whereon. In these three verses are the three several works of Virgil intended, for in teaching his flocks to feed, is meant his Æglogues. In labouring of lands, is his Bucolics. In singing of wars and deadly dread, is his divine Æneis figured.

In derring-do, in manhood and chivalry.

For ever. He sheweth the cause why poets were wont to be had in such honour of noble men, that is, that by them their worthiness and valour should through their famous poesies be commended to all posterities. Wherefore it is said, that Achilles had never been so famous, as he is, but for Homer's immortal verses, which is the only advantage which he had of Hector. And also that Alexander the Great, coming to his tomb in Sigeus, with natural tears blessed him, that ever was his hap to be honoured with so excellent a poet's work, as so renowned and ennobled only by his means. Which being declared in a most eloquent oration of Tully's, is of Petrarch no less worthily set forth in a sonnet:

"Giunto Alexandro a la famosa tomba
Del fero Achille, sospirando disse:
O fortunato, che si chiara tromba Trovasti," &c.

And that such account hath been always made of poets, as well sheweth this, that the worthy Scipio, in all his wars against Carthage and Numantia, had evermore in his company, and that in a most familiar sort, the good old poet Ennius; as also that Alexander destroying Thebes, when he was informed that the famous lyric poet Pindarus was born in that city, not only commanded straitly, that no man should, upon pain of death, do any violence to that house, by fire or otherwise: but also specially spared most, and some highly rewarded, that were of his kin. So favoured he the only name of a poet, which praise otherwise was in the same man no less famous, that when he came to ransacking of king Darius' coffers, whom he lately had overthrown, he found in a little coffer of silver the two books of Homer's works, as laid up there for special jewels and richesse, which he taking thence, put one of them daily in his bosom, and the other every night laid under his pillow. Such honour have poets always found in the sight of princes and noble men, which this author here very well sheweth, as elsewhere more notably.

But after. He sheweth the cause of contempt of poetry to be idleness, and baseness of mind.

Pent, shut up in sloth, as in a coop or cage.

Tom Piper, an ironical sarcasmus, spoken in derision of these rude wits, which make more account of a rhyming ribald, than of skill grounded upon learning and judgement.

Ne breast, the meaner sort of men.

Her piecéd pinions, unperfect skill: spoken with humble modesty.

As soot as swan. The comparison seemeth to be strange, for the swan hath ever won small commendation for her sweet singing: but it is said of the learned, that the swan, a little before her death, singeth most pleasantly, as prophesying by a secret instinct her near destiny. As well saith the poet elsewhere in one of his sonnets:

"The silver swan doth sing before her dying day,
    As she that feels the deep delight that is in death," &c.

Immortal mirror, beauty, which is an excellent object of poetical spirits, as appeareth by the worthy Petrarch, saying,

"Fiorir faceva il mio debile ingegno,
    A la sua ombra, e crescer ne gli affanni."

A caitiff corage, a base and abject mind.

For lofty love. I think this playing with the letter to be rather a fault than a figure, as well in our English tongue, as it hath been always in the Latin called *Cacozelon*.

A vacant, imitateth Mantuan's saying, "vacuum curis divina cerebrum Poscit."

Lavish cups. Resembleth the common verse, "Fœcundi calices quem non fecere disertum."

O if my. He seemeth here to be ravished with a poetical fury. For (if one rightly mark) the numbers rise so full, and the verse groweth so big, that it seemeth he had forgot the meanness of shepherd's state and style.

Wild ivy, for it is dedicated to Bacchus, and therefore it is said, that the Mænades (that is Bacchus' frantic priestesses) used in their sacrifice to carry *thyrsos*, which were pointed staves or javelins, wrapped about with ivy.

In buskin. It was the manner of poets and players in tragedies to wear buskins, as also in comedies to use stocks and light shoes. So that the buskin in poetry is used for tragical matter, as is said in Virgil, "Sola Sophocleo tua carmina digna cothurno." And the like in Horace, "Magnum loqui, nitique cothurno."

Quaint, strange. Bellona, the goddess of battle, that is, Pallas, which may therefore well be called quaint, for that (as Lucian saith) when Jupiter her father was in travail of her, he caused his son Vulcan with his axe to hew his head. Out of which leaped forth lustily a valiant damsel armed at all points, whom seeing Vulcan so fair and comely, lightly leaping to her, proffered her some courtesy, which the lady disdaining, shaked her spear at him, and threatened his sauciness. Therefore such strangeness is well applied to her.

Equipage, order.

Tides, seasons.

Charm, temper and order; for charms were wont to be made by verses, as Ovid saith, "Aut si carminibus."

NOVEMBER

EMBLEM

Hereby is meant, as also in the whole course of this æglogue, that poetry is a divine instinct, and unnatural rage, passing the reach of common reason. Whom Piers answereth *epiphonematicos*, as admitting the excellency of the skill, whereof in Cuddie he had already had a taste.

NOVEMBER

ÆGLOGA UNDECIMA. ARGUMENT

IN *this xi. æglogue he bewaileth the death of some maiden of great blood, whom he calleth Dido. The personage is secret, and to me altogether unknown, albe of himself I often required the same. This æglogue is made in imitation of Marot his song, which he made upon the death of Lois the French queen; but far passing his reach, and in mine opinion all other the æglogues of this book.*

THENOT. COLIN

The. Colin, my dear, when shall it please thee sing,
  As thou were wont, songs of some jouissance?
  Thy Muse too long slumb'reth in sorrowing,
  Lullèd asleep through love's misgovernance.
  Now somewhat sing, whose endless sovenance
  Among the shepherds' swains may aye remain,
  Whether thee list thy lovèd lass advance,
  Or honour Pan with hymns of higher vein.
Col. Thenot, now nis the time of merrymake,
  Nor Pan to hery, nor with love to play;
  Sike mirth in May is meetest for to make,
  Or summer shade, under the cockèd hay.
  But now sad winter welkèd hath the day,
  And Phœbus, weary of his yearly task,
  Ystablèd hath his steeds in lowly lay,
  And taken up his inn in Fish's hask.
  Thilk sullein season sadder plight doth ask,
  And loatheth sike delights as thou dost praise:
  The mournful Muse in mirth now list ne mask,
  As she was wont in youth and summer days:
  But if thou algate lust light virelays,
  And looser songs of love to underfong,
  Who but thyself deserves sike poet's praise?
  Relive thy oaten pipes that sleepen long.

The. The nightingale is sovereign of song,
  Before him sits the titmouse silent be:
And I, unfit to thrust in skilful throng,
  Should Colin make judge of my foolery?
Nay, better learn of hem that learned be,
  And han be watered at the Muses' well:
The kindly dew drops from the higher tree,
  And wets the little plants that lowly dwell.
But if sad winter's wrath, and season chill,
  Accord not with thy Muse's merriment,
To sadder times thou may'st attune thy quill,
  And sing of sorrow and death's dreariment.
For dead is Dido, dead, alas! and drent;
Dido! the great shepherd his daughter shene.
The fairest may she was that ever went,
Her like she has not left behind I ween:
And, if thou wilt bewail my woeful teen,
I shall thee give yond cosset for thy pain;
And, if thy rhymes as round and rueful bene
As those that did thy Rosalind complain,
Much greater gifts for guerdon thou shalt gain,
Than kid or cosset, which I thee bynempt.
Then up, I say, thou jolly shepherd swain,
Let not my small demand be so contempt.

Col. Thenot, to that I choose thou dost me tempt;
But ah! too well I wot my humble vein,
And how my rhymes bene rugged and unkempt;
Yet, as I con, my conning I will strain.

"Up, then, Melpomene! the mournful'st Muse of nine,
Such cause of mourning never hadst afore;
Up, grisly ghosts! and up my rueful rhyme!
Matter of mirth now shalt thou have no more;
For dead she is, that mirth thee made of yore.
    Dido, my dear, alas! is dead,
    Dead, and lieth wrapt in lead.
    O heavy herse!
Let streaming tears be pouréd out in store;
    O careful verse!

"Shepherds, that by your flocks on Kentish downs abide,
Wail ye this woeful waste of Nature's wark;

NOVEMBER

Wail we the wight whose presence was our pride;
Wail we the wight whose absence is our cark;
The sun of all the world is dim and dark:
    The earth now lacks her wonted light,
    And all we dwell in deadly night.
    O heavy herse!
Break we our pipes, that shrilled as loud as lark;
    O careful verse!

"Why do we longer live, (ah, why live we so long?)
Whose better days Death hath shut up in woe?
The fairest flower our girlond all among
Is faded quite, and into dust ygo.
Sing now, ye shepherds' daughters, sing no mo
    The songs that Colin made you in her praise,
    But into weeping turn your wanton lays.
    O heavy herse!
Now is time to die. Nay, time was long ygo:
    O careful verse!

"Whence is it, that the flow'ret of the field doth fade,
And lieth buried long in winter's bale;
Yet, soon as spring his mantle hath displayed,
It flow'reth fresh, as it should never fail?
But thing on earth that is of most avail,
    As virtue's branch and beauty's bud,
    Reliven not for any good.
    O heavy herse!
The branch once dead, the bud eke needs must quail;
    O careful verse!

"She, while she was, (that was, a woeful word to sayn!)
For beauty's praise and pleasance had no peer;
So well she couth the shepherds entertain
With cakes and cracknels, and such country cheer:
Ne would she scorn the simple shepherd's swain
    For she would call him often heame,
    And give him curds and clotted cream.
    O heavy herse!
Als Colin Clout she would not once disdain
    O careful verse!

"But now sike happy cheer is turned to heavy chance,
Such pleasance now displaced by dolour's dint:

All music sleeps, where death doth lead the dance,
And shepherds' wonted solace is extinct.
The blue in black, the green in gray is tinct;
   The gaudy girlonds deck her grave,
   The faded flowers her corse embrave.
   O heavy herse!
Mourn now, my Muse, now mourn with tears besprint;
   O careful verse!

"O thou great shepherd, Lobbin, how great is thy grief!
Where bene the nosegays that she dight for thee?
The coloured chaplets wrought with a chief,
The knotted rush-rings, and gilt rosemary?
For she deeméd nothing too dear for thee.
   Ah! they bene all yclad in clay;
   One bitter blast blew all away.
   O heavy herse!
Thereof nought remains but the memory;
   O careful verse!

"Ay me! that dreary Death should strike so mortal stroke,
That can undo Dame Nature's kindly course;
The faded locks fall from the lofty oak,
The floods do gasp, for driéd is their source,
And floods of tears flow in their stead perforce:
   The mantled meadows mourn,
   Their sundry colours turn.
   O heavy herse!
The heavens do melt in tears without remorse;
   O careful verse!

"The feeble flocks in field refuse their former food,
And hang their heads as they would learn to weep;
The beasts in forest wail as they were wood,
Except the wolves, that chase the wand'ring sheep,
Now she is gone that safely did hem keep:
   The turtle on the baréd branch
   Laments the wound that Death did launch.
   O heavy herse!
And Philomel her song with tears doth steep;
   O careful verse!

"The water nymphs, that wont with her to sing and
      dance,
And for her girlond olive branches bear,
Now baleful boughs of cypress doen advance;
The Muses, that were wont green bays to wear,
Now bringen bitter elder branches sere;
   The fatal sisters eke repent
   Her vital thread so soon was spent.
   O heavy herse!
Mourn now, my Muse, now mourn with heavy cheer,
   O careful verse!

"O! trustless state of earthly things, and slipper hope
Of mortal men, that swink and sweat for nought,
And, shooting wide, do miss the markéd scope;
Now have I learned (a lesson dearly bought)
That nis on earth assurance to be sought;
   For what might be in earthly mould,
   That did her buried body hold.
   O heavy herse!
Yet saw I on the bier when it was brought;
   O careful verse!

"But maugre Death, and dreaded sisters' deadly spite,
And gates of hell, and fiery furies' force,
She hath the bonds broke of eternal night,
Her soul unbodied of the burdenous corse.
Why then weeps Lobbin so without remorse?
   O Lob! thy loss no longer lament;
   Dido nis dead, but into heaven hent.
   O happy herse!
Cease now, my Muse, now cease thy sorrow's source;
   O joyful verse!

"Why wail we then? why weary we the gods with
      plaints,
As if some evil were to her betight?
She reigns a goddess now among the saints,
That whilom was the saint of shepherds' light,
And is installéd now in heaven's height.
   I see thee, blessed soul, I see
   Walk in Elysian fields so free.

O happy herse!
Might I once come to thee (O that I might!);
  O joyful verse!

"Unwise and wretched men, to weet what's good or ill,
We deem of death as doom of ill desert;
But knew we, fools, what it us brings until,
Die would we daily, once it to expert!
No danger there the shepherd can astert;
  Fair fields and pleasant lays there bene;
  The fields aye fresh, the grass aye green.
O happy herse!
Make haste, ye shepherds, thither to revert:
  O joyful verse!

"Dido is gone afore (whose turn shall be the next?);
There lives she with the blessed gods in bliss,
There drinks she nectar with ambrosia mixt,
And joys enjoys that mortal men do miss.
The honour now of highest gods she is,
  That whilom was poor shepherds' pride,
  While here on earth she did abide.
O happy herse!
Cease now, my song, my woe now wasted is;
  O joyful verse!"

The. Ay, frank shepherd, how bene thy verses meint
With doleful pleasance, so as I ne wot
Whether rejoice or weep for great constraint!
Thine be the cosset, well hast thou it got.
Up, Colin up! enough thou mournéd hast;
Now gins to mizzle, hie we homeward fast.

COLIN'S EMBLEM

La mort ny mord.

GLOSS

Jouissance, mirth.
Sovenance, remembrance.
Hery, honour.
Welked, shortened or impaired. As the moon being in the wane is said of Lydgate to welk.
In lowly lay, according to the season of the month November, when the sun draweth low in the south toward his tropic or return.

NOVEMBER

In Fish's hask, the sun reigneth, that is, in the sign Pisces all November: a hask is a wicker pad, wherein they use to carry fish.

Virelays, a light kind of song.

Be watered, for it is a saying of poets, that they have drunk of the Muses' well Castalias, whereof was before sufficiently said.

Dreariment, dreary and heavy cheer.

The great shepherd is some man of high degree, and not, as some vainly suppose, God Pan. The person both of the shepherd and of Dido is unknown, and closely buried in the author's conceit. But out of doubt I am, that it is not Rosalind, as some imagine: for he speaketh soon after of her a'so.

Shene, fair and shining.

May, for maid.

Teen, sorrow.

Guerdon, reward.

Bynempt, bequeathed.

Cosset, a lamb brought up without the dam.

Unkempt, incompti. Not combed, that is, rude and unhandsome.

Melpomene, the sad and wailful Muse, used of poets in honour of tragedies: as saith Virgil, "Melpomene tragico proclamat mœsta boatu."

Up grisly ghosts, the manner of tragical poets, to call for help of furies, and damned ghosts: so is Hecuba of Euripides, and Tantalus brought in of Seneca. And the rest of the rest.

Herse is the solemn obsequy in funerals.

Waste of, decay of so beautiful a piece.

Cark, care.

Ah why, an elegant epanorthosis, as also soon after: nay, time was long ago.

Floweret, a diminutive for a little flower. This is a notable and sententious comparison, *a minore ad majus*.

Reliven not, live not again, s. not in their earthly bodies: for in heaven they enjoy their due reward.

The branch. He meaneth Dido, who being as it were the main branch now withered, the buds, that is, beauty, (as he said afore) can no more flourish.

With cakes, fit for shepherds' banquets.

Heame, for home, after the northern pronouncing.

Tinct, dyed or stained.

The gaudy. The meaning is, that the things which were the ornaments of her life are made the honour of her funeral, as is used in burials.

Lobbin, the name of a shepherd, which seemeth to have been the lover and dear friend of Dido.

Rush-rings, agreeable for such base gifts.

Faded locks, dried leaves. As if Nature herself bewailed the death of the maid.

Source, spring.

Mantled meadows, for the sundry flowers are like a mantle or coverlet wrought with many colours.

Philomel, the nightingale: whom the poets feign once to have been a lady of great beauty, till, being ravished by her sister's husband, she desired to be turned into a bird of her name, whose complaints be very well set forth of Ma. George Gascoigne, a witty gentleman, and the very chief of our late rhymers, who, and if some parts of learning wanted not, (albe it is well known he altogether wanted not learning) no doubt would have attained to the excellency of those famous poets. For gifts of wit and natural promptness appear in him abundantly.

Cypress, used of the old Paynims in the furnishing of their funeral pomp, and properly the sign of all sorrow and heaviness.

The fatal sisters, Clotho, Lachesis, and Atropos, daughters of Herebus and the Night, whom the poets feign to spin the life of man, as it were a long thread, which they draw out in length, till his fatal hour and timely death be come; but if by other casualty his days be abridged, then one of them, that is, Atropos, is said to have cut the thread in twain. Hereof cometh a common verse:

"Clotho colum bajulat, Lachesis trahit, Atropos occat."

O trustless, a gallant exclamation, moralized with great wisdom, and passionate with great affection.

Bier, a frame, whereon they use to lay the dead corse.

Furies, of poets are feigned to be three, Persephone, Alecto, and Megæra, which are said to be the authors of all evil and mischief.

Eternal night is death or darkness of hell.

Betight, happened.

I see, a lively icon or representation, as if he saw her in heaven present.

Elysian fields be devised of poets to be a place of pleasure like Paradise, where the happy souls do rest in peace and eternal happiness.

Die would, the very express saying of Plato *in Phædone.*

Astert, befall unawares.

Nectar and ambrosia, be feigned to be the drink and food of the gods: ambrosia they liken to manna in Scripture, and nectar to be white like cream, whereof is a proper tale of Hebe, that spilt a cup of it, and stained the heavens, as yet appeareth. But I have already discoursed that at large in my commentary upon the *Dreams* of the same author.

Meint, mingled.

EMBLEM

Which is as much to say, as *Death biteth not.* For although by course of nature we be born to die, and being ripened with age, as with a timely harvest, we must be gathered in time, or else of our selves we fall like rotted ripe fruit from the tree: yet death is not to be counted for evil, nor (as the poet said a little before) as doom of ill desert. For though the trespass of the first man brought death into the world, as the guerdon of sin, yet being overcome by the death of one that died for all, it is now made (as Chaucer saith) the green pathway to life. So that it agreeth well with that was said, that Death biteth not, that is, hurteth not at all.

DECEMBER

ÆGLOGA DUODECIMA. ARGUMENT

This *æglogue* (*even as the first began*) *is ended with a complaint of Colin to God Pan; wherein, as weary of his former ways, he proportioneth his life to the four seasons of the year; comparing his youth to the spring time, when he was fresh and free from love's folly. His manhood to the summer, which, he saith, was consumed with great heat and excessive drouth, caused through a comet or blazing star, by which he meaneth love; which passion is commonly compared to such flames and immoderate heat. His riper years he resembleth to an unseasonable harvest, wherein the fruits fall ere they be ripe. His latter age to winter's chill and frosty season, now drawing near to his last end.*

  The gentle shepherd sat beside a spring,
  All in the shadow of a bushy brere,
  That Colin hight, which well could pipe and sing,
  For he of Tityrus his songs did lere:
   There, as he sat in secret shade alone,
   Thus gan he make of love his piteous moan.

  "O sovereign Pan! thou god of shepherds all,
  Which of our tender lambkins takest keep,
  And, when our flocks into mischance mought fall,
  Dost save from mischief the unwary sheep:
   Als of their masters hast no less regard
   Than of the flocks, which thou dost watch and ward:

  "I thee beseech (so be thou deign to hear
  Rude ditties, tuned to shepherd's oaten reed,
  Or if I ever sonnet sung so clear,
  As it with pleasance mought thy fancy feed)
   Hearken awhile, from thy green cabinet,
   The rural song of careful Colinet.

  "Whilom in youth, when flowered my joyful spring,
  Like swallow swift I wand'red here and there;
  For heat of heedless lust me so did sting,
  That I of doubted danger had no fear:
   I went the wasteful woods and forest wide,
   Withouten dread of wolves to bene espied.

"I wont to range amid the mazy thicket,
And gather nuts to make me Christmas game,
And joyéd oft to chase the trembling pricket,
Or hunt the heartless hare till she were tame.
  What reckéd I of wintry age's waste?—
  Then deeméd I my spring would ever last.

"How often have I scaled the craggy oak,
All to dislodge the raven of her nest?
How have I weariéd with many a stroke
The stately walnut-tree, the while the rest
  Under the tree fell all for nuts at strife?
  For ylike to me was liberty and life.

"And for I was in thilk same looser years,
(Whether the Muse so wrought me from my birth,
Or I too much believed my shepherd peers,)
Somedeal ybent to song and music's mirth,
  A good old shepherd, Wrenock was his name,
  Made me by art more cunning in the same.

"From thence I durst in derring-do compare
With shepherd's swain whatever fed in field;
And, if that Hobbinol right judgement bear,
To Pan his own self pipe I need not yield:
  For, if the flocking nymphs did follow Pan,
  The wiser Muses after Colin ran.

"But, ah! such pride at length was ill repaid:
The shepherds' god (perdie god was he none)
My hurtless pleasance did me ill upbraid;
My freedom lorn, my life he left to moan:
  Love they him calléd that gave me checkmate.
  But better mought they have behote him Hate,

"Then gan my lovely spring bid me farewell,
And summer season sped him to display
(For love then in the Lion's house did dwell)
The raging fire that kindled at his ray.
  A comet stirred up that unkindly heat,
  That reignéd (as men said) in Venus' seat.

"Forth was I led, not as I wont afore,
When choice I had to choose my wand'ring way,
But whither luck and love's unbridled lore
Would lead me forth on Fancy's bit to play:

The bush my bed, the bramble was my bower,
The woods can witness many a woeful stour.

"Where I was wont to seek the honey bee,
Working her formal rooms in waxen frame,
The grisly toad-stool grown there mought I see,
And loathéd paddocks lording on the same:
    And where the chanting birds lulled me asleep,
    The ghastly owl her grievous inn doth keep."

"Then as the spring gives place to elder time,
And bringeth forth the fruit of summer's pride;
Also my age, now passéd youngthly prime,
To things of riper season self applied,
    And learned of lighter timber cotes to frame,
    Such as might save my sheep and me from shame.

"To make fine cages for the nightingale,
And baskets of bulrushes, was my wont:
Who to entrap the fish in winding sale
Was better seen, or hurtful beasts to hont?
    I learnéd als the signs of heaven to ken,
    How Phœbe fails, where Venus sits, and when.

"And triéd time yet taught me greater things;
The sudden rising of the raging seas,
The sooth of birds by beating of their wings,
The power of herbs, both which can hurt and ease,
    And which be wont t' enrage the restless sheep,
    And which be wont to work eternal sleep.

"But, ah! unwise and witless Colin Clout,
That kidst the hidden kinds of many a weed,
Yet kidst not e'en to cure thy sore heart-root,
Whose rankling wound as yet does rifely bleed.
    Why livest thou still, and yet hast thy death's wound
    Why diest thou still, and yet alive art found?

"Thus is my summer worn away and wasted,
Thus is my harvest hastened all too rath;
The ear that budded fair is burnt and blasted,
And all my hopéd gain is turned to scath:
    Of all the seed that in my youth was sown
    Was nought but brakes and brambles to be mown.

"My boughs with bloosmes that crownéd were at first,
And promiséd of timely fruit such store,
Are left both bare and barren now at erst;
The flatt'ring fruit is fallen to ground before,
And rotted ere they were half mellow ripe;
My harvest waste, my hope away did wipe.

"The fragrant flowers, that in my garden grew,
Bene witheréd, as they had been gathered long;
Their roots bene driéd up for lack of dew,
Yet dewed with tears they han be ever among.
   Ah! who has wrought my Rosalind this spite,
   To spill the flowers that should her girlond dight?

"And I, that whilom wont to frame my pipe
Unto the shifting of the shepherd's foot,
Sike follies now have gathered as too ripe,
And cast hem out as rotten and unsoot.
   The looser lass I cast to please no more;
   One if I please, enough is me therefore.

"And thus of all my harvest-hope I have
Nought reapéd but a weedy crop of care;
Which, when I thought have thresht in swelling sheave,
Cockle for corn, and chaff for barley, bare:
   Soon as the chaff should in the fan be fined,
   All was blown away of the wavering wind.

"So now my year draws to his latter term,
My spring is spent, my summer burnt up quite;
My harvest hastes to stir up winter stern,
And bids him claim with rigorous rage his right:
   So now he storms with many a sturdy stour;
   So now his blust'ring blast each coast doth scour.

"The careful cold hath nipt my rugged rind,
And in my face deep furrows eld hath pight:
My head besprent with hoary frost I find,
And by mine eye the crow his claw doth write:
   Delight is laid abed; and pleasure past;
   No sun now shines; clouds han all overcast.

"Now leave, ye shepherds' boys, your merry glee;
My Muse is hoarse and weary of this stound;

DECEMBER

Here will I hang my pipe upon this tree:
Was never pipe of reed did better sound.
 Winter is come that blows the bitter blast,
 And after winter dreary death does haste.

"Gather together ye my little flock,
My little flock, that was to me so lief;
Let me, ah! let me in your folds ye lock,
Ere the breme winter breed you greater grief.
 Winter is come, that blows the baleful breath,
 And after winter cometh timely death.

"Adieu, delights, that lullèd me asleep;
Adieu, my dear, whose love I bought so dear;
Adieu, my little lambs and lovèd sheep;
Adieu, ye woods, that oft my witness were:
 Adieu, good Hobbinol, that was so true,
 Tell Rosalind, her Colin bids her adieu."

COLIN'S EMBLEM

Vivitur ingenio: cætera mortis erunt.

GLOSS

Tityrus, Chaucer, as hath been oft said.
Lambkins, young lambs.
Als of their, seemeth to express Virgil's verse:

"Pan curat oves oviumque magistros."

Deign, vouchsafe.
Cabinet, Colinet, diminutives.
Mazy, for they be like to a maze whence it is hard to get out again.
Peers, fellows and companions.
Music, that is poetry, as Terence saith, "Qui artem tractant musicam," speaking of poets.
Derring-do, aforesaid.
Lion's house. He imagineth simply that Cupid, which is love, had his abode in the hot sign Leo, which is in the midst of summer; a pretty allegory; whereof the meaning is, that love in him wrought an extraordinary heat of lust.
His ray, which is Cupid's beam or flames of love.
A comet, a blazing star, meant of beauty, which was the cause of his hot love.
Venus, the goddess of beauty or pleasure. Also a sign in heaven, as it is here taken. So he meaneth that beauty, which hath always aspect to Venus, was the cause of his unquietness in love.

Where I was. A fine description of the change of his life and liking, for all things now seemed to him to have altered their kindly course.

Lording. Spoken after the manner of paddocks and frogs sitting, which is indeed lordly, not removing nor looking once aside, unless they be stirred.

Then as. The second part, that is, his manhood.

Cotes, sheepcotes, for such be the exercises of shepherds.

Sale, or sallow, a kind of wood like willow, fit to wreath and bind in leaps to catch fish withal.

Phœbe fails, the eclipse of the moon, which is always in Cauda, or Capite Draconis, signs in heaven.

Venus, s. Venus star, otherwise called Hesperus, and Vesper, and Lucifer, both because he seemeth to be one of the brightest stars, and also first riseth, and setteth last. All which skill in stars being convenient for shepherds to know, Theocritus and the rest use.

Raging seas. The cause of the swelling and ebbing of the sea cometh of the course of the moon, sometimes increasing, sometimes waning and decreasing.

Sooth of birds, a kind of soothsaying used in elder times, which they gathered by the flying of birds: first (as is said) invented by the Tuscans, and from them derived to the Romans who, as it is said in Livy, were so superstitiously rooted in the same, that they agreed that every nobleman should put his son to the Tuscans, by them to be brought up in that knowledge.

Of herbs. That wondrous things be wrought by herbs, as well appeareth by the common working of them in our bodies, as also by the wonderful enchantments and sorceries that have been wrought by them, insomuch that it is said that Circe, a famous sorceress, turned men into sundry kinds of beasts and monsters, and only by herbs: as the poet saith:

"Dea sæva potentibus herbis," &c.

Kidst, knewest.

Ear, of corn.

Scath, loss, hindrance.

The fragrant flowers, sundry studies and laudable parts of learning, wherein our poet is seen, be they witness which are privy to this study.

Ever among, ever and anon.

Thus is my. The third part, wherein is set forth his ripe years as an untimely harvest that bringeth little fruit.

So now my year. The last part, wherein is described his age, by comparison of wintry storms.

Careful cold, for care is said to cool the blood.

Glee, mirth.

Hoary frost, a metaphor of hoary hairs scattered like to a gray frost.

Breme, sharp and bitter.

Adieu delights, is a conclusion of all: where in six verses he comprehendeth briefly all that was touched in this book. In the first verse his delights of youth generally: in the second, the love of Rosalind: in the third, the keeping of sheep, which is the argument of all the æglogues: in the fourth, his complaints: and in the last two, his professed friendship and good will to his good friend Hobbinol.

DECEMBER

EMBLEM

The meaning whereof is, that all things perish and come to their last end, but works of learned wits and monuments of poetry abide for ever. And therefore Horace of his Odes, a work though full indeed of great wit and learning yet of no so great weight and importance, boldly saith,

"Exegi monimentum ære perennius,
 Quod nec imber edax, nec aquilo vorax," &c.

Therefore let not be envied, that this poet in his epilogue saith, he hath made a calendar that shall endure as long as time, &c., following the ensample of Horace and Ovid in the like.

"Grande opus exegi, quod nec Jovis ira, nec ignis,
 Nec ferum poterit nec edax abolere vetustas," &c.

Lo! I have made a calendar for every year,
That steel in strength, and time in durance, shall outwear;
And, if I markéd well the starrës revolution,
It shall continue till the world's dissolution,
To teach the ruder shepherd how to feed his sheep,
And from the falser's fraud his folded flock to keep.

Go, little calendar! thou hast a free passport;
Go but a lowly gate amongst the meaner sort:
Dare not to match thy pipe with Tityrus his style,
Nor with the Pilgrim that the Ploughman played awhile;
But follow them far off, and their high steps adore:
The better please, the worse despise; I ask no more.

MERCE NON MERCEDE

COMPLAINTS

CONTAINING SUNDRY SMALL POEMS
OF THE
WORLD'S VANITY

WHEREOF THE NEXT PAGE MAKETH MENTION

BY ED. SP.

A NOTE OF THE SUNDRY POEMS CONTAINED IN THIS VOLUME

1. *The Ruins of Time.*
2. *The Tears of the Muses.*
3. *Virgil's Gnat.*
4. *Prosopopoia, or Mother Hubbard's Tale.*
5. *The Ruins of Rome: by Bellay.*
6. *Muiopotmos, or The Tale of the Butterfly.*
7. *Visions of the World's Vanity.*
8. *Bellay's Visions.*
9. *Petrarch's Visions.*

THE PRINTER TO THE GENTLE READER

SINCE my late setting forth of the *Faerie Queene*, finding that it hath found a favourable passage amongst you, I have sithence endeavoured by all good means (for the better increase and accomplishment of your delights,) to get into my hands such small poems of the same author's, as I heard were dispersed abroad in sundry hands, and not easy to be come by, by himself; some of them having been diversly embezzled and purloined from him since his departure over sea. Of the which I have, by good means, gathered together these few parcels present, which I have caused to be imprinted altogether, for that they all seem to contain like matter of argument in them; being all complaints and meditations of the world's vanity, very grave and profitable. To which effect I understand that he besides wrote sundry others, namely *Ecclesiastes* and *Canticum Canticorum* translated, *A Sen-night's Slumber*, *The Hell of Lovers*, *His Purgatory*, being all dedicated to ladies; so as it may seem he meant them all to one volume. Besides some other pamphlets loosely scattered abroad: as *The Dying Pelican*, *The Hours of the Lord*, *The Sacrifice of a Sinner*, *The Seven Psalms*, &c., which when I can, either by himself or otherwise, attain to, I mean likewise for your favour sake to set forth. In the meantime, praying you gently to accept of these, and graciously to entertain the new poet, *I take leave.*

THE RUINS OF TIME

DEDICATED TO THE RIGHT NOBLE AND BEAUTIFUL LADY

THE LADY MARY

COUNTESS OF PEMBROKE

Most honourable and bountiful Lady, there be long sithens deep sowed in my breast the seed of most entire love and humble affection unto that most brave knight, your noble brother deceased; which, taking root, began in his lifetime somewhat to bud forth, and to shew themselves to him, as then in the weakness of their first spring; and would in their riper strength (had it pleased high God till then to draw out his days) spired forth fruit of more perfection. But since God hath disdained the world of that most noble spirit, which was the hope of all learned men, and the patron of my young Muses, together with him both their hope of any further fruit was cut off, and also the tender delight of those their first blossoms nipped and quite dead. Yet, sithens my late coming into England, some friends of mine, (which might much prevail with me, and indeed command me) knowing with how strait bands of duty I was tied to him, as also bound unto that noble house, (of which the chief hope then rested in him) have sought to revive them by upbraiding me, for that I have not shewed any thankful remembrance towards him or any of them, but suffer their names to sleep in silence and forgetfulness. Whom chiefly to satisfy or else to avoid that foul blot of unthankfulness, I have conceived this small poem, intituled by a general name of *The World's Ruins*; yet specially intended to the renowning of that noble race, from which both you and he sprang, and to the eternizing of some of the chief of them late deceased. The which I dedicate unto your Ladyship as whom it most specially concerneth; and to whom I acknowledge myself bounden by many singular favours and great graces. I pray for your honourable happiness; and so humbly kiss your hands.

Your Ladyship's ever
humbly at command,
E. S.

It chancéd me one day beside the shore
Of silver streaming Thamesis to be,
Nigh where the goodly Verlame stood of yore.
Of which there now remains no memory,
Nor any little monument to see,
By which the traveller, that fares that way,
"This once was she," may warnéd be to say.

There, on the other side, I did behold
A woman sitting, sorrowfully wailing,
Rending her yellow locks, like wiry gold
About her shoulders carelessly down trailing,
And streams of tears from her fair eyes forth railing:
In her right hand a broken rod she held,
Which towards heaven she seemed on high to weld.

Whether she were one of that river's nymphs,
Which did the loss of some dear love lament,
I doubt; or one of those three fatal imps
Which draw the days of men forth in extent;
Or th' ancient genius of that city brent:
But, seeing her so piteously perplexed,
I (to her calling) asked what her so vexed.

"Ah! what delight" (quoth she) "in earthly thing,
Or comfort can I, wretched creature, have?
Whose happiness the heavens envying,
From highest stair to lowest step me drave,
And have in mine own bowels made my grave,
That of all nations now I am forlorn,
The world's sad spectacle, and Fortune's scorn."

Much was I movéd at her piteous plaint,
And felt my heart nigh riven in my breast
With tender ruth to see her sore constraint;
That, shedding tears awhile, I still did rest.
And after did her name of her request,
"Name have I none" (quoth she) "nor any being,
Bereft of both by Fate's unjust decreeing.

"I was that city, which the garland wore
Of Britain's pride, delivered unto me
By Roman victors, which it won of yore;
Though nought at all but ruins now I be,
And lie in mine own ashes, as ye see,
Verlame I was: what boots it that I was,
Sith now I am but weeds and wasteful grass?

"O vain world's glory! and unsteadfast state
Of all that lives on face of sinful earth!
Which, from their first until their utmost date,
Taste no one hour of happiness or mirth;
But like as at the ingate of their birth

They crying creep out of their mother's womb,
So wailing back go to their woeful tomb.

"Why then doth flesh, a bubble-glass of breath,
Hunt after honour and advancement vain,
And rear a trophy for devouring death,
With so great labour and long lasting pain,
As if his days for ever should remain?
Sith all that in this world is great or gay
Doth as a vapour vanish, and decay.

"Look back, who list, unto the former ages,
And call to count what is of them become:
Where be those learned wits and antique sages,
Which of all wisdom knew the perfect sum?
Where those great warriors, which did overcome
The world with conquest of their might and main,
And made one meare of th' earth and of their reign?

"What now is of th' Assyrian Lioness,
Of whom no footing now on earth appears?
What of the Persian Bear's outrageousness,
Whose memory is quite worn out with years,
Who of the Grecian Leopard now aught hears,
That overran the east with greedy power,
And left his whelps their kingdoms to devour?

"And where is that same great seven-headed beast,
That made all nations vassals of her pride,
To fall before her feet at her behest,
And in the neck of all the world did ride?
Where doth she all that wondrous wealth now hide?
With her own weight down pressèd now she lies,
And by her heaps her hugeness testifies.

"O Rome! thy ruin I lament and rue,
And in thy fall my fatal overthrow,
That whilom was, whilst heavens with equal view
Deigned to behold me and their gifts bestow,
The picture of thy pride in pompous show;
And of the whole world as thou wast the empress,
So I of this small northern world was princess.

"To tell the beauty of my buildings fair,
Adorned with purest gold and precious stone;
To tell my riches, and endowments rare,
That by my foes are now all spent and gone;
To tell my forces, matchable to none,
Were but lost labour, that few would believe,
And with rehearsing would me more aggrieve.

"High towers, fair temples, goodly theatres,
Strong walls, rich porches, princely palaces,
Large streets, brave houses, sacred sepulchres,
Sure gates, sweet gardens, stately galleries,
Wrought with fair pillars and fine imageries;
All those (O pity!) now are turned to dust,
And overgrown with black oblivion's rust.

"Thereto for warlike power, and people's store,
In Britanny was none to match with me,
That many often did abie full sore;
Ne Troynovant, though elder sister she,
With my great forces might comparéd be:
That stout Pendragon to his peril felt,
Who in a siege seven years about me dwelt.

"But long ere this, Bunduca, Britoness,
Her mighty host against my bulwarks brought,
Bunduca, that victorious conqueress,
That, lifting up her brave heroic thought
'Bove woman's weakness, with the Romans fought,
Fought, and in field against them thrice prevailed;
Yet was she foiled, whenas she me assailed.

"And though at last by force I conquered were
Of hardy Saxons, and became their thrall,
Yet was I with much bloodshed bought full dear,
And priced with slaughter of their general;
The monument of whose sad funeral,
For wonder of the world, long in me lasted,
But now to nought through spoil of time is wasted.

"Wasted it is, as if it never were;
And all the rest, that me so honoured made
And of the world admiréd ev'rywhere,

Is turned to smoke, that doth to nothing fade;
And of that brightness now appears no shade,
But grisly shades, such as do haunt in hell
With fearful fiends, that in deep darkness dwell.

"Where my high steeples whilom used to stand,
On which the lordly falcon wont to tower,
There now is but an heap of lime and sand,
For the shriek-owl to build her baleful bower:
And where the nightingale wont forth to pour
Her restless plaints, to comfort wakeful lovers,
There now haunt yelling mews and whining plovers.

"And where the crystal Thamis wont to slide
In silver channel, down along the lea,
About whose flowery banks on either side
A thousand nymphs, with mirthful jollity,
Were wont to play, from all annoyance free,
There now no river's course is to be seen,
But moorish fens, and marshes ever green.

"Seems, that that gentle river for great grief
Of my mishaps, which oft I to him plained,
Or for to shun the horrible mischief,
With which he saw my cruel foes me pained,
And his pure streams with guiltless blood oft stained;
From my unhappy neighbourhood far fled,
And his sweet waters away with him led.

"There also, where the wingéd ships were seen
In liquid waves to cut their foamy way,
And thousand fishers numb'red to have been
In that wide lake looking for plenteous prey
Of fish, which they with baits used to betray,
Is now no lake, nor any fishers' store,
Nor ever ship shall sail there any more.

"They all are gone, and all with them is gone;
Ne aught to me remains, but to lament
My long decay, which no man else doth moan,
And mourn my fall with doleful dreariment.
Yet it is comfort in great languishment,
To be bemoanéd with compassion kind,
And mitigates the anguish of the mind.

"But me no man bewaileth, but in game,
Ne sheddeth tears from lamentable eye;
Nor any lives that mentioneth my name
To be rememb'red of posterity,
Save one that, maugre Fortune's injury,
And Time's decay, and Envy's cruel tort,
Hath writ my record in true-seeming sort.

"Camden! the nourice of antiquity,
And lantern unto late succeeding age,
To see the light of simple verity
Buried in ruins, through the great outrage
Of her own people led with warlike rage:
Camden! though Time all monuments obscure,
Yet thy just labours ever shall endure.

"But why (unhappy wight!) do I thus cry,
And grieve that my remembrance quite is rased
Out of the knowledge of posterity,
And all my antique monuments defaced?
Sith I do daily see things highest placed,
So soon as Fates their vital thread have shorn,
Forgotten quite as they were never born.

"It is not long, since these two eyes beheld
A mighty prince, of most renownéd race,
Whom England high in count of honour held,
And greatest ones did sue to gain his grace;
Of greatest ones he, greatest in his place,
Sate in the bosom of his sovereign,
And *Right and loyal* did his word maintain.

"I saw him die, I saw him die, as one
Of the mean people, and brought forth on bier;
I saw him die, and no man left to moan
His doleful fate, that late him lovéd dear:
Scarce any left to close his eyelids near;
Scarce any left upon his lips to lay
The sacred sod, or requiem to say.

"O! trustless state of miserable men,
That build your bliss on hope of earthly thing,
And vainly think yourselves half happy then,
When painted faces with smooth flattering
Do fawn on you, and your wide praises sing;

THE RUINS OF TIME

And, when the courting masker louteth low,
Him true in heart and trusty to you trow.

"All is but feignéd, and with ochre dyed,
That every shower will wash and wipe away;
All things do change that under heaven abide,
And after death all friendship doth decay:
Therefore, whatever man bear'st worldly sway,
Living, on God, and on thyself rely,
For, when thou diest, all shall with thee die.

"He now is dead, and all is with him dead,
Save what in heaven's storehouse he uplaid:
His hope is failed, and come to pass his dread,
And evil men, now dead, his deeds upbraid:
Spite bites the dead, that living never bayed.
He now is gone, the whiles the fox is crept
Into the hole, the which the badger swept.

"He now is dead, and all his glory gone,
And all his greatness vapouréd to nought,
That as a glass upon the water shone,
Which vanished quite, so soon as it was sought:
His name is worn already out of thought,
Ne any poet seeks him to revive,
Yet many poets honoured him alive.

"Ne doth his Colin, careless Colin Clout,
Care now his idle bagpipe up to raise,
Ne tell his sorrow to the list'ning rout
Of shepherd grooms, which wont his songs to praise:
Praise whoso list, yet I will him dispraise,
Until he quite him of this guilty blame.
Wake, shepherd's boy, at length awake for shame!

"And whoso else did goodness by him gain,
And whoso else his bounteous mind did try,
Whether he shepherd be, or shepherd's swain,
(For many did, which do it now deny,)
Awake, and to his song a part apply:
And I, the whilst you mourn for his decease,
Will with my mourning plaints your plaint increase.

"He died, and after him his brother died,
His brother prince, his brother noble peer,
That whilst he livéd was of none envide,
And dead is now, as living, counted dear,
Dear unto all that true affection bear:
But unto thee most dear, O dearest dame!
His noble spouse, and paragon of fame.

"He, whilst he livéd, happy was through thee,
And, being dead, is happy now much more;
Living, that linkéd chanced with thee to be,
And dead, because him dead thou dost adore
As living, and thy lost dear love deplore.
So whilst that thou, fair flower of chastity,
Dost live, by thee thy lord shall never die.

"Thy lord shall never die, the whiles this verse
Shall live, and surely it shall live for ever:
For ever it shall live, and shall rehearse
His worthy praise, and virtues dying never,
Though death his soul do from his body sever;
And thou thyself herein shalt also live:
Such grace the heavens do to my verses give.

"Ne shall his sister, ne thy father die,
Thy father, that good earl of rare renown,
And noble patron of weak poverty;
Whose great good deeds, in country and in town,
Have purchased him in heaven an happy crown,
Where he now liveth in eternal bliss,
And left his son t' ensue those steps of his.

"He, noble bud, his grandsire's lively heir,
Under the shadow of thy countenance
Now gins to shoot up fast, and flourish fair
In learned arts, and goodly governance,
That him to highest honour shall advance.
Brave imp of Bedford! grow apace in bounty,
And count of wisdom more than of thy county.

"Ne may I let thy husband's sister die,
That goodly lady, sith she eke did spring
Out of his stock and famous family,

THE RUINS OF TIME

Whose praises I to future age do sing;
And forth out of her happy womb did bring
The sacred brood of learning and all honour;
In whom the heavens poured all their gifts upon her.

"Most gentle spirit, breathéd from above
Out of the bosom of the Maker's bliss,
In whom all bounty and all virtuous love
Appearéd in their native properties,
And did enrich that noble breast of his
With treasure passing all this worldës worth,
Worthy of heaven itself, which brought it forth.

"His blessed spirit, full of power divine
And influence of all celestial grace,
Loathing this sinful earth and earthly slime,
Fled back too soon unto his native place;
Too soon for all that did his love embrace,
Too soon for all this wretched world, whom he
Robbed of all right and true nobility.

"Yet, ere his happy soul to heaven went
Out of this fleshly gaol, he did devise
Unto his heavenly Maker to present
His body, as a spotless sacrifice;
And chose that guilty hands of enemies
Should pour forth th' off'ring of his guiltless blood:
So life exchanging for his country's good.

"O noble spirit! live there ever blessed,
The world's late wonder, and the heaven's new joy;
Live ever there, and leave me here distressed
With mortal cares and cumbrous world's annoy!
But, where thou dost that happiness enjoy,
Bid me, O! bid me quickly come to thee,
That happy there I may thee always see.

"Yet, whilst the Fates afford me vital breath,
I will it spend in speaking of thy praise,
And sing to thee, until that timely death
By Heaven's doom do end my earthly days:
Thereto do thou my humble spirit raise,
And into me that sacred breath inspire,
Which thou there breathest perfect and entire.

"Then will I sing: but who can better sing
Than thine own sister, peerless lady bright,
Which to thee sings with deep heart's sorrowing,
Sorrowing temperéd with dear delight,
That her to hear I feel my feeble sprite
Robbéd of sense, and ravishéd with joy:
O sad joy, made of mourning and annoy!

"Yet will I sing: but who can better sing
Than thou thyself, thine own self's valiance,
That, whilst thou livedst, madest the forests ring,
And fields resound, and flocks to leap and dance,
And shepherds leave their lambs unto mischance,
To run thy shrill Arcadian pipe to hear:
O, happy were those days, thrice happy were!

"But now, more happy thou, and wretched we
Which want the wonted sweetness of thy voice,
Whiles thou, now in Elysian fields so free,
With Orpheus, and with Linus, and the choice
Of all that ever did in rhymes rejoice,
Conversest, and dost hear their heavenly lays,
And they hear thine, and thine do better praise.

"So there thou livest, singing evermore,
And here thou livest, being ever song
Of us, which living lovéd thee afore,
And now thee worship 'mongst that blessed throng
Of heavenly poets and heroës strong.
So thou both here and there immortal art,
And everywhere through excellent desart.

"But such as neither of themselves can sing,
Nor yet are sung of others for reward,
Die in obscure oblivion, as the thing
Which never was, ne ever with regard
Their names shall of the later age be heard,
But shall in rusty darkness ever lie,
Unless they mentioned be with infamy.

"What booteth it to have been rich alive?
What to be great? what to be gracious?
When after death no token doth survive

Of former being in this mortal house,
But sleeps in dust, dead and inglorious,
Like beast whose breath but in his nostrils is,
And hath no hope of happiness or bliss.

"How many great ones may rememb'red be,
Which in their days most famously did flourish;
Of whom no word we hear, nor sign now see,
But as things wiped out with a sponge to perish,
Because they living caréd not to cherish
No gentle wits, through pride or covetise,
Which might their names for ever memorize.

"Provide therefore (ye princes) whilst ye live,
That of the Muses ye may friended be,
Which unto men eternity do give;
For they be daughters of Dame Memory
And Jove, the father of eternity,
And do those men in golden thrones repose,
Whose merits they to glorify do choose.

"The sevenfold iron gates of grisly hell,
And horrid house of sad Proserpina,
They able are with power of mighty spell
To break, and thence the souls to bring away
Out of dread darkness to eternal day,
And them immortal make, which else would die
In foul forgetfulness, and nameless lie.

"So whilom raiséd they the puissant brood
Of golden girt Alcmena, for great merit,
Out of the dust, to which the Œtæan wood
Had him consumed, and spent his vital spirit,
To highest heaven, where now he doth inherit
All happiness in Hebe's silver bower,
Chosen to be her dearest paramour.

"So raised they eke fair Leda's warlike twins,
And interchangéd life unto them lent,
That, when th' one diës, th' other then begins
To shew in heaven his brightness orient;
And they, for pity of the sad waymént
Which Orpheus for Eurydice did make
Her back again to life sent for his sake.

"So happy are they, and so fortunate,
Whom the Pierian sacred sisters love,
That freed from bands of impacáble fate,
And power of death, they live for aye above,
Where mortal wrecks their bliss may not remove;
But with the gods, for former virtues' meed,
On nectar and ambrosia do feed.

"For deeds do die, however nobly done,
And thoughts of men do as themselves decay;
But wise words, taught in numbers for to run,
Recorded by the Muses, live for aye;
Ne may with storming showers be washed away,
Ne bitter-breathing winds with harmful blast,
Nor age, nor envy, shall them ever waste.

"In vain do earthly princes, then, in vain,
Seek with pyramidës to heaven aspired,
Or huge colosses built with costly pain,
Or brazen pillars never to be fired,
Or shrines made of the metal most desired,
To make their memories for ever live;
For how can mortal immortality give?

"Such one Mausolus made, the world's great wonder,
But now no remnant doth thereof remain:
Such one Marcellus, but was torn with thunder:
Such one Lysippus, but is worn with rain:
Such one King Edmond, but was rent for gain.
All such vain monuments of earthly mass,
Devoured of Time, in time to nought do pass.

"But Fame with golden wings aloft doth fly,
Above the reach of ruinous decay,
And with brave plumes doth beat the azure sky,
Admired of base-born men from far away:
Then, whoso will with virtuous deeds assay
To mount to heaven, on Pegasus must ride,
And with sweet poets' verse be glorified.

"For not to have been dipt in Lethe lake,
Could save the son of Thetis from to die;
But that blind bard did him immortal make

With verses, dipt in dew of Castaly;
Which made the eastern conqueror to cry,
O fortunate young man, whose virtue found
So brave a trump, thy noble acts to sound!

"Therefore in this half happy I do read
Good Melibee, that hath a poet got
To sing his living praises being dead,
Deserving never here to be forgot,
In spite of envy that his deeds would spot:
Since whose decease, learning lies unregarded,
And men of arms do wander unrewarded.

"Those two be those two great calamities,
That long ago did grieve the noble sprite
Of Solomon with great indignities,
Who whilom was alive the wisest wight:
But now his wisdom is disprovéd quite;
For he, that now wields all things at his will,
Scorns th' one and th' other in his deeper skill.

"O grief of griefs! O gall of all good hearts!
To see that virtue should despiséd be
Of him, that first was raised for virtuous parts,
And now, broad spreading like an aged tree,
Lets none shoot up that nigh him planted be:
O let the man, of whom the Muse is scorned,
Nor alive nor dead be of the Muse adorned!

"O vile world's trust! that with such vain illusion
Hath so wise men bewitcht, and overkest,
That they see not the way of their confusion.
O vainness! to be added to the rest,
That do my soul with inward grief infest:
Let them behold the piteous fall of me,
And in my case their own ensample see.

"And whoso else that sits in highest seat
Of this world's glory, worshippéd of all,
Ne feareth change of Time, not Fortune's threat,
Let him behold the horror of my fall,
And his own end unto remembrance call;
That of like ruin he may warnéd be,
And in himself be moved to pity me."

Thus having ended all her piteous plaint,
With doleful shrieks she vanishéd away,
That I, through inward sorrow wexen faint,
And all astonishéd with deep dismay,
For her departure, had no word to say;
But sate long time in senseless sad affright,
Looking still, if I might of her have sight.

Which when I misséd, having lookéd long,
My thought returnéd grievéd home again,
Renewing her complaint with passion strong,
For ruth of that same woman's piteous pain;
Whose words recording in my troubled brain,
I felt such anguish wound my feeble heart,
That frozen horror ran through every part.

So inly grieving in my groaning breast,
And deeply musing at her doubtful speech,
Whose meaning much I laboured forth to wrest,
Being above my slender reason's reach;
At length, by demonstration me to teach,
Before mine eyes strange sights presented were,
Like tragic pageants seeming to appear.

I

I saw an image, all of massy gold,
Placéd on high upon an altar fair,
That all, which did the same from far behold,
Might worship it, and fall on lowest stair.
Not that great idol might with this compare,
To which th' Assyrian tyrant would have made
The holy brethren falsely to have prayed.

But th' altar, on the which this image stayed,
Was (O great pity!) built of brittle clay,
That shortly the foundation decayed,
With showers of heaven and tempests worn away;
Then down it fell, and low in ashes lay,
Scornéd of every one, which by it went;
That I, it seeing, dearly did lament.

II

Next unto this a stately tower appeared,
Built all of richest stone that might be found,

THE RUINS OF TIME

And nigh unto the heavens in height upreared,
But placéd on a plot of sandy ground:
Not that great tower, which is so much renowned
For tongues' confusion in Holy Writ,
King Ninus' work, might be compared to it.

But O vain labours of terrestrial wit,
That builds so strongly on so frail a soil,
As with each storm does fall away, and flit,
And gives the fruit of all your travails' toil
To be the prey of Time, and Fortune's spoil!
I saw this tower fall suddenly to dust,
That nigh with grief thereof my heart was brust.

III

Then did I see a pleasant paradise,
Full of sweet flowers and daintiest delights,
Such as on earth man could not more devise,
With pleasures choice to feed his cheerful sprites:
Not that, which Merlin by his magic sleights
Made for the gentle Squire, to entertain
His fair Belphœbe, could this garden stain.

But O short pleasure, bought with lasting pain!
Why will hereafter any flesh delight
In earthly bliss, and joy in pleasures vain,
Since that I saw this garden wasted quite,
That where it was scarce seeméd any sight?
That I, which once that beauty did behold,
Could not from tears my melting eyes withhold.

IV

Soon after this a giant came in place,
Of wondrous power, and of exceeding stature,
That none durst view the horror of his face,
Yet was he mild of speech, and meek of nature:
Not he, which in despite of his Creator
With railing terms defied the Jewish host,
Might with this mighty one in hugeness boast;

For from the one he could to th' other coast,
Stretch his strong thighs, and th' ocean overstride,
And reach his hand into his enemies' host.

But see the end of pomp and fleshly pride!
One of his feet unwares from him did slide,
That down he fell into the deep abyss,
Where drowned with him is all his earthly bliss.

V

Then did I see a bridge, made all of gold,
Over the sea from one to other side,
Withouten prop or pillar it t' uphold,
But like the coloured rainbow archéd wide:
Not that great arch, which Trajan edified,
To be a wonder to all age ensuing,
Was matchable to this in equal viewing.

But (ah!) what boots it to see earthly thing
In glory, or in greatness to excel,
Sith Time doth greatest things to ruin bring?
This goodly bridge, one foot not fast'ned well,
Gan fail, and all the rest down shortly fell,
Ne of so brave a building aught remained,
That grief thereof my spirit greatly pained.

VI

I saw two bears, as white as any milk,
Lying together in a mighty cave,
Of mild aspect, and hair as soft as silk,
That savage nature seeméd not to have,
Nor after greedy spoil of blood to crave:
Two fairer beasts might not elsewhere be found,
Although the compassed world were sought around.

But what can long abide above this ground
In state of bliss, or steadfast happiness?
The cave, in which these bears lay sleeping sound,
Was but earth, and with her own weightiness
Upon them fell, and did unwares oppress;
That, for great sorrow of their sudden fate,
Henceforth all world's felicity I hate.

¶ Much was I troubled in my heavy sprite,
At sight of these sad spectacles forepast,
That all my senses were bereavéd quite,
And I in mind remainéd sore aghast,
Distraught 'twixt fear and pity; when at last

THE RUINS OF TIME

I heard a voice, which loudly to me called,
That with the sudden shrill I was appalled.

"Behold" (said it) "and by ensample see,
That all is vanity and grief of mind,
Ne other comfort in this world can be,
But hope of heaven, and heart to God inclined:
For all the rest must needs be left behind."
With that it bad me, to the other side
To cast mine eye, where other sights I spied.

I

Upon that famous river's further shore,
There stood a snowy swan of heavenly hue,
And gentle kind, as ever fowl afore;
A fairer one in all the goodly crew
Of white Strymonian brood might no man view:
There he most sweetly sung the prophecy
Of his own death in doleful elegy.

At last, when all his mourning melody
He ended had, that both the shores resounded,
Feeling the fit that him forewarned to die,
With lofty flight above the earth he bounded,
And out of sight to highest heaven mounted:
Where now he is become an heavenly sign;
There now the joy is his, here sorrow mine.

II

Whilst thus I lookéd, lo! adown the lea
I saw an harp strung all with silver twine,
And made of gold and costly ivory,
Swimming, that whilom seeméd to have been
The harp on which Dan Orpheus was seen
Wild beasts and forests after him to lead,
But was th' harp of Philisides now dead.

At length out of the river it was reared
And borne above the clouds to be divined,
Whilst all the way most heavenly noise was heard
Of the strings, stirréd with the warbling wind,
That wrought both joy and sorrow in my mind:
So now in heaven a sign it doth appear,
The Harp well known beside the northern Bear.

III

Soon after this I saw, on th' other side,
A curious coffer made of heben wood,
That in it did most precious treasure hide,
Exceeding all this baser worldës good:
Yet through the overflowing of the flood
It almost drownéd was, and done to nought,
That sight thereof much grieved my pensive thought.

At length, when most in peril it was brought,
Two angels, down descending with swift flight,
Out of the swelling stream it lightly caught,
And 'twixt their blessed arms it carried quite
Above the reach of any living sight:
So now it is transformed into that star
In which all heavenly treasures lockéd are.

IV

Looking aside I saw a stately bed,
Adornéd all with costly cloth of gold,
That might for any prince's couch be red,
And deckt with dainty flowers, as if it shold
Be for some bride, her joyous night to hold:
Therein a goodly virgin sleeping lay;
A fairer wight saw never summer's day.

I heard a voice that calléd far away,
And her awaking bad her quickly dight,
For lo! her bridegroom was in ready ray
To come to her, and seek her love's delight.
With that she started up with cheerful sight,
When suddenly both bed and all was gone,
And I in languor left there all alone.

V

Still as I gazéd, I beheld where stood
A knight all armed, upon a wingéd steed;
The same that bred was of Medusa's blood,
On which Dan Perseus, born of heavenly seed,
The fair Andromeda from peril freed:
Full mortally this knight ywounded was,
That streams of blood forth flowéd on the grass.

THE RUINS OF TIME

Yet was he deckt (small joy to him, alas!)
With many garlands for his victories,
And with rich spoils, which late he did purcháse
Through brave achievements from his enemies;
Fainting at last through long infirmities,
He smote his steed, that straight to heaven him bore,
And left me here his loss for to deplore.

VI

Lastly I saw an ark of purest gold
Upon a brazen pillar standing high,
Which th' ashes seemed of some great prince to hold,
Enclosed therein for endless memory
Of him, whom all the world did glorify:
Seemed the heavens with the earth did disagree,
Whether should of those ashes keeper be.

At last meseemed wing-footed Mercury,
From heaven descending to appease their strife,
The ark did bear with him above the sky,
And to those ashes gave a second life,
To live in heaven where happiness is rife:
At which the earth did grieve exceedingly,
And I for dole was almost like to die.

L'Envoy

Immortal spirit of Philisides,
Which now art made the heaven's ornament,
That whilom wast the worldës chief'st riches,
Give leave to him that loved thee to lament
His loss, by lack of thee to heaven hent,
And with last duties of this broken verse,
Broken with sighs, to deck thy sable hearse.

And ye, fair lady, th' honour of your days,
And glory of the world your high thoughts scorn,
Vouchsafe this monument of his last praise
With some few silver-dropping tears t' adorn;
And as ye be of heavenly offspring born,
So unto heaven let your high mind aspire,
And loathe this dross of sinful world's desire!

THE TEARS OF THE MUSES
BY ED. SP.

TO THE RIGHT HONOURABLE
THE LADY STRANGE

Most brave and noble Lady, the things that make ye so much honoured of the world as ye be, are such, as (without my simple lines' testimony) are thoroughly known to all men; namely, your excellent beauty, your virtuous behaviour, and your noble match with that most honourable Lord, the very pattern of right nobility. But the causes for which ye have thus deserved of me to be honoured (if honour it be at all) are, both your particular bounties, and also some private bands of affinity, which it hath pleased your ladyship to acknowledge. Of which whenas I found myself in no part worthy, I devised this last slender means, both to intimate my humble affection to your Ladyship, and also to make the same universally known to the world; that by honouring you they might know me, and by knowing me they might honour you. Vouchsafe, noble Lady, to accept this simple remembrance, though not worthy of yourself, yet such as, perhaps, by good acceptance thereof, ye may hereafter cull out a more meet and memorable evidence of your own excellent deserts. So, recommending the same to your Ladyship's good liking, I humbly take leave.

Your Ladyship's humbly ever,
ED. SP.

    Rehearse to me, ye sacred sisters nine,
The golden brood of great Apollo's wit,
Those piteous plaints and sorrowful sad tine,
Which late ye pouréd forth as ye did sit
Beside the silver springs of Helicone,
Making your music of heart-breaking moan.

    For since the time that Phœbus' foolish son
Ythunderéd, through Jove's avengeful wrath,
For traversing the chariot of the sun
Beyond the compass of his 'pointed path,
Of you, his mournful sisters, was lamented,
Such mournful tunes were never since invented.

THE TEARS OF THE MUSES

Nor since that fair Calliope did lose
Her lovéd twins, the darlings of her joy,
Her Palici, whom her unkindly foes,
The Fatal Sisters, did for spite destroy,
Whom all the Muses did bewail long space,
Was ever heard such wailing in this place.

For all their groves, which with the heavenly noises
Of their sweet instruments were wont to sound,
And th' hollow hills, from which their silver voices
Were wont redoubled echoes to rebound,
Did now rebound with nought but rueful cries,
And yelling shrieks thrown up into the skies.

The trembling streams, which wont in channels clear
To rumble gently down with murmur soft,
And were by them right tuneful taught to bear
A bass's part amongst their concerts oft,
Now, forced to overflow with brackish tears,
With troublous noise did dull their dainty ears.

The joyous nymphs and lightfoot faëries
Which thither came to hear their music sweet,
And to the measure of their melodies
Did learn to move their nimble-shifting feet,
Now, hearing them so heavily lament,
Like heavily lamenting from them went.

And all that else was wont to work delight
Through the divine infusion of their skill,
And all that else seemed fair and fresh in sight,
So made by nature for to serve their will,
Was turnéd now to dismal heaviness,
Was turnéd now to dreadful ugliness.

Ay me! what thing on earth, that all thing breeds,
Might be the cause of so impatient plight?
What fury, or what fiend with felon deeds
Hath stirred up so mischievous despight?
Can grief then enter into heavenly hearts,
And pierce immortal breasts with mortal smarts?

Vouchsafe ye then, whom only it concerns,
To me those secret causes to display;
For none but you, or who of you it learns,

Can rightfully arede so doleful lay.
Begin, thou eldest sister of the crew,
And let the rest in order thee ensue.

Clio. Hear, thou great father of the gods on high,
That most art dreaded for thy thunder darts;
And thou, our sire, that reign'st in Castaly
And Mount Parnasse, the god of goodly arts:
Hear, and behold the miserable state
Of us, thy daughters, doleful desolate.

Behold the foul reproach and open shame,
The which is day by day unto us wrought
By such as hate the honour of our name,
The foes of learning and each gentle thought;
They, not contented us themselves to scorn,
Do seek to make us of the world forlorn,

Ne only they that dwell in lowly dust,
The sons of darkness and of ignorance,
But they, whom thou, great Jove, by doom unjust
Didst to the type of honour erst advance:
They now, puft up with sdeignful insolence,
Despise the brood of blessed sapience.

The sectaries of my celestial skill,
That wont to be the world's chief ornament,
And learned imps that wont to shoot up still,
And grow to height of kingdom's government,
They underkeep, and with their spreading arms
Do beat their buds, that perish through their harms.

It most behoves the honourable race
Of mighty peers true wisdom to sustain,
And with their noble countenance to grace
The learned foreheads, without gifts or gain;
Or rather learn'd themselves behoves to be,
That is the garland of nobility.

But (ah!) all otherwise they do esteem
Of th' heavenly gift of wisdom's influence,
And to be learned it a base thing deem:
Base-minded they that want intelligence;
For God himself for wisdom most is praised,
And men to God thereby are nighest raised.

But they do only strive themselves to raise
Through pompous pride, and foolish vanity:
In th' eyes of people they put all their praise,
And only boast of arms and ancestry:
But virtuous deeds, which did those arms first give
To their grandsires, they care not to achieve.

So I, that do all noble feats profess
To register, and sound in trump of gold,
Through their bad doings, or base slothfulness,
Find nothing worthy to be writ, or told;
For better far it were to hide their names,
Than telling them to blazon out their blames.

So shall succeeding ages have no light
Of things forepast, nor monuments of time;
And all that in this world is worthy hight
Shall die in darkness, and lie hid in slime:
Therefore I mourn with deep heart's sorrowing,
Because I nothing noble have to sing.

With that she rained such store of streaming tears,
That could have made a stony heart to weep;
And all her sisters rent their golden hairs,
And their fair faces with salt humour steep.
So ended she, and then the next anew,
Began her grievous plaint as doth ensue.

Melpomene. O! who shall pour into my swollen eyes
A sea of tears that never may be dried,
A brazen voice that may with shrilling cries
Pierce the dull heavens and fill the aër wide,
And iron sides that sighing may endure,
To wail the wretchedness of world impure?

Ah, wretched world! the den of wickedness,
Deformed with filth and foul iniquity;
Ah, wretched world! the house of heaviness,
Filled with the wrecks of mortal misery;
Ah, wretched world! and all that is therein,
The vassals of God's wrath, and slaves of sin.

Most miserable creature under sky
Man without understanding doth appear;
For all this world's affliction he thereby,

And Fortune's freaks, is wisely taught to bear:
Of wretched life the only joy she is,
And th' only comfort in calamities.

She arms the breast with constant patience
Against the bitter throws of dolour's darts:
She solaceth with rules of sapience
The gentle minds, in midst of worldly smarts:
When he is sad, she seeks to make him merry,
And doth refresh his sprites when they be weary.

But he that is of reason's skill bereft,
And wants the staff of wisdom him to stay,
Is like a ship in midst of tempest left
Withouten helm or pilot her to sway:
Full sad and dreadful is that ship's event;
So is the man that wants intendiment.

Why then do foolish men so much despise
The precious store of this celestial riches?
Why do they banish us, that patronize
The name of learning?   Most unhappy wretches!
The which lie drowned in deep wretchedness,
Yet do not see their own unhappiness.

My part it is and my professéd skill
The stage with tragic buskin to adorn,
And fill the scene with plaint, and outcries shrill
Of wretched persons to misfortune born;
But none more tragic matter I can find
Than this, of men deprived of sense and mind.

For all man's life meseems a tragedy,
Full of sad sights and sore catastrophes;
First coming to the world with weeping eye,
Where all his days, like dolorous trophies,
Are heapt with spoils of fortune and of fear,
And he at last laid forth on baleful bier.

So all with rueful spectacles is filled,
Fit for Megæra or Persephone;
But I that in true tragedies am skilled,
The flower of wit, find nought to busy me:
Therefore I mourn, and pitifully moan,
Because that mourning matter I have none

Then gan she woefully to wail, and wring
Her wretched hands in lamentable wise;
And all her sisters, thereto answering,
Threw forth loud shrieks and dreary doleful cries.
So rested she; and then the next in rew
Began her grievous plaint, as doth ensue.

Thalia. Where be the sweet delights of learning's treasure
That wont with comic sock to beautify
The painted theatres, and fill with pleasure
The list'ners' eyes and ears with melody;
In which I late was wont to reign as queen,
And mask in mirth with graces well beseen?

O! all is gone; and all that goodly glee,
Which wont to be the glory of gay wits,
Is laid abed, and nowhere now to see;
And in her room unseemly Sorrow sits,
With hollow brows and grisly countenance,
Marring my joyous gentle dalliance.

And him beside sits ugly Barbarism,
And brutish Ignorance, ycrept of late
Out of dread darkness of the deep abysm.
Where being bred, he light and heaven does hate:
They in the minds of men now tyrannize,
And the fair scene with rudeness foul disguise.

All places they with folly have possest,
And with vain toys the vulgar entertain;
But me have banishéd, with all the rest
That whilom wont to wait upon my train,
Fine Counterfeasance, and unhurtful Sport,
Delight, and Laughter, deckt in seemly sort.

All these, and all that else the comic stage
With seasoned wit and goodly pleasance graced,
By which man's life in his likest imáge
Was limnéd forth, are wholly now defaced;
And those sweet wits, which wont the like to frame,
Are now despised, and made a laughing game.

And he, the man whom Nature self had made
To mock herself, and Truth to imitate,
With kindly counter under mimic shade,

Our pleasant Willy, ah! is dead of late:
With whom all joy and jolly merriment
Is also deaded, and in dolour drent.

Instead thereof scoffing Scurrility,
And scornful Folly with Contempt is crept,
Rolling in rhymes of shameless ribaldry
Without regard, or due decorum kept;
Each idle wit at will presumes to make,
And doth the learned's task upon him take.

But that same gentle spirit, from whose pen
Large streams of honey and sweet nectar flow,
Scorning the boldness of such base-born men,
Which dare their follies forth so rashly throw,
Doth rather choose to sit in idle cell,
Than so himself to mockery to sell.

So am I made the servant of the many,
And laughing-stock of all that list to scorn;
Not honouréd nor caréd for of any,
But loathed of losels as a thing forlorn:
Therefore I mourn and sorrow with the rest,
Until my cause of sorrow be redrest.

Therewith she loudly did lament and shrike,
Pouring forth streams of tears abundantly;
And all her sisters, with compassion like,
The breaches of her singults did supply.
So rested she; and then the next in rew
Began her grievous plaint, as doth ensue.

Euterpe. Like as the darling of the summer's pride,
Fair Philomel, when winter's stormy wrath
The goodly fields, that erst so gay were dyed
In colours divers, quite despoiléd hath,
All comfortless doth hide her cheerless head
During the time of that her widowhead:

So we, that erst were wont in sweet accord
All places with our pleasant notes to fill,
Whilst favourable times did us afford
Free liberty to chant our charms at will,
All comfortless upon the baréd bough,
Like woeful culvers, do sit wailing now.

For far more bitter storm than winter's stour
The beauty of the world hath lately wasted,
And those fresh buds, which wont so fair to flower,
Hath marréd quite, and all their blossoms blasted;
And those young plants, which wont with fruit t' abound,
Now without fruit or leaves are to be found.

A stony coldness hath benumbed the sense
And lively spirits of each living wight,
And dimmed with darkness their intelligence,
Darkness more than Cimmerians' daily night:
And monstrous error, flying in the air,
Hath marred the face of all that seeméd fair.

Image of hellish horror, Ignorance,
Born in the bosom of the black abyss,
And fed with furies' milk for sustenance
Of his weak infancy, begot amiss
By yawning Sloth on his own mother Night:
So he his sons both sire and brother hight.

He, armed with blindness and with boldness stout,
(For blind is bold) hath our fair light defaced;
And, gathering unto him a ragged rout
Of fauns and satyrs, hath our dwellings rased
And our chaste bowers, in which all virtue reigned,
With brutishness and beastly filth hath stained.

The sacred springs of horsefoot Helicon,
So oft bedewéd with our learned lays,
And speaking streams of pure Castalion,
The famous witness of our wonted praise,
They trampled have with their foul footings' tread,
And like to troubled puddles have them made.

Our pleasant groves, which planted were with pains,
That with our music wont so oft to ring,
And arbours sweet, in which the shepherds' swains
Were wont so oft their pastorals to sing,
They have cut down, and all their pleasance marred,
That now no pastoral is to be heard.

Instead of them, foul goblins and shriek-owls
With fearful howling do all places fill;
And feeble Echo now laments and howls

The dreadful accents of their outcries shrill.
So all is turnéd into wilderness,
Whilst Ignorance the Muses doth oppress.

And I, whose joy was erst with spirit full
To teach the warbling pipe to sound aloft,
My spirits now dismayed with sorrow dull
Do moan my misery with silence soft:
Therefore I mourn and wail incessantly,
Till please the heavens afford me remedy.

Therewith she wailéd with exceeding woe,
And piteous lamentation did make;
And all her sisters, seeing her do so,
With equal plaints her sorrow did partake.
So rested she; and then the next in rew
Began her grievous plaint, as doth ensue.

Terpsichore. Whoso hath in the lap of soft delight
Been long time lulled, and fed with pleasures sweet,
Fearless through his own fault or Fortune's spite
To tumble into sorrow and regreet,
If chance him fall into calamity,
Finds greater burthen of his misery.

So we that erst in joyance did abound,
And in the bosom of all bliss did sit,
Like virgin queens, with laurel garlands crowned
For virtue's meed and ornament of wit,
Sith Ignorance our kingdom did confound,
Be now become most wretched wights on ground.

And in our royal thrones, which lately stood
In th' hearts of men to rule them carefully,
He now hath placéd his accurséd brood,
By him begotten of foul Infamy;
Blind Error, scornful Folly, and base Spite,
Who hold by wrong that we should have by right.

They to the vulgar sort now pipe and sing,
And make them merry with their fooleries;
They cheerly chant, and rhymes at random fling,

THE TEARS OF THE MUSES

The fruitful spawn of their rank fantasies:
They feed the ears of fools with flattery,
And good men blame, and losels magnify.

All places they do with their toys possess,
And reign in liking of the multitude;
The schools they fill with fond newfangleness,
And sway in court with pride and rashness rude;
'Mongst simple shepherds they do boast their skill,
And say their music matcheth Phœbus' quill.

The noble hearts to pleasures they allure,
And tell their prince that learning is but vain:
Fair ladies' loves they spot with thoughts impure,
And gentle minds with lewd delights distain;
Clerks they to loathly idleness entice,
And fill their books with discipline of vice.

So everywhere they rule, and tyrannize,
For their usurpéd kingdoms' maintenance,
The whiles we silly maids, whom they despise
And with reproachful scorn discountenance,
From our own native heritage exiled,
Walk through the world of every one reviled.

Nor any one doth care to call us in,
Or once vouchsafeth us to entertain,
Unless some one perhaps of gentle kin,
For pity's sake compassion our pain,
And yield us some relief in this distress;
Yet to be so relieved is wretchedness.

So wander we all careful comfortless,
Yet none doth care to comfort us at all;
So seek we help our sorrow to redress,
Yet none vouchsafes to answer to our call;
Therefore we mourn and pitiless complain,
Because none living pitieth our pain.

With that she wept and woefully waymented,
That naught on earth her grief might pacify;
And all the rest her doleful din augmented
With shrieks and groans and grievous agony.

So ended she; and then the next in rew
Began her piteous plaint, as doth ensue.

Erato. Ye gentle spirits, breathing from above,
Where ye in Venus' silver bower were bred,
Thoughts half divine, full of the fire of love,
With beauty kindled, and with pleasure fed,
Which ye now in security possess,
Forgetful of your former heaviness;

Now change the tenor of your joyous lays,
With which ye use your loves to deify,
And blazon forth an earthly beauty's praise
Above the compass of the archéd sky:
Now change your praises into piteous cries,
And eulogies turn into elegies.

Such as ye wont, whenas those bitter stounds
Of raging love first gan you to torment,
And launch your hearts with lamentable wounds
Of secret sorrow and sad languishment,
Before your loves did take you unto grace;
Those now renew, as fitter for this place.

For I that rule in measure moderate
The tempest of that stormy passion,
And use to paint in rhymes the troublous state
Of lovers' life in likest fashion,
Am put from practice of my kindly skill,
Banished by those that Love with lewdness fill.

Love wont to be schoolmaster of my skill,
And the deviceful matter of my song;
Sweet Love devoid of villainy or ill,
But pure and spotless, as at first he sprong
Out of th' Almighty's bosom, where he nests;
From thence infuséd into mortal breasts.

Such high conceit of that celestial fire,
The base-born brood of blindness cannot guess,
Ne ever dare their dunghill thoughts aspire
Unto so lofty pitch of perfectness,
But rhyme at riot, and do rage in love;
Yet little wot what doth thereto behove.

Fair Cytheree, the mother of delight,
And queen of beauty, now thou may'st go pack;
For lo! thy kingdom is defacéd quite,
Thy sceptre rent, and power put to wrack;
And thy gay son, that wingéd god of love,
May now go prune his plumes like rufféd dove.

And ye three twins, to light by Venus brought,
The sweet companions of the Muses late,
From whom whatever thing is goodly thought,
Doth borrow grace, the fancy to aggrate;
Go beg with us, and be companions still,
As heretofore of good, so now of ill.

For neither you nor we shall any more
Find entertainment or in court or school;
For that which was accounted heretofore
The learned's meed is now lent to the fool:
He sings of love, and maketh loving lays,
And they him hear, and they him highly praise.

With that she pouréd forth a brackish flood
Of bitter tears, and made exceeding moan;
And all her sisters, seeing her sad mood,
With loud laments her answered all at one.
So ended she; and then the next in rew
Began her grievous plaint, as doth ensue.

Calliope. To whom shall I my evil case complain
  Or tell the anguish of my inward smart,
  Sith none is left to remedy my pain,
  Or deigns to pity a perplexéd heart;
  But rather seeks my sorrow to augment
  With foul reproach, and cruel banishment?

For they, to whom I uséd to apply
  The faithful service of my learned skill,
  The goodly offspring of Jove's progeny,
  That wont the world with famous acts to fill;
  Whose living praises in heroic style,
  It is my chief profession to compile;

They, all corrupted through the rust of Time
That doth all fairest things on earth deface,
Or through unnoble sloth, or sinful crime,
That doth degenerate the noble race,
Have both desire of worthy deeds forlorn,
And name of learning utterly do scorn.

Ne do they care to have the ancestry
Of th' old heroës memorized anew;
Ne do they care that late posterity
Should know their names, or speak their praises due.
But die forgot from whence at first they sprong,
As they themselves shall be forgot ere long.

What boots it then to come from glorious
Forefathers, or to have been nobly bred?
What odds 'twixt Irus and old Inachus,
'Twixt best and worst, when both alike are dead:
If none of neither mention should make,
Nor out of dust their memories awake?

Or who would ever care to do brave deed,
Or strive in virtue others to excel,
If none should yield him his deservéd meed,
Due praise, that is the spur of doing well?
For if good were not praiséd more than ill,
None would choose goodness of his own free will.

Therefore the nurse of virtue I am hight,
And golden trumpet of eternity,
That lowly thoughts lift up to heaven's height,
And mortal men have power to deify:
Bacchus and Hercules I raised to heaven,
And Charlemagne amongst the starrës seven.

But now I will my golden clarion rend,
And will henceforth immortalize no more;
Sith I no more find worthy to commend
For prize of value, or for learned lore:
For noble peers, whom I was wont to raise,
Now only seek for pleasure, naught for praise.

Their great revénues all in sumptuous pride
They spend, that naught to learning they may spare:
And the rich fee, which poets wont divide,
Now parasites and sycophants do share:
Therefore I mourn and endless sorrow make,
Both for myself and for my sisters' sake.

With that she loudly gan to wail and shrike,
And from her eyes a sea of tears did pour;
And all her sisters, with compassion like,
Did more increase the sharpness of her shower.
So ended she; and then the next in rew
Began her plaint, as doth herein ensue.

Urania. What wrath of gods, or wicked influence
Of stars conspiring wretched men t' afflict,
Hath poured on earth this noyous pestilence,
That mortal minds doth inwardly infect
With love of blindness and of ignorance,
To dwell in darkness without sovenance?

What difference 'twixt man and beast is left,
When th' heavenly light of knowledge is put out,
And th' ornaments of wisdom are bereft?
Then wand'reth he in error and in doubt,
Unweeting of the danger he is in,
Through flesh's frailty, and deceit of sin.

In this wide world in which they, wretches, stray,
It is the only comfort which they have,
It is their light, their loadstar, and their day;
But hell, and darkness, and the grisly grave,
Is ignorance, the enemy of grace,
That minds of men born heavenly doth debase.

Through knowledge we behold the world's creation,
How in his cradle first he fost'red was;
And judge of Nature's cunning operation,
How things she forméd of a formless mass:
By knowledge we do learn ourselves to know,
And what to man, and what to God, we owe

From hence we mount aloft unto the sky,
And look into the crystal firmament:
There we behold the heaven's great hierarchy,
The stars' pure light, the spheres' swift movëment,
The spirits and intelligences fair,
And angels waiting on th' Almighty's chair.

And there, with humble mind and high insight,
Th' eternal Maker's majesty we view,
His love, his truth, his glory, and his might,
And mercy more than mortal men can view.
O sovereign Lord! O sovereign happiness,
To see thee, and thy mercy measureless!

Such happiness have they that do embrace
The precepts of my heavenly discipline;
But shame and sorrow and accursèd case
Have they that scorn the school of arts divine,
And banish me, which do profess the skill
To make men heavenly wise through humbled will.

However yet they me despise and spite,
I feed on sweet contentment of my thought,
And please myself with mine own self-delight,
In contemplation of things heavenly wrought:
So, loathing earth, I look up to the sky,
And, being driven hence, I thither fly.

Thence I behold the misery of men,
Which want the bliss that wisdom would them breed,
And like brute beasts do lie in loathsome den
Of ghostly darkness, and of ghastly dreed;
For whom I mourn, and for myself complain,
And for my sisters eke whom they disdain.

With that she wept and wailed so piteously,
As if her eyes had been two springing wells;
And all the rest, her sorrow to supply,
Did throw forth shrieks and cries and dreary yells.
So ended she; and then the next in rew
Began her mournful plaint, as doth ensue.

Polyhymnia. A doleful case desires a doleful song,
  Without vain art or curious complements;
  And squalid Fortune, into baseness flong,
  Doth scorn the pride of wonted ornaments:
  Then fittest are these ragged rhymes for me,
  To tell my sorrows that exceeding be.

For the sweet numbers and melodious measures,
  With which I wont the wingéd words to tie,
  And make a tuneful diapase of pleasures,
  Now being let to run at liberty
  By those which have no skill to rule them right,
  Have now quite lost their natural delight.

Heaps of huge words uphoarded hideously,
  With horrid sound though having little sense,
  They think to be chief praise of poetry;
  And, thereby wanting due intelligence,
  Have marred the face of goodly poesy,
  And made a monster of their fantasy.

Whilom in ages past none might profess
  But princes and high priests that secret skill;
  The sacred laws therein they wont express,
  And with deep oracles their verses fill:
  Then was she held in sovereign dignity,
  And made the nursling of nobility.

But now nor prince nor priest doth her maintain,
  But suffer her profanéd for to be
  Of the base vulgar, that with hands unclean
  Dares to pollute her hidden mystery;
  And treadeth under foot her holy things,
  Which was the care of kesars and of kings.

One only lives, her age's ornament,
  And mirror of her Maker's majesty,
  That with rich bounty, and dear cherishment,
  Supports the praise of noble poesy;
  Ne only favours them which it profess,
  But is herself a peerless poetress.

Most peerless prince, most peerless poetress,
The true Pandora of all heavenly graces,
Divine Elisa, sacred emperess!
Live she for ever, and her royal places
Be filled with praises of divinest wits,
That her eternize with their heavenly writs!

Some few beside this sacred skill esteem,
Admirers of her glorious excellence;
Which, being light'ned with her beauty's beam,
Are thereby filled with happy influence;
And lifted up above the worldës gaze,
To sing with angels her immortal praise.

But all the rest, as born of savage brood,
And having been with acorns always fed,
Can no whit savour this celestial food,
But with base thoughts are into blindness led,
And kept from looking on the lightsome day:
For whom I wail and weep all that I may.

Eftsoons such store of tears she forth did pour,
As if she all to water would have gone;
And all her sisters, seeing her sad stour,
Did weep and wail, and made exceeding moan,
And all their learned instruments did break:
The rest, untold, no living tongue can speak.

VIRGIL'S GNAT

LONG SINCE DEDICATED

TO THE MOST NOBLE AND EXCELLENT LORD

THE EARL OF LEICESTER

LATE DECEASED

WRONGED, yet not daring to express my pain,
To you (great lord) the causer of my care,
In cloudy tears my case I thus complain
Unto yourself, that only privy are:
  But if that any Œdipus unware
Shall chance, through power of some divining sprite,
To read the secret of this riddle rare,
And know the purport of my evil plight,
Let him rest pleasèd with his own insight,
Ne further seek to glose upon the text;
For grief enough it is to grievèd wight
To feel his fault, and not be further vext.
  But what so by myself may not be showen,
May by this gnat's complaint be easily knowen.

WE now have played (Augustus) wantonly,
Tuning our song unto a tender Muse,
And, like a cobweb weaving slenderly,
Have only played: let thus much then excuse
This gnat's small poem, that th' whole history
Is but a jest, though envy it abuse:
But who such sports and sweet delights doth blame,
Shall lighter seem than this gnat's idle name.

Hereafter, when as season more secure
Shall bring forth fruit, this Muse shall speak to thee
In bigger notes, that may thy sense allure,
And for thy worth frame some fit poesy:
The golden offspring of Latona pure,
And ornament of great Jove's progeny,
Phœbus shall be the author of my song,
Playing on ivory harp with silver strung

He shall inspire my verse with gentle mood
Of poet's prince, whether he woon beside
Fair Xanthus sprinkled with Chimæra's blood,
Or in the woods of Astery abide;
Or whereas Mount Parnasse, the Muses' bood,
Doth his broad forehead like two horns divide,
And the sweet waves of sounding Castaly
With liquid foot doth slide down easily.

Wherefore, ye sisters, which the glory be
Of the Pierian streams, fair Naiades,
Go too, and, dancing all in company,
Adorn that god: and thou holy Pales,
To whom the honest care of husbandry
Returneth by continual success,
Have care for to pursue his footing light
Through the wide woods and groves, with green leaves dight.

Professing thee, I lifted am aloft
Betwixt the forest wide and starry sky:
And thou, most dread (Octavius), which oft
To learned wits givest courage worthily,
O come (thou sacred child), come sliding soft,
And favour my beginnings graciously;
For not these leaves do sing that dreadful stound,
When giants' blood did stain Phlegræan ground.

Nor how th' half-horsy people, Centaurs hight,
Fought with the bloody Lapithas at bord:
Nor how the East with tyrannous despight
Burnt th' Attic towers, and people slew with sword;
Nor how Mount Athos through exceeding might
Was diggéd down; nor iron bands abord
The Pontic sea by their huge navy cast,
My volume shall renown, so long since past.

Nor Hellespont trampled with horses' feet,
When flocking Persians did the Greeks affray;
But my soft Muse, as for her power more meet,
Delights (with Phœbus' friendly leave) to play
An easy running verse with tender feet.
And thou (dread sacred child), to thee alway,

VIRGIL'S GNAT

Let everlasting lightsome glory strive,
Through the world's endless ages to survive.

And let an happy room remain for thee
'Mongst heavenly ranks, where blessed souls do rest;
And let long lasting life with joyous glee,
As thy due meed that thou deservest best,
Hereafter many years rememb'red be
Amongst good men, of whom thou oft are blest
Live thou for ever in all happiness!
But let us turn to our first business.

The fiery sun was mounted now on hight
Up to the heavenly towers, and shot eachwhere
Out of his golden chariot glistering light;
And fair Aurora, with her rosy hair,
The hateful darkness now had put to flight;
Whenas the shepherd, seeing day appear,
His little goats gan drive out of their stalls,
To feed abroad where pasture best befalls.

To an high mountain's top he with them went,
Where thickest grass did clothe the open hills.
They now amongst the woods and thickets ment,
Now in the valleys wand'ring at their wills,
Spread themselves far abroad through each descent,
Some on the soft green grass feeding their fills,
Some, clamb'ring through the hollow cliffs on high,
Nibble the bushy shrubs which grow thereby.

Others the utmost boughs of trees do crop,
And browse the woodbine twigs that freshly bud;
This with full bit doth catch the utmost top
Of some soft willow, or new growen stud;
This with sharp teeth the bramble leaves doth lop,
And chaw the tender prickles in her cud;
The whiles another high doth overlook
Her own like image in a crystal brook.

O! the great happiness, which shepherds have,
Whoso loathes not too much the poor estate,
With mind that ill use doth before deprave,
Ne measures all things by the costly rate

Of riotise, and semblants outward brave!
No such sad cares, as wont to macerate
And rend the greedy minds of covetous men,
Do ever creep into the shepherd's den.

Ne cares he if the fleece, which him arrays,
Be not twice steepéd in Assyrian dye:
Ne glistering of gold, which underlays
The summer beams, do blind his gazing eye;
Ne pictures' beauty, nor the glancing rays
Of precious stones, whence no good cometh by;
Ne yet his cup embost with imagery
Of Bætus' or of Alcon's vanity.

Ne aught the whelky pearls esteemeth he,
Which are from Indian seas brought far away;
But with pure breast from careful sorrow free,
On the soft grass his limbs doth oft display,
In sweet spring time, when flowers' variety
With sundry colours paints the sprinkled lay:
There, lying all at ease from guile or spite,
With pipe of fenny reeds doth him delight.

There he, lord of himself, with palm bedight,
His looser locks doth wrap in wreath of vine:
There his milk-dropping goats be his delight,
And fruitful Pales, and the forest green,
And darksome caves in pleasant valleys pight,
Whereas continual shade is to be seen,
And where fresh springing wells, as crystal neat,
Do always flow to quench his thirsty heat.

O! who can lead, then, a more happy life
Than he, that with clean mind, and heart sincere,
No greedy riches knows nor bloody strife,
No deadly fight of warlike fleet doth fear;
Ne runs in peril of foes' cruel knife,
That in the sacred temples he may rear
A trophy of his glittering spoils and treasure,
Or may abound in riches above measure.

Of him his God is worshipt with his scythe,
And not with skill of craftsman polishéd:

He joys in groves, and makes himself full blithe
With sundry flowers in wild fields gatheréd;
Ne frankincense he from Panchæa buy'th:
Sweet Quiet harbours in his harmless head,
And perfect Pleasure builds her joyous bower,
Free from sad cares that rich men's hearts devour.

This all his care, this all his whole endeavour,
To this his mind and senses he doth bend,
How he may flow in Quiet's matchless treasure,
Content with any food that God doth send;
And how his limbs, resolved through idle leisure,
Unto sweet sleep he may securely lend
In some cool shadow from the scorching heat,
The whiles his flock their chawéd cuds do eat.

O flocks! O fauns! and O ye pleasant springs
Of Tempe! where the country nymphs are rife,
Through whose not costly care each shepherd sings
As merry notes upon his rustic fife,
As that Ascræan bard, whose fame now rings
Through the wide world, and leads as joyful life;
Free from all troubles and from worldly toil,
In which fond men do all their days turmoil.

In such delights whilst thus his careless time
This shepherd drives, upleaning on his bat,
And on shrill reeds chanting his rustic rhyme,
Hyperion, throwing forth his beams full hot,
Into the highest top of heaven gan climb,
And, the world parting by an equal lot,
Did shed his whirling flames on either side,
As the great Ocean doth himself divide.

Then gan the shepherd gather into one
His straggling goats, and drave them to a ford,
Whose cærule stream, rumbling in pebble stone,
Crept under moss as green as any gourd.
Now had the sun half heaven overgone,
When he his herd back from that water-ford
Drave, from the force of Phœbus' boiling ray,
Into thick shadows, there themselves to lay.

Soon as he them placed in thy sacred wood
(O Delian goddess!) saw, to which of yore
Came the bad daughter of old Cadmus' brood,
Cruel Agave, flying vengeance sore
Of king Nyctelius for the guilty blood
Which she with curséd hands had shed before;
There she half frantic, having slain her son,
Did shroud herself, like punishment to shun.

Here also playing on the grassy green,
Wood-gods, and satyrs, and swift dryadës,
With many fairies oft were dancing seen.
Not so much did Dan Orpheus repress
The streams of Hebrus with his songs, I ween,
As that fair troop of woody goddesses
Stayed thee (O Peneus!), pouring forth to thee
From cheerful looks great mirth and gladsome glee.

The very nature of the place, resounding
With gentle murmur of the breathing air,
A pleasant bower with all delight abounding
In the fresh shadow did for them prepare,
To rest their limbs with weariness redounding.
For first the high palm trees, with branches fair,
Out of the lowly valleys did arise,
And high shoot up their heads into the skies.

And them amongst the wicked lotus grew,
Wicked for holding guilefully away
Ulysses' men, whom rapt with sweetness new,
Taking to host, it quite from him did stay;
And eke those trees, in whose transforméd hue
The sun's sad daughters wailed the rash decay
Of Phaeton, whose limbs, with lightning rent,
They, gathering up, with sweet tears did lament.

And that same tree, in which Demophoon,
By his disloyalty lamented sore,
Eternal hurt left unto many one:
Whom als accompanied the oak, of yore
Through fatal charms transformed to such an one;
The oak, whose acorns were our food, before
That Ceres' seed of mortal men were known,
Which first Triptoleme taught how to be sown.

VIRGIL'S GNAT

Here also grew the rougher-rinded pine,
The great Argoan ship's brave ornament,
Whom Golden Fleece did make an heavenly sign;
Which coveting, with his high top's extent,
To make the mountains touch the stars divine,
Decks all the forest with embellishment;
And the black holm that loves the wat'ry vale;
And the sweet cypress, sign of deadly bale.

Amongst the rest the clamb'ring ivy grew,
Knitting his wanton arms with grasping hold,
Lest that the poplar happely should rue
Her brother's strokes, whose boughs she doth enfold
With her lithe twigs, till they the top surview,
And paint with pallid green her buds of gold.
Next did the myrtle tree to her approach,
Not yet unmindful of her old reproach.

But the small birds, in their wide boughs embow'ring,
Chanted their sundry tunes with sweet consent;
And under them a silver spring, forth pouring
His trickling streams, a gentle murmur sent;
Thereto the frogs, bred in the slimy scouring
Of the moist moors, their jarring voices bent,
And shrill grasshoppers chirpéd them around:
All which the airy Echo did resound.

In this so pleasant place this shepherd's flock
Lay everywhere, their weary limbs to rest,
On every bush, and every hollow rock,
Where breathe on them the whistling wind mote best;
The whiles the shepherd self, tending his stock,
Sate by the fountain side, in shade to rest,
Where gentle slumb'ring sleep oppresséd him
Displayed on ground, and seizéd every limb.

Of treachery or trains nought took he keep,
But, loosely on the grassy green dispread,
His dearest life did trust to careless sleep;
Which, weighing down his drooping drowsy head,
In quiet rest his molten heart did steep,
Devoid of care, and fear of all falsehead;
Had not inconstant Fortune, bent to ill,
Bid strange mischance his quietness to spill.

For at his wonted time in that same place
An huge great serpent, all with speckles pied,
To drench himself in moorish slime did trace,
There from the boiling heat himself to hide:
He, passing by with rolling wreathéd pace,
With brandisht tongue the empty air did gride,
And wrapt his scaly boughts with fell despight,
That all things seemed appalléd at his sight.

Now, more and more having himself enrolled,
His glittering breast he lifteth up on high,
And with proud vaunt his head aloft doth hold;
His crest above, spotted with purple dye,
On every side did shine like scaly gold;
And his bright eyes, glancing full dreadfully,
Did seem to flame out flakes of flashing fire,
And with stern looks to threaten kindled ire.

Thuswise long time he did himself dispace
There round about, whenas at last he spied,
Lying along before him in that place,
That flock's grand captain and most trusty guide:
Eftsoons more fierce in visage, and in pace,
Throwing his fiery eyes on every side,
He cometh on, and all things in his way
Full sternly rends that might his passage stay.

Much he disdains that any one should dare
To come unto his haunt; for which intent
He inly burns, and gins straight to prepare
The weapons, which Nature to him hath lent:
Felly he hisseth, and doth fiercely stare,
And hath his jaws with angry spirits rent,
That all his tract with bloody drops is stained
And all his folds are now in length outstrained.

Whom, thus at point preparéd, to prevent,
A little nursling of the humid air,
A gnat, unto the sleepy shepherd went;
And, marking where his eyelids twinkling rare
Shewed the two pearls which sight unto him lent,
Through their thin coverings appearing fair,
His little needle there infixing deep,
Warned him awake, from death himself to keep.

Wherewith enraged he fiercely gan upstart,
And with his hand him rashly bruising slew
As in avengement of his heedless smart,
That straight the spirit out of his senses flew,
And life out of his members did depart:
When, suddenly casting aside his view,
He spied his foe with felonous intent,
And fervent eyes to his destruction bent.

All suddenly dismayed, and heartless quite,
He fled aback, and catching hasty hold
Of a young alder hard beside him pight,
It rent, and straight about him gan behold
What god or Fortune would assist his might.
But whether god or Fortune made him bold
It's hard to read: yet hardy will he had
To overcome, that made him less adrad.

The scaly back of that most hideous snake
Enwrappéd round, oft feigning to retire
And oft him to assail, he fiercely strake
Whereas his temples did his crest-front tire;
And, for he was but slow, did sloth off-shake
And gazing ghastly on (for fear and ire
Had blent so much his sense, that less he feared;)
Yet when he saw him slain, himself he cheered.

By this the night forth from the darksome bower
Of Herebus her teeméd steeds gan call,
And lazy Vesper in his timely hour
From golden Œta gan proceed withal;
Whenas the shepherd after this sharp stour,
Seeing the doubled shadows low to fall,
Gathering his straying flock, does homeward fare,
And unto rest his weary joints prepare.

Into whose sense so soon as lighter sleep
Was entered, and now loosing every limb,
Sweet slumb'ring dew in carelessness did steep,
The image of that gnat appeared to him,
And in sad terms gan sorrowfully weep,
With grisly countenance and visage grim,
Wailing the wrong which he had done of late,
Instead of good, hast'ning his cruel fate.

Said he: "What have I, wretch, deserv'd, that thus
Into this bitter bale I am outcast,
Whilst that thy life more dear and precíous thus
Was than mine own, so long as it did last?
I now, in lieu of pains so gracíous,
Am tost in th' air with every windy blast:
Thou, safe deliveréd from sad decay,
Thy careless limbs in loose sleep dost display.

"So livest thou; but my poor wretched ghost
Is forced to ferry over Lethe's river,
And spoiled of Charon to and fro am tost.
Seest thou not how all places quake and quiver,
Light'ned with deadly lamps on every post?
Tisiphone eachwhere doth shake and shiver
Her flaming fire-brand, encount'ring me,
Whose locks uncombéd cruel adders be.

"And Cerberus, whose many mouths do bay
And bark out flames, as if on fire he fed;
Adown whose neck, in terrible array,
Ten thousand snakes crawling about his head
Do hang in heaps, that horribly affray,
And bloody eyes do glister fiery red;
He oftentimes me dreadfully doth threaten
With painful torments to be sorely beaten.

"Ay me! that thanks so much should fail of meed;
For that I thee restored to life again,
Even from the door of death and deadly dreed!
Where then is now the guerdon of my pain?
Where the reward of my so piteous deed?
The praise of pity vanisht is in vain,
And th' antique faith of Justice long agone
Out of the land is fled away and gone.

"I saw another's fate approaching fast,
And left mine own his safëty to tender;
Into the same mishap I now am cast,
And shunned destruction doth destruction render:
Not unto him that never hath trespast,
But punishment is due to the offender.
Yet let destruction be the punishment,
So long as thankful will may it relent.

"I carried am into waste wilderness,
Waste wilderness, amongst Cimmerian shades,
Where endless pains and hideous heaviness
Is round about me heapt in darksome glades;
For there huge Othos sits in sad distress,
Fast bound with serpents that him oft invades;
Far off beholding Ephialtes tied,
Which once assayed to burn this world so wide.

"And there is mournful Tityus, mindful yet
Of thy displeasure, O Latona fair!
Displeasure too implacable was it,
That made him meat for wild fowls of the air.
Much do I fear among such fiends to sit;
Much do I fear back to them to repair,
To the black shadows of the Stygian shore,
Where wretched ghosts sit wailing evermore.

"There next the utmost brink doth he abide,
That did the banquets of the gods bewray,
Whose throat through thirst to nought nigh being dried,
His sense to seek for ease turns every way:
And he, that in avengement of his pride
For scorning to the sacred gods to pray,
Against a mountain rolls a mighty stone,
Calling in vain for rest, and can have none.

"Go ye with them, go, cursed damosels,
Whose bridal torches foul Erinnys tined;
And Hymen, at your spousals sad, foretells
Tidings of death and massacre unkind:
With them that cruel Colchid mother dwells,
The which conceived in her revengeful mind
With bitter wounds her own dear babes to slay,
And murd'red troops upon great heaps to lay.

"There also those two Pandionian maids,
Calling on Itys, Itys! evermore,
Whom, wretched boy, they slew with guilty blades
For whom the Thracian king lamenting sore,
Turned to a lapwing, foully them upbraids,
And fluttering round about them still does soar:
There now they all eternally complain
Of others' wrong, and suffer endless pain.

"But the two brethren born of Cadmus' blood,
Whilst each does for the sovereignty contend,
Blind through ambition, and with vengeance wood,
Each doth against the other's body bend
His cursèd steel, of neither well withstood,
And with wide wounds their carcasses doth rend;
That yet they both do mortal foes remain,
Sith each with brother's bloody hand was slain.

"Ah (welladay!), there is no end of pain,
Nor change of labour may entreated be;
Yet I beyond all these am carried fain,
Where other powers far different I see,
And must pass over to th' Elysian plain:
There grim Persephone, encount'ring me,
Doth urge her fellow Furies earnestly
With their bright firebrands me to terrify.

"There chaste Alceste lives inviolate,
Free from all care, for that her husband's days
She did prolong by changing fate for fate.
Lo! there lives also the immortal praise
Of womankind, most faithful to her mate,
Penelope; and from her far aways
A rueless rout of young men which her wooed,
All slain with darts, lie wallowed in their blood.

"And sad Eurydice thence now no more
Must turn to life, but there detainèd be
For looking back, being forbid before:
Yet was the guilt thereof, Orpheus, in thee.
Bold sure he was, and worthy spirit bore,
That durst those lowest shadows go to see,
And could believe that anything could please
Fell Cerberus, or Stygian powers appease:

"Ne feared the burning waves of Phlegethon,
Nor those same mournful kingdoms, compassèd
With rusty horror and foul fashíon;
And deep-digged vaults; and Tartar coverèd
With bloody night, and dark confusíon;
And judgement seats, whose judge is deadly dread,
A judge, that after death doth punish sore
The faults which life hath trespassèd before.

"But valiant fortune made Dan Orpheus bold:
For the swift running rivers still did stand,
And the wild beasts their fury did withhold,
To follow Orpheus' music through the land:
And th' oaks, deep grounded in the earthly mould,
Did move, as if they could him understand;
And the shrill woods, which were of sense bereaved,
Through their hard bark his silver sound received.

"And eke the moon her hasty steeds did stay,
Drawing in teams along the starry sky;
And didst (O monthly virgin!) thou delay
Thy nightly course, to hear his melody?
The same was able with like lovely lay
The queen of hell to move as easily,
To yield Eurydice unto her fere
Back to be borne, though it unlawful were.

"She (lady), having well before approved
The fiends to be too cruel and severe,
Observed th' appointed way, as her behoved,
Ne ever did her eyesight turn arear,
Ne ever spake, ne cause of speaking moved;
But, cruel Orpheus, thou much crueller,
Seeking to kiss her, brok'st the gods' decree,
And thereby mad'st her ever damned to be.

"Ah! but sweet love of pardon worthy is,
And doth deserve to have small faults remitted,
If hell at least things lightly done amiss
Knew how to pardon, when aught is omitted;
Yet are ye both receivéd into bliss,
And to the seats of happy souls admitted:
And you beside the honourable band
Of great heroës do in order stand.

"There be the two stout sons of Æacus,
Fierce Peleus, and the hardy Telamon,
Both seeming now full glad and joyëous
Through their sire's dreadful jurisdiction,
Being the judge of all that horrid house:
And both of them, by strange occasíon,
Renowned in choice of happy marríage
Through Venus' grace, and virtue's carríage.

"For th' one was ravisht of his own bondmaid,
The fair Ixíone captíved from Troy;
But th' other was with Thetis' love assayed,
Great Nereus his daughter and his joy.
On this side them there is a young man laid,
Their match in glory, mighty, fierce, and coy;
That from th' Argolic ships with furious ire
Bet back the fury of the Trojan fire.

"O! who would not recount the strong divorces
Of that great war, which Trojans oft beheld?
And oft beheld the warlike Greekish forces,
When Teucrian soil with bloody rivers swelled,
And wide Sigean shores were spread with corses,
And Simois and Xanthus blood outwelled;
Whilst Hector ragéd with outrageous mind,
Flames, weapons, wounds, in Greeks' fleet to have tined.

"For Ida self, in aid of that fierce fight,
Out of her mountains minist'red supplies;
And, like a kindly nurse, did yield (for spite)
Store of firebrands out of her nurseries
Unto her foster-children, that they might
Inflame the navy of their enemies,
And all the Rhœtean shore to ashes turn,
Where lay the ships which they did seek to burn.

"'Gainst which the noble son of Telamon
Opposed himself, and, thwarting his huge shield,
Them battle bad, 'gainst whom appeared anon
Hector, the glory of the Trojan field:
Both fierce and furious in contention
Encount'red, that their mighty strokes so shrilled,
As the great clap of thunder which doth rive
The rattling heavens, and clouds asunder drive.

"So th' one with fire and weapons did contend
To cut the ships from turning home again
To Argos; th' other strove for to defend
The force of Vulcan with his might and main.
Thus th' one Æacid did his fame extend;
But th' other joyed, that, on the Phrygian plain
Having the blood of vanquisht Hector shed,
He compassed Troy thrice with his body dead.

VIRGIL'S GNAT

"Again great dole on either party grew,
That him to death unfaithful Paris sent;
And also him that false Ulysses slew,
Drawn into danger through close ambushment;
Therefore from him Laertes' son his view
Doth turn aside, and boasts his good event
In working of Strymonian Rhesus' fall,
And eft in Dolon's subtil surprisall.

"Again the dreadful Cicones him dismay,
And black Læstrygones, a people stout:
Then greedy Scylla, under whom there bay
Many great bandogs which her gird about:
Then do the Ætnean Cyclops him affray,
And deep Charybdis gulfing in and out:
Lastly the squalid lakes of Tartary,
And grisly fiends of hell him terrify.

"There also goodly Agamemnon boasts,
The glory of the stock of Tantalus,
And famous light of all the Greekish hosts;
Under whose conduct most victorious,
The Doric flames consumed the Iliac posts.
Ah! but the Greeks themselves, more dolorous,
To thee, O Troy! paid penance for thy fall;
In th' Hellespont being nigh drownéd all.

"Well may appear, by proof of their mischance,
The changeful turning of men's slippery state,
That none whom Fortune freely doth advance
Himself therefore to heaven should elevate;
For lofty type of honour, through the glance
Of Envy's dart, is down in dust prostrate,
And all that vaunts in worldly vanity
Shall fall through Fortune's mutability.

"Th' Argolic power returning home again,
Enricht with spoils of th' Ericthonian tower,
Did happy wind and weather entertain,
And with good speed the foamy billows scour:
No sign of storm, no fear of future pain,
Which soon ensuéd them with heavy stour.
Nereis to the seas a token gave,
The whiles their crooked keels the surges clave.

"Suddenly, whether through the gods' decree,
Or hapless rising of some froward star,
The heavens on every side enclouded be:
Black storms and fogs are blowen up from far,
That now the pilot can no loadstar see,
But skies and seas do make most dreadful war;
The billows striving to the heavens to reach,
And th' heavens striving them for to impeach.

"And in avengement of their bold attempt,
Both sun and stars and all the heavenly powers
Conspire in one to wreak their rash contempt,
And down on them to fall from highest towers:
The sky, in pieces seeming to be rent,
Throws lightning forth, and hail, and harmful showers;
That death on every side to them appears
In thousand forms, to work more ghastly fears.

"Some in the greedy floods are sunk and drent;
Some on the rocks of Caphareus are thrown;
Some on th' Euboic cliffs in pieces rent;
Some scatt'red on the Hercæan shores unknown;
And many lost, of whom no monument
Remains, nor memory is to be shown:
Whilst all the purchase of the Phrygian prey,
Tost on salt billows, round about doth stray.

"Here many other like heroës be,
Equal in honour to the former crew,
Whom ye in goodly seats may placéd see,
Descended all from Rome by lineage due;
From Rome, that holds the world in sovereignty,
And doth all nations unto her subdue:
Here Fabii and Decii do dwell,
Horatii that in virtue did excel.

"And here the antique fame of stout Camill
Doth ever live; and constant Curtius,
Who, stiffly bent his vowéd life to spill
For country's health, a gulf most hideous
Amidst the town with his own corpse did fill,
T' appease the powers; and prudent Mucius,
Who in his flesh endured the scorching flame,
To daunt his foe by ensample of the same.

VIRGIL'S GNAT

"And here wise Curius, companion
Of noble virtues, lives in endless rest;
And stout Flaminius, whose devotion
Taught him the fire's scorned fury to detest;
And here the praise of either Scipion
Abides in highest place above the best,
To whom the ruined walls of Carthage vowed,
Trembling their forces, sound their praises loud.

"Live they for ever through their lasting praise!
But I, poor wretch, am forcéd to return
To the sad lakes that Phœbus' sunny rays
Do never see, where souls do always mourn;
And by the wailing shores to waste my days,
Where Phlegethon with quenchless flames doth burn;
By which just Minos righteous souls doth sever
From wicked ones, to live in bliss for ever.

"Me therefore thus the cruel fiends of hell,
Girt with long snakes, and thousand iron chains,
Through doom of that their cruel judge compel
With bitter torture, and impatient pains,
Cause of my death and just complaint to tell:
For thou art he whom my poor ghost complains
To be the author of her ill unwares,
That careless hear'st my intolerable cares.

"Them therefore as bequeathing to the wind,
I now depart, returning to thee never,
And leave this lamentable plaint behind:
But do thou haunt the soft down-rolling river,
And wild green woods and fruitful pastures mind;
And let the flitting air my vain words sever."
Thus having said, he heavily departed
With piteous cry, that any would have smarted.

Now, when the slothful fit of life's sweet rest
Had left the heavy shepherd, wondrous cares
His inly grievéd mind full sore opprest;
That baleful sorrow he no longer bears
For that gnat's death, which deeply was imprest,
But bends whatever power his aged years
Him lent, yet being such as through their might
He lately slew his dreadful foe in fight.

By that same river lurking under green,
Eftsoons he gins to fashion forth a place;
And, squaring it in compass well beseen,
There plotteth out a tomb by measured space:
His iron-headed spade then making clean,
To dig up sods out of the flow'ry grass,
His work he shortly to good purpose brought,
Like as he had conceived it in his thought.

An heap of earth he hoarded up on high,
Enclosing it with banks on every side,
And thereupon did raise full busily
A little mount, of green turfs edified;
And on the top of all, that passers by
Might it behold, the tomb he did provide
Of smoothest marble stone in order set,
That never might his lucky 'scape forget.

And round about he taught sweet flowers to grow:
The rose engrainéd in pure scarlet dye;
The lily fresh, and violet below;
The marigold, and cheerful rosemary;
The Spartan myrtle, whence sweet gum does flow;
The purple hyacinth, and fresh costmary;
And saffron, sought for in Cilician soil;
And laurel, th' ornament of Phœbus' toil.

Fresh rhododaphne, and the Sabine flower,
Matching the wealth of th' ancient frankincense;
And pallid ivy, building his own bower;
And box, yet mindful of his old offence;
Red amaranthus, luckless paramour;
Oxeye still green, and bitter patience;
Ne wants there pale Narcisse, that, in a well
Seeing his beauty, in love with it fell.

And whatsoever other flower of worth,
And whatso other herb of lovely hue,
The joyous spring out of the ground brings forth,
To clothe herself in colours fresh and new,
He planted there, and reared a mount of earth,
In whose high front was writ as doth ensue.

To thee, small gnat, in lieu of his life saved,
The shepherd hath thy death's record engraved.

PROSOPOPOIA:

OR

MOTHER HUBBARD'S TALE
BY ED. SP.

DEDICATED TO THE RIGHT HONOURABLE, THE
LADY COMPTON AND MOUNTEAGLE

Most fair and virtuous Lady; having often sought opportunity by some good means to make known to your Ladyship the humble affection and faithful duty, which I have always professed, and am bound to bear to that house, from whence ye spring, I have at length found occasion to remember the same, by making a simple present to you of these my idle labours; which having long sithens composed in the raw conceit of my youth, I lately amongst other papers lighted upon, and was by others, which liked the same, moved to set them forth. Simple is the device, and the composition mean, yet carrieth some delight, even the rather because of the simplicity and meanness thus personated. The same I beseech your Ladyship take in good part, as a pledge of that profession which I have made to you; and keep with you until, with some other more worthy labour, I do redeem it out of your hands, and discharge my utmost duty. Till then, wishing your Ladyship all increase of honour and happiness, I humbly take leave.

Your Ladyship's ever humbly,

ED. SP.

It was the month in which the righteous maid,
That for disdain of sinful world's upbraid
Fled back to heaven, whence she was first conceived,
Into her silver bower the sun received;
And the hot Sirian dog on him awaiting,
After the chaféd Lion's cruel baiting,
Corrupted had th' air with his noisome breath,
And poured on th' earth plague, pestilence, and death.
Amongst the rest a wicked malady
Reigned amongst men, that many did to die,
Deprived of sense and ordinary reason;
That it to leeches seeméd strange and geason.

My fortune was, 'mongst many others mo,
To be partaker of their common woe;
And my weak body set on fire with grief,
Was robbed of rest and natural relief.
In this ill plight there came to visit me
Some friends, who, sorry my sad case to see,
Began to comfort me in cheerful wise,
And means of gladsome solace to devise:
But seeing kindly sleep refuse to do
His office, and my feeble eyes forgo,
They sought my troubled sense how to deceive
With talk, that might unquiet fancies reave;
And, sitting all in seats about me round,
With pleasant tales (fit for that idle stound)
They cast in course to waste the weary hours.
Some told of ladies, and their paramours;
Some of brave knights, and their renownéd squires;
Some of the faeries and their strange attires;
And some of giants, hard to be believed;
That the delight thereof me much relieved.
Amongst the rest a good old woman was,
Hight Mother Hubbard, who did far surpass
The rest in honest mirth, that seemed her well:
She, when her turn was come her tale to tell,
Told of a strange adventure, that betided
Betwixt the fox and th' ape by him misguided,
The which, for that my sense it greatly pleased,
All were my spirit heavy and diseased,
I'll write in terms as she the same did say,
So well as I her words remember may.
No Muse's aid me needs hereto to call;
Base is the style, and matter mean withal.

  Whilom (said she) before the world was civil,
The fox and th' ape, disliking of their evil
And hard estate, determinéd to seek
Their fortunes far abroad, like with his like,
For both were crafty and unhappy witted;
Two fellows might nowhere be better fitted.
The fox, that first this cause of grief did find,
Gan first thus plain his case with words unkind.
"Neighbour ape, and my gossip eke beside
(Both two sure bands in friendship to be tied),
To whom may I more trustily complain

MOTHER HUBBARD'S TALE

The evil plight that doth me sore constrain,
And hope thereof to find due remedy?
Hear, then, my pain and inward agony.
Thus many years I now have spent and worn
In mean regard, and basest fortune's scorn,
Doing my country service as I might,
No less, I dare say, than the proudest wight;
And still I hopéd to be up advanced,
For my good parts; but still it has mischanced.
Now therefore that no longer hope I see,
But froward fortune still to follow me,
And losels lifted up where I did look,
I mean to turn the next leaf of the book:
Yet, ere that any way I do betake,
I mean my gossip privy first to make."
"Ah! my dear gossip" (answered then the ape),
"Deeply do your sad words my wits awhape,
Both for because your grief doth great appear,
And eke because myself am touchéd near:
For I likewise have wasted much good time,
Still waiting to preferment up to climb,
Whilst others always have before me stept,
And from my beard the fat away have swept;
That now unto despair I gin to grow,
And mean for better wind about to throw.
Therefore to me, my trusty friend, arede
Thy counsel: two is better than one head."
"Certes" (said he) "I mean me to disguise
In some strange habit, after uncouth wise;
Or like a pilgrim, or a lymiter,
Or like a gipsen, or a juggeler,
And so to wander to the worldës end,
To seek my fortune, where I may it mend:
For worse than that I have I cannot meet.
Wide is the world, I wot, and every street
Is full of fortunes, and adventures strange,
Continually subject unto change.
Say, my fair brother now, if this device
Doth like you, or may you to like entice."
"Surely" (said th' ape) "it likes me wondrous well;
And would ye not poor fellowship expel,
Myself would offer you t' accompany
In this adventure's chanceful jeopardy:

For to wex old at home in idleness
Is disadvent'rous, and quite fortuneless;
Abroad, where change is, good may gotten be."
    The fox was glad, and quickly did agree:
So both resolved, the morrow next ensuing,
So soon as day appeared to people's viewing,
On their intended journey to proceed;
And overnight whatso thereto did need
Each did prepare, in readiness to be.
The morrow next, so soon as one might see
Light out of heaven's windows forth to look,
Both their habiliments unto them took,
And put themselves (a' God's name) on their way;
Whenas the ape, beginning well to weigh
This hard adventure, thus began t' advise.
"Now rede, Sir Reynold, as ye be right wise,
What course ye ween is best for us to take,
That for ourselves we may a living make.
Whether shall we profess some trade or skill,
Or shall we vary our device at will,
Even as new occasion appears?
Or shall we tie ourselves for certain years
To any service, or to any place?
For it behoves, ere that into the race
We enter, to resolve first hereupon."
    "Now surely, brother" (said the fox anon),
"Ye have this matter motionéd in season;
For everything that is begun with reason
Will come by ready means unto his end,
But things miscounselléd must needs miswend.
Thus therefore I advise upon the case,
That not to any certain trade or place,
Nor any man, we should ourselves apply;
For why should he that is at liberty
Make himself bond? sith then we are free born,
Let us all servile base subjection scorn;
And as we be sons of the world so wide,
Let us our father's heritage divide,
And challenge to ourselves our portions due
Of all the patrimony, which a few
Now hold in hugger-mugger in their hand,
And all the rest do rob of good and land.
For now a few have all, and all have nought,

Yet all be brethren ylike dearly bought:
There is no right in this partition,
Ne was it so by institution
Ordainéd first, ne by the law of Nature,
But that she gave like blessing to each creature,
As well of worldly livelode as of life,
That there might be no difference nor strife,
Nor aught called mine or thine: thrice happy then
Was the condition of mortal men.
That was the golden age of Saturn old,
But this might better be the world of gold;
For without gold now nothing will be got,
Therefore (if please you) this shall be our plot:
We will not be of any occupation;
Let such vile vassals, born to base vocation,
Drudge in the world, and for their living droil,
Which have no wit to live withouten toil;
But we will walk about the world at pleasure,
Like two free men, and make our ease our treasure.
Free men some beggars call, but they be free,
And they which call them so more beggars be;
For they do swink and sweat to feed the other,
Who live like lords of that which they do gather,
And yet do never thank them for the same,
But as their due by nature do it claim.
Such will we fashion both ourselves to be,
Lords of the world; and so will wander free
Whereso us listeth, uncontrolled of any:
Hard is our hap, if we (amongst so many)
'Light not on some that may our state amend;
Seldom but some good cometh ere the end."

Well seemed the ape to like this ordinance;
Yet, well considering of the circumstance,
As pausing in great doubt, awhile he stayed,
And afterwards with grave advisement said:
"I cannot, my lief brother, like but well
The purpose of the complot which ye tell;
For well I wot (compared to all the rest
Of each degree) that beggars' life is best:
And they, that think themselves the best of all,
Oft-times to begging are content to fall.
But this I wot withal, that we shall run
Into great danger, like to be undone,

Thus wildly to wander in the world's eye,
Withouten passport or good warranty,
For fear lest we like rogues should be reputed,
And for ear-markéd beasts abroad be bruited.
Therefore, I rede that we our counsels call,
How to prevent this mischief ere it fall,
And how we may, with most security,
Beg amongst those that beggars do defy."
"Right well, dear gossip, ye adviséd have,"
(Said then the fox) "but I this doubt will save;
For ere we farther pass I will devise
A passport for us both in fittest wise,
And by the names of soldiers us protect:
That now is thought a civil begging sect.
Be you the soldier, for you likest are
For manly semblance, and small skill in war:
I will but wait on you, and, as occasion
Falls out, myself fit for the same will fashion."

  The passport ended, both they forward went;
The ape clad soldier-like, fit for th' intent,
In a blue jacket with a cross of red
And many slits, as if that he had shed
Much blood through many wounds therein received,
Which had the use of his right arm bereaved.
Upon his head an old Scotch cap he wore,
With a plume feather all to pieces tore:
His breeches were made after the new cut,
Al Portugese, loose like an empty gut;
And his hose broken high above the heeling,
And his shoes beaten out with travelling.
But neither sword nor dagger he did bear;
Seems that no foe's revengement he did fear:
Instead of them a handsome bat he held,
On which he leanéd, as one far in eld.
Shame light on him, that through so false illusion,
Doth turn the name of soldiers to abusion,
And that, which is the noblest mystery,
Brings to reproach and common infamy!
Long they thus travelléd, yet never met
Adventure which might them a-working set;
Yet many ways they sought, and many tried,
Yet for their purposes none fit espied.
At last they chanced to meet upon the way

A simple husbandman in garments gray;
Yet though his vesture were but mean and base,
A good yeoman he was of honest place,
And more for thrift did care than for gay clothing:
Gay without good is good hearts' greatest loathing.
The fox him spying, had the ape him dight
To play his part, for lo! he was in sight
That (if he erred not,) should them entertain,
And yield them timely profit for their pain.
Eftsoons the ape himself gan up to rear,
And on his shoulders high his bat to bear,
As if good service he were fit to do;
But little thrift for him he did it to:
And stoutly forward he his steps did strain,
That like a handsome swain it him became.
  Whenas they nigh approachéd, that good man,
Seeing them wander loosely, first began
T' inquire of custom, what and whence they were?
To whom the ape, "I am a soldier,
That late in wars have spent my dearest blood,
And in long service lost both limbs and good;
And now, constrained that trade to overgive,
I driven am to seek some means to live:
Which might it you in pity please t' afford,
I would be ready, both in deed and word,
To do you faithful service all my days.
This iron world" (that same he weeping says)
"Brings down the stoutest hearts to lowest state;
For misery doth bravest minds abate,
And make them seek for that they wont to scorn,
Of fortune and of hope at once forlorn."
The honest man, that heard him thus complain,
Was grieved as he had felt part of his pain;
And, well disposed him some relief to show,
Asked if in husbandry he aught did know,
To plough, to plant, to reap, to rake, to sow,
To hedge, to ditch, to thrash, to thatch, to mow?
Or to what labour else he was prepared,
For husband's life is laborous and hard?
Whenas the ape him heard so much to talk
Of labour, that did from his liking balk,
He would have slipt the collar handsomely,
And to him said: "Good sir, full glad am I,

To take what pains may any living wight;
But my late maiméd limbs lack wonted might
To do their kindly services as needeth.
Scarce this right hand the mouth with diet feedeth,
So that it may no painful work endure,
Ne to strong labour can itself inure:
But if that any other place you have,
Which asks small pains, but thriftiness to save,
Or care to overlook, or trust to gather,
Ye may me trust as your own ghostly father."

With that the husbandman gan him avise,
That it for him were fittest exercise
Cattle to keep, or grounds to oversee;
And askéd him, if he could willing be
To keep his sheep, or to attend his swine,
Or watch his mares, or take his charge of kine?
"Gladly" (said he) "whatever such-like pain
Ye put on me, I will the same sustain;
But gladliest I of your fleecy sheep
(Might it you please) would take on me the keep.
For ere that unto arms I me betook,
Unto my father's sheep I used to look,
That yet the skill thereof I have not lost:
Thereto right well this curdog, by my cost,"
(Meaning the fox) "will serve my sheep to gather,
And drive to follow after their bell-wether."
The husbandman was meanly well content
Trial to make of his endeavourment;
And, home him leading, lent to him the charge
Of all his flock, with liberty full large,
Giving accompt of th' annual increase
Both of their lambs, and of their woolly fleece.
Thus is this ape become a shepherd swain,
And the false fox his dog (God give them pain!)
For ere the year have half his course outrun,
And do return from whence he first begun,
They shall him make an ill accompt of thrift.
Now whenas Time, flying with wingës swift,
Expiréd had the term, that these two javels
Should render up a reck'ning of their travels
Unto their master, which it of them sought,
Exceedingly they troubled were in thought,
Ne wist what answer unto him to frame,

MOTHER HUBBARD'S TALE

Ne how to 'scape great punishment, or shame,
For their false treason and vile thievery:
For not a lamb of all their flock's supply
Had they to shew; but, ever as they bred,
They slew them, and upon their fleshes fed;
For that disguiséd dog loved blood to spill,
And drew the wicked shepherd to his will.
So 'twixt them both they not a lambkin left,
And when lambs failed the old sheep's lives they reft;
That how t' acquit themselves unto their lord
They were in doubt, and flatly set abord.
The fox then counselled th' ape for to require
Respite till morrow t' answer his desire;
For time's delay new hope of help still breeds.
The goodman granted, doubting nought their deeds,
And bad next day that all should ready be:
But they more subtil meaning had than he;
For the next morrow's meed they closely meant,
For fear of afterclaps, for to prevent:
And that same evening, when all shrouded were
In careless sleep, they without care or fear
Cruelly fell upon their flock in fold,
And of them slew at pleasure what they wold.
Of which whenas they feasted had their fill,
For a full complement of all their ill,
They stole away, and took their hasty flight,
Carried in clouds of all-concealing night.

So was the husbandman left to his loss,
And they unto their fortune's change to toss:
After which sort they wanderéd long while,
Abusing many through their cloakéd guile,
That at the last they gan to be descried
Of every one, and all their sleights espied.
So as their begging now them failéd quite,
For none would give, but all men would them wite:
Yet would they take no pains to get their living,
But seek some other way to gain by giving,
Much like to begging, but much better named,
For many beg which are thereof ashamed.
And now the fox had gotten him a gown,
And th' ape a cassock sidelong hanging down;
For they their occupation meant to change,
And now in other state abroad to range:

For, since their soldier's pass no better sped,
They forged another, as for clerks book-read,
Who passing forth, as their adventures fell,
Through many haps, which needs not here to tell,
At length chanced with a formal priest to meet,
Whom they in civil manner first did greet,
And after asked an alms for God's dear love.
The man straightway his choler up did move,
And with reproachful terms gan them revile,
For following that trade so base and vile;
And asked what licence, or what pass they had?
"Ah!" (said the ape, as sighing wondrous sad)
"It's an hard case, when men of good deserving
Must either driven be perforce to sterving,
Or askéd for their pass by every squib,
That list at will them to revile or snib:
And yet (God wot) small odds I often see,
'Twixt them that ask, and them that askéd be.
Nath'less, because you shall not us misdeem,
But that we are as honest as we seem,
Ye shall our passport at your pleasure see,
And then ye will (I hope) well movéd be."
Which when the priest beheld, he viewed it near,
As if therein some text he studying were,
But little else (God wot) could thereof skill;
For read he could not evidence, nor will.
Ne tell a written word, ne write a letter,
Ne make one tittle worse, ne make one better:
Of such deep learning little had he need,
Ne yet of Latin, ne of Greek, that breed
Doubts 'mongst divines, and difference of texts,
From whence arise diversity of sects,
And hateful heresies, of God abhorred:
But this good sir did follow the plain word,
Ne meddled with their controversies vain:
All his care was, his service well to sayn,
And to read hom'lies upon holidays;
When that was done, he might attend his plays:
An easy life, and fit high God to please.

He, having overlooked their pass at ease,
Gan at the length them to rebuke again,
That no good trade of life did entertain,
But lost their time in wand'ring loose abroad;

MOTHER HUBBARD'S TALE

Seeing the world, in which they bootless bode,
Had ways enough for all therein to live;
Such grace did God unto his creatures give.
Said then the fox: "Who hath the world not tried,
From the right way full eath may wander wide:
We are but novices, new come abroad,
We have not yet the tract of any trode,
Nor on us taken any state of life,
But ready are of any to make preif.
Therefore might please you, which the world have proved,
Us to advise, which forth but lately moved,
Of some good course that we might undertake;
Ye shall for ever us your bondmen make."
The priest gan wex half proud to be so prayed,
And thereby willing to afford them aid;
"It seems" (said he) "right well that ye be clerks,
Both by your witty words, and by your works.
Is not that name enough to make a living
To him that hath a whit of Nature's giving?
How many honest men see ye arise
Daily thereby, and grow to goodly prize?
To deans, to archdeacons, to commissaries,
To lords, to principals, to prebendaries;
All jolly prelates, worthy rule to bear,
Whoever them envý: yet spite bites near.
Why should ye doubt, then, but that ye likewise
Might unto some of those in time arise?
In the meantime to live in good estate,
Loving that love, and hating those that hate;
Being some honest curate, or some vicar
Content with little in condition sicker."
"Ah! but" (said th' ape) "the charge is wondrous great,
To feed men's souls, and hath an heavy threat."
"To feed men's souls" (quoth he) "is not in man;
For they must feed themselves, do what we can.
We are but charged to lay the meat before:
Eat they that list, we need to do no more.
But God it is that feeds them with his grace,
The bread of life poured down from heavenly place.
Therefore said he, that with the budding rod
Did rule the Jews, *All shall be taught of God*.
That same hath Jesus Christ now to him raught,
By whom the flock is rightly fed, and taught:

He is the Shepherd, and the Priest is he;
We but his shepherd swains ordained to be.
Therefore herewith do not yourself dismay;
Ne is the pains so great, but bear ye may,
For not so great, as it was wont of yore,
It's nowadays, ne half so strait and sore.
They whilom uséd duly every day
Their service and their holy things to say,
At morn and even, besides their anthems sweet,
Their penny masses, and their complines meet,
Their diriges, their trentals, and their shrifts,
Their memories, their singings, and their gifts.
Now all those needless works are laid away;
Now once a week, upon the Sabbath day,
It is enough to do our small devotion,
And then to follow any merry motion.
Ne are we tied to fast, but when we list;
Ne to wear garments base of woollen twist,
But with the finest silks us to array,
That before God we may appear more gay,
Resembling Aaron's glory in his place:
For far unfit it is, that person base
Should with vile clothes approach God's majesty,
Whom no uncleanness may approachen nigh;
Or that all men, which any master serve,
Good garments for their service should deserve;
But he that serves the Lord of hosts most high,
And that in highest place, t' approach him nigh,
And all the people's prayers to present
Before his throne, as on ambassage sent
Both to and fro, should not deserve to wear
A garment better than of wool or hair.
Beside, we may have lying by our sides
Our lovely lasses, or bright shining brides:
We be not tied to wilful chastity,
But have the gospel of free liberty."

By that he ended had his ghostly sermon,
The fox was well induced to be a parson,
And of the priest eftsoons gan to inquire,
How to a benefice he might aspire.
"Marry, there" (said the priest) "is art indeed:
Much good deep learning one thereout may read;
For that the ground-work is, and end of all,

How to obtain a beneficial.
First, therefore, when ye have in handsome wise
Yourself attiréd, as you can devise,
Then to some nobleman yourself apply,
Or other great one in the worldës eye,
That hath a zealous disposition
To God, and so to his religion.
There must thou fashion eke a godly zeal,
Such as no carpers may contrare reveal;
For each thing feignéd ought more wary be.
There thou must walk in sober gravity,
And seem as saint-like as Saint Radegund:
Fast much, pray oft, look lowly on the ground,
And unto every one do courtesy meek:
These looks (nought saying) do a benefice seek,
And be thou sure one not to lack ere long.
But if thee list unto the court to throng,
And there to hunt after the hopéd prey,
Then must thou thee dispose another way:
For there thou needs must learn to laugh, to lie,
To face, to forge, to scoff, to company,
To crouch, to please, to be a beetle-stock
Of thy great master's will, to scorn, or mock.
So may'st thou chance mock out a benefice,
Unless thou canst one conjure by device,
Or cast a figure for a bishopric;
And if one could, it were but a school trick.
These be the ways by which without reward
Livings in court be gotten, though full hard·
For nothing there is done without a fee:
The courtier needs must recompenséd be
With a benevolence, or have in gage
The primitias of your parsonage:
Scarce can a bishopric forpass them by,
But that it must be gelt in privity.
Do not thou therefore seek a living there,
But of more private persons seek elsewhere,
Whereas thou may'st compound a better penny,
Ne let thy learning questioned be of any.
For some good gentleman, that hath the right
Unto his church for to present a wight,
Will cope with thee in reasonable wise;
That if the living yearly do arise

To forty pound, that then his youngest son
Shall twenty have, and twenty thou hast won:
Thou hast it won, for it is of frank gift,
And he will care for all the rest to shift,
Both that the bishop may admit of thee,
And that therein thou may'st maintainéd be.
This is the way for one that is unlearned
Living to get, and not to be discerned.
But they, that are great clerks, have nearer ways,
For learning sake to living them to raise;
Yet many eke of them (God wot) are driven
T' accept a benefice in pieces riven.
How say'st thou (friend), have I not well discoursed
Upon this common-place (though plain, not worst)?
Better a short tale than a bad long shriving.
Needs any more to learn to get a living?"
  "Now sure, and by my halidom," (quoth he)
"Ye a great master are in your degree:
Great thanks I yield you for your discipline,
And do not doubt but duly to incline
My wits thereto, as ye shall shortly hear."
The priest him wished good speed, and well to fare:
So parted they, as either's way them led.
But th' ape and fox ere long so well them sped,
Through the priest's wholesome counsel lately taught,
And through their own fair handling wisely wrought,
That they a benefice 'twixt them obtained;
And crafty Reynold was a priest ordained,
And th' ape his parish clerk procured to be.
Then made they revel rout and goodly glee;
But, ere long time had passéd, they so ill
Did order their affairs, that th' evil will
Of all their parish'ners they had constrained;
Who to the Ordinary of them complained,
How foully they their offices abused,
And them of crimes and heresies accused,
That pursuivants he often for them sent;
But they neglected his commandëment.
So long persisted obstinate and bold,
Till at the length he publishéd to hold
A visitation, and them cited thither:
Then was high time their wits about to gather.
What did they then, but made a composition

With their next neighbour priest, for light condition,
To whom their living they resignéd quite
For a few pence, and ran away by night.
  So passing through the country in disguise,
They fled far off, where none might them surprise;
And after that long strayéd here and there,
Through every field and forest far and near,
Yet never found occasion for their turn,
But almost starved did much lament and mourn.
At last they chanced to meet upon the way
The mule all deckt in goodly rich array,
With bells and bosses that full loudly rung,
And costly trappings that to ground down hung.
Lowly they him saluted in meek wise;
But he through pride and fatness gan despise
Their meanness; scarce vouchsafed them to requite.
Whereat the fox, deep groaning in his sprite,
Said: "Ah! Sir Mule, now blessed be the day,
That I see you so goodly and so gay
In your attires, and eke your silken hide
Filled with round flesh, that every bone doth hide.
Seems that in fruitful pastures ye do live,
Or Fortune doth you secret favour give."
"Foolish fox" (said the mule) "thy wretched need
Praiseth the thing that doth thy sorrow breed:
For well I ween, thou canst not but envý
My wealth, compared to thine own misery,
That art so lean and meagre waxen late,
That scarce thy legs uphold thy feeble gait."
"Ay me!" (said then the fox) "whom evil hap
Unworthy in such wretchedness doth wrap,
And makes the scorn of other beasts to be:
But rede (fair sir, of grace) from whence come ye;
Or what of tidings you abroad do hear?
News may perhaps some good unweeting bear."
"From royal court I lately came" (said he),
"Where all the bravery that eye may see,
And all the happiness that heart desire,
Is to be found: he nothing can admire,
That hath not seen that heaven's portraiture.
But tidings there is none, I you assure,
Save that which common is, and known to all,
That courtiers, as the tide, do rise and fall."

"But tell us" (said the ape), "we do you pray,
Who now in court doth bear the greatest sway,
That, if such fortune do to us befall,
We may seek favour of the best of all?"
"Marry," (said he) "the highest now in grace
Be the wild beasts, that swiftest are in chase;
For in their speedy course and nimble flight
The lion now doth take the most delight;
But chiefly joys on foot them to behold,
Enchased with chain and circulet of gold.
So wild a beast so tame ytaught to be,
And buxom to his bands, is joy to see;
So well his golden circlet him beseemeth.
But his late chain his liege unmeet esteemeth;
For so brave beasts she loveth best to see
In the wild forest ranging fresh and free.
Therefore if fortune thee in court to live,
In case thou ever there wilt hope to thrive,
To some of these thou must thyself apply;
Else as a thistle-down in th' air doth fly,
So vainly shalt thou to and fro be tost,
And lose thy labour and thy fruitless cost.
And yet full few which follow them, I see,
For virtue's bare regard advancéd be,
But either for some gainful benefit,
Or that they may for their own turns be fit.
Nath'less perhaps ye things may handle so,
That ye may better thrive than thousands mo."

"But" (said the ape) "how shall we first come in,
That after we may favour seek to win?"
"How else" (said he) "but with a good bold face,
And with big words, and with a stately pace,
That men may think of you in general,
That to be in you which is not at all:
For not by that which is, the world now deemeth,
(As it was wont) but by that same that seemeth.
Ne do I doubt but that ye well can fashion
Yourselves thereto, according to occasion.
So fare ye well; good courtiers may ye be!"
So, proudly neighing, from them parted he.
Then gan this crafty couple to devise,
How for the court themselves they might aguise;
For thither they themselves meant to address,

In hope to find there happier success.
So well they shifted, that the ape anon
Himself had clothéd like a gentleman,
And the sly fox, as like to be his groom,
That to the court in seemly sort they come;
Where the fond ape, himself uprearing high
Upon his tiptoes, stalketh stately by,
As if he were some great magnifico,
And boldly doth amongst the boldest go;
And his man Reynold, with fine counterfeasance,
Supports his credit and his countenance.
Then gan the courtiers gaze on every side,
And stare on him, with big looks basin-wide,
Wond'ring what mister wight he was, and whence:
For he was clad in strange accoutrements,
Fashioned with quaint devices, never seen
In court before, yet there all fashions bene;
Yet he them in newfangleness did pass,
But his behaviour altogether was
Alla Turchesca, much the more admired;
And his looks lofty, as if he aspired
To dignity and sdeigned the low degree;
That all which did such strangeness in him see
By secret means gan of his state inquire,
And privily his servant thereto hire:
Who, throughly armed against such coverture,
Reported unto all, that he was sure
A noble gentleman of high regard,
Which through the world had with long travel fared,
And seen the manners of all beasts on ground;
Now here arrived, to see if like he found.

Thus did the ape at first him credit gain,
Which afterwards he wisely did maintain
With gallant show, and daily more augment
Through his fine feats and courtly complement;
For he could play, and dance, and vault, and spring,
And all that else pertains to revelling,
Only through kindly aptness of his joints.
Besides, he could do many other points,
The which in court him servéd to good stead;
For he 'mongst ladies could their fortunes read
Out of their hands, and merry leasings tell,
And juggle finely, that became him well.

But he so light was at legerdemain,
That what he toucht came not to light again;
Yet would he laugh it out, and proudly look,
And tell them that they greatly him mistook.
So would he scoff them out with mockery,
For he therein had great felicity;
And with sharp quips joyed others to deface,
Thinking that their disgracing did him grace:
So whilst that other like vain wits he pleased,
And made to laugh, his heart was greatly eased.
But the right gentle mind would bite his lip
To hear the javel so good men to nip;
For, though the vulgar yield an open ear,
And common courtiers love to gibe and fleer
At everything which they hear spoken ill,
And the best speeches with ill meaning spill,
Yet the brave courtier, in whose beauteous thought
Regard of honour harbours more than aught,
Doth loathe such base condition, to backbite
Any's good name for envy or despite:
He stands on terms of honourable mind,
Ne will be carried with the common wind
Of court's inconstant mutability,
Ne after every tattling fable fly;
But hears and sees the follies of the rest,
And thereof gathers for himself the best.
He will not creep, nor crouch with feignéd face,
But walks upright with comely steadfast pace,
And unto all doth yield due courtesy;
But not with kisséd hand below the knee,
As that same apish crew is wont to do:
For he disdains himself t' embase thereto.
He hates foul leasings, and vile flattery,
Two filthy blots in noble gentry;
And loathful idleness he doth detest,
The canker-worm of every gentle breast;
The which to banish with fair exercise
Of knightly feats, he daily doth devise;
Now managing the mouths of stubborn steeds,
Now practising the proof of warlike deeds,
Now his bright arms assaying, now his spear,
Now the nigh aiméd ring away to bear.
At other times he casts to sue the chase

Of swift wild beasts, or run on foot a race,
T' enlarge his breath (large breath in arms most needful),
Or else by wrestling to wex strong and heedful,
Or his stiff arms to stretch with yewen bow,
And manly legs, still passing to and fro,
Without a gownéd beast him fast beside,
A vain ensample of the Persian pride;
Who, after he had won th' Assyrian foe,
Did ever after scorn on foot to go.
    Thus when this courtly gentleman with toil
Himself hath weariéd, he doth recoil
Unto his rest, and there with sweet delight
Of music's skill revives his toiléd sprite;
Or else with loves, and ladies' gentle sports,
The joy of youth, himself he recomfórts;
Or lastly, when the body list to pause,
His mind unto the Muses he withdraws:
Sweet lady Muses, ladies of delight,
Delights of life, and ornaments of light!
With whom he close confers with wise discourse,
Of Nature's works, of heaven's continual course,
Of foreign lands, of people different,
Of kingdoms' change, of divers government,
Of dreadful battles of renownéd knights;
With which he kindleth his ambitious sprites
To like desire and praise of noble fame,
The only upshot whereto he doth aim:
For all his mind on honour fixéd is,
To which he levels all his purposes.
And in his prince's service spends his days,
Not so much for to gain, or for to raise
Himself to high degree, as for His Grace,
And in his liking to win worthy place,
Through due deserts and comely carriage,
In whatso please employ his personage,
That may be matter meet to gain him praise:
For he is fit to use in all assays,
Whether for arms and warlike amenance,
Or else for wise and civil governance.
For he is practised well in policy,
And thereto doth his courting most apply:
To learn the interdeal of princes strange,
To mark th' intent of counsels, and the change

Of states, and eke of private men somewhile,
Supplanted by fine falsehood and fair guile;
Of all the which he gathereth what is fit
T' enrich the storehouse of his powerful wit,
Which through wise speeches and grave conference
He daily ekes, and brings to excellence.
  Such is the rightful courtier in his kind,
But unto such the ape lent not his mind:
Such were for him no fit companions,
Such would descry his lewd conditions;
But the young lusty gallants he did choose
To follow, meet to whom he might disclose
His witless pleasance, and ill-pleasing vein.
A thousand ways he them could entertain,
With all the thriftless games that may be found;
With mumming and with masking all around,
With dice, with cards, with billiards far unfit,
With shuttlecocks, misseeming manly wit,
With courtesans, and costly riotise,
Whereof still somewhat to his share did rise:
Nor, them to pleasure, would he sometimes scorn
A pander's coat (so basely was he born).
Thereto he could fine loving verses frame,
And play the poet oft. But ah! for shame,
Let not sweet poets' praise, whose only pride
Is virtue to advance, and vice deride,
Be with the work of losels' wit defamed,
Ne let such verses poetry be named:
Yet he the name on him would rashly take,
Maugre the sacred Muses, and it make
A servant to the vile affection
Of such, as he depended most upon;
And with the sugary sweet thereof allure
Chaste ladies' ears to fantasies impure.
  To such delights the noble wits he led
Which him relieved, and their vain humours fed
With fruitless follies and unsound delights.
But if perhaps into their noble sprites
Desire of honour or brave thought of arms
Did ever creep, then with his wicked charms
And strong conceits he would it drive away,
Ne suffer it to house there half a day.
And whenso love of letters did inspire

Their gentle wits, and kindle wise desire,
That chiefly doth each noble mind adorn,
Then he would scoff at learning, and eke scorn
The sectaries thereof, as people base
And simple men, which never came in place
Of world's affairs, but, in dark corners mewed,
Mutt'red of matters as their books them shewed,
Ne other knowledge ever did attain,
But with their gowns their gravity maintain.
From them he would his impudent lewd speech
Against God's holy ministers oft reach,
And mock divines and their profession.
What else then did he by progression,
But mock high God himself, whom they profess?
But what cared he for God, or godliness?
All his care was himself how to advance,
And to uphold his courtly countenance
By all the cunning means he could devise:
Were it by honest ways, or otherwise,
He made small choice; yet sure his honesty
Got him small gains, but shameless flattery,
And filthy brocage, and unseemly shifts,
And borrow base, and some good ladies' gifts:
But the best help, which chiefly him sustained,
Was his man Reynold's purchase which he gained
For he was schooled by kind in all the skill
Of close conveyance, and each practice ill
Of cozenage and cleanly knavery,
Which oft maintained his master's bravery.
Besides, he used another slippery sleight,
In taking on himself, in common sight,
False personages fit for every stead,
With which he thousands cleanly cozenéd:
Now like a merchant, merchants to deceive,
With whom his credit he did often leave
In gage for his gay master's hopeless debt:
Now like a lawyer, when he land would let,
Or sell fee-simples in his master's name,
Which he had never, nor aught like the same.
Then would he be a broker, and draw in
Both wares and money, by exchange to win:
Then would he seem a farmer, that would sell
Bargains of woods, which he did lately fell,

Or corn, or cattle, or such other ware,
Thereby to cozen men not well aware:
Of all the which there came a secret fee,
To th' ape, that he his countenance might be.

  Besides all this, he used oft to beguile
Poor suitors, that in court did haunt somewhile;
For he would learn their business secretly,
And then inform his master hastily,
That he by means might cast them to prevent,
And beg the suit the which the other meant.
Or otherwise false Reynold would abuse
The simple suitor, and wish him to choose
His master, being one of great regard
In court, to compass any suit not hard,
In case his pains were recompensed with reason.
So would he work the silly man by treason
To buy his master's frivolous good will,
That had not power to do him good or ill.
So pitiful a thing is suitor's state!
Most miserable man, whom wicked fate
Hath brought to court, to sue for had-I-wist,
That few have found, and many one hath missed!
Full little knowest thou, that hast not tried,
What hell it is in suing long to bide:
To lose good days, that might be better spent;
To waste long nights in pensive discontent;
To speed to-day, to be put back to-morrow;
To feed on hope, to pine with fear and sorrow;
To have thy prince's grace, yet want her peers';
To have thy asking, yet wait many years;
To fret thy soul with crosses and with cares;
To eat thy heart through comfortless despairs;
To fawn, to crouch, to wait, to ride, to run,
To spend, to give, to want, to be undone.
Unhappy wight, born to disastrous end,
That doth his life in so long 'tendance spend!

  Whoever leaves sweet home, where mean estate
In safe assurance, without strife or hate,
Finds all things needful for contentment meek,
And will to court for shadows vain to seek,
Or hope to gain, himself will a daw try:
That curse God send unto mine enemy!
For none but such as this bold ape, unblest,

Can ever thrive in that unlucky quest;
Or such as hath a Reynold to his man,
That by his shifts his master furnish can.
But yet this fox could not so closely hide
His crafty feats, but that they were descried
At length by such as sate in justice seat,
Who for the same him foully did entreat;
And having worthily him punishéd,
Out of the court for ever banishéd.
And now the ape, wanting his huckster man,
That wont provide his necessaries, gan
To grow into great lack, ne could uphold
His countenance in those his garments old;
Ne new ones could he easily provide,
Though all men him uncaséd gan deride,
Like as a puppet placéd in a play,
Whose part once past all men bid take away:
So that he driven was to great distress,
And shortly brought to hopeless wretchedness.
Then, closely as he might, he cast to leave
The Court, not asking any pass or leave;
But ran away in his rent rags by night,
Ne ever stayed in place, ne spake to wight,
Till that the fox, his copesmate, he had found,
To whom complaining his unhappy stound,
At last again with him in travel joined,
And with him fared some better chance to find.

So in the world long time they wanderéd,
And mickle want and hardness sufferéd;
That them repented much so foolishly
To come so far to seek for misery,
And leave the sweetness of contented home,
Though eating hips, and drinking watery foam.
Thus as they them complainéd to and fro,
Whilst through the forest reckless they did go,
Lo! where they spied, how, in a gloomy glade,
The lion sleeping lay in secret shade,
His crown and sceptre lying him beside,
And having doffed for heat his dreadful hide:
Which when they saw, the ape was sore afraid,
And would have fled with terror all dismayed,
But him the fox with hardy words did stay,
And bad him put all cowardice away:

For now was time (if ever they would hope)
To aim their counsels to the fairest scope,
And them for ever highly to advance,
In case the good, which their own happy chance
Them freely off'red, they would wisely take.
Scarce could the ape yet speak, so did he quake;
Yet, as he could, he asked how good might grow
Where nought but dread and death do seem in show?
"Now," (said he) "whiles the lion sleepeth sound,
May we his crown and mace take from the ground,
And eke his skin, the terror of the wood,
Wherewith we may ourselves (if we think good)
Make kings of beasts, and lords of forests all
Subject unto that power imperial."
"Ah! but" (said the ape) "who is so bold a wretch,
That dare his hardy hand to those outstretch,
Whenas he knows his meed, if he be spied,
To be a thousand deaths, and shame beside?"
"Fond ape!" (said then the fox) "into whose breast
Never crept thought of honour, nor brave gest,
Who will not venture life a king to be,
And rather rule and reign in sovereign see,
Than dwell in dust inglorious and base,
Where none shall name the number of his place?
One joyous hour in blissful happiness,
I choose before a life of wretchedness.
Be therefore counselléd herein by me,
And shake off this vile-hearted cowardry.
If he awake, yet is not death the next,
For we may colour it with some pretext
Of this, or that, that may excuse the crime:
Else we may fly; thou to a tree may'st climb,
And I creep underground, both from his reach:
Therefore be ruled to do as I do teach."

The ape, that erst did nought but chill and quake,
Now gan some courage unto him to take,
And was content to attempt that enterprise,
Tickled with glory and rash covetise:
But first gan question, whether should essay
Those royal ornaments to steal away.
"Marry, that shall yourself," (quoth he thereto)
"For ye be fine and nimble it to do;
Of all the beasts, which in the forests be,

Is not a fitter for this turn than ye:
Therefore, my own dear brother, take good heart,
And ever think a kingdom is your part."
Loth was the ape, though praiséd, to adventer,
Yet faintly gan into his work to enter,
Afraid of every leaf that stirred him by,
And every stick that underneath did lie,
Upon his tiptoes nicely he upwent,
For making noise, and still his ear he lent
To every sound that under heaven blew;
Now went, now stopt, now crept, now backward drew
That it good sport had been him to have eyed:
Yet at the last, (so well he him applied)
Through his fine handling, and his cleanly play,
He all those royal signs had stol'n away,
And with the fox's help them borne aside
Into a secret corner unespied.
Whither whenas they came they fell at words,
Whether of them should be the lord of lords:
For th' ape was strifeful, and ambitious;
And the fox guileful, and most covetous;
That neither pleaséd was to have the reign
'Twixt them divided into even twain,
But either (algates) would be lords alone;
For love and lordship bide no paragon.
"I am most worthy," (said the ape) "sith I
For it did put my life in jeopardy:
Thereto I am in person and in stature
Most like a man, the lord of every creature,
So that it seemeth I was made to reign,
And born to be a kingly sovereign."
"Nay" (said the fox), "Sir Ape, you are astray:
For though to steal the diadem away
Were the work of your nimble hand, yet I
Did first devise the plot by policy;
So that it wholly springeth from my wit:
For which also I claim myself more fit
Than you to rule; for government of state
Will without wisdom soon be ruinate.
And where ye claim yourself for outward shape
Most like a man, man is not like an ape
In his chief parts, that is, in wit and spirit;
But I therein most like to him do merit,

For my sly wiles and subtil craftiness,
The title of the kingdom to possess.
Nath'less (my brother) since we passéd are
Unto this point, we will appease our jar;
And I with reason meet will rest content,
That ye shall have both crown and government,
Upon condition, that ye ruléd be
In all affairs, and counselléd by me;
And that ye let none other ever draw
Your mind from me, but keep this as a law:
And hereupon an oath unto me plight."

The ape was glad to end the strife so light,
And thereto swore; for who would not oft swear,
And oft unswear, a diadem to bear?
Then freely up those royal spoils he took,
Yet at the lion's skin he inly quook;
But it dissembléd, and upon his head
The crown, and on his back the skin he did,
And the false fox him helpéd to array.
Then when he was all dight he took his way
Into the forest, that he might be seen
Of the wild beasts in his new glory sheen.
There the two first whom he encount'red were
The sheep and th' ass, who, stricken both with fear
At sight of him, gan fast away to fly;
But unto them the fox aloud did cry,
And in the king's name bad them both to stay,
Upon the pain that thereof follow may.
Hardly, nath'less, were they restrainéd so,
Till that the fox forth toward them did go,
And there dissuaded them from needless fear,
For that the king did favour to them bear;
And therefore dreadless bad them come to court,
For no wild beasts should do them any tort
There or abroad; ne would his Majesty
Use them but well, with gracious clemency,
As whom he knew to him both fast and true.
So he persuaded them, with homage due
Themselves to humble to the ape prostrate,
Who, gently to them bowing in his gait,
Receivéd them with cheerful entertain.
Thenceforth proceeding with his princely train,
He shortly met the tiger, and the boar,

MOTHER HUBBARD'S TALE

Which with the simple camel ragéd sore
In bitter words, seeking to take occasion
Upon his fleshly corpse to make invasion:
But soon as they this mock-king did espy,
Their troublous strife they stinted by and by,
Thinking indeed that it the lion was.
He then, to prove whether his power would pass
As current, sent the fox to them straightway,
Commanding them their cause of strife bewray;
And, if that wrong on either side there were,
That he should warn the wronger to appear
The morrow next at court, it to defend;
In the meantime upon the king t' attend.
The subtil fox so well his message said,
That the proud beasts him readily obeyed:
Whereby the ape in wondrous stomach wox,
Strongly encouraged by the crafty fox,
That king indeed himself he shortly thought,
And all the beasts him feared as they ought,
And followéd unto his palace high;
Where taking congé, each one by and by
Departed to his home in dreadful awe,
Full of the feared sight which late they saw.

 The ape, thus seizéd of the regal throne,
Eftsoons by counsel of the fox alone,
Gan to provide for all things in assurance,
That so his rule might longer have endurance.
First to his gate he 'pointed a strong guard,
That none might enter but with issue heard:
Then, for the safeguard of his personage,
He did appoint a warlike equipage
Of foreign beasts, not in the forest bred,
But part by land and part by water fed;
For tyranny is with strange aid supported.
Then unto him all monstrous beasts resorted,
Bred of two kinds, as griffons, minotaurs,
Crocodiles, dragons, beavers, and centaurs:
With those himself he strength'ned mightily,
That fear he need no force of enemy.
Then gan he rule and tyrannize at will,
Like as the fox did guide his graceless skill;
And all wild beasts made vassals of his pleasures,
And with their spoils enlarged his private treasures.

No care of justice, nor no rule of reason,
No temperance, nor no regard of season,
Did thenceforth ever enter in his mind;
But cruelty, the sign of currish kind,
And sdeignful pride, and wilful arrogance:
Such follows those whom Fortune doth advance.

But the false fox most kindly played his part;
For whatsoever mother-wit or art
Could work, he put in proof: no practice sly,
No counterpoint of cunning policy,
No reach, no breach, that might him profit bring,
But he the same did to his purpose wring.
Nought suffered he the ape to give or grant,
But through his hand must pass the fiant.
All offices, all leases by him leapt,
And of them all whatso he liked he kept.
Justice he sold injustice for to buy,
And for to purchase for his progeny.
Ill might it prosper that ill gotten was;
But, so he got it, little did he pass.
He fed his cubs with fat of all the soil,
And with the sweat of others' sweating toil;
He crammèd them with crumbs of benefices,
And filled their mouths with meeds of malefices:
He clothèd them with all colours, save white,
And loaded them with lordships and with might,
So much as they were able well to bear,
That with the weight their backs nigh broken were:
He chaff'red chairs in which churchmen were set,
And breach of laws to privy farm did let:
No statute so establishéd might be,
Nor ordinance so needful, but that he
Would violate, though not with violence,
Yet under colour of the confidence
The which the ape reposed in him alone,
And reck'ned him the kingdom's corner-stone.
And ever, when he aught would bring to pass,
His long experience the platform was:
And, when he aught not pleasing would put by,
The cloak was care of thrift, and husbandry,
For to increase the common treasure's store;
But his own treasure he increaséd more,
And lifted up his lofty towers thereby,

That they began to threat the neighbour sky;
The whiles the prince's palaces fell fast
To ruin (for what thing can ever last?)
And whilst the other peers, for poverty,
Were forced their ancient houses to let lie,
And their old castles to the ground to fall,
Which their forefathers, famous over-all,
Had founded for the kingdom's ornament,
And for their memory's long monument:
But he no count made of nobility,
Nor the wild beasts whom arms did glorify,
The realm's chief strength and garland of the crown.
All these through feignéd crimes he thrust adown,
Or made them dwell in darkness of disgrace;
For none, but whom he list, might come in place.

   Of men of arms he had but small regard,
But kept them low, and strainéd very hard.
For men of learning little he esteemed;
His wisdom he above their learning deemed.
As for the rascal commons least he cared,
For not so common was his bounty shared:
"Let God," (said he) "if please, care for the many,
I for myself must care before else any."
So did he good to none, to many ill,
So did he all the kingdom rob and pill,
Yet none durst speak, ne none durst of him plain,
So great he was in grace, and rich through gain.
Ne would he any let to have access
Unto the prince, but by his own address,
For all that else did come were sure to fail.
Yet would he further none but for avail;
For on a time the sheep, to whom of yore
The fox had promiséd of friendship store,
What time the ape the kingdom first did gain,
Came to the court, her case there to complain;
How that the wolf, her mortal enemy,
Had sithence slain her lamb most cruelly,
And therefore craved to come unto the king,
To let him know the order of the thing.
"Soft, goody sheep!" (then said the fox) "not so:
Unto the king so rash ye may not go;
He is with greater matter busiéd
Than a lamb, or the lamb's own mother's head.

Ne, certes, may I take it well in part,
That ye my cousin wolf so foully thwart,
And seek with slander his good name to blot;
For there was cause, else do it he would not:
Therefore surcease, good dame, and hence depart."
So went the sheep away with heavy heart:
So many mo, so every one was used,
That to give largely to the box refused.

Now when high Jove, in whose almighty hand
The care of kings and power of empires stand,
Sitting one day within his turret high,
From whence he views, with his black-lidded eye,
Whatso the heaven in his wide vault contains,
And all that in the deepest earth remains,
And troubled kingdom of wild beasts beheld,
Whom not their kindly sovereign did weld,
But an usurping ape, with guile suborned,
Had all subversed, he sdeignfully it scorned
In his great heart, and hardly did refrain,
But that with thunderbolts he had him slain,
And driven down to hell, his duest meed:
But, him avising, he that dreadful deed
Forbore, and rather chose with scornful shame
Him to avenge, and blot his brutish name
Unto the world, that never after any
Should of his race be void of infamy;
And his false counsellor, the cause of all,
To damn to death, or dole perpetual,
From whence he never should be quit, nor stalled.
Forthwith he Mercury unto him called,
And bad him fly with never-resting speed
Unto the forest, where wild beasts do breed,
And there inquiring privily, to learn
What did of late chance happen to the lion stern,
That he ruled not the empire, as he ought?
And whence were all those plaints unto him brought
Of wrongs, and spoils, by savage beasts committed?
Which done, he bad the lion be remitted
Into his seat, and those same treachours vile
Be punishéd for their presumptuous guile.

The son of Maia, soon as he received
That word, straight with his azure wings he cleaved
The liquid clouds, and lucid firmament;

Ne stayed, till that he came with steep descent
Unto the place where his prescript did show.
There stooping, like an arrow from a bow,
He soft arrivéd on the grassy plain,
And fairly pacéd forth with easy pain,
Till that unto the palace nigh he came.
Then gan he to himself new shape to frame;
And that fair face, and that ambrosial hue,
Which wonts to deck the gods' immortal crew
And beautify the shiny firmament,
He doffed, unfit for that rude rabblement.
So, standing by the gates in strange disguise,
He gan inquire of some in secret wise,
Both of the king, and of his government,
And of the fox, and his false blandishment.
And evermore he heard each one complain
Of foul abuses both in realm and reign;
Which yet to prove more true he meant to see,
And an eye-witness of each thing to be.
Then on his head his dreadful hat he dight,
Which maketh him invisible in sight,
And mocketh th' eyes of all the lookers on,
Making them think it but a vision.
Through power of that he runs through enemies' swerds;
Through power of that he passeth through the herds
Of ravenous wild beasts, and doth beguile
Their greedy mouths of the expected spoil;
Through power of that his cunning thieveries
He wonts to work, that none the same espies;
And, through the power of that, he putteth on
What shape he list in apparition.
That on his head he wore, and in his hand
He took Caduceus, his snaky wand,
With which the damnéd ghosts he governeth,
And furies rules, and Tartare tempereth.
With that he causeth sleep to seize the eyes,
And fear the hearts of all his enemies;
And, when him list, an universal night
Throughout the world he makes on every wight;
As when his sire with Alcumena lay.

   Thus dight, into the court he took his way,
Both through the guard, which never him descried,
And through the watchmen, who him never spied.

Thenceforth he passed into each secret part,
Whereas he saw, that sorely grieved his heart,
Each place abounding with foul injuries,
And filled with treasure racked with robberies;
Each place defiled with blood of guiltless beasts,
Which had been slain to serve the ape's behests:
Gluttony, malice, pride, and covetise,
And lawlessness reigning with riotise;
Besides the infinite extortíons,
Done through the fox's great oppressíons,
That the complaints thereof could not be told.
Which when he did with loathful eyes behold,
He would no more endure, but came his way,
And cast to seek the lion where he may,
That he might work the avengement for this shame
On those two caitives, which had bred him blame.
And, seeking all the forest busily,
At last he found, where sleeping he did lie.
The wicked weed, which there the fox did lay,
From underneath his head he took away,
And then him waking, forcéd up to rise.
The lion looking up gan him avise,
As one late in a trance, what had of long
Become of him: for fantasy is strong.
"Arise," (said Mercury) "thou sluggish beast,
That here liest senseless, like the corpse deceased,
The whilst thy kingdom from thy head is rent,
And thy throne royal with dishonour blent:
Arise, and do thyself redeem from shame,
And be avenged on those that breed thy blame."

Thereat enragéd, soon he gan upstart,
Grinding his teeth, and grating his great heart;
And, rousing up himself, for his rough hide
He gan to reach, but nowhere it espied.
Therewith he gan full terribly to roar,
And chafed at that indignity right sore.
But when his crown and sceptre both he wanted,
Lord! how he fumed, and swelled, and raged, and panted;
And threat'ned death, and thousand deadly dolours,
To them that had purloined his princely honours.
With that in haste, disrobéd as he was,
He toward his own palace forth did pass;
And all the way he roaréd as he went,

That all the forest with astonishment
Thereof did tremble, and the beasts therein
Fled fast away from that so dreadful din.
At last he came unto his mansion,
Where all the gates he found fast locked anon,
And many warders round about them stood.
With that he roared aloud, as he were wood,
That all the palace quakéd at the stound,
As if it quite were riven from the ground,
And all within were dead and heartless left:
And th' ape himself, as one whose wits were reft,
Fled here and there, and every corner sought,
To hide himself from his own fearéd thought.
But the false fox, when he the lion heard,
Fled closely forth, straightway of death afeard,
And to the lion came, full lowly creeping,
With feignéd face, and wat'ry eyne half weeping,
T' excuse his former treason and abusion,
And turning all unto the ape's confusion.
Nath'less the royal beast forbore believing,
But bad him stay at ease till further prieving.

Then, when he saw no entrance to him granted,
Roaring yet louder that all hearts it daunted,
Upon those gates with force he fiercely flew,
And, rending them in pieces, felly slew
Those warders strange, and all that else he met.
But th' ape still flying he nowhere might get:
From room to room, from beam to beam he fled
All breathless, and for fear now almost dead;
Yet him at last the lion spied, and caught,
And forth with shame unto his judgement brought.
Then all the beasts he caused assembled be,
To hear their doom, and sad ensample see.
The fox, first author of that treachery,
He did uncase, and then away let fly:
But th' ape's long tail (which then he had) he quite
Cut off, and both ears paréd of their height;
Since which all apes but half their ears have left,
And of their tails are utterly bereft.

So Mother Hubbard her discourse did end,
Which pardon me, if I amiss have penned;
For weak was my remembrance it to hold,
And bad her tongue that it so bluntly told.

THE RUINS OF ROME

BY BELLAY

I

Ye heavenly spirits, whose ashy cinders lie
Under deep ruins, with huge walls opprest,
But not your praise, the which shall never die
Through your fair verses, ne in ashes rest;
If so be shrilling voice of wight alive
May reach from hence to depth of darkest hell,
Then let those deep abysses open rive,
That ye may understand my shrieking yell.
Thrice having seen under the heavens' veil
Your tombs' devoted compass over-all,
Thrice unto you with loud voice I appeal,
And for your antique fury here do call,
    The whiles that I with sacred horror sing
    Your glory, fairest of all earthly thing!

II

Great Babylon her haughty walls will praise,
And sharpéd steeples high shot up in air;
Greece will the old Ephesian buildings blaze,
And Nilus' nurslings their pyramidës fair:
The same yet vaunting Greece will tell the story
Of Jove's great image in Olympus placed;
Mausolus' work will be the Carians' glory;
And Crete will boast the labyrinth, now rased:
The antique Rhodian will likewise set forth
The great Colosse, erect to Memory;
And what else in the world is of like worth,
Some greater learned wit will magnify:
    But I will sing above all monuments
    Seven Roman Hills, the world's Seven Wonderments.

III

Thou stranger, which for Rome in Rome here seekest,
And nought of Rome in Rome perceiv'st at all,

These same old walls, old arches, which thou seest,
Old palaces, is that which Rome men call.
Behold what wreck, what ruin, and what waste,
And how that she, which with her mighty power
Tamed all the world, hath tamed herself at last;
The prey of Time, which all things doth devour!
Rome now of Rome is th' only funeral,
And only Rome of Rome hath victory;
Ne aught save Tiber hast'ning to his fall
Remains of all.   O world's inconstancy!
   That which is firm doth flit and fall away,
   And that is flitting doth abide and stay.

IV

She, whose high top above the stars did soar,
One foot on Thetis, th' other on the Morning,
One hand on Scythia, th' other on the Moor,
Both heaven and earth in roundness compassing;
Jove fearing, lest if she should greater grow,
The giants old should once again uprise,
Her whelmed with hills, these seven hills, which be now
Tombs of her greatness which did threat the skies:
Upon her head he heapt Mount Saturnal,
Upon her belly th' antique Palatine,
Upon her stomach laid Mount Quirinal,
On her left hand the noisome Esquiline,
   And Cælian on the right; but both her feet
   Mount Viminal and Aventine do meet.

V

Who lists to see whatever nature, art,
And heaven could do, O Rome! thee let him see,
In case thy greatness he can guess in heart,
By that which but the picture is of thee.
Rome is no more: but if the shade of Rome
May of the body yield a seeming sight,
It's like a corse drawn forth out of the tomb
By magic skill out of eternal night.
The corpse of Rome in ashes is entombed,
And her great spirit, rejoinéd to the spirit
Of this great mass, is in the same enwombed;
But her brave writings, which her famous merit

In spite of Time out of the dust doth rear,
Do make her idol through the world appear.

VI

Such as the Berecynthian goddess bright,
In her swift chariot with high turrets crowned,
Proud that so many gods she brought to light;
Such was this city in her good days found:
This city, more than that great Phrygian mother
Renowned for fruit of famous progeny,
Whose greatness by the greatness of none other,
But by herself, her equal match could see.
Rome only might to Rome comparéd be,
And only Rome could make great Rome to tremble:
So did the gods by heavenly doom decree,
That other earthly power should not resemble
   Her that did match the whole earth's puissance,
   And did her courage to the heavens advance.

VII

Ye sacred ruins, and ye tragic sights,
Which only do the name of Rome retain,
Old monuments, which of so famous sprites
The honour yet in ashes do maintain:
Triumphant arcs, spires, neighbours to the sky,
That you to see doth th' heaven itself appal,
Alas! by little ye to nothing fly,
The people's fable, and the spoil of all:
And though your frames do for a time make war
'Gainst Time, yet Time in time shall ruinate
Your works and names, and your last relics mar.
My sad desires, rest therefore moderate:
   For if that Time make end of things so sure,
   It als will end the pain which I endure.

VIII

Through arms and vassals Rome the world subdued,
That one would ween that one sole city's strength
Both land and sea in roundness had surviewed,
To be the measure of her breadth and length:
This people's virtue yet so fruitful was
Of virtuous nephews, that posterity,
Striving in power their grandfathers to pass,

The lowest earth joined to the heaven high;
To th' end that, having all parts in their power,
Nought from the Roman Empire might be quight;
And that though Time doth commonwealths devour,
Yet no time should so low embase their height,
  That her head, earthed in her foundations deep,
  Should not her name and endless honour keep.

IX

Ye cruel stars, and eke ye gods unkind,
Heaven envious, and bitter stepdame Nature!
Be it by fortune, or by course of kind,
That ye do weld th' affairs of earthly creature;
Why have your hands long sithence travailéd
To frame this world that doth endure so long?
Or why were not these Roman palaces
Made of some matter no less firm and strong?
I say not, as the common voice doth say,
That all things which beneath the moon have being
Are temporal, and subject to decay:
But I say rather, though not all agreeing
  With some that ween the contrary in thought,
  That all this whole shall one day come to nought.

X

As that brave son of Æson, which by charms
Achieved the Golden Fleece in Colchid land,
Out of the earth engend'red men of arms
Of dragon's teeth, sown in the sacred sand;
So this brave town, that in her youthly days
An hydra was of warriors glorious,
Did fill with her renownéd nurslings' praise
The fiery sun's both one and other house:
But they at last, there being then not living
An Hercules so rank seed to repress,
Amongst themselves with cruel fury striving,
Mowed down themselves with slaughter merciless;
  Renewing in themselves that rage unkind,
  Which whilom did those earthborn brethren blind.

XI

Mars, shaming to have given so great head
To his offspring, that mortal puissance,

Puffed up with pride of Roman hardihead,
Seemed above heaven's power itself to advance;
Cooling again his former kindled heat,
With which he had those Roman spirits filled,
Did blow new fire, and with enflaméd breath
Into the Gothic cold hot rage instilled.
Then gan that nation, th' earth's new giant brood,
To dart abroad the thunderbolts of war,
And beating down these walls with furious mood
Into her mother's bosom, all did mar;
  To th' end that none, all were it Jove his sire,
  Should boast himself of the Romane Empire.

XII

Like as whilom the children of the earth
Heaped hills on hills to scale the starry sky,
And fight against the gods of heavenly birth,
Whiles Jove at them his thunderbolts let fly,
All suddenly with lightning overthrown,
The furious squadrons down to ground did fall,
That th' earth under her children's weight did groan,
And th' heavens in glory triumphed over all:
So did that haughty front, which heapéd was
On these seven Roman hills, itself uprear
Over the world, and lift her lofty face
Against the heaven, that gan her force to fear.
  But now these scornéd fields bemoan her fall,
  And gods secure fear not her force at all.

XIII

Nor the swift fury of the flames aspiring,
Nor the deep wounds of victor's raging blade,
Nor ruthless spoil of soldiers blood-desiring,
The which so oft thee (Rome) their conquest made;
Ne stroke on stroke of Fortune variable,
Ne rust of age hating continuance,
Nor wrath of gods, nor spite of men unstable,
Nor thou opposed against thine own puissance;
Nor th' horrible uproar of winds high blowing,
Nor swelling streams of that god snaky-paced,
Which hath so often with his overflowing
Thee drenchéd, have thy pride so much abased;

But that this nothing, which they have thee left,
Makes the world wonder what they from thee reft.

XIV

As men in summer fearless pass the ford
Which is in winter lord of all the plain,
And with his tumbling streams doth bear aboard
The ploughman's hope and shepherd's labour vain:
And as the coward beasts use to despise
The noble lion after his life's end,
Whetting their teeth, and with vain foolhardise
Daring the foe that cannot him defend:
And as at Troy most dastards of the Greeks
Did brave about the corpse of Hector cold;
So those, which whilom wont with pallid cheeks
The Roman triumphs' glory to behold,
　Now on these ashy tombs shew boldness vain,
　And, conquered, dare the conqueror disdain.

XV

Ye pallid spirits, and ye ashy ghosts,
Which, joying in the brightness of your day,
Brought forth those signs of your presumptuous boasts
Which now their dusty relics do bewray;
Tell me, ye spirits (sith the darksome river
Of Styx, not passable to souls returning,
Enclosing you in thrice three wards for ever,
Do not restrain your images still mourning),
Tell me then (for perhaps some one of you
Yet here above him secretly doth hide),
Do ye not feel your torments to accrue,
When ye sometimes behold the ruined pride
　Of these old Roman works, built with your hands,
　Now to become nought else but heapéd sands?

XVI

Like as ye see the wrathful sea from far
In a great mountain heapt with hideous noise,
Eftsoons of thousand billows should'red near,
Against a rock to break with dreadful poise:
Like as ye see fell Boreas with sharp blast
Tossing huge tempests through the troubled sky,
Eftsoons having his wide wings spent in waste,

To stop his weary cáreer suddenly:
And as ye see huge flames spread diversly,
Gathered in one up to the heavens to spire,
Eftsoons consumed to fall down feebily,
So whilom did this monarchy aspire,
 As waves, as wind, as fire, spread over all,
 Till it by fatal doom adown did fall.

XVII

So long as Jove's great bird did make his flight,
Bearing the fire with which heaven doth us fray,
Heaven had not fear of that presumptuous might
With which the giants did the gods assay;
But all so soon as scorching sun had brent
His wings which wont the earth to overspread,
The earth out of her massy womb forth sent
That antique horror, which made heaven adread.
Then was the German raven in disguise
That Roman eagle seen to cleave asunder,
And towards heaven freshly to arise
Out of these mountains, now consumed to powder;
 In which the fowl that serves to bear the lightning
 Is now no more seen flying, nor alighting.

XVIII

These heaps of stones, these old walls, which ye see,
Were first enclosures but of savage soil;
And these brave palaces, which mast'red be
Of Time, were shepherds' cottages somewhile.
Then took the shepherds kingly ornaments,
And the stout hind armed his right hand with steel:
Eftsoons their rule of yearly presidents
Grew great, and six months greater a great deal;
Which, made perpetual, rose to so great might,
That thence th' imperial eagle rooting took,
Till th' heaven itself, opposing 'gainst her might,
Her power to Peter's súccessor betook;
 Who, shepherd-like, (as fates the same foreseeing)
 Doth shew that all things turn to their first being.

XIX

All that is perfect, which th' heaven beautifies;
All that's imperfect, born below the moon;

All that doth feed our spirits and our eyes,
And all that doth consume our pleasures soon;
All the mishap the which our days outwears,
All the good hap of th' oldest times afore,
Rome, in the time of her great ancestors,
Like a Pandora, lockéd long in store.
But Destiny this huge chaos turmoiling,
In which all good and evil was enclosed,
Their heavenly virtues from these woes assoiling,
Carried to heaven, from sinful bondage losed;
  But their great sins, the causers of their pain,
  Under these antique ruins yet remain.

XX

No otherwise than rainy cloud, first fed
With earthly vapours gathered in the air,
Eftsoons in compass archt, to steep his head,
Doth plunge himself in Tethys' bosom fair;
And, mounting up again from whence he came,
With his great belly spreads the dimméd world,
Till at the last, dissolving his moist frame,
In rain, or snow, or hail, he forth is hurled;
This city, which was first but shepherds' shade,
Uprising by degrees, grew to such height,
That queen of land and sea herself she made.
At last, not able to bear so great weight,
  Her power, disperst through all the world, did vade;
  To shew that all in th' end to nought shall fade.

XXI

The same, which Pyrrhus and the puissance
Of Afric could not tame, that same brave city,
Which, with stout courage armed against mischance,
Sustained the shock of common enmity;
Long as her ship, tossed with so many freaks,
Had all the world in arms against her bent,
Was never seen, that any fortune's wreaks
Could break her course begun with brave intent.
But, when the object of her virtue failed,
Her power itself against itself did arm;
As he that having long in tempest sailed,
Fain would arrive, but cannot for the storm,
  If too great wind against the port him drive,
  Doth in the port itself his vessel rive.

XXII

When that brave honour of the Latin name,
Which meared her rule with Africa, and Byze,
With Thames' inhabitants of noble fame,
And they which see the dawning day arise;
Her nurslings did with mutinous uproar
Hearten against herself her conquered spoil,
Which she had won from all the world afore,
Of all the world was spoiled within a while:
So, when the compassed course of the universe
In six and thirty thousand years is run,
The bands of th' elements shall back reverse
To their first discord, and be quite undone;
   The seeds, of which all things at first were bred,
   Shall in great Chaos' womb again be hid.

XXIII

O wary wisdom of the man, that would
That Carthage towers from spoil should be forborne,
To th' end that his victorious people should
With cank'ring leisure not be overworn:
He well foresaw how that the Roman courage,
Impatient of pleasure's faint desires,
Through idleness would turn to civil rage,
And be herself the matter of her fires;
For, in a people given all to ease,
Ambition is engend'red easily;
As, in a vicious body, gross disease
Soon grows through humours' superfluity,
   That came to pass, when swoll'n with plenty's pride,
   Nor prince, nor peer, nor kin they would abide,

XXIV

If the blind fury, which wars breedeth oft,
Wonts not t' enrage the hearts of equal beasts,
Whether they fare on foot, or fly aloft,
Or arméd be with claws, or scaly crests,
Which fell Erinnys, with hot burning tongs,
Did gripe your hearts with noisome rage imbued,
That each to other working cruel wrongs,
Your blades in your own bowels you imbrued?
Was this (ye Romans) your hard destiny,
Or some old sin, whose unappeaséd guilt

Poured vengeance forth on you eternally?
Or brother's blood, the which at first was spilt
  Upon your walls, that God might not endure
  Upon the same to set foundation sure?

XXV

O that I had the Thracian poet's harp,
For to awake out of th' infernal shade
Those antique Cæsars, sleeping long in dark,
The which this ancient city whilom made!
Or that I had Amphion's instrument,
To quicken, with his vital notes' accord,
The stony joints of these old walls now rent,
By which th' Ausonian light might be restored!
Or that at least I could, with pencil fine,
Fashion the portraits of these palaces,
By pattern of great Virgil's spirit divine!
I would essay with that which in me is,
  To build, with level of my lofty style,
  That which no hands can evermore compile.

XXVI

Who list the Roman greatness forth to figure,
Him needeth not to seek for usage right
Of line, or lead, or rule, or square, to measure
Her length, her breadth, her deepness, or her height;
But him behoves to view in compass round
All that the Ocean grasps in his long arms;
Be it where the yearly star doth scorch the ground,
Or where cold Boreas blows his bitter storms.
Rome was th' whole world, and all the world was Rome,
And if things named their names do equalize,
When land and sea ye name, then name ye Rome;
And, naming Rome, ye land and sea comprise:
  For th' ancient plot of Rome, displayéd plain,
  The map of all the wide world doth contain.

XXVII

Thou that at Rome astonisht dost behold
The antique pride which menacéd the sky,
These haughty heaps, these palaces of old,
These walls, these arcs, these baths, these temples high;

Judge, by these ample ruins' view, the rest
The which injurious Time hath quite outworn,
Since of all workmen held in reck'ning best;
Yet these old fragments are for patterns born:
Then also mark how Rome, from day to day,
Repairing her decayéd fashíon,
Renews herself with buildings rich and gay;
That one would judge, that the Romane dæmon
  Doth yet himself with fatal hand enforce,
  Again on foot to rear her pouldred corse.

XXVIII

He that hath seen a great oak dry and dead,
Yet clad with relics of some trophies old,
Lifting to heaven her aged hoary head,
Whose foot in ground hath left but feeble hold,
But half disbowelled lies above the ground,
Shewing her wreathéd roots, and naked arms,
And on her trunk, all rotten and unsound,
Only supports herself for meat of worms;
And, though she owe her fall to the first wind,
Yet of the devout people is adored,
And many young plants spring out of her rind:
Who such an oak hath seen, let him record
  That such this city's honour was of yore,
  And 'mongst all cities flourishéd much more.

XXIX

All that which Egypt whilom did devise,
All that which Greece their temples to embrave
After th' Ionic, Attic, Doric guise;
Or Corinth skilled in curious works to grave;
All that Lysippus' practic art could form,
Apelles' wit, or Phidias his skill,
Was wont this ancient city to adorn,
And the heaven itself with her wide wonders fill;
All that which Athens ever brought forth wise,
All that which Afric ever brought forth strange,
All that which Asia ever had of price,
Was here to see. O marvellous great change!
  Rome, living, was the world's sole ornament,
  And, dead, is now the world's sole monument.

XXX

Like as the seeded field green grass first shows,
Then from green grass into a stalk doth spring,
And from a stalk into an ear forth-grows,
Which ear the fruitful grain doth shortly bring;
And as in season due the husband mows
The waving locks of those fair yellow ears,
Which, bound in sheaves, and laid in comely rows,
Upon the naked fields in stacks he rears:
So grew the Roman Empire by degree,
Till that barbarian hands it quite did spill,
And left of it but these old marks to see,
Of which all passers-by do somewhat pill:
  As they which glean, the relics use to gather,
  Which th' husbandman behind him chanced to scatter.

XXXI

That same is now nought but a champaign wide,
Where all this world's pride once was situate.
No blame to thee, whosoever dost abide
By Nile, or Gange, or Tigre, or Euphrate;
Ne Afric thereof guilty is, nor Spain,
Nor the bold people by the Thamis' brinks,
Nor the brave warlike brood of Alemain,
Nor the born soldier which Rhine running drinks:
Thou only cause, O civil fury, art,
Which, sowing in th' Emathian fields thy spite,
Didst arm thy hand against thy proper heart:
To th' end that when thou wast in greatest height,
  To greatness grown, through long prosperity,
  Thou then adown might'st fall more horribly.

XXXII

Hope ye, my verses, that posterity
Of age ensuing shall you ever read?
Hope ye, that ever immortality
So mean harp's work may challenge for her meed?
If under heaven any endurance were,
These monuments, which not in paper writ,
But in porphýre and marble do appear,
Might well have hoped to have obtainéd it.
Nath'less my lute, whom Phœbus deigned to give,

Cease not to sound these old antiquities;
For if that Time do let thy glory live,
Well may'st thou boast, however base thou be,
   That thou art first, which of thy nation sung
   Th' old honour of the people gownéd long.

L'Envoy

Bellay, first garland of free poesy
That France brought forth, though fruitful of brave wits,
Well worthy thou of immortality,
That long hast travailed, by thy learned writs,
Old Rome out of her ashes to revive,
And give a second life to dead decays!
Needs must he all eternity survive,
That can to other give eternal days:
Thy days therefore are endless, and thy praise
Excelling all that ever went before.
And, after thee, gins Bartas high to raise
His heavenly Muse, th' Almighty to adore.
   Live, happy spirits, th' honour of your name,
   And fill the world with never-dying fame!

MUIOPOTMOS

OR THE

FATE OF THE BUTTERFLY

BY ED. SP.

DEDICATED TO THE MOST FAIR AND VIRTUOUS LADY

THE LADY CAREY

MOST brave and bountiful Lady, for so excellent favours as I have received at your sweet hands, to offer these few leaves, as in recompense, should be as to offer flowers to the gods for their divine benefits. Therefore I have determined to give myself wholly to you, as quite abandoned from myself, and absolutely vowed to your services: which in all right is ever held for full recompense of debt or damage, to have the person yielded. My person I wot well how little worth it is. But the faithful mind and humble zeal which I bear unto your Ladyship may perhaps be more of price, as may please you to account and use the poor service thereof; which taketh glory to advance your excellent parts and noble virtues, and to spend itself in honouring you: not so much for your great bounty to myself, which yet may not be unminded; nor for name or kindred's sake by you vouchsafed, being also regardable; as for that honourable name, which ye have by your brave deserts purchased to yourself, and spread in the mouths of all men: with which I have also presumed to grace my verses, and under your name to commend to the world this small poem, the which beseeching your Ladyship to take in worth, and of all things therein according to your wonted graciousness to make a mild construction, I humbly pray for your happiness.

Your Ladyship's ever humbly,
E. S.

I SING of deadly dolorous debate,
Stirred up through wrathful Nemesis' despight,
Betwixt two mighty ones of great estate,
Drawn into arms, and proof of mortal fight,
Through proud ambition and heart-swelling hate,
Whilst neither could the other's greater might
And sdeignful scorn endure; that from small jar
Their wraths at length broke into open war.

The root whereof and tragical effect,
Vouchsafe, O thou the mournful'st Muse of nine!
That wont'st the tragic stage for to direct,
In funeral complaints and wailful tine,
Reveal to me, and all the means detect,
Through which sad Clarion did at last decline
To lowest wretchedness. And is there then
Such rancour in the hearts of mighty men?

Of all the race of silver-wingéd flies
Which do possess the empire of the air,
Betwixt the centred earth and azure skies,
Was none more favourable, nor more fair,
Whilst heaven did favour his felicities,
Than Clarion, the eldest son and heir
Of Muscarol; and in his father's sight
Of all alive did seem the fairest wight.

With fruitful hope his aged breast he fed
Of future good, which his young toward years,
Full of brave courage and bold hardihead,
Above th' ensample of his equal peers,
Did largely promise, and to him fore-red,
(Whilst oft his heart did melt in tender tears)
That he in time would sure prove such an one,
As should be worthy of his father's throne.

The fresh young fly, in whom the kindly fire
Of lustful youth began to kindle fast,
Did much disdain to subject his desire
To loathsome sloth, or hours in ease to wast,
But joy'd to range abroad in fresh attire,
Through the wide compass of the airy coast;
And, with unwearied wings, each part t' inquire
Of the wide rule of his renownéd sire.

For he so swift and nimble was of flight,
That from this lower tract he dared to stie
Up to the clouds, and thence with pinions light
To mount aloft unto the crystal sky,
To view the workmanship of heaven's height:
Whence, down descending, he along would fly
Upon the streaming rivers, sport to find;
And oft would dare to tempt the troublous wind.

So on a summer's day, when season mild
With gentle calm the world had quieted,
And high in heaven Hyperion's fiery child
Ascending did his beams abroad dispread,
Whiles all the heavens on lower creatures smiled,
Young Clarion, with vauntful lustihead,
After his guise did cast abroad to fare:
And thereto gan his furnitures prepare.

His breastplate first, that was of substance pure,
Before his noble heart he firmly bound,
That mought his life from iron death assure,
And ward his gentle corpse from cruel wound;
For it by art was framéd to endure
The bite of baleful steel and bitter stound,
No less than that which Vulcan made to shield
Achilles' life from fate of Troyan field.

And then about his shoulders broad he threw
An hairy hide of some wild beast, whom he
In savage forest by adventure slew,
And reft the spoil his ornament to be;
Which, spreading all his back, with dreadful view
Made all that him so horrible did see
Think him Alcides with the lion's skin,
When the Nemæan conquest he did win.

Upon his head his glistering burganet,
The which was wrought by wonderous device
And curiously engraven, he did set:
The metal was of rare and passing price;
Not Bilbo steel, nor brass from Corinth fet,
Nor costly orichalc from strange Phœnice,
But such as could both Phœbus' arrows ward,
And th' hailing darts of heaven beating hard.

Therein two deadly weapons fixt he bore,
Strongly outlancéd towards either side,
Like two sharp spears his enemies to gore:
Like as a warlike brigandine, applied
To fight, lays forth her threatful pikes afore,
The engines which in them sad death do hide:
So did this fly outstretch his fearful horns,
Yet so as him their terror more adorns.

Lastly his shiny wings as silver bright,
Painted with thousand colours, passing far
All painters' skill, he did about him dight:
Not half so many sundry colours are
In Iris' bow, ne heaven doth shine so bright,
Distinguishéd with many a twinkling star;
Nor Juno's bird in her eye-spotted train
So many goodly colours doth contain.

Ne (may it be withouten peril spoken?)
The Archer God, the son of Cytheree,
That joys on wretched lovers to be wroken,
And heapéd spoils of bleeding hearts to see,
Bears in his wings so many a changeful token.
Ah, my liege lord! forgive it unto me,
If aught against thine honour I have told;
Yet sure those wings were fairer manifold.

Full many a lady fair, in court full oft
Beholding them, him secretly envíde,
And wished that two such fans, so silken soft
And golden fair, her love would her provide;
Or that, when them the gorgeous fly had doft,
Some one, that would with grace be gratified,
From him would steal them privily away,
And bring to her so precíous a prey.

Report is, that dame Venus, on a day
In spring, when flowers do clothe the fruitful ground,
Walking abroad with all her nymphs to play,
Bad her fair damsels, flocking her around,
To gather flowers her forehead to array:
Amongst the rest a gentle nymph was found,
Hight Astery, excelling all the crew
In courteous usage and unstainéd hue;

Who being nimbler jointed than the rest,
And more industrious, gatheréd more store
Of the field's honour than the others' best;
Which they in secret hearts envýing sore,
Told Venus, when her as the worthiest
She praised, that Cupid (as they heard before)
Did lend her secret aid, in gathering
Into her lap the children of the spring.

Whereof the goddess gathering jealous fear,
Not yet unmindful how not long ago
Her son to Psyche secret love did bear,
And long it close concealed, till mickle woe
Thereof arose, and many a rueful tear,
Reason with sudden rage did overgo;
And, giving hasty credit to th' accuser,
Was led away of them that did abuse her.

Eftsoons that damsel, by her heavenly might,
She turned into a wingéd butterfly,
In the wide air to make her wand'ring flight;
And all those flowers, with which so plenteously
Her lap she filléd had, that bred her spight,
She placéd in her wings, for memory
Of her pretended crime, though crime none were:
Since which that fly them in her wings doth bear.

Thus the fresh Clarion, being ready dight,
Unto his journey did himself address,
And with good speed began to take his flight:
Over the fields, in his frank lustiness,
And all the champaign o'er he soaréd light;
And all the country wide he did possess,
Feeding upon their pleasures bounteously,
That none gainsaid, nor none did him envý.

The woods, the rivers, and the meadows green,
With his air-cutting wings he measured wide,
Ne did he leave the mountains bare unseen,
Nor the rank grassy fens' delights untried.
But none of these, however sweet they bene,
Might please his fancy, nor him cause t' abide:
His choiceful sense with every change doth flit:
No common things may please a wavering wit.

To the gay gardens his unstaid desire
Him wholly carried, to refresh his sprites:
There lavish Nature, in her best attire,
Pours forth sweet odours and alluring sights;
And Art, with her contending, doth aspire
T' excel the natural with made delights;
And all, that fair or pleasant may be found,
In riotous excess doth there abound.

There he arriving round about doth fly,
From bed to bed, from one to other border,
And takes survey, with curious busy eye,
Of every flower and herb there set in order:
Now this, now that, he tasteth tenderly,
Yet none of them he rudely doth disorder,
Ne with his feet their silken leaves deface,
But pastures on the pleasures of each place.

And evermore, with most variety
And change of sweetness (for all change is sweet),
He casts his glutton sense to satisfy,
Now sucking of the sap of herb most meet,
Or of the dew which yet on them does lie,
Now in the same bathing his tender feet;
And then he percheth on some branch thereby,
To weather him, and his moist wings to dry.

And then again he turneth to his play,
To spoil the pleasures of that paradise;
The wholesome sage, and lavender still gray,
Rank-smelling rue, and cummin good for eyes,
The roses reigning in the pride of May,
Sharp hyssop, good for green wounds' remedies,
Fair marigolds, and bees-alluring thyme,
Sweet marjoram, and daisies decking prime:

Cool violets, and orpine growing still,
Embathéd balm, and cheerful galingale,
Fresh costmary and breathful camomill,
Dull poppy, and drink-quick'ning setuale,
Vein-healing vervain, and head-purging dill,
Sound savory, and basil hearty-hale,
Fat coleworts, and comforting perseline,
Cold lettuce, and refreshing rosmarine.

And whatso else of virtue good or ill
Grew in this garden, fetch from far away,
Of every one he takes, and tastes at will,
And on their pleasures greedily doth prey.
Then, when he hath both played and fed his fill,
In the warm sun he doth himself embay,
And there him rests in riotous suffisance
Of all his gladfulness, and kingly joyance.

MUIOPOTMOS

What more felicity can fall to creature
Then to enjoy delight with liberty,
And to be lord of all the works of Nature,
To reign in th' air from th' earth to highest sky,
To feed on flowers and weeds of glorious feature,
To take whatever thing doth please the eye?
Who rests not pleaséd with such happiness,
Well worthy he to taste of wretchedness.

But what on earth can long abide in state,
Or who can him assure of happy day,
Sith morning fair may bring foul evening late,
And least mishap the most bliss alter may?
For thousand perils lie in close await
About us daily, to work our decay;
That none, except a god, or god him guide,
May them avoid, or remedy provide.

And whatso heavens in their secret doom
Ordainéd have, how can frail fleshly wight
Forecast, but it must needs to issue come?
The sea, the air, the fire, the day, the night,
And th' armies of their creatures all and some
Do serve to them, and with importune might
War against us, the vassals of their will.
Who then can save what they dispose to spill?

Not thou, O Clarion! though fairest thou
Of all thy kind, unhappy happy fly,
Whose cruel fate is woven even now
Of Jove's own hand, to work thy misery.
Ne may thee help the many hearty vow,
Which thy old sire with sacred piety
Hath pouréd forth for thee, and th' altars sprent:
Nought may thee save from heaven's avengëment.

It fortunéd (as heavens had behight)
That in this garden, where young Clarion
Was wont to solace him, a wicked wight,
The foe of fair things, th' author of confusion,
The shame of Nature, the bondslave of spite,
Had lately built his hateful mansion;
And, lurking closely, in await now lay,
How he might any in his trap betray.

But when he spied the joyous butterfly
In this fair plot dispacing to and fro,
Fearless of foes and hidden jeopardy,
Lord! how he gan for to bestir him tho,
And to his wicked work each part apply.
His heart did yearn against his hated foe,
And bowels so with rankling poison swelled,
That scarce the skin the strong contagion held.

The cause why he this fly so malicéd
Was (as in stories it is written found)
For that his mother, which him bore and bred,
The most fine-fing'red workwoman on ground,
Arachne, by his means was vanquishéd
Of Pallas, and in her own skill confound,
When she with her for excellence contended,
That wrought her shame, and sorrow never ended.

For the Tritonian goddess, having heard
Her blazéd fame which all the world had filled,
Came down to prove the truth, and due reward
For her praiseworthy workmanship to yield;
But the presumptuous damsel rashly dared
The goddess self to challenge to the field,
And to compare with her in curious skill
Of works with loom, with needle, and with quill.

Minerva did the challenge not refuse,
But deigned with her the paragon to make:
So to their work they sit, and each doth choose
What story she will for her tapet take.
Arachne figured how Jove did abuse
Europa like a bull, and on his back
Her through the sea did bear; so lively seen,
That it true sea, and true bull, ye would ween.

She seemed still back unto the land to look,
And her playfellows' aid to call, and fear
The dashing of the waves, that up she took
Her dainty feet, and garments gathered near;
But (Lord!) how she in every member shook,
Whenas the land she saw no more appear,
But a wild wilderness of waters deep:
Then gan she greatly to lament and weep.

Before the bull she pictured wingéd Love,
With his young brother Sport, light fluttering
Upon the waves, as each had been a dove;
The one his bow and shafts, the other spring
A burning tead about his head did move,
As in their sire's new love both triumphing:
And many nymphs about them flocking round,
And many tritons which their horns did sound.

And round about her work she did empale
With a fair border wrought of sundry flowers,
Enwoven with an ivy-winding trail:
A goodly work, full fit for kingly bowers;
Such as Dame Pallas, such as Envy pale,
That all good things with venomous tooth devours,
Could not accuse.   Then gan the goddess bright
Herself likewise unto her work to dight.

She made the story of the old debate
Which she with Neptune did for Athens try:
Twelve gods do sit around in royal state,
And Jove in midst with awful majesty,
To judge the strife between them stirréd late:
Each of the gods, by his like visnomy
Eath to be known; but Jove above them all,
By his great looks and power imperial.

Before them stands the god of seas in place,
Claiming that sea-coast city as his right.
And strikes the rocks with his three-forkéd mace;
Whenceforth issues a warlike steed in sight,
The sign by which he challengeth the place;
That all the gods, which saw his wondrous might,
Did surely deem the victory his due:
But seldom seen, forejudgement proveth true.

Then to herself she gives her ægid shield,
And steeléd spear, and morion on her head,
Such as she oft is seen in warlike field:
Then sets she forth, how with her weapon dread
She smote the ground, the which straight forth did yield
A fruitful olive tree, with berries spread,
That all the gods admired: then all the story
She compassed with a wreath of olives hoary.

Amongst these leaves she made a butterfly,
With excellent device and wondrous sleight,
Flutt'ring among the olives wantonly,
That seemed to live, so like it was in sight:
The velvet nap which on his wings doth lie,
The silken down with which his back is dight,
His broad outstretchéd horns, his hairy thighs,
His glorious colours, and his glistering eyes.

Which when Arachne saw, as overlaid
And masteréd with workmanship so rare,
She stood astonied long, ne aught gainsaid;
And with fast-fixéd eyes on her did stare,
And by her silence, sign of one dismayed,
The victory did yield her as her share:
Yet did she inly fret and felly burn,
And all her blood to poisonous rancour turn:

That shortly from the shape of womanhead,
Such as she was when Pallas she attempted,
She grew to hideous shape of drearihead,
Pinéd with grief of folly late repented:
Eftsoons her white straight legs were alteréd
To crooked crawling shanks, of marrow emptied;
And her fair face to foul and loathsome hue,
And her fine corpse to a bag of venom grew.

This curséd creature, mindful of that old
Infested grudge, the which his mother felt,
So soon as Clarion he did behold,
His heart with vengeful malice inly swelt;
And weaving straight a net with many a fold
About the cave in which he lurking dwelt,
With fine small cords about it stretchéd wide,
So finely spun that scarce they could be spied.

Not any damsel, which her vaunteth most
In skilful knitting of soft silken twine,
Nor any weaver, which his work doth boast
In diaper, in damask, or in line,
Nor any skilled in workmanship embost,
Nor any skilled in loops of fing'ring fine,
Might in their divers cunning ever dare
With this so curious network to compare.

Ne do I think, that that same subtil gin,
The which the Lemnian god framed craftily,
Mars sleeping with his wife to compass in,
That all the gods with common mockery
Might laugh at them, and scorn their shameful sin,
Was like to this. This same he did apply
For to entrap the careless Clarion,
That ranged eachwhere without suspicion.

Suspicion of friend, nor fear of foe
That hazarded his health, had he at all,
But walked at will, and wand'red to and fro,
In the pride of his freedom principal:
Little wist he his fatal future woe,
But was secure: the liker he to fall.
He likest is to fall into mischance,
That is regardless of his governance.

Yet still Aragnol (so his foe was hight)
Lay lurking covertly him to surprise;
And all his gins, that him entangle might,
Dress'd in good order as he could devise.
At length, the foolish fly, without foresight,
As he that did all danger quite despise,
Toward those parts came flying carelessly,
Where hidden was his hateful enemy.

Who, seeing him, with secret joy therefore
Did tickle inwardly in every vein;
And his false heart, fraught with all treason's store,
Was filled with hope his purpose to obtain:
Himself he close upgathered more and more
Into his den, that his deceitful train
By his there being might not be bewrayed,
Ne any noise, ne any motion made.

Like as a wily fox, that having spied
Where on a sunny bank the lambs do play,
Full closely creeping by the hinder side,
Lies in ambushment of his hopéd prey,
Ne stirreth limb; till, seeing ready tide,
He rusheth forth, and snatcheth quite away
One of the little younglings unawares:
So to his work Aragnol him prepares.

Who now shall give unto my heavy eyes
A well of tears, that all may overflow?
Or where shall I find lamentable cries,
And mournful tunes enough my grief to show?
Help, O thou tragic Muse! me to devise
Notes sad enough t' express this bitter throe:
For lo! the dreary stound is now arrived,
That of all happiness hath us deprived.

The luckless Clarion, whether cruel Fate
Or wicked Fortune faultless him misled,
Or some ungracious blast, out of the gate
Of Æole's reign, perforce him drove on head,
Was (O sad hap, and hour unfortunate!)
With violent swift flight forth carriéd
Into the curséd cobweb, which his foe
Had framéd for his final overthrow.

There the fond fly, entangled, struggled long,
Himself to free thereout; but all in vain:
For striving more, the more in laces strong
Himself he tied, and wrapt his wingës twain
In limy snares the subtil loops among;
That in the end he breathless did remain,
And, all his youngthly forces idly spent,
Him to the mercy of th' avenger lent.

Which when the grisly tyrant did espy,
Like a grim lion rushing with fierce might
Out of his den, he seizéd greedily
On the resistless prey; and with fell spite,
Under the left wing struck his weapon sly
Into his heart, that his deep-groaning sprite
In bloody streams forth fled into the air,
His body left the spectacle of care.

VISIONS OF THE WORLD'S VANITY

I

One day, whiles that my daily cares did sleep,
My spirit, shaking off her earthly prison,
Began to enter into meditation deep
Of things exceeding reach of common reason;
Such as this age, in which all good is geason,
And all that humble is, and mean debased,
Hath brought forth in her last declining season,
Grief of good minds, to see goodness disgraced!
On which whenas my thought was throughly placed
Unto my eyes strange shews presented were,
Picturing that which I in mind embraced,
That yet those sights impassion me full near.
  Such as they were (fair lady!) take in worth,
  That when time serves may bring things better forth.

II

In summer's day, when Phœbus fairly shone,
I saw a bull as white as driven snow,
With gilden horns embowéd like the moon,
In a fresh flowering meadow lying low:
Up to his ears the verdant grass did grow,
And the gay flowers did offer to be eaten;
But he with fatness so did overflow,
That he all wallowed in the weeds down beaten.
Ne cared with them his dainty lips to sweeten;
Till that a brize, a scornéd little creature,
Through his fair hide his angry sting did threaten,
And vext so sore, that all his goodly feature
  And all his plenteous pasture nought him pleased:
  So by the small the great is oft diseased.

III

Beside the fruitful shore of muddy Nile,
Upon a sunny bank outstretchéd lay,
In monstrous length, a mighty crocodile,
That, crammed with guiltless blood and greedy prey

Of wretched people travelling that way,
Thought all things less than his disdainful pride.
I saw a little bird called Tedula,
The least of thousands which on earth abide,
That forced this hideous beast to open wide
The grisly gates of his devouring hell,
And let him feed, as Nature did provide,
Upon his jaws, that with black venom swell.
    Why then should greatest things the least disdain,
    Sith that so small so mighty can constrain?

IV

The kingly bird, that bears Jove's thunderclap,
One day did scorn the simple scarabee,
Proud of his highest service, and good hap,
That made all other fowls his thralls to be:
The silly fly, that no redress did see,
Spied where the eagle built his tow'ring nest,
And, kindling fire within the hollow tree,
Burnt up his young ones, and himself distrest;
Ne suff'red him in any place to rest,
But drove in Jove's own lap his eggs to lay;
Where gathering also filth him to infest,
Forced with the filth his eggs to fling away:
    For which whenas the fowl was wroth, said Jove,
    "Lo! how the least the greatest may reprove."

V

Toward the sea turning my troubled eye,
I saw the fish (if fish I may it clepe)
That makes the sea before his face to fly,
And with his flaggy fins doth seem to sweep
The foamy waves out of the dreadful deep,
The huge Leviathan, dame Nature's wonder,
Making his sport, that many makes to weep:
A sword-fish small him from the rest did sunder,
That, in his throat him pricking softly under,
His wide abyss him forcéd forth to spew,
That all the sea did roar like heaven's thunder,
And all the waves were stained with filthy hue.
    Hereby I learnéd have not to despise
    Whatever thing seems small in common eyes.

VI

An hideous dragon, dreadful to behold,
Whose back was armed against the dint of spear
With shields of brass that shone like burnisht gold,
And forkéd sting that death in it did bear,
Strove with a spider his unequal peer;
And bad defiance to his enemy.
The subtil vermin, creeping closely near,
Did in his drink shed poison privily;
Which, through his entrails spreading diversly,
Made him to swell, that nigh his bowels brust,
And him enforced to yield the victory,
That did so much in his own greatness trust.
  O! how great vainness is it then to scorn
    The weak, that hath the strong so oft forlorn!

VII

High on a hill a goodly cedar grew,
Of wondrous length, and straight proportion,
That far abroad her dainty odours threw;
'Mongst all the daughters of proud Libanon,
Her match in beauty was not any one.
Shortly within her inmost pith there bred
A little wicked worm, perceived of none,
That on her sap and vital moisture fed:
Thenceforth her garland so much honouréd
Began to die, (O great ruth for the same!)
And her fair locks fell from her lofty head,
That shortly bald and baréd she became.
  I, which this sight beheld, was much dismayed
    To see so goodly thing so soon decayed.

VIII

Soon after this I saw an elephant,
Adorned with bells and bosses gorgeously,
That on his back did bear (as battailant)
A gilden tower, which shone exceedingly;
That he himself through foolish vanity,
Both for his rich attire and goodly form,
Was pufféd up with passing surquedry,
And shortly gan all other beasts to scorn.
Till that a little ant, a silly worm,

Into his nostrils creeping, so him pained,
That casting down his towers, he did deform
Both borrowed pride, and native beauty stained.
  Let therefore nought that great is therein glory,
  Sith so small thing his happiness may vary.

IX

Looking far forth into the ocean wide,
A goodly ship with banners bravely dight,
And flag in her top-gallant, I espied
Through the main sea making her merry flight:
Fair blew the wind into her bosom right;
And th' heavens lookéd lovely all the while,
That she did seem to dance, as in delight,
And at her own felicity did smile.
All suddenly there clove unto her keel
A little fish, that men called Remora,
Which stopt her course, and held her by the heel,
That wind nor tide could move her thence away.
  Strange thing, meseemeth, that so small a thing
  Should able be so great an one to wring.

X

A mighty lion, lord of all the wood,
Having his hunger throughly satisfied
With prey of beasts and spoil of living blood,
Safe in his dreadless den him thought to hide:
His sternness was his praise, his strength his pride,
And all his glory in his cruel claws.
I saw a wasp, that fiercely him defied,
And bad him battle even to his jaws:
Sore he him stung, that it the blood forth draws,
And his proud heart is filled with fretting ire:
In vain he threats his teeth, his tail, his paws,
And from his bloody eyes doth sparkle fire:
  That dead himself he wisheth for despight.
  So weakest may annoy the most of might!

XI

What time the Roman Empire bore the reign
Of all the world and flourished most in might,
The nations gan their sovereignty disdain,
And cast to quit them from their bondage quite:

So, when all shrouded were in silent night,
The Gauls were, by corrupting of a maid,
Possessed nigh of the Capitol through sleight,
Had not a goose the treachery bewrayed,
If then a goose great Rome from ruin stayed,
And Jove himself, the patron of the place,
Preserved from being to his foes betrayed;
Why do vain men mean things so much deface,
   And in their might repose their most assurance,
   Sith nought on earth can challenge long endurance?

XII

When these sad sights were overpast and gone,
My sprite was greatly movéd in her rest,
With inward ruth and dear affectíon,
To see so great things by so small distrest.
Thenceforth I gan in my engrievéd breast,
To scorn all difference of great and small,
Sith that the greatest often are opprest,
And unawares do into danger fall.
And ye, that read these ruins tragical,
Learn by their loss to love the low degree;
And, if that Fortune chance you up to call
To honour's seat, forget not what you be:
   For he, that of himself is most secure,
   Shall find his state most fickle and unsure.

THE VISIONS OF BELLAY

I

It was the time, when rest, soft sliding down
From heaven's height into men's heavy eyes,
In the forgetfulness of sleep doth drown
The careful thoughts of mortal miseries;
Then did a ghost before mine eyes appear,
On that great river's bank, that runs by Rome;
Which, calling me by name, bad me to rear
My looks to heaven whence all good gifts do come,
And crying loud, "Lo! now behold" (quoth he)
"What under this great temple placéd is:
Lo, all is nought but flying vanity!"
So I, that know this world's inconstancies,
    Sith only God surmounts all Time's decay,
    In God alone my confidence do stay.

II

On high hill's top I saw a stately frame,
An hundred cubits high by just assize,
With hundred pillars fronting fair the same,
All wrought with diamond after Doric wise:
Nor brick nor marble was the wall in view,
But shining crystal, which from top to base
Out of her womb a thousand rayons threw
On hundred steps of Afric gold's enchase:
Gold was the parget; and the ceiling bright
Did shine all scaly with great plates of gold;
The floor of jasp and emerald was dight.
O world's vainesse! Whiles thus I did behold,
    An earthquake shook the hill from lowest seat,
    And overthrew this frame with ruin great.

III

Then did a sharpéd spire of diamond bright,
Ten feet each way in square, appear to me,
Justly proportioned up unto his height,
So far as archer might his level see:

The top thereof a pot did seem to bear,
Made of the metal, which we most do honour;
And in this golden vessel couchéd were
The ashes of a mighty emperor:
Upon four corners of the base were pight,
To bear the frame, four great lions of gold:
A worthy tomb for such a worthy wight.
Alas, this world doth nought but grievance hold!
  I saw a tempest from the heaven descend,
    Which this brave monument with flash did rend.

IV

I saw raised up on ivory pillars tall,
Whose bases were of richest metal's wark,
The chapters alabaster, the friezes crystal,
The double front of a triumphal arc:
On each side portrayed was a Victory,
Clad like a nymph, that wings of silver wears,
And in triumphant chair was set on high,
The ancient glory of the Roman peers.
No work it seemed of earthly craftsman's wit,
But rather wrought by his own industry,
That thunder-darts for Jove his sire doth fit.
Let me no more see fair thing under sky,
  Sith that mine eyes have seen so fair a sight
  With sudden fall to dust consuméd quite.

V

Then was the fair Dodonian tree far seen,
Upon seven hills to spread his gladsome gleam
And conquerors bedeckéd with his green,
Along the banks of the Ausonian stream:
There many an ancient trophy was addrest,
And many a spoil, and many a goodly show,
Which that brave race's greatness did attest,
That whilom from the Troyan blood did flow.
Ravisht I was so rare a thing to view;
When lo! a barbarous troop of clownish fone
The honour of these noble boughs down threw,
Under the wedge I heard the trunk to groan;
  And, since, I saw the root in great disdain
  A twin of forkéd trees send forth again.

VI

I saw a wolf under a rocky cave
Nursing two whelps; I saw her little ones
In wanton dalliance the teat to crave,
While she her neck wreathed from them for the nones.
I saw her range abroad to seek her food,
And roaming through the field with greedy rage
T' imbrue her teeth and claws with lukewarm blood
Of the small herds, her thirst for to assuage.
I saw a thousand huntsmen, which descended
Down from the mountains bord'ring Lombardy,
That with an hundred spears her flank wide rended.
I saw her on the plain outstretchéd lie,
   Throwing out thousand throbs in her own soil:
   Soon on a tree uphanged I saw her spoil.

VII

I saw the bird that can the sun endure,
With feeble wings essay to mount on hight;
By more and more she gan her wings t' assure,
Following th' ensample of her mother's sight:
I saw her rise, and with a larger flight
To pierce the clouds, and with wide pinions
To measure the most haughty mountain's height,
Until she raught the gods' own mansions:
There was she lost; when sudden I beheld,
Where, tumbling through the air in fiery fold,
All flaming down she on the plain was felled,
And soon her body turned to ashes cold.
   I saw the fowl, that doth the light despise,
   Out of her dust like to a worm arise.

VIII

I saw a river swift, whose foamy billows
Did wash the ground-work of an old great wall;
I saw it covered all with grisly shadows,
That with black horror did the air appal:
Thereout a strange beast with seven heads arose,
That towns and castles under her breast did cour,
And seemed both milder beasts and fiercer foes
Alike with equal ravine to devour.
Much was I mazed, to see this monster's kind

In hundred forms to change his fearful hue;
Whenas at length I saw the wrathful wind,
Which blows cold storms, burst out of Scythian mew,
    That 'sperst these clouds; and in so short as thought,
    This dreadful shape was vanishéd to nought.

IX

Then all astonied with this mighty ghost,
An hideous body big and strong I saw,
With side-long beard, and locks down hanging loast,
Stern face, and front full of Saturn-like awe,
Who, leaning on the belly of a pot,
Poured forth a water, whose out-gushing flood
Ran bathing all the creeky shore aflot,
Whereon the Troyan prince spilt Turnus' blood:
And at his feet a bitch-wolf suck did yield
To two young babes. His left the palm tree stout,
His right hand did the peaceful olive wield;
And head with laurel garnisht was about.
    Sudden both palm and olive fell away,
    And fair green laurel branch did quite decay.

X

Hard by a river's side a virgin fair,
Folding her arms to heaven with thousand throbs,
And outraging her cheeks and golden hair,
To falling river's sound thus tuned her sobs.
"Where is" (quoth she) "this whilom honoured face?
Where the great glory and the ancient praise,
In which all world's felicity had place,
When gods and men my honour up did raise?
Sufficed it not that civil wars me made
The whole world's spoil, but that this hydra new,
Of hundred Hercules to be assayed,
With seven heads, budding monstrous crimes anew,
    So many Neros and Caligulas
    Out of these crooked shores must daily raise?"

XI

Upon an hill a bright flame I did see
Waving aloft with triple point to sky,
Which, like incense of precious cedar tree,
With balmy odours filled th' air far and nigh.

A bird all white, well feathered on each wing,
Hereout up to the throne of gods did fly,
And all the way most pleasant notes did sing,
Whilst in the smoke she unto heaven did stie.
Of this fair fire the scattered rays forth threw
On every side a thousand shining beams:
When sudden dropping of a silver dew
(O grievous chance!) gan quench those precious flames;
  That it, which erst so pleasant scent did yield,
  Of nothing now but noyous sulphur smelled.

XII

I saw a spring out of a rock forth rail,
As clear as crystal 'gainst the sunny beams,
The bottom yellow, like the golden grail
That bright Pactolus washeth with his streams;
It seemed that Art and Nature had assembled
All pleasure there, for which man's heart could long;
And there a noise alluring sleep soft trembled,
Of many accords more sweet than mermaids' song:
The seats and benches shone as ivory,
And hundred nymphs sate side by side about;
When from nigh hills, with hideous outcry,
A troop of satyrs in the place did rout,
  Which with their villain feet the stream did ray,
  Threw down the seats, and drove the nymphs away.

XIII

Much richer than that vessel seemed to be,
Which did to that sad Florentine appear,
Casting mine eyes far off, I chanced to see
Upon the Latin coast herself to rear:
But suddenly arose a tempest great,
Bearing close envy to these riches rare,
Which gan assail this ship with dreadful threat,
This ship to which none other might compare:
And finally the storm impetuous
Sunk up these riches, second unto none,
Within the gulf of greedy Nereus.
I saw both ship and mariners each one,
  And all that treasure, drownéd in the main:
  But I the ship saw after raised again.

XIV

Long having deeply groaned these visions sad,
I saw a city like unto that same
Which saw the messenger of tidings glad;
But that on sand was built the goodly frame:
It seemed her top the firmament did rase,
And no less rich than fair, right worthy sure
(If aught here worthy) of immortal days,
Or if aught under heaven might firm endure.
Much wond'red I to see so fair a wall:
When from the northern coast a storm arose,
Which breathing fury from his inward gall
On all which did against his course oppose,
    Into a cloud of dust 'sperst in the air
    The weak foundations of this city fair.

XV

At length, even at the time when Morpheus
Most truly doth unto our eyes appear,
Weary to see the heavens still wavering thus,
I saw Typhœus' sister coming near,
Whose head, full bravely with a morion hid,
Did seem to match the gods in majesty.
She, by a river's bank that swift down slid,
Over all the world did raise a trophy high,
An hundred vanquisht kings under her lay,
With arms bound at their backs in shameful wise.
Whilst I thus mazéd was with great affray,
I saw the heavens in war against her rise:
    Then down she stricken fell with clap of thunder,
    That with great noise I waked in sudden wonder.

THE VISIONS OF PETRARCH

FORMERLY TRANSLATED

I

Being one day at my window all alone,
So many strange things happened me to see,
As much it grieveth me to think thereon.
At my right hand a hind appeared to me.
So fair as mought the greatest god delight;
Two eager dogs did her pursue in chase,
Of which the one was black, the other white:
With deadly force so in their cruel race
They pincht the haunches of that gentle beast,
That at the last, and in short time, I spied,
Under a rock, where she, alas, opprest,
Fell to the ground, and there untimely died.
  Cruel death vanquishing so noble beauty,
  Oft makes me wail so hard a destiny.

II

After, at sea a tall ship did appear,
Made all of heben and white ivory;
The sails of gold, of silk the tackle were:
Mild was the wind, calm seemed the sea to be,
The sky eachwhere did shew full bright and fair:
With rich treasures this gay ship freighted was:
But sudden storm did so turmoil the air,
And tumbled up the sea, that she (alas)
Strake on a rock, that under water lay,
And perishéd past all recovery.
O, how great ruth, and sorrowful assay,
Doth vex my spirit with perplexity,
  Thus in a moment to see lost and drowned,
  So great riches as like cannot be found!

III

The heavenly branches did I see arise
Out of the fresh and lusty laurel tree,
Amidst the young green wood: of Paradise
Some noble plant I thought myself to see:

THE VISIONS OF PETRARCH

Such store of birds therein yshrouded were,
Chanting in shade their sundry melody,
That with their sweetness I was ravisht near.
While on this laurel fixéd was mine eye,
The sky gan everywhere to overcast,
And dark'ned was the welkin all about,
When sudden flash of heaven's fire outbrast,
And rent this royal tree quite by the root;
   Which makes me much and ever to complain;
   For no such shadow shall be had again.

IV

Within this wood, out of a rock did rise
A spring of water, mildly rumbling down,
Whereto approachéd not in any wise
The homely shepherd, nor the ruder clown;
But many Muses, and the nymphs withal,
That sweetly in accord did tune their voice
To the soft sounding of the water's fall:
That my glad heart thereat did much rejoice.
But while herein I took my chief delight,
I saw (alas) the gaping earth devour
The spring, the place, and all clean out of sight;
Which yet aggrieves my heart even to this hour,
   And wounds my soul with rueful memory,
   To see such pleasures gone so suddenly.

V

I saw a phœnix in the wood alone,
With purple wings, and crest of golden hue;
Strange bird he was, whereby I thought anon,
That of some heavenly wight I had the view;
Until he came unto the broken tree,
And to the spring, that late devouréd was.
What say I more? each thing at last we see
Doth pass away: the phœnix there, alas,
Spying the tree destroyed, the water dried,
Himself smote with his beak, as in disdain,
And so forthwith in great despight he died,
That yet my heart burns in exceeding pain,
   For ruth and pity of so hapless plight:
   O let mine eyes no more see such a sight!

VI

At last so fair a lady did I spy,
That thinking yet on her I burn and quake;
On herbs and flowers she walkéd pensively,
Mild, but yet love she proudly did forsake.
White seemed her robes, yet woven so they were,
As snow and gold together had been wrought:
Above the waist a dark cloud shrouded her,
A stinging serpent by the heel her caught;
Wherewith she languisht as the gathered flower;
And well assured she mounted up to joy.
Alas, on earth so nothing doth endure,
But bitter grief and sorrowful annoy:
    Which make this life wretched and miserable,
    Tosséd with storms of fortune variable!

VII

When I behold this tickle trustless state
Of vain world's glory, flitting to and fro,
And mortal men tosséd by troublous fate
In restless seas of wretchedness and woe;
I wish I might this weary life forgo,
And shortly turn unto my happy rest,
Where my free spirit might not any moe
Be vext with sights, that do her peace molest.
And ye, fair lady, in whose bounteous breast
All heavenly grace and virtue shrinéd is,
When ye these rhymes do read, and view the rest,
Loathe this base world, and think of heaven's bliss:
    And though ye be the fairest of God's creatures,
    Yet think, that death shall spoil your goodly features.

DAPHNAÏDA

AN ELEGY

UPON THE DEATH OF THE NOBLE AND VIRTUOUS

DOUGLAS HOWARD

DAUGHTER AND HEIR OF HENRY LORD HOWARD, VISCOUNT BYNDON
AND WIFE OF ARTHUR GORGES, ESQUIRE

DEDICATED TO THE RIGHT HONOURABLE THE LADY

HELENA, MARQUESS OF NORTHAMPTON

BY ED. SP.

I HAVE the rather presumed humbly to offer unto your Honour the dedication of this little poem, for that the noble and virtuous gentlewoman of whom it is written, was by match near allied, and in affection greatly devoted, unto your Ladyship. The occasion why I wrote the same, was as well the great good fame which I heard of her deceased, as the particular goodwill which I bear unto her husband Master Arthur Gorges, a lover of learning and virtue, whose house, as your Ladyship by marriage hath honoured, so do I find the name of them, by many notable records, to be of great antiquity in this realm, and such as have ever borne themselves with honourable reputation to the world, and unspotted loyalty to their prince and country: besides, so lineally are they descended from the Howards, as that the Lady Anne Howard, eldest daughter to John Duke of Norfolk, was wife to Sir Edmund, mother to Sir Edward, and grandmother to Sir William and Sir Thomas Gorges, knights: and therefore I do assure myself that no due honour done to the White Lion, but will be most grateful to your Ladyship, whose husband and children do so nearly participate with the blood of that noble family. So in all duty I recommend this pamphlet', and the good acceptance thereof, to your honourable favour and protection. London, this first of January, 1591.

Your Honour's humbly ever,

ED. SP.

WHATEVER man be he whose heavy mind,
With grief of mournful great mishap opprest,
Fit matter for his cares increase would find,
Let read the rueful plaint herein exprest,
Of one (I ween) the woeful'st man alive,
Even sad Alcyon, whose empiercéd breast
Sharp sorrow did in thousand pieces rive.

But whoso else in pleasure findeth sense,
Or in this wretched life doth take delight,
Let him be banished far away from hence;
Nor let the sacred Sisters here be hight,
Though they of sorrow heavily can sing;
For even their heavy song would breed delight;
But here no tunes, save sobs and groans, shall ring.

Instead of them, and their sweet harmony,
Let those three fatal Sisters, whose sad hands
Do weave the direful threads of destiny,
And in their wrath break off the vital bands,
Approach hereto; and let the dreadful Queen
Of Darkness deep come from the Stygian strands,
And grisly ghosts, to hear the doleful teen.

In gloomy evening, when the weary sun,
After his day's long labour drew to rest,
And sweaty steeds, now having overrun
The compassed sky, gan water in the west,
I walked abroad to breathe the freshing air
In open fields, whose flowering pride, opprest
With early frosts, had lost their beauty fair.

There came unto my mind a troublous thought,
Which daily doth my weaker wit possess,
Nor lets it rest until it forth have brought
Her long-borne infant, fruit of heaviness,
Which she conceivéd hath through meditation
Of this world's vainness and life's wretchedness,
That yet my soul it deeply doth impassion.

So as I muséd on the misery
In which men live, and I of many most
Most miserable man; I did espy
Where towards me a sorry wight did cost,

Clad all in black, that mourning did bewray,
And Jacob staff in hand devoutly crossed,
Like to some pilgrim come from far away.

His careless locks uncombéd and unshorn,
Hung long adown, and beard all overgrown,
That well he seemed to be some wight forlorn;
Down to the earth his heavy eyes were thrown,
As loathing light; and ever as he went
He sighéd soft, and inly deep did groan,
As if his heart in pieces would have rent.

Approaching nigh, his face I viewéd near,
And by the semblant of his countenance
Meseemed I had his person seen elsewhere,
Most like Alcyon seeming at a glance;
Alcyon he, the jolly shepherd swain
That wont full merrily to pipe and dance,
And fill with pleasance every wood and plain.

Yet half in doubt, because of his disguise,
I softly said, "Alcyon!" Therewithal
He looked aside as in disdainful wise;
Yet stayéd not, till I again did call:
Then, turning back, he said, with hollow sound,
"Who is it that doth name me, woeful thrall,
The wretched'st man that treads this day on ground?"

"One, whom like woefulness, impresséd deep,
Hath made fit mate thy wretched case to hear,
And given like cause with thee to wail and weep;
Grief finds some ease by him that like does bear.
Then stay, Alcyon, gentle shepherd! stay,"
(Quoth I) "till thou have to my trusty ear
Committed what thee doth so ill apay."

"Cease, foolish man!" (said he, half wrathfully)
"To seek to hear that which cannot be told,
For the huge anguish, which doth multiply
My dying pains, no tongue can well unfold;
Ne do I care that any should bemoan
My hard mishap, or any weep that wold,
But seek alone to weep, and die alone."

"Then be it so," (quoth I) "that thou are bent
To die alone, unpitiéd, unplained;
Yet, ere thou die, it were convenient
To tell the cause which thee thereto constrained,
Lest that the world thee dead accuse of guilt,
And say, when thou of none shalt be maintained,
That thou for secret crime thy blood hast spilt."

"Who life does loathe, and longs to be unbound
From the strong shackles of frail flesh," quoth he,
"Nought cares at all what they, that live on ground,
Deem the occasion of his death to be;
Rather desires to be forgotten quite,
Than question made of his calamity,
For heart's deep sorrow hates both life and light.

"Yet since so much thou seem'st to rue my grief,
And carest for one that for himself cares nought,
(Sign of thy love, though nought for my relief,
For my relief exceedeth living thought)
I will to thee this heavy case relate:
Then hearken well till it to end be brought,
For never didst thou hear more hapless fate.

"Whilom I used (as thou right well dost know)
My little flock on western downs to keep,
Not far from whence Sabrina's stream doth flow,
And flowery banks with silver liquor steep;
Nought cared I then for worldly change or chance,
For all my joy was on my gentle sheep,
And to my pipe to carol and to dance.

"It there befell, as I the fields did range
Fearless and free, a fair young lioness,
White as the native rose before the change
Which Venus' blood did in her leaves impress,
I spiéd playing on the grassy plain
Her youthful sports and kindly wantonness,
That did all other beasts in beauty stain.

"Much was I movéd at so goodly sight,
Whose like before mine eye had seldom seen,
And gan to cast how I her compass might,
And bring to hand that yet had never been;

So well I wrought with mildness and with pain,
That I her caught disporting on the green,
And brought away fast bound with silver chain.

"And afterwards I handled her so fair,
That though by kind she stout and savage were,
For being born an ancient lion's heir,
And of the race that all wild beasts do fear,
Yet I her framed, and won so to my bent,
That she became so meek and mild of cheer,
As the least lamb in all my flock that went:

"For she in field, wherever I did wend,
Would wend with me, and wait by me all day;
And all the night that I in watch did spend,
If cause required, or else in sleep, if nay,
She would all night by me or watch or sleep,
And evermore when I did sleep or play,
She of my flock would take full wary keep.

"Safe then, and safest were my silly sheep,
Ne feared the wolf, ne feared the wildest beast,
All were ydrowned in careless quiet deep;
My lovely lioness without behest
So careful was for them, and for my good,
That when I wakéd, neither most nor least
I found miscarried or in plain or wood.

"Oft did the shepherds, which my hap did hear,
And oft their lasses, which my luck envíde,
Daily resort to me from far and near,
To see my lioness, whose praises wide
Were spread abroad; and when her worthiness
Much greater than the rude report they tried,
They her did praise, and my good fortune bless.

"Long thus I joyed in my happiness,
And well did hope my joy would have no end.
But oh, fond man! that in world's fickleness,
Reposedst hope, or weenedst her thy friend
That glories most in mortal miseries,
And daily doth her changeful counsels bend
To make new matter fit for tragedies;

DAPHNAÏDA

"For whilst I was thus without dread or doubt,
A cruel satyr with his murd'rous dart,
Greedy of mischief, ranging all about,
Gave her the fatal wound of deadly smart,
And reft fro me my sweet companion,
And reft fro me my love, my life, my heart:
My lioness (ah, woe is me!) is gone!

"Out of the world thus was she reft away,
Out of the world, unworthy such a spoil,
And borne to heaven, for heaven a fitter prey;
Much fitter than the lion, which with toil
Alcides slew, and fixed in firmament:
Her now I seek throughout this earthly soil,
And seeking miss, and missing do lament."

Therewith he gan afresh to wail and weep,
That I for pity of his heavy plight
Could not abstain mine eyes with tears to steep;
But, when I saw the anguish of his sprite
Some deal allayed, I him bespake again:
"Certes, Alcyon, painful is thy plight,
That it in me breeds almost equal pain.

"Yet doth not my dull wit well understand
The riddle of thy lovéd lioness;
For rare it seems in reason to be scanned,
That man, who doth the whole world's rule possess,
Should to a beast his noble heart embase,
And be the vassal of his vassaless;
Therefore more plain arede this doubtful case."

Then sighing sore, "Daphne thou knew'st," quoth he,
"She now is dead!" ne more endured to say,
But fell to ground for great extremity;
That I, beholding it, with deep dismay
Was much appalled, and, lightly him uprearing,
Revokéd life, that would have fled away,
All were myself, through grief, in deadly drearing.

Then gan I him to comfort all my best,
And with mild counsel strove to mitigate
The stormy passion of his troubled breast,
But he thereby was more impassionate;

As stubborn steed, that is with curb restrained,
Becomes more fierce and fervent in his gait;
And, breaking forth at last, thus dearnly plained:

I

"What man henceforth that breatheth vital air
Will honour heaven, or heavenly powers adore,
Which so unjustly do their judgements share
'Mongst earthly wights, as to afflict so sore
The innocent, as those which do transgress,
And do not spare the best or fairest, more
Than worst or foulest, but do both oppress?

"If this be right, why did they then create
The world so fair, sith fairness is neglected?
Or why be they themselves immaculate,
If purest things be not by them respected?
She fair, she pure, most fair, most pure she was,
Yet was by them as thing impure rejected;
Yet she in pureness heaven itself did pass.

"In pureness and in all celestial grace,
That men admire in goodly womankind,
She did excel, and seemed of angels' race,
Living on earth like angel new divined,
Adorned with wisdom and with chastity,
And all the dowries of a noble mind,
Which did her beauty much more beautify.

"No age hath bred (since fair Astræa left
The sinful world) more virtue in a wight;
And when she parted hence, with her she reft
Great hope, and robbed her race of bounty quite.
Well may the shepherd lasses now lament;
For double loss by her hath on them light,
To lose both her and bounty's ornament.

"Ne let Elisa, royal shepherdess,
The praises of my parted love envý,
For she hath praises in all plenteousness
Poured upon her, like showers of Castaly,
By her own shepherd, Colin, her own shepherd,
That her with heavenly hymns doth deify,
Of rustic Muse full hardly to be bettered.

"She is the rose, the glory of the day,
And mine the primrose in the lowly shade:
Mine, ah! not mine; amiss I mine did say:
Not mine, but His, which mine awhile her made:
Mine to be His, with Him to live for aye.
O that so fair a flower so soon should fade,
And through untimely tempest fall away!

"She fell away in her first age's spring,
Whilst yet her leaf was green, and fresh her rind,
And whilst her branch fair blossoms forth did bring,
She fell away against all course of kind.
For age to die is right, but youth is wrong;
She fell away like fruit blown down with wind.
Weep, shepherd! weep, to make my undersong.

II

"What heart so stony hard but that would weep,
And pour forth fountains of incessant tears?
What Timon but would let compassion creep
Into his breast, and pierce his frozen ears?
Instead of tears, whose brackish bitter well
I wasted have, my heart-blood dropping wears,
To think to ground how that fair blossom fell.

"Yet fell she not as one enforced to die,
Ne died with dread and grudging discontent,
But as one toiled with travail down doth lie,
So lay she down, as if to sleep she went,
And closed her eyes with careless quietness;
The whiles soft death away her spirit hent,
And soul assoiled from sinful fleshliness.

"Yet ere that life her lodging did forsake,
She, all resolved, and ready to remove,
Calling to me (ay me!) this wise bespake;
'Alcyon! ah, my first and latest love!
Ah! why does my Alcyon weep and mourn,
And grieve my ghost, that ill mote him behove,
As if to me had chanced some evil turn!

"'I, since the messenger is come for me,
That summons souls unto the bridal feast
Of his great Lord, must needs depart from thee,

And straight obey his sovereign behest;
Why should Alcyon then so sore lament
That I from misery shall be released,
And freed from wretched long imprisonment!

"'Our days are full of dolour and disease,
Our life afflicted with incessant pain,
That nought on earth may lessen or appease;
Why then should I desire here to remain!
Or why should he, that loves me, sorry be
For my deliverance, or at all complain
My good to hear, and toward joys to see!

"'I go, and long desiréd have to go;
I go with gladness to my wishéd rest,
Whereas no world's sad care nor wasting woe
May come their happy quiet to molest;
But saints and angels in celestial thrones
Eternally Him praise that hath them blest;
There shall I be amongst those blessed ones.

"'Yet, ere I go, a pledge I leave with thee
Of the late love the which betwixt us passed,
My young Ambrosia; in lieu of me,
Love her; so shall our love for ever last.
Thus, dear! adieu, whom I expect ere long.'—
So having said, away she softly passed:
Weep, shepherd! weep, to make mine undersong.

III

"So oft as I record those piercing words,
Which yet are deep engraven in my breast,
And those last deadly accents, which like swords
Did wound my heart, and rend my bleeding chest,
With those sweet sug'red speeches do compare,
The which my soul first conquered and possessed,
The first beginners of my endless care:

"And when those pallid cheeks and ashy hue,
In which sad Death his portraiture had writ,
And when those hollow eyes and deadly view,
On which the cloud of ghastly night did sit,

I match with that sweet smile and cheerful brow,
Which all the world subduéd unto it,
How happy was I then, and wretched now!

"How happy was I when I saw her lead
The shepherds' daughters dancing in a round!
How trimly would she trace and softly tread
The tender grass, with rosy garland crowned!
And when she list advance her heavenly voice,
Both nymphs and muses nigh she made astound,
And flocks and shepherds causéd to rejoice.

"But now, ye shepherd lasses, who shall lead
Your wand'ring troops, or sing your virelays?
Or who shall dight your bowers, sith she is dead
That was the lady of your holidays?
Let now your bliss be turnéd into bale,
And into plaints convert your joyous plays,
And with the same fill every hill and dale.

"Let bagpipe nevermore be heard to shrill,
That may allure the senses to delight,
Ne ever shepherd sound his oaten quill
Unto the many that provoke them might
To idle pleasance; but let ghastliness
And dreary horror dim the cheerful light,
To make the image of true heaviness:

"Let birds be silent on the naked spray,
And shady woods resound with dreadful yells;
Let streaming floods their hasty courses stay,
And parching drouth dry up the crystal wells;
Let th' earth be barren, and bring forth no flowers,
And th' air be filled with noise of doleful knells,
And wand'ring spirits walk untimely hours.

"And Nature, nurse of every living thing,
Let rest herself from her long weariness,
And cease henceforth things kindly forth to bring,
But hideous monsters full of ugliness;
For she it is that hath me done this wrong,
No nurse, but stepdame, cruel, merciless.
Weep, shepherd! weep, to make my undersong.

IV

"My little flock, whom erst I loved so well,
And wont to feed with finest grass that grew,
Feed ye henceforth on bitter astrophel,
And stinking smallage, and unsavoury rue;
And, when your maws are with those weeds corrupted,
Be ye the prey of wolves; ne will I rue
That with your carcasses wild beasts be glutted.

"Ne worse to you, my silly sheep, I pray,
Ne sorer vengeance wish on you to fall
Than to myself, for whose confused decay
To careless heavens I do daily call;
But heavens refuse to hear a wretch's cry;
And cruel Death doth scorn to come at call,
Or grant his boon that most desires to die.

"The good and righteous he away doth take,
To plague th' unrighteous which alive remain;
But the ungodly ones he doth forsake,
By living long to multiply their pain;
Else surely death should be no punishment,
As the Great Judge at first did it ordain,
But rather riddance from long languishment.

"Therefore, my Daphne they have ta'en away;
For worthy of a better place was she:
But me unworthy willéd here to stay,
That with her lack I might tormented be.
Sith then they so have ord'red, I will pay
Penance to her, according their decree,
And to her ghost do service day by day.

"For I will walk this wand'ring pilgrimage,
Throughout the world from one to other end,
And in affliction waste my better age:
My bread shall be the anguish of my mind,
My drink the tears which fro mine eyes do rain,
My bed the ground that hardest I may find;
So will I wilfully increase my pain.

"And she, my love that was, my saint that is,
When she beholds from her celestial throne
(In which she joyeth in eternal bliss)

My bitter penance, will my case bemoan,
And pity me that living thus do die;
For heavenly spirits have compassion
On mortal men, and rue their misery.

"So when I have with sorrow satisfied
Th' importune Fates, which vengeance on me seek,
And th' heavens with long languor pacified,
She, for pure pity of my sufferance meek,
Will send for me, for which I daily long,
And will till then my painful penance eke.
Weep, shepherd! weep, to make my undersong.

v

"Henceforth I hate whatever Nature made,
And in her workmanship no pleasure find,
For they be all but vain, and quickly fade;
So soon as on them blows the northern wind,
They tarry not, but flit and fall away,
Leaving behind them nought but grief of mind,
And mocking such as think they long will stay.

"I hate the heaven, because it doth withhold
Me from my love, and eke my love from me;
I hate the earth, because it is the mould
Of fleshly slime and frail mortality;
I hate the fire, because to nought it flies;
I hate the air, because sighs of it be;
I hate the sea, because it tears supplies.

"I hate the day, because it lendeth light
To see all things, and not my love to see;
I hate the darkness and the dreary night,
Because they breed sad balefulness in me;
I hate all times, because all times do fly
So fast away, and may not stayéd be,
But as a speedy post that passeth by.

"I hate to speak, my voice is spent with crying;
I hate to hear, loud plaints have dulled mine ears;
I hate to taste, for food withholds my dying;
I hate to see, mine eyes are dimmed with tears;

I hate to smell, no sweet on earth is left;
I hate to feel, my flesh is numbed with fears:
So all my senses from me are bereft.

"I hate all men, and shun all womankind;
The one, because as I they wretched are;
The other, for because I do not find
My love with them, that wont to be their star:
And life I hate, because it will not last;
And death I hate, because it life doth mar;
And all I hate that is to come or past.

"So all the world, and all in it I hate,
Because it changeth ever to and fro,
And never standeth in one certain state,
But still unsteadfast, round about doth go
Like a mill-wheel in midst of misery,
Driven with streams of wretchedness and woe,
That dying lives, and living still does die.

"So do I live, so do I daily die,
And pine away in self-consuming pain!
Sith she that did my vital powers supply,
And feeble spirits in their force maintain,
Is fetched fro me, why seek I to prolong
My weary days in dolour and disdain?
Weep, shepherd! weep, to make my undersong.

VI

"Why do I longer live in life's despite,
And do not die then in despite of death;
Why do I longer see this loathsome light
And do in darkness not abridge my breath,
Sith all my sorrow should have end thereby,
And cares find quiet? Is it so uneath
To leave this life, or dolorous to die?

"To live I find it deadly dolorous,
For life draws care, and care continual woe;
Therefore to die must needs be joyëous,
And wishful thing this sad life to forgo:
But I must stay; I may it not amend,
My Daphne hence departing bad me so;
She bad me stay, till she for me did send.

"Yet, whilst I in this wretched vale do stay
My weary feet shall ever wand'ring be,
That still I may be ready on my way
Whenas her messenger doth come for me;
Ne will I rest my feet for feebleness,
Ne will I rest my limbs for fraïlty,
Ne will I rest mine eyes for heaviness.

"But, as the mother of the gods, that sought
For fair Eurydice, her daughter dear,
Throughout the world, with woeful heavy thought;
So will I travel whilst I tarry here,
Ne will I lodge, ne will I ever lin,
Ne, whenas drooping Titan draweth near
To loose his team, will I take up my inn.

"Ne sleep (the harbinger of weary wights)
Shall ever lodge upon mine eyelids more;
Ne shall with rest refresh my fainting sprites,
Nor failing force to former strength restore:
But I will wake and sorrow all the night
With Philumene, my fortune to deplore;
With Philumene, the partner of my plight.

"And ever as I see the stars to fall,
And underground to go to give them light
Which dwell in darkness, I to mind will call
How my fair star (that shined on me so bright)
Fell suddenly and faded underground;
Since whose departure, day is turned to night,
And night without a Venus star is found.

"But soon as day doth shew his dewy face,
And calls forth men unto their toilsome trade,
I will withdraw me to some darksome place,
Or some deep cave, or solitary shade;
There will I sigh, and sorrow all day long,
And the huge burden of my cares unlade.
Weep, shepherd! weep, to make my undersong.

VII

"Henceforth mine eyes shall nevermore behold
Fair thing on earth, ne feed on false delight
Of aught that framéd is of mortal mould,
Sith that my fairest flower is faded quite;

For all I see is vain and transitory,
Ne will be held in any steadfast plight,
But in a moment lose their grace and glory.

"And ye fond men! on Fortune's wheel that ride,
Or in aught under heaven repose assurance,
Be it riches, beauty, or honour's pride,
Be sure that they shall have no long endurance,
But ere ye be aware will flit away;
For nought of them is yours, but th' only usance
Of a small time, which none ascertain may.

"And ye, true lovers! whom disastrous chance
Hath far exiléd from your ladies' grace,
To mourn in sorrow and sad sufferance,
When ye do hear me in that desert place
Lamenting loud my Daphne's elegy,
Help me to wail my miserable case,
And when life parts vouchsafe to close mine eye.

"And ye, more happy lovers! which enjoy
The presence of your dearest loves' delight,
When ye do hear my sorrowful annoy,
Yet pity me in your impassioned sprite,
And think that such mishap, as chanced to me,
May happen unto the most happiest wight;
For all men's states alike unsteadfast be.

"And ye, my fellow-shepherds! which do feed
Your careless flocks on hills and open plains,
With better fortune than did me succeed,
Remember yet my undeservéd pains;
And, when ye hear that I am dead or slain,
Lament my lot, and tell your fellow-swains
That sad Alcyon died in life's disdain.

"And ye, fair damsels! shepherds' dear delights,
That with your loves do their rude hearts possess,
Whenas my hearse shall happen to your sights,
Vouchsafe to deck the same with cyparess;
And ever sprinkle brackish tears among,
In pity of my undeserved distress,
The which I, wretch, enduréd have this long.

"And ye, poor pilgrims! that with restless toil
Weary yourselves in wand'ring desert ways,
Till that you come where ye your vows assoil,
When passing by ye read these woeful lays,
On my grave written, rue my Daphne's wrong,
And mourn for me that languish out my days.
Cease, shepherd! cease, and end thy undersong."

Thus when he ended had his heavy plaint,
The heaviest plaint that ever I heard sound,
His cheeks wexed pale, and sprites began to faint
As if again he would have fallen to ground;
Which when I saw, I (stepping to him light)
Amovéd him out of his stony swound,
And gan him to recomfort as I might.

But he no way recomforted would be,
Nor suffer solace to approach him nigh,
But casting up a sdeignful eye at me,
That in his trance I would not let him lie,
Did rend his hair, and beat his blubb'red face,
As one disposéd wilfully to die,
That I sore grieved to see his wretched case.

Then when the pang was somewhat overpast,
And the outrageous passion nigh appeased,
I him desired, sith day was overcast,
And dark night fast approached, to be pleased
To turn aside unto my cabinet,
And stay with me, till he were better eased
Of that strong stound which him so sore beset.

But by no means I could him win thereto,
Ne longer him entreat with me to stay,
But without taking leave he forth did go
With stagg'ring pace and dismal looks dismay,
As if that Death he in the face had seen,
Or hellish hags had met upon the way:
But what of him became I cannot ween.

COLIN CLOUT'S COME HOME AGAIN
BY ED. SPENSER

TO THE RIGHT WORTHY AND NOBLE KNIGHT

SIR WALTER RALEIGH

CAPTAIN OF HER MAJESTY'S GUARD, LORD WARDEN OF THE STANNARIES, AND LIEUTENANT OF THE COUNTY OF CORNWALL

SIR, that you may see that I am not always idle as ye think, though not greatly well occupied, nor altogether undutiful, though not precisely officious, I make you present of this simple pastoral, unworthy of your higher conceit for the meanness of the style, but agreeing with the truth in circumstance and matter. The which I humbly beseech you to accept in part of payment of the infinite debt in which I acknowledge myself bounden unto you, for your singular favours and sundry good turns, shewed to me at my late being in England, and with your good countenance protect against the malice of evil mouths, which are always wide open to carp at and misconstrue my simple meaning. I pray continually for your happiness. From my house of Kilcolman, the 27 of December, 1591.

Yours very humbly,

ED. SP.

THE shepherd's boy (best knowen by that name)
That after Tityrus first sung his lay,
Lays of sweet love, without rebuke or blame,
Sate (as his custom was) upon a day,
Charming his oaten pipe unto his peers,
The shepherd swains that did about him play:
Who all the while, with greedy listful ears,
Did stand astonished at his curious skill,
Like heartless deer, dismayed with thunder's sound.
At last, whenas he pipéd had his fill,
He rested him: and, sitting then around,
One of those grooms (a jolly groom was he,
As ever pipéd on an oaten reed,
And loved this shepherd dearest in degree,
Hight Hobbinol) gan thus to him arede.
  "Colin, my lief, my life, how great a loss
Had all the shepherds' nation by thy lack:

And I, poor swain, of many, greatest cross!
That, sith thy Muse first since thy turning back
Was heard to sound as she was wont on high,
Hast made us all so blessed and so blithe.
Whilst thou wast hence, all dead in dole did lie:
The woods were heard to wail full many a sithe,
And all their birds with silence to complain:
The fields with faded flowers did seem to mourn,
And all their flocks from feeding to refrain:
The running waters wept for thy return,
And all their fish with languor did lament:
But now both woods and fields and floods revive,
Sith thou art come, their cause of merriment,
That us, late dead, has made again alive.
But were it not too painful to repeat
The passéd fortunes, which to thee befell
In thy late voyage, we thee would entreat,
Now at thy leisure them to us to tell."

To whom the shepherd gently answered thus:
"Hobbin, thou temptest me to that I couet:
For good passéd newly to discuss,
By double usury doth twice renew it.
And since I saw that angel's blessed eye,
Her world's bright sun, her heaven's fairest light,
My mind, full of my thoughts' satiety,
Doth feed on sweet contentment of that sight:
Since that same day in nought I take delight,
Ne feeling have in any earthly pleasure,
But in remembrance of that glorious bright,
My life's sole bliss, my heart's eternal treasure.
Wake then, my pipe; my sleepy Muse, awake;
Till I have told her praises lasting long:
Hobbin desires, thou may'st it not forsake;—
Hark then, ye jolly shepherds, to my song."

With that they all gan throng about him near,
With hungry ears to hear his harmony:
The whiles their flocks, devoid of danger's fear,
Did round about them feed at liberty.

"One day" (quoth he) "I sat (as was my trade)
Under the foot of Mole, that mountain hoar,
Keeping my sheep amongst the cooly shade
Of the green alders by the Mulla's shore;
There a strange shepherd chanced to find me out,

Whether alluréd with my pipe's delight,
Whose pleasing sound yshrilléd far about,
Or thither led by chance, I know not right:
Whom when I askéd from what place he came,
And how he hight, himself he did yclepe
The Shepherd of the Ocëan by name,
And said he came far from the main-sea deep.
He, sitting me beside in that same shade,
Provokéd me to play some pleasant fit;
And, when he heard the music which I made,
He found himself full greatly pleased at it:
Yet, emuling my pipe, he took in hond
My pipe, before that emuléd of many,
And played thereon; (for well that skill he conned)
Himself as skilful in that art as any.
He piped, I sung; and, when he sung, I piped;
By change of turns, each making other merry;
Neither envýing other, nor envíed,
So pipéd we, until we both were weary."

There interrupting him, a bonny swain,
That Cuddy hight, him thus atween bespake:
"And, should it not thy ready course restrain,
I would request thee, Colin, for my sake,
To tell what thou didst sing, when he did play;
For well I ween it worth recounting was,
Whether it were some hymn, or moral lay,
Or carol made to praise thy lovéd lass."

"Nor of my love, nor of my lass" (quoth he)
"I then did sing, as then occasion fell:
For love had me forlorn, forlorn of me,
That made me in that desert choose to dwell.
But of my river Bregog's love I sung,
Which to the shiny Mulla he did bear,
And yet doth bear, and ever will, so long
As water doth within his banks appear."

"Of fellowship" (said then that bonny boy)
"Record to us that lovely lay again:
The stay whereof shall nought these ears annoy,
Who all that Colin makes do covet fain."

"Hear then" (quoth he) "the tenor of my tale,
In sort as I it to that shepherd told:
No leasing new, nor grandam's fable stale,
But ancient truth confirmed with credence old.

"Old father Mole, (Mole hight that mountain gray
That walls the north side of Armulla dale)
He had a daughter fresh as flower of May,
Which gave that name unto that pleasant vale;
Mulla, the daughter of old Mole, so hight
The nymph, which of that water-course has charge,
That, springing out of Mole, doth run down right
To Buttevant, where, spreading forth at large,
It giveth name unto that ancient city,
Which Kilnemullah clepéd is of old;
Whose ragged ruins breed great ruth and pity
To travellers, which it from far behold.
Full fain she loved, and was beloved full fain
Of her own brother river, Bregog hight,
So hight because of this deceitful train
Which he with Mulla wrought to win delight.
But her old sire more careful of her good,
And meaning her much better to prefer,
Did think to match her with the neighbour flood,
Which Allo hight, Broad-water calléd far;
And wrought so well with his continual pain,
That he that river for his daughter won:
The dower agreed, the day assignéd plain,
The place appointed where it should be done.
Nath'less the nymph her former liking held;
For love will not be drawn, but must be led;
And Bregog did so well her fancy weld,
That her good will he got her first to wed.
But for her father, sitting still on high,
Did warily still watch which way she went,
And eke from far observed, with jealous eye,
Which way his course the wanton Bregog bent;
Him to deceive, for all his watchful ward,
The wily lover did devise this sleight:
First into many parts his stream he shared,
That, whilst the one was watched, the other might
Pass unespied to meet her by the way;
And then, besides, those little streams so broken
He underground so closely did convey,
That of their passage doth appear no token,
Till they into the Mulla's water slide.
So secretly did he his love enjoy,
Yet not so secret, but it was descried,

COLIN'S COME HOME AGAIN

And told her father by a shepherd's boy.
Who, wondrous wroth, for that so foul despight,
In great avenge did roll down from his hill
Huge mighty stones, the which encumber might
Hi passage, and his water-courses spill.
So of a river, which he was of old,
He none was made, but scatt'red all to nought;
And, lost among those rocks into him rolled,
Did lose his name: so dear his love he bought."

Which having said, him Thestylis bespake:
"Now by my life this was a merry lay,
Worthy of Colin self, that did it make.
But rede now eke, of friendship I thee pray,
What ditty did that other shepherd sing:
For I do covet most the same to hear,
As men use most to covet foreign thing."

"That shall I eke" (quoth he) "to you declare:
His song was all a lamentable lay
Of great unkindness, and of usage hard,
Of Cynthia the Lady of the Sea,
Which from her presence faultless him debarred.
And ever and anon, with singults rife,
He criéd out, to make his undersong:
'Ah! my love's queen, and goddess of my life,
Who shall me pity, when thou dost me wrong?'"

Then gan a gentle bonny lass to speak,
That Marin hight: "Right well he sure did plain,
That could great Cynthia's sore displeasure break,
And move to take him to her grace again.
But tell on further, Colin, as befell
'Twixt him and thee, that thee did hence dissuade."

"When thus our pipes we both had wearied well,"
(Quoth he) "and each an end of singing made,
He gan to cast great liking to my lore,
And great disliking to my luckless lot,
That banished had myself, like wight forlore,
Into that waste, where I was quite forgot.
The which to leave, thenceforth he counselled me,
Unmeet for man, in whom was aught regardful,
And wend with him, his Cynthia to see;
Whose grace was great, and bounty most rewardful.
Besides her peerless skill in making well,
And all the ornaments of wondrous wit,

Such as all womankind did far excel;
Such as the world admired, and praiséd it.
So what with hope of good, and hate of ill,
He me persuaded forth with him to fare.
Nought took I with me, but mine oaten quill:
Small needments else need shepherd to prepare.
So to the sea we came; the sea, that is
A world of waters heapéd up on high,
Rolling like mountains in wide wilderness,
Horrible, hideous, roaring with hoarse cry."

"And is the sea" (quoth Corydon) "so fearful?"

"Fearful much more" (quoth he) "than heart can fear:
Thousand wild beasts with deep mouths gaping direful
Therein still wait poor passengers to tear.
Who life doth loathe, and longs Death to behold,
Before he die, already dead with fear,
And yet would live with heart half stony cold,
Let him to sea, and he shall see it there.
And yet as ghastly dreadful, as it seems,
Bold men, presuming life for gain to sell,
Dare tempt that gulf, and in those wand'ring streams
Seek ways unknown, ways leading down to hell.
For, as we stood there waiting on the strand,
Behold! an huge great vessel to us came,
Dancing upon the waters back to land,
As if it scorned the danger of the same;
Yet was it but a wooden frame and frail,
Glued together with some subtil matter.
Yet had it arms and wings, and head and tail,
And life to move itself upon the water.
Strange thing! how bold and swift the monster was,
That neither cared for wind, nor hail, nor rain,
Nor swelling waves, but thorough them did pass
So proudly, that she made them roar again.
The same aboard us gently did receive,
And without harm us far away did bear,
So far that land, our mother, us did leave,
And nought but sea and heaven to us appear.
Then heartless quite, and full of inward fear,
That shepherd I besought to me to tell,
Under what sky, or in what world we were,
In which I saw no living people dwell.

COLIN'S COME HOME AGAIN

Who, me recomforting all that he might,
Told me that that same was the regiment
Of a great shepherdess, that Cynthia hight,
His liege, his lady, and his life's regént.—
  "If then" (quoth I) "a shepherdess she be,
Where be the flocks and herds, which she doth keep?
And where may I the hills and pastures see,
On which she useth for to feed her sheep?"
  "These be the hills," (quoth he) "the surges high,
On which fair Cynthia her herds doth feed:
Her herds be thousand fishes with their fry,
Which in the bosom of the billows breed.
Of them the shepherd which hath charge in chief,
Is Triton, blowing loud his wreathéd horn:
At sound whereof, they all for their relief
Wend to and fro at evening and at morn.
And Proteus eke with him does drive his herd
Of stinking seals and porpoises together,
With hoary head and dewy-dropping beard,
Compelling them which way he list, and whether.
And, I among the rest, of many least,
Have in the ocean charge to me assigned;
Where I will live or die at her behest,
And serve and honour her with faithful mind.
Besides an hundred nymphs all heavenly born,
And of immortal race, do still attend
To wash fair Cynthia's sheep, when they be shorn,
And fold them up, when they have made an end.
Those be the shepherds which my Cynthia serve
At sea, beside a thousand moe at land:
For land and sea my Cynthia doth deserve
To have in her commandëment at hand."
  Thereat I wond'red much, till, wond'ring more
And more, at length we land far off descried:
Which sight much gladded me; for much afore
I feared, lest land we never should have eyed.
Thereto our ship her course directly bent,
As if the way she perfectly had known.
We Lundy pass; by that same name is meant
An island, which the first to west was shown.
From thence another world of land we kenned,
Floating amid the sea in jeopardy,
And round about with mighty white rocks hemmed,

Against the sea's encroaching cruelty.
Those same, the shepherd told me, were the fields
In which dame Cynthia her landherds fed;
Fair goodly fields, than which Armulla yields
None fairer, nor more fruitful to be red:
The first, to which we nigh approachéd, was
An high headland thrust far into the sea,
Like to an horn, whereof the name it has,
Yet seemed to be a goodly pleasant lea:
There did a lofty mount at first us greet,
Which did a stately heap of stones uprear,
That seemed amid the surges for to fleet,
Much greater than that frame, which us did bear;
There did our ship her fruitful womb unlade,
And put us all ashore on Cynthia's land."

"What land is that thou meant," (then Cuddy said)
"And is there other than whereon we stand?"

"Ah! Cuddy," (then quoth Colin) "thou's a fon,
That hast not seen least part of Nature's work:
Much more there is unkenned than thou dost con,
And much more that does from men's knowledge lurk.
For that same land much larger is than this,
And other men and beasts and birds doth feed:
There fruitful corn, fair trees, fresh herbage is,
And all things else that living creatures need.
Besides most goodly rivers there appear,
No whit inferior to thy Fanchin's praise,
Or unto Allo, or to Mulla clear:
Nought hast thou, foolish boy, seen in thy days."

"But if that land be there" (quoth he) "as here,
And is their heaven likewise there all one?
And, if like heaven, be heavenly graces there,
Like as in this same world where we do won?"

"Both heaven and heavenly graces do much more"
(Quoth he) "abound in that same land than this:
For there all happy peace and plenteous store
Conspire in one to make contented bliss.
No wailing there nor wretchedness is heard,
No bloody issues nor no leprosies,
No grisly famine, nor no raging swerd,
No nightly bordrags, nor no hue and cries;
The shepherds there abroad may safely lie,
On hills and downs, withouten dread or danger:

No ravenous wolves the goodman's hope destroy,
Nor outlaws fell affray the forest ranger.
There learned arts do flourish in great honour,
And poets' wits are had in peerless price:
Religion hath lay power to rest upon her,
Advancing virtue and suppressing vice.
For end, all good, all grace there freely grows,
Had people grace it gratefully to use:
For God His gifts there plenteously bestows,
But graceless men them greatly do abuse."

"But say on further" (then said Corylas)
"The rest of thine adventures, that betided."

"Forth on our voyage we by land did pass,"
(Quoth he) "as that same shepherd still us guided,
Until that we to Cynthia's presence came:
Whose glory greater than my simple thought,
I found much greater than the former fame;
Such greatness I cannot compare to aught:
But if I her like aught on earth might read,
I would her liken to a crown of lillies
Upon a virgin bride's adornéd head,
With roses dight and goolds and daffadillies;
Or like the circlet of a turtle true,
In which all colours of the rainbow be;
Or like fair Phœbe's garland shining new,
In which all pure perfection one may see.
But vain it is to think, by paragon
Of earthly things, to judge of things divine:
Her power, her mercy, and her wisdom, none
Can deem, but who the Godhead can define.
Why then do I, base shepherd, bold and blind,
Presume the things so sacred to profane?
More fit it is t' adore, with humble mind,
The image of the heavens in shape humane."

With that Alexis broke his tale asunder,
Saying: "By wond'ring at thy Cynthia's praise,
Colin, thyself thou mak'st us more to wonder,
And her upraising dost thyself upraise.
But let us hear what grace she shewéd thee,
And how that shepherd strange thy cause advanced."

"The Shepherd of the Ocëan" (quoth he)
"Unto that goddess grace me first enhanced,
And to mine oaten pipe inclined her ear,

That she thenceforth therein gan take delight;
And it desired at timely hours to hear,
All were my notes but rude and roughly dight;
For not by measure of her own great mind,
And wondrous worth, she mott my simple song,
But joyed that country shepherd aught could find
Worth hearkening to, amongst the learned throng."

"Why?" (said Alexis then) "what needeth she
That is so great a shepherdess herself,
And hath so many shepherds in her fee,
To hear thee sing, a simple silly elf?
Or be the shepherds which do serve her lazy,
That they list not their merry pipes apply?
Or be their pipes untunable and crazy,
That they cannot her honour worthily?"

"Ah! nay" (said Colin), "neither so, nor so:
For better shepherds be not under sky,
Nor better able, when they list to blow
Their pipes aloud, her name to glorify.
There is good Harpalus, now woxen aged
In faithful service of fair Cynthia:
And there is Corydon, though meanly waged,
Yet ablest wit of most I know this day.
And there is sad Alcyon bent to mourn,
Though fit to frame an everlasting ditty,
Whose gentle sprite for Daphne's death doth turn
Sweet lays of love to endless plaints of pity.
Ah! pensive boy, pursue that brave conceit
In thy sweet *Eglantine of Meriflure*;
Lift up thy notes unto their wonted height,
That may thy Muse and mates to mirth allure.
There eke is Palin worthy of great praise,
Albe he envy at my rustic quill:
And there is pleasing Alcon, could he raise
His tunes from lays to matter of more skill.
And there is old Palemon free from spite
Whose careful pipe may make the hearer rue:
Yet he himself may ruéd be more right,
That sung so long until quite hoarse he grew.
And there is Alabaster, throughly taught
In all this skill, though knowen yet to few;
Yet, were he known to Cynthia as he ought,
His *Eliseis* would be read anew.

Who lives that can match that heroic song,
Which he hath of that mighty princess made?
O dreaded Dread, do not thyself that wrong,
To let thy fame lie so in hidden shade:
But call it forth, O call him forth to thee,
To end thy glory which he hath begun:
That, when he finished hath as it should be,
No braver poem can be under sun.
Nor Po nor Tiber's swans so much renowned,
Nor all the brood of Greece so highly praised,
Can match that Muse when it with bays is crowned
And to the pitch of her perfection raised.
And there is a new shepherd late upsprong,
The which doth all afore him far surpass;
Appearing well in that well-tunéd song,
Which late he sung unto a scornful lass.
Yet doth his trembling Muse but lowly fly,
As daring not to rashly mount on hight,
And doth her tender plumes as yet but try
In love's soft lays and looser thoughts' delight.
Then rouse thy feathers quickly, Daniel,
And to what course thou please thyself advance:
But most, meseems, thy accent will excel
In tragic plaints and passionate mischance.
And there that Shepherd of the Ocean is,
That spends his wit in love's consuming smart:
Full sweetly temp'red is that Muse of his,
That can empierce a prince's mighty heart.
There also is (ah no, he is not now!),
But since I said he is, he quite is gone,
Amyntas quite is gone, and lies full low,
Having his Amaryllis left to moan.
Help, O ye shepherds, help ye all in this,
Help Amaryllis this her loss to mourn:
Her loss is yours, your loss Amyntas is,
Amyntas, flower of shepherds' pride forlorn:
He whilst he livéd was the noblest swain
That ever pipéd in an oaten quill:
Both did he other, which could pipe, maintain,
And eke could pipe himself with passing skill.
And there, though last not least, is Aetion,
A gentler shepherd may nowhere be found:
Whose Muse, full of high thought's invention,

Doth like himself heroically sound.
All these, and many others mo remain,
Now after Astrophel is dead and gone:
But while as Astrophel did live and reign,
Amongst all these was none his paragon.
All these do flourish in their sundry kind,
And do their Cynthia immortal make:
Yet found I liking in her royal mind,
Not for my skill, but for that shepherd's sake."

    Then spake a lovely lass, hight Lucida:
"Shepherd, enough of shepherds thou hast told,
Which favour thee, and honour Cynthia:
But of so many nymphs, which she doth hold
In her retinue, thou hast nothing said;
That seems, with none of them thou favour foundest,
Or art ingrateful to each gentle maid,
That none of all their due deserts resoundest."

    "Ah far be it" (quoth Colin Clout) "fro me,
That I of gentle maids should ill deserve!
For that myself I do profess to be
Vassal to one, whom all my days I serve;
The beam of beauty sparkled from above,
The flower of virtue and pure chastity,
The blossom of sweet joy and perfect love,
The pearl of peerless grace and modesty:
To her my thoughts I daily dedicate,
To her my heart I nightly martyrize:
To her my love I lowly do prostrate,
To her my life I wholly sacrifice:
My thought, my heart, my love, my life is she,
And I hers ever only, ever one:
One ever I all vowéd hers to be,
One ever I, and others' never none."

    Then thus Melissa said: "Thrice happy maid,
Whom thou dost so enforce to deify:
That woods, and hills, and valleys thou hast made
Her name to echo unto heaven high.
But say, who else vouchsaféd thee of grace?"

    "They all" (quoth he) "me gracéd goodly well,
That all I praise; but in the highest place,
Urania, sister unto Astrophel,
In whose brave mind, as in a golden coffer,
All heavenly gifts and riches lockéd are;

More rich than pearls of Ind, or gold of Opher,
And in her sex more wonderful and rare.
Ne less praiseworthy I Theana rede,
Whose goodly beams though they be overdight
With mourning stole of careful widowhead,
Yet through that darksome veil do glister bright;
She is the well of bounty and brave mind,
Excelling most in glory and great light:
She is the ornament of womankind,
And court's chief garland with all virtues dight.
Therefore great Cynthia her in chiefest grace
Doth hold, and next unto herself advance,
Well worthy of so honourable place,
For her great worth and noble governance.
Ne less praiseworthy is her sister dear,
Fair Marian, the Muses' only darling:
Whose beauty shineth as the morning clear,
With silver dew upon the roses pearling.
Ne less praiseworthy is Mansilia,
Best known by bearing up great Cynthia's train:
That same is she to whom Daphnaïda
Upon her niece's death I did complain:
She is the pattern of true womanhead,
And only mirror of feminity:
Worthy next after Cynthia to tread,
As she is next her in nobility.
Ne less praiseworthy Galathea seems
Than best of all that honourable crew,
Fair Galathea with bright shining beams,
Inflaming feeble eyes that her do view.
She there then waited upon Cynthia,
Yet there is not her won; but here with us
About the borders of our rich Coshma,
Now made of Maa the nymph delicíous.
Ne less praiseworthy fair Neæra is,
Neæra ours, not theirs, though there she be;
For of the famous Shure the nymph she is,
For high desert advanced to that degree.
She is the blossom of grace and courtesy,
Adornéd with all honourable parts:
She is the branch of true nobility,
Beloved of high and low with faithful hearts.
Ne less praiseworthy Stella do I rede,

Though nought my praises of her needed are,
Whom verse of noblest shepherd lately dead
Hath praised and raised above each other star.
Ne less praiseworthy are the sisters three,
The honour of the noble family:
Of which I meanest boast myself to be,
And most that unto them I am so nigh:
Phyllis, Charillis, and sweet Amaryllis.
Phyllis, the fair, is eldest of the three:
The next to her is bountiful Charillis:
But th' youngest is the highest in degree.
Phyllis, the flower of rare perfection,
Fair spreading forth her leaves with fresh delight,
That, with their beauty's amorous reflection,
Bereave of sense each rash beholder's sight.
But sweet Charillis is the paragon
Of peerless price, and ornament of praise,
Admired of all, yet envièd of none,
Through the mild temperance of her goodly rays.
Thrice happy do I hold thee, noble swain,
The which art of so rich a spoil possessed,
And, it embracing dear without disdain,
Hast sole possession in so chaste a breast!
Of all the shepherds' daughters which there be,
And yet there be the fairest under sky,
Or that elsewhere I ever yet did see,
A fairer nymph yet never saw mine eye:
She is the pride and primrose of the rest,
Made by the Maker self to be admired;
And like a goodly beacon high addressed
That is with sparks of heavenly beauty fired.
But Amaryllis, whether fortunate
Or else unfortunate may I arede,
That freëd is from Cupid's yoke by fate,
Since which she doth new bands' adventure dread;—
Shepherd, whatever thou hast heard to be
In this or that praised diversly apart,
In her thou may'st them all assembled see,
And sealed up in the treasure of her heart.
Ne thee less worthy, gentle Flavia,
For thy chaste life and virtue I esteem:
Ne thee less worthy, courteous Candida,
For thy true love and loyalty I deem.

Besides yet many mo that Cynthia serve,
Right noble nymphs, and high to be commended:
But, if I all should praise as they deserve,
This sun would fail me ere I half had ended.
Therefore, in closure of a thankful mind,
I deem it best to hold eternally
Their bounteous deeds and noble favours shrined,
Than by discourse them to indignify."

So having said, Aglaura him bespake:
"Colin, well worthy were those goodly favours
Bestowed on thee, that so of them dost make,
And them requitest with thy thankful labours.
But of great Cynthia's goodness, and high grace,
Finish the story which thou hast begun."

"More eath" (quoth he) "it is in such a case
How to begin, than know how to have done.
For every gift, and every goodly meed,
Which she on me bestowed, demands a day;
And every day, in which she did a deed,
Demands a year it duly to display.
Her words were like a stream of honey fleeting,
The which doth softly trickle from the hive,
Able to melt the hearer's heart unweeting,
And eke to make the dead again alive.
Her deeds were like great clusters of ripe grapes,
Which load the branches of the fruitful vine;
Off'ring to fall into each mouth that gapes,
And fill the same with store of timely wine.
Her looks were like beams of the morning sun,
Forth looking through the windows of the east,
When first the fleecy cattle have begun
Upon the pearléd grass to make their feast.
Her thoughts are like the fume of frankincense,
Which from a golden censer forth doth rise,
And throwing forth sweet odours mounts fro thence
In rolling globes up to the vaulted skies.
There she beholds, with high aspiring thought,
The cradle of her own creatíon,
Amongst the seats of angels heavenly wrought
Much like an angel in all form and fashion."

"Colin," (said Cuddy then) "thou hast forgot
Thyself, meseems, too much, to mount so high:
Such lofty flight base shepherd seemeth not,

From flocks and fields, to angels and to sky."

"True," (answered he) "but her great excellence
Lifts me above the measure of my might:
That, being filled with furious insolence,
I feel myself like one yrapt in sprite.
For when I think of her, as oft I ought,
Then want I words to speak it fitly forth:
And, when I speak of her what I have thought,
I cannot think according to her worth:
Yet will I think of her, yet will I speak,
So long as life my limbs doth hold together;
And whenas death these vital bands shall break,
Her name recorded I will leave for ever.
Her name in every tree I will endoss,
That, as the trees do grow, her name may grow:
And in the ground eachwhere will it engross,
And fill with stones, that all men may it know.
The speaking woods, and murmuring waters' fall,
Her name I'll teach in knowen terms to frame:
And eke my lambs, when for their dams they call,
I'll teach to call for Cynthia by name.
And long while after I am dead and rotten,
Amongst the shepherds' daughters dancing round,
My lays made of her shall not be forgotten,
But sung by them with flowery garlands crowned.
And ye, whoso ye be, that still survive,
Whenas ye hear her memory renewed,
Be witness of her bounty here alive,
Which she to Colin her poor shepherd shewed."

Much was the whole assembly of those herds
Moved at his speech, so feelingly he spake:
And stood awhile astonished at his words,
Till Thestylis at last their silence brake,
Saying: "Why, Colin, since thou found'st such grace
With Cynthia and all her noble crew,
Why didst thou ever leave that happy place,
In which such wealth might unto thee accrue;
And back returnedst to this barren soil,
Where cold and care and penury do dwell,
Here to keep sheep, with hunger and with toil?
Most wretched he, that is and cannot tell."

"Happy indeed" (said Colin) "I him hold,
That may that blesséd presence still enjoy,

Of fortune and of envy uncontrolled,
Which still are wont most happy states t' annoy:
But I, by that which little while I proved,
Some part of those enormities did see,
The which in court continually hoved,
And followed those which happy seemed to be.
Therefore I, silly man, whose former days
Had in rude fields been altogether spent,
Durst not adventure such unknown ways,
Nor trust the guile of Fortune's blandishment;
But rather chose back to my sheep to turn,
Whose utmost hardness I before had tried,
Than, having learned repentance late, to mourn
Amongst those wretches which I there descried."

"Shepherd," (said Thestylis) "it seems of spite
Thou speakest thus 'gainst their felicity,
Which thou envíest, rather than of right
That aught in them blameworthy thou dost spy."

"Cause have I none" (quoth he) "of cank'red will
To 'quite them ill, that me demeaned so well:
But self-regard of private good or ill
Moves me of each, so as I found, to tell
And eke to warn young shepherds' wand'ring wit,
Which, through report of that life's painted bliss,
Adandon quiet home to seek for it,
And leave their lambs to loss, misled amiss.
For, sooth to say, it is no sort of life,
For shepherd fit to lead in that same place,
Where each one seeks with malice, and with strife,
To thrust down other into foul disgrace,
Himself to raise: and he doth soonest rise
That best can handle his deceitful wit
In subtil shifts, and finest sleights devise,
Either by sland'ring his well-deeméd name,
Through leasings lewd, and feignéd forgery;
Or else by breeding him some blot of blame,
By creeping close into his secrecy;
To which him needs a guileful hollow heart,
Maskéd with fair dissembling courtesy,
A filéd tongue, furnished with terms of art,
No art of school, but courtiers' schoolery.
For arts of school have there small countenance,
Counted but toys to busy idle brains;

And there professors find small maintenance,
But to be instruments of others' gains.
Ne is there place for any gentle wit,
Unless to please itself it can apply;
But should'red is, or out of door quite shit,
As base, or blunt, unmeet for melody.
For each man's worth is measured by his weed,
As harts by horns, or asses by their ears:
Yet asses bene not all whose ears exceed,
Nor yet all harts that horns the highest bears;
For highest looks have not the highest mind,
Nor haughty words most full of highest thoughts:
But are like bladders blowen up with wind,
That being pricked do vanish into noughts.
Even such is all their vaunted vanity,
Nought else but smoke, and fumeth soon away.
Such is their glory that in simple eye
Seem greatest, when their garments are most gay.
So they themselves for praise of fools do sell,
And all their wealth for painting on a wall;
With price whereof they buy a golden bell,
And purchase highest rooms in bower and hall:
Whiles single Truth and simple Honesty
Do wander up and down despised of all;
Their plain attire such glorious gallantry
Disdains so much, that none them in doth call."

"Ah! Colin," (then said Hobbinol) "the blame
Which thou imputest, is too general,
As if not any gentle wit of name
Nor honest mind might there be found at all.
For well I wot, sith I myself was there,
To wait on Lobbin, (Lobbin well thou knewest,)
Full many worthy ones then waiting were,
As everelse in prince's court thou viewest.
Of which among you many yet remain,
Whose names I cannot readily now guess:
Those that poor suitors' papers do retain,
And those that skill of medicine profess,
And those that do to Cynthia expound
The ledden of strange languages in charge:
For Cynthia doth in sciences abound,
And gives to their professors stipends large.
Therefore unjustly thou dost wite them all,

For that which thou mislikedst in a few."
  "Blame is" (quoth he) "more blameless general,
Than that which private errors doth pursue;
For well I wot, that there amongst them be
Full many persons of right worthy parts,
Both for report of spotless honesty,
And for profession of all learned arts,
Whose praise hereby no whit impairéd is,
Though blame do light on those that faulty be;
For all the rest do most-what fare amiss,
And yet their own misfaring will not see:
For either they be pufféd up with pride,
Or fraught with envy that their galls do swell,
Or they their days to idleness divide,
Or drownded lie in Pleasure's wasteful well,
In which like moldwarps nuzzling still they lurk,
Unmindful of chief parts of manliness;
And do themselves, for want of other work,
Vain votaries of lazy Love profess,
Whose service high so basely they ensue,
That Cupid self of them ashaméd is,
And must'ring all his men in Venus' view,
Denies them quite for servitors of his."
  "And is Love then" (said Corylas) "once known
In court, and his sweet lore professéd there?
I weenéd sure he was our god alone,
And only wonned in fields and forests here."
  "Not so" (quoth he), "Love most aboundeth there.
For all the walls and windows there are writ,
All full of Love, and love, and love my dear,
And all their talk and study is of it.
Ne any there doth brave or valiant seem,
Unless that some gay mistress' badge he bears:
Ne any one himself doth aught esteem,
Unless he swim in love up to the ears.
But they of Love, and of his sacred lere,
(As it should be) all otherwise devise,
Than we poor shepherds are accustomed here,
And him do sue and serve all otherwise:
For with lewd speeches, and licentious deeds,
His mighty mysteries they do profane,
And use his idle name to other needs,
But as a complement for courting vain.

So him they do not serve as they profess,
But make him serve to them for sordid uses:
Ah! my dread lord, that dost liege hearts possess,
Avenge thyself on them for their abuses.
But we poor shepherds, whether rightly so,
Or thought our rudeness into error led,
Do make religion how we rashly go
To serve that god, that is so greatly dread;
For him the greatest of the gods we deem,
Born without sire or couples of one kind;
For Venus' self doth solely couples seem,
Both male and female through commixture joined;
So pure and spotless Cupid forth she brought,
And in the gardens of Adonis nursed:
Where growing he his own perfection wrought,
And shortly was of all the gods the first.
Then got he bow and shafts of gold and lead,
In which so fell and puissant he grew,
That Jove himself his power began to dread,
And, taking up to heaven, him godded new.
From thence he shoots his arrows everywhere
Into the world, at random as he will,
On us frail men, his wretched vassals here,
Like as himself us pleaseth save or spill.
So we him worship, so we him adore
With humble hearts to heaven uplifted high,
That to true loves he may us evermore
Prefer, and of their grace us dignify:
Ne is there shepherd, ne yet shepherds' swain,
Whatever feeds in forest or in field,
That dare with evil deed or leasing vain
Blaspheme his power, or terms unworthy yield."

"Shepherd, it seems that some celestial rage
Of love" (quoth Cuddy) "is breathed into thy breast,
That poureth forth these oracles so sage
Of that high power, wherewith thou art possessed.
But never wist I till this present day,
Albe of Love I always humbly deemed,
That he was such an one as thou dost say,
And so religiously to be esteemed.
Well may it seem, by this thy deep insight,
That of that god the priest thou shouldest be,
So well thou wot'st the mystery of his might,

As if his godhead thou didst present see."
"Of Love's perfection perfectly to speak,
Or of his nature rightly to define,
Indeed" (said Colin) "passeth reason's reach,
And needs his priest t' express his power divine.
For long before the world he was ybore,
And bred above in Venus' bosom dear:
For by his power the world was made of yore,
And all that therein wondrous doth appear.
For how should else things so far from attone,
And so great enemies as of them be,
Be ever drawn together into one
And taught in such accordance to agree?
Through him the cold began to covet heat,
And water fire; the light to mount on high,
And th' heavy down to peize; the hungry t' eat,
And voidness to seek full satiety.
So, being former foes, they wexéd friends,
And gan by little learn to love each other:
So, being knit, they brought forth other kinds
Out of the fruitful womb of their great mother.
Then first gan heaven out of darkness dread
For to appear, and brought forth cheerful day:
Next gan the earth to shew her naked head,
Out of deep waters which her drowned alway:
And, shortly after, every living wight
Crept forth like worms out of her slimy nature.
Soon as on them the sun's life-giving light
Had pouréd kindly heat and formal feature,
Thenceforth they gan each one his like to love,
And like himself desire for to beget:
The lion chose his mate, the turtle-dove
Her dear, the dolphin his own dolphinet;
But man, that had the spark of reason's might
More than the rest to rule his passíon,
Chose for his love the fairest in his sight,
Like as himself was fairest by creation.
For beauty is the bait which with delight
Doth man allure for to enlarge his kind;
Beauty, the burning lamp of heaven's light,
Darting her beams into each feeble mind:
Against whose power nor god nor man can find
Defence, ne ward the danger of the wound;

But, being hurt, seek to be medicined
Of her that first did stir that mortal stound.
Then do they cry and call to Love apace,
With prayers loud importuning the sky,
Whence he them hears; and, when he list shew grace
Does grant them grace that otherwise would die.
So Love is lord of all the world by right,
And rules the creatures by his powerful saw:
All being made the vassals of his might,
Through secret sense which thereto doth them draw.
Thus ought all lovers of their lord to deem,
And with chaste heart to honour him alway:
But whoso else doth otherwise esteem,
Are outlaws, and his lore do disobey.
For their desire is base, and doth not merit
The name of love, but of disloyal lust:
Ne 'mongst true lovers they shall place inherit,
But as exiles out of his court be thrust."

So having said, Melissa spake at will:
"Colin, thou now full deeply hast divined
Of love and beauty; and, with wondrous skill,
Hast Cupid self depainted in his kind.
To thee are all true lovers greatly bound,
That dost their cause so mightily defend:
But most, all women are thy debtors found,
That dost their bounty still so much commend."

"That ill" (said Hobbinol) "they him requite,
For having lovéd ever one most dear:
He is repaid with scorn and foul despight,
That irks each gentle heart which it doth hear."

"Indeed" (said Lucid) "I have often heard
Fair Rosalind of divers foully blamed
For being to that swain too cruel hard,
That her bright glory else hath much defamed.
But who can tell what cause had that fair maid
To use him so that uséd her so well;
Or who with blame can justly her upbraid
For loving not? for who can love compel?
And, sooth to say, it is foolhardy thing,
Rashly to witen creatures so divine;
For demigods they be and first did spring
From heaven, though graffed in frailness feminine.
And well I wot, that oft I heard it spoken,

COLIN'S COME HOME AGAIN

How one, that fairest Helen did revile,
Through judgement of the gods to bene ywroken,
Lost both his eyes and so remained long while,
Till he recanted had his wicked rhymes,
And made amends to her with treble praise,
Beware therefore, ye grooms, I rede betimes,
How rashly blame of Rosalind ye raise."

"Ah! shepherds," (then said Colin) "ye ne weet
How great a guilt upon your heads ye draw,
To make so bold a doom, with words unmeet,
Of things celestial which ye never saw.
For she is not like as the other crew
Of shepherds' daughters which amongst you be,
But of divine regard and heavenly hue,
Excelling all that ever ye did see.
Not then to her that scornéd thing so base,
But to myself the blame that looked so high:
So high her thoughts as she herself have place,
And loathe each lowly thing with lofty eye.
Yet so much grace let her vouchsafe to grant
To simple swain, sith her I may not love:
Yet that I may her honour paravant,
And praise her worth, though far my wit above.
Such grace shall be some guerdon for the grief
And long affliction which I have endured:
Such grace sometimes shall give me some relief,
And ease of pain which cannot be recured.
And ye, my fellow-shepherds, which do see
And hear the languors of my too long dying,
Unto the world for ever witness be,
That hers I die, nought to the world denying,
This simple trophy of her great conquest."—

So, having ended, he from ground did rise,
And after him uprose eke all the rest:
All loth to part, but that the glooming skies
Warned them to draw their bleating flocks to rest.

ASTROPHEL

A PASTORAL ELEGY

UPON THE DEATH OF THE MOST NOBLE AND VALOROUS KNIGHT
SIR PHILIP SIDNEY

DEDICATED TO THE MOST BEAUTIFUL AND VIRTUOUS LADY
THE COUNTESS OF ESSEX

SHEPHERDS, that wont, on pipes of oaten reed,
Oft-times to plain your love's concealéd smart;
And with your piteous lays have learned to breed
Compassion in a country lass's heart:
Hearken, ye gentle shepherds, to my song,
And place my doleful plaint your plaints among.

To you alone I sing this mournful verse,
The mournful'st verse that ever man heard tell:
To you whose softened hearts it may empierce
With dolour's dart for death of Astrophel.
To you I sing and to none other wight,
For well I wot my rhymes bene rudely dight.

Yet as they bene, if any nicer wit
Shall hap to hear, or covet them to read:
Think he, that such are for such ones most fit,
Made not to please the living but the dead.
And if in him found pity ever place,
Let him be moved to pity such a case.

A GENTLE shepherd born in Arcady,
Of gentlest race that ever shepherd bore,
About the grassy banks of Hæmony
Did keep his sheep, his little stock and store:
Full carefully he kept them day and night,
In fairest fields, and Astrophel he hight.

Young Astrophel, the pride of shepherds' praise,
Young Astrophel, the rustic lasses' love:
Far passing all the pastors of his days,
In all that seemly shepherd might behove.

In one thing only failing of the best,
That he was not so happy as the rest.

For from the time that first the nymph his mother
Him forth did bring, and taught her lambs to feed;
A slender swain, excelling far each other,
In comely shape, like her that did him breed,
He grew up fast in goodness and in grace,
And doubly fair wox both in mind and face.

Which daily more and more he did augment,
With gentle usage and demeanour mild:
That all men's hearts with secret ravishment
He stole away, and weetingly beguiled.
Ne spite itself, that all good things doth spill,
Found aught in him that she could say was ill.

His sports were fair, his joyance innocent,
Sweet without sour, and honey without gall:
And he himself seemed made for merriment,
Merrily masking both in bower and hall.
There was no pleasure nor delightful play,
When Astrophel soever was away.

For he could pipe, and dance, and carol sweet,
Amongst the shepherds in their shearing feast;
As summer's lark that with her song doth greet
The dawning day forth coming from the east.
And lays of love he also could compose:
Thrice happy she, whom he to praise did choose.

Full many maidens often did him woo,
Them to vouchsafe amongst his rhymes to name,
Or make for them as he was wont to do
For her that did his heart with love inflame.
For which they promiséd to dight for him
Gay chapelets of flowers and garlands trim.

And many a nymph both of the wood and brook
Soon as his oaten pipe began to shrill,
Both crystal wells and shady groves forsook,
To hear the charms of his enchanting skill;
And brought him presents, flowers if it were prime,
Or mellow fruit if it were harvest time.

But he for none of them did care a whit,
Yet wood-gods for them often sighéd sore:
Ne for their gifts unworthy of his wit,
Yet not unworthy of the country's store.
For one alone he cared, for one he sigh't,
His life's desire, and his dear love's delight.

Stella the fair, the fairest star in sky,
As fair as Venus or the fairest fair
(A fairer star saw never living eye),
Shot her sharp-pointed beams through purest air.
Her he did love, her he alone did honour,
His thoughts, his rhymes, his songs were all upon her.

To her he vowed the service of his days,
On her he spent the riches of his wit:
For her he made hymns of immortal praise,
Of only her he sung, he thought, he writ.
Her, and but her, of love he worthy deemed;
For all the rest but little he esteemed.

Ne her with idle words alone he wooed.
And verses vain, (yet verses are not vain,)
But with brave deeds to her sole service vowed,
And bold achievements her did entertain.
For both in deeds and words he nurt'red was,
Both wise and hardy (too hardy, alas!)

In wrestling nimble, and in running swift,
In shooting steady, and in swimming strong:
Well made to strike, to throw, to leap, to lift,
And all the sports that shepherds are among.
In every one he vanquisht every one,
He vanquisht all, and vanquisht was of none.

Besides, in hunting such felicity,
Or rather infelicity, he found,
That every field and forest far away
He sought, where savage beasts do most abound.
No beast so savage but he could it kill;
No chase so hard, but he therein had skill.

Such skill, matched with such courage as he had,
Did prick him forth with proud desire of praise

ASTROPHEL

To seek abroad, of danger nought ydrad,
His mistress' name, and his own fame to raise.
What needeth peril to be sought abroad,
Since round about us it doth make abode!

It fortunéd as he that perilous game
In foreign soil pursuéd far away,
Into a forest wide and waste he came,
Where store he heard to be of savage prey.
So wide a forest and so waste as this,
Nor famous Ardeyn, nor foul Arlo, is.

There his well-woven toils, and subtil trains,
He laid the brutish nation to enwrap:
So well he wrought with practice and with pains,
That he of them great troops did soon entrap.
Full happy man (misweening much) was he,
So rich a spoil within his power to see.

Eftsoons, all heedless of his dearest hale,
Full greedily into the herd he thrust,
To slaughter them, and work their final bale,
Lest that his toil should of their troops be brust.
Wide wounds amongst them nany one he made,
Now with his sharp boar-spear, now with his blade.

His care was all how he them all might kill,
That none might 'scape (so partial unto none):
Ill mind so much to mind another's ill,
As to become unmindful of his own.
But pardon that unto the cruel skies,
That from himself to them withdrew his eyes.

So as he raged amongst that beastly rout,
A cruel beast of most accurséd brood
Upon him turned (despair makes cowards stout,)
And, with fell tooth accustoméd to blood,
Launchéd his thigh with so mischievous might,
That it both bone and mucles rivéd quite.

So deadly was the dint and deep the wound,
And so huge streams of blood thereout did flow,
That he enduréd not the direful stound,
But on the cold dear earth himself did throw;

The whiles the captive herd his nets did rend,
And, having none to let, to wood did wend.

Ah! where were ye this while, his shepherd peers,
To whom alive was nought so dear as he:
And ye, fair maids, the matches of his years,
Which in his grace did boast you most to be!
Ah! where were ye, when he of you had need,
To stop his wound that wondrously did bleed!

Ah! wretched boy, the shape of drearihead,
And sad ensample of man's sudden end:
Full little faileth but thou shalt be dead,
Unpitiéd, unplained, of foe or friend:
Whilst none is nigh, thine eyelids up to close,
And kiss thy lips like faded leaves of rose.

A sort of shepherds, suing of the chase,
As they the forest rangéd on a day,
By fate or fortune came unto the place,
Whereas the luckless boy yet bleeding lay;
Yet bleeding lay, and yet would still have bled,
Had not good hap those shepherds thither led.

They stopped his wound, (too late to stop it was!)
And in their arms then softly did him rear:
Then (as he willed) unto his lovéd lass,
His dearest love, him dolefully did bear.
The dolefull'st bier that ever man did see,
Was Astrophel, but dearest unto me!

She, when she saw her love in such a plight,
With cruddled blood and filthy fore deformed,
That wont to be with flowers and garlands dight,
And her dear favours dearly well adorned;
Her face, the fairest face that eye mote see,
She likewise did deform, like him to be.

Her yellow locks that shone so bright and long,
As sunny beams in fairest summer's day,
She fiercely tore, and with outrageous wrong
From her red cheeks the roses rent away;
And her fair breast, the treasury of joy,
She spoiled thereof, and filléd with annoy.

His pallid face, impicturéd with death,
She bathéd oft with tears, and driéd oft:
And with sweet kisses sucked the wasting breath
Out of his lips like lilies pale and soft:
And oft she called to him, who answered nought,
But only by his looks did tell his thought.

The rest of her impatíent regret,
And piteous moan the which she for him made,
No tongue can tell, nor any forth can set,
But he whose heart like sorrow did invade.
At last, when pain his vital powers had spent,
His wasted life her weary lodge forwent.

Which when she saw, she stayéd not a whit,
But after him did make untimely haste:
Forthwith her ghost out of her corpse did flit,
And followéd her mate like turtle chaste,
To prove that Death their hearts cannot divide,
Which living were in love so firmly tied.

The gods, which all things see, this same beheld,
And, pitying this pair of lovers true,
Transforméd them, there lying on the field,
Into one flower that is both red and blue;
It first grows red, and then to blue doth fade,
Like Astrophel, which thereinto was made.

And in the midst thereof a star appears,
As fairly formed as any star in skies;
Resembling Stella in her freshest years,
Forth darting beams of beauty from her eyes:
And all the day it standeth full of deow,
Which is the tears that from her eyes did flow.

That herb of some Starlight is called by name,
Of others Penthia, though not so well:
But thou, wherever thou dost find the same,
From this day forth do call it Astrophel:
And whensoever thou it up dost take,
Do pluck it softly for that shepherd's sake.

Hereof when tidings far abroad did pass,
The shepherds all which lovéd him full dear,
And sure full dear of all he lovéd was,
Did thither flock to see what they did hear.
And when that piteous spectacle they viewed,
The same with bitter tears they all bedewed.

And every one did make exceeding moan,
With inward anguish and great grief opprest:
And every one did weep and wail, and moan,
And means devised to shew his sorrow best.
That from that hour, since first on grassy green
Shepherds kept sheep, was not like mourning seen.

But first his sister that Clorinda hight,
The gentlest shepherdess that lives this day,
And most resembling both in shape and sprite
Her brother dear, began this doleful lay.
Which, lest I mar the sweetness of the verse,
In sort as she it sung I will rehearse.

THE DOLEFUL LAY OF CLORINDA

*(These verses are supposed to have been written by Mary Countess of
Pembroke, sister to Sir Philip Sidney)*

Ay me, to whom shall I my case complain,
That may compassion my impatient grief!
Or where shall I unfold my inward pain,
That my enriven heart may find relief!
    Shall I unto the heavenly powers it show?
    Or unto earthly men that dwell below?

To heavens? ah, they alas, the authors were,
And workers of my unremédied woe:
For they foresee what to us happens here,
And they foresaw, yet suff'red this be so.
    From them comes good, from them comes also ill;
    That which they made, who can them warn to spill?

To men? ah, they alas, like wretched be,
And subject to the heavens' ordinance:
Bound to abide whatever they decree,
Their best redress is their best sufferance.
    How then can they, like wretched, comfort me,
    The which no less need comforted to be?

Then to myself will I my sorrow mourn,
Sith none alive like sorrowful remains:
And to myself my plaints shall back return,
To pay their usury with doubled pains.
    The woods, the hills, the rivers, shall resound
    The mournful accent of my sorrow's ground.

Woods, hills, and rivers, now are desolate,
Sith he is gone the which them all did grace:
And all the fields do wail their widow state,
Sith death their fairest flower did late deface.
    The fairest flower in field that ever grew,
    Was Astrophel; that was, we all may rue.

What cruel hand of cursèd foe unknown,
Hath cropt the stalk which bore so fair a flower?
Untimely cropt, before it well were grown,
And clean defacèd in untimely hour.
  Great loss to all that ever him did see,
  Great loss to all, but greatest loss to me!

Break now your garlands, O ye shepherds' lasses,
Sith the fair flower, which them adorned, is gone:
The flower, which them adorned, is gone to ashes,
Never again let lass put garland on.
  Instead of garland, wear sad cypress now,
  And bitter elder, broken from the bough.

Ne ever sing the love-lays which he made;
Who ever made such lays of love as he?
Ne ever read the riddles, which he said
Unto yourselves, to make you merry glee.
  Your merry glee is now laid all abed,
  Your merrymaker now, alas, is dead.

Death, the devourer of all world's delight,
Hath robbèd you, and reft fro me my joy:
Both you and me, and all the world he quite
Hath robbed of joyance, and left sad annoy.
  Joy of the world, and shepherds' pride was he!
  Shepherds, hope never like again to see!

O Death! thou hast us of such riches reft,
Tell us at least, what hast thou with it done?
What is become of him whose flower here left
Is but the shadow of his likeness gone?
  Scarce like the shadow of that which he was,
  Nought like, but that he like a shade did pass.

But that immortal spirit, which was deckt
With all the dowries of celestial grace,
By sovereign choice from th' heavenly quires select,
And lineally derived from angels' race,
  O! what is now of it become arede.
  Ay me! can so divine a thing be dead?

Ah! no: it is not dead, ne can it die,
But lives for aye, in blissful Paradise:
Where like a new-born babe it soft doth lie,
In bed of lilies wrapt in tender wise;

And compassed all about with roses sweet.
And dainty violets from head to feet.

There thousand birds, all of celestial brood,
To him do sweetly carol day and night;
And with strange notes, of him well understood,
Lull him asleep in angelic delight;
    Whilst in sweet dream to him presented be
    Immortal beauties, which no eye may see.

But he them sees, and takes exceeding pleasure
Of their divine aspécts, appearing plain,
And kindling love in him above all measure;
Sweet love, still joyous, never feeling pain:
    For what so goodly form he there doth see,
    He may enjoy from jealous rancour free.

There liveth he in everlasting bliss,
Sweet spirit never fearing more to die:
Ne dreading harm from any foes of his,
Ne fearing savage beasts' more cruelty.
    Whilst we here, wretches, wail his private lack,
    And with vain vows do often call him back.

But live thou there, still happy, happy spirit,
And give us leave thee here thus to lament!
Not thee that dost thy heaven's joy inherit,
But our own selves that here in dole are drent.
    Thus do we weep and wail, and wear our eyes,
    Mourning, in others, our own miseries.

WHICH when she ended had, another swain
Of gentle wit and dainty sweet device,
Whom Astrophel full dear did entertain,
Whilst here he lived, and held in passing price,
Hight Thestylis, began his mournful turn:
And made the Muses in his song to mourn.

And after him full many other mo,
As every one in order loved him best,
Gan dight themselves t' express their inward woe,
With doleful lays unto the time addrest:
The which I here in order will rehearse,
As fittest flowers to deck his mournful hearse.

AMORETTI AND EPITHALAMION

WRITTEN NOT LONG SINCE BY

EDMUND SPENSER

TO THE RIGHT WORSHIPFUL

SIR ROBERT NEEDHAM, KNIGHT

SIR, to gratulate your safe return from Ireland, I had nothing so ready, nor thought anything so meet, as these sweet conceited sonnets, the deed of that well-deserving gentleman, Master Edmund Spenser: whose name sufficiently warranting the worthiness of the work, I do more confidently presume to publish it in his absence, under your name, to whom (in my poor opinion) the patronage thereof doth in some respects properly appertain. For, besides your judgement and delight in learned poesy, this gentle Muse, for her former perfection long wished for in England, now at the length crossing the seas in your happy company, (though to yourself unknown) seemeth to make choice of you, as meetest to give her deserved countenance, after her return: entertain her, then, (right worshipful) in sort best beseeming your gentle mind, and her merit, and take in worth my good will herein, who seek no more but to shew myself yours in all dutiful affection.

W. P.

TO THE AUTHOR

Dark is the day, when Phœbus' face is shrouded,
And weaker sights may wander soon astray:
But, when they see his glorious rays unclouded,
With steady steps they keep the perfect way:
So, while this Muse in foreign lands doth stay,
Invention weeps, and pens are cast aside,
The time, like night, deprived of cheerful day;
And few do write, but (ah!) too soon may slide.
Then, hie thee home, that art our perfect guide,
And with thy wit illustrate England's fame,
Daunting thereby our neighbours' ancient pride,
That do, for poesy, challenge chiefest name:
   So we that live, and ages that succeed,
   With great applause thy learned works shall read.

G. W., SENIOR.

Ah! Colin, whether on the lowly plain,
Piping to shepherds thy sweet roundelays:
Or whether singing, in some lofty vein,
Heroic deeds of past or present days;
Or whether in thy lovely mistress' praise,
Thou list to exercise thy learned quill;
Thy Muse hath got such grace and power to please,
With rare invention, beautified by skill,
As who therein can ever joy their fill!
O! therefore let that happy Muse proceed
To climb the height of Virtue's sacred hill,
Where endless honour shall be made thy meed:
  Because no malice of succeeding days
  Can rase those records of thy lasting praise.

G. W., J<small>R</small>.

I

HAPPY ye leaves! whenas those lily hands,
Which hold my life in their dead-doing might,
Shall handle you, and hold in love's soft bands,
Like captives trembling at the victor's sight.
And happy lines! on which, with starry light,
Those lamping eyes will deign sometimes to look,
And read the sorrows of my dying sprite,
Written with tears in heart's close-bleeding book.
And happy rhymes! bathed in the sacred brook
Of Helicon, whence she derivéd is;
When ye behold that angel's blesséd look,
My soul's long-lackéd food, my heaven's bliss;
  Leaves, lines, and rhymes, seek her to please alone,
  Whom if ye please, I care for other none!

II

Unquiet thought! whom at the first I bred
Of th' inward bale of my love-pinéd heart;
And sithens have with sighs and sorrows fed,
Till greater than my womb thou woxen art:
Break forth at length out of the inner part,
In which thou lurkest like to viper's brood;
And seek some succour both to ease my smart,
And also to sustain thyself with food.
But, if in presence of that fairest proud
Thou chance to come, fall lowly at her feet;

And, with meek humblesse and afflicted mood,
Pardon for thee, and grace for me, entreat:
    Which if she grant, then live, and my love cherish:
    If not, die soon; and I with thee will perish.

III

The sovereign beauty which I do admire,
Witness the world how worthy to be praised!
The light whereof hath kindled heavenly fire
In my frail spirit, by her from baseness raised;
That, being now with her huge brightness dazed,
Base thing I can no more endure to view:
But, looking still on her, I stand amazed
At wondrous sight of so celestial hue.
So when my tongue would speak her praises due,
It stoppéd is with thought's astonishment;
And, when my pen would write her titles true,
It ravisht is with fancy's wonderment:
    Yet in my heart I then both speak and write
    The wonder that my wit cannot indite.

IV

New year, forth looking out of Janus' gate,
Doth seem to promise hope of new delight:
And, bidding th' old adieu, his passéd date
Bids all old thoughts to die in dumpish sprite:
And, calling forth out of sad winter's night
Fresh Love, that long hath slept in cheerless bower,
Wills him awake, and soon about him dight
His wanton wings and darts of deadly power.
For lusty Spring now in his timely hour
Is ready to come forth, him to receive;
And warns the earth with divers-coloured flower
To deck herself, and her fair mantle weave.
    Then you, fair flower! in whom fresh youth doth reign,
    Prepare yourself new love to entertain.

V

Rudely thou wrongest my dear heart's desire,
In finding fault with her too portly pride:
The thing which I do most in her admire,
Is of the world unworthy most envide:

For in those lofty looks is close implied
Scorn of base things, and sdeign of foul dishonour:
Threat'ning rash eyes which gaze on her so wide,
That loosely they ne dare to look upon her.
Such pride is praise, such portliness is honour,
That bold'ned innocence bears in her eyes;
And her fair countenance, like a goodly banner,
Spreads in defiance of all enemies.
   Was never in this world aught worthy tried,
     Without some spark of such self-pleasing pride.

VI

Be nought dismayed that her unmovéd mind
Doth still persist in her rebellious pride:
Such love, not like to lusts of baser kind,
The harder won, the firmer will abide.
The dureful oak, whose sap is not yet dried,
Is long ere it conceive the kindling fire;
But, when it once doth burn, it doth divide
Great heat, and makes his flames to heaven aspire.
So hard it is to kindle new desire
In gentle breast, that shall endure for ever:
Deep is the wound, that dints the parts entire
With chaste affects that naught but death can sever;
   Then think not long in taking little pain
     To knit the knot, that ever shall remain.

VII

Fair eyes! the mirror of my mazéd heart,
What wondrous virtue is contained in you,
The which both life and death forth from you dart,
Into the object of your mighty view?
For when ye mildly look with lovely hue,
Then is my soul with life and love inspired:
But when ye lower, or look on me askew,
Then do I die, as one with lightning fired.
But, since that life is more than death desired,
Look ever lovely, as becomes you best;
That your bright beams, of my weak eyes admired,
May kindle living fire within my breast.
   Such life should be the honour of your light,
   Such death the sad ensample of your might.

VIII

More than most fair, full of the living fire,
Kindled above unto the Maker near;
No eyes but joys, in which all powers conspire,
That to the world nought else be counted dear;
Through your bright beams doth not the blinded guest
Shoot out his darts to base affections wound;
But angels come to lead frail minds to rest
In chaste desires, on heavenly beauty bound.
You frame my thoughts, and fashion me within;
You stop my tongue, and teach my heart to speak;
You calm the storm that passion did begin,
Strong through your cause, but by your virtue weak.
  Dark is the world, where your light shinéd never;
  Well is he born, that may behold you ever.

IX

Long-while I sought to what I might compare
Those powerful eyes, which lighten my dark sprite;
Yet find I nought on earth, to which I dare
Resemble th' image of their goodly light.
Not to the sun: for they do shine by night;
Nor to the moon: for they are changéd never;
Nor to the stars: for they have purer sight;
Nor to the fire: for they consume not ever;
Nor to the lightning: for they still persever;
Nor to the diamond: for they are more tender;
Nor unto crystal: for nought may them sever;
Nor unto glass: such baseness mought offend her.
  Then to the Maker's self they likest be,
  Whose light doth lighten all that here we see.

X

Unrighteous Lord of Love, what law is this,
That me thou makest thus tormented be,
The whiles she lordeth in licentious bliss,
Of her free will, scorning both thee and me?
See! how the tyranness doth joy to see
The huge massacres which her eyes do make;
And humbled hearts brings captive unto thee,
That thou of them may'st mighty vengeance take.
But her proud heart do thou a little shake,
And that high look, with which she doth control

All this world's pride, bow to a baser make,
And all her faults in thy black book enrol:
    That I may laugh at her in equal sort,
      As she doth laugh at me, and makes my pain her sport.

XI

Daily when I do seek and sue for peace,
And hostages do offer for my truth;
She, cruel warrior, doth herself address
To battle, and the weary war renew'th;
Ne will be moved with reason, or with ruth,
To grant small respite to my restless toil;
But greedily her fell intent pursu'th,
Of my poor life to make unpitied spoil.
Yet my poor life, all sorrows to assoil,
I would her yield, her wrath to pacify:
But then she seeks, with torment and turmoil,
To force me live, and will not let me die.
    All pain hath end, and every war hath peace;
    But mine, no price nor prayer may surcease.

XII

One day I sought with her heart-thrilling eyes
To make a truce, and terms to entertain:
All fearless then of so false enemies,
Which sought me to entrap in treason's train.
So, as I then disarmèd did remain,
A wicked ambush which lay hidden long
In the close covert of her guileful eyen,
Thence breaking forth, did thick about me throng.
Too feeble I t' abide the brunt so strong,
Was forced to yield myself into their hands;
Who, me captiving strait with rigorous wrong,
Have ever since me kept in cruel bands.
    So, lady, now to you I do complain,
    Against your eyes, that justice I may gain.

XIII

In that proud port, which her so goodly graceth,
Whiles her fair face she rears up to the sky,
And to the ground her eyelids low embaseth,
Most goodly temperature ye may descry;

Mild humblesse, mixt with awful majesty.
For, looking on the earth whence she was born,
Her mind rememb'reth her mortality,
Whatso is fairest shall to earth return.
But that same lofty countenance seems to scorn
Base thing, and think how she to heaven may climb;
Treading down earth as loathsome and forlorn,
That hinders heavenly thoughts with drossy slime.
    Yet lowly still vouchsafe to look on me;
    Such lowliness shall make you lofty be.

XIV

Return again, my forces late dismayed,
Unto the siege by you abandoned quite.
Great shame it is to leave, like one afraid,
So fair a piece, for one repulse so light.
'Gainst such strong castles needeth greater might
Then those small forts which ye were wont belay:
Such haughty minds, inured to hardy fight,
Disdain to yield unto the first assay.
Bring therefore all the forces that ye may,
And lay incessant battery to her heart;
Plaints, prayers, vows, ruth, sorrow, and dismay;
Those engines can the proudest love convert:
    And, if those fail, fall down and die before her;
    So dying live, and living do adore her.

XV

Ye tradeful merchants, that with weary toil
Do seek most precious things to make your gain;
And both the Indias of their treasure spoil;
What needeth you to seek so far in vain?
For lo, my love doth in herself contain
All this world's riches that may far be found:
If sapphires, lo, her eyes be sapphires plain;
If rubies, lo, her lips be rubies sound;
If pearls, her teeth be pearls, both pure and round;
If ivory, her forehead ivory ween;
If gold, her locks are finest gold on ground;
If silver, her fair hands are silver sheen:
    But that which fairest is, but few behold,
    Her mind adorned with virtues manifold.

AMORETTI

XVI

One day as I unwarily did gaze
On those fair eyes, my love's immortal light;
The whiles my 'stonisht heart stood in amaze,
Through sweet illusion of her looks' delight;
I mote perceive how, in her glancing sight,
Legions of loves with little wings did fly;
Darting their deadly arrows, fiery bright,
At every rash beholder passing by.
One of those archers closely I did spy,
Aiming his arrow at my very heart:
When suddenly, with twinkle of her eye,
The damsel broke his misintended dart.
    Had she not so done, sure I had been slain,
    Yet as it was, I hardly 'scaped with pain.

XVII

The glorious portrait of that angel's face,
Made to amaze weak men's confuséd skill,
And this world's worthless glory to embase,
What pen, what pencil, can express her fill?
For though he colours could devise at will,
And eke his learned hand at pleasure guide,
Lest, trembling, it his workmanship should spill,
Yet many wondrous things there are beside:
The sweet eye-glances, that like arrows glide;
The charming smiles, that rob sense from the heart;
The lovely pleasance, and the lofty pride,
Cannot expresséd be by any art.
    A greater craftsman's hand thereto doth need,
    That can express the life of things indeed.

XVIII

The rolling wheel that runneth often round,
The hardest steel, in tract of time doth tear:
And drizzling drops, that often do redound,
The firmest flint doth in continuance wear:
Yet cannot I, with many a dropping tear
And long entreaty, soften her hard heart;
That she will once vouchsafe my plaint to hear,
Or look with pity on my painful smart;
But, when I plead, she bids me play my part;
And when I weep, she says, Tears are but water,

And when I sigh, she says, I know the art;
And when I wail, she turns herself to laughter.
  So do I weep, and wail, and plead in vain,
  Whiles she as steel and flint doth still remain.

XIX

The merry cuckoo, messenger of spring,
His trumpet shrill hath thrice already sounded,
That warns all lovers wait upon their king,
Who now is coming forth with garland crownéd.
With noise whereof the quire of birds resounded,
Their anthems sweet, deviséd of Love's praise,
That all the woods their echoes back rebounded,
As if they knew the meaning of their lays.
But 'mongst them all, which did Love's honour raise,
No word was heard of her that most it ought;
But she his precept proudly disobeys,
And doth his idle message set at nought.
  Therefore, O Love, unless she turn to thee
  Ere cuckoo end, let her rebel be!

XX

In vain I seek and sue to her for grace,
And do mine humbled heart before her pour;
The whiles her foot she in my neck doth place,
And tread my life down in the lowly flower.
And yet the lion that is lord of power,
And reigneth over every beast in field,
In his most pride disdaineth to devour
The silly lamb that to his might doth yield,
But she, more cruel, and more savage wild,
Then either lion or the lioness,
Shames not to be with guiltless blood defiled,
But taketh glory in her cruelness.
  Fairest than fairest! let none ever say,
    That ye were blooded in a yielded prey.

XXI

Was it the work of Nature or of Art,
Which temp'red so the feature of her face,
That pride and meekness, mixt by equal part,
Do both appear t' adorn her beauty's grace?

For with mild pleasance, which doth pride displace,
She to her love doth lookers' eyes allure;
And, with stern countenance, back again doth chase
Their looser looks that stir up lusts impure;
With such strange terms her eyes she doth inure,
That, with one look, she doth my life dismay;
And with another doth it straight recure;
Her smile me draws; her frown me drives away.
   Thus doth she train and teach me with her looks;
   Such art of eyes I never read in books!

XXII

This holy season, fit to fast and pray,
Men to devotion ought to be inclined:
Therefore, I likewise, on so holy day,
For my sweet saint some service fit will find.
Her temple fair is built within my mind,
In which her glorious image placéd is;
On which my thoughts do day and night attend,
Like sacred priests that never think amiss!
There I to her, as th' author of my bliss,
Will build an altar to appease her ire;
And on the same my heart will sacrifice,
Burning in flames of pure and chaste desire:
   The which vouchsafe, O goddess, to accept,
   Amongst thy dearest relics to be kept.

XXIII

Penelope, for her Ulysses' sake,
Devised a web her wooers to deceive;
In which the work that she all day did make,
The same at night she did again unreave:
Such subtil craft my damsel doth conceive,
Th' importune suit of my desire to shun:
For all that I in many days do weave,
In one short hour I find by her undone.
So, when I think to end that I begun,
I must begin and never bring to end:
For with one look she spills that long I spun;
And with one word my whole year's work doth rend
   Such labour like the spider's web I find,
   Whose fruitless work is broken with least wind.

XXIV

When I behold that beauty's wonderment,
And rare perfection of each goodly part;
Of Nature's skill the only complement;
I honour and admire the Maker's art.
But when I feel the bitter baleful smart,
Which her fair eyes unwares do work in me,
That death out of their shiny beams do dart;
I think that I a new Pandora see,
Whom all the gods in counsel did agree
Into this sinful world from heaven to send;
That she to wicked men a scourge should be,
For all their faults with which they did offend.
    But, since ye are my scourge, I will entreat,
    That for my faults ye will me gently beat.

XXV

How long shall this like dying life endure,
And know no end of her own misery,
But waste and wear away in terms unsure,
'Twixt fear and hope depending doubtfully!
Yet better were at once to let me die,
And shew the last ensample of your pride;
Than to torment me thus with cruelty,
To prove your power, which I too well have tried.
But yet if in your hard'ned breast ye hide
A close intent at last to shew me grace,
Then all the woes and wrecks which I abide,
As means of bliss I gladly will embrace;
    And wish that more and greater they might be,
    That greater meed at last may turn to me.

XXVI

Sweet is the rose, but grows upon a brere;
Sweet is the juniper, but sharp his bough;
Sweet is the eglantine, but pricketh near;
Sweet is the fir-bloom, but his branch is rough;
Sweet is the cypress, but his rind is tough;
Sweet is the nut, but bitter is his pill;
Sweet is the broom-flower, but yet sour enough:
And sweet is moly, but his root is ill.
So every sweet with sour is temp'red still,
That maketh it be coveted the more:

For easy things, that may be got at will,
Most sorts of men do set but little store.
    Why then should I account of little pain,
    That endless pleasure shall unto me gain!

XXVII

Fair proud! now tell me, why should fair be proud,
Sith all world's glory is but dross unclean,
And in the shade of death itself shall shroud,
However now thereof ye little ween!
That goodly idol, now so gay beseen,
Shall doff her flesh's borrowed fair attire,
And be forgot as it had never been;
That many now much worship and admire!
Ne any then shall after it inquire,
Ne any mention shall thereof remain,
But what this verse, that never shall expire,
Shall to you purchase with her thankless pain!
    Fair! be no longer proud of that shall perish;
    But that, which shall you make immortal, cherish.

XXVIII

The laurel-leaf, which you this day do wear,
Gives me great hope of your relenting mind:
For since it is the badge which I do bear,
Ye, bearing it, do seem to me inclined:
The power thereof, which oft in me I find,
Let it likewise your gentle breast inspire
With sweet infusion, and put you in mind
Of that proud maid, whom now those leaves attire:
Proud Daphne, scorning Phœbus' lovely fire,
On the Thessalian shore from him did fly:
For which the gods, in their revengeful ire,
Did her transform into a laurel-tree.
    Then fly no more, fair love, from Phœbus' chase,
    But in your breast his leaf and love embrace.

XXIX

See! how the stubborn damsel doth deprave
My simple meaning with disdainful scorn;
And by the bay, which I unto her gave,
Accounts myself her captive quite forlorn.

The bay (quoth she) is of the victors borne,
Yielded them by the vanquisht as their meeds,
And they therewith do poets' heads adorn,
To sing the glory of their famous deeds.
But sith she will the conquest challenge needs,
Let her accept me as her faithful thrall;
That her great triumph, which my skill exceeds,
I may in trump of fame blaze over-all.
   Then would I deck her head with glorious bays,
   And fill the world with her victorious praise.

XXX

My love is like to ice, and I to fire;
How comes it then that this her cold so great
Is not dissolved through my so hot desire,
But harder grows the more I her entreat!
Or how comes it that my exceeding heat
Is not delayed by her heart-frozen cold;
But that I burn much more in boiling sweat,
And feel my flames augmented manifold!
What more miraculous thing may be told,
That fire, which all things melts, should harden ice;
And ice, which is congealed with senseless cold,
Should kindle fire by wonderful device!
   Such is the power of love in gentle mind,
   That it can alter all the course of kind.

XXXI

Ah! why hath Nature to so hard a heart
Given so goodly gifts of beauty's grace!
Whose pride depraves each other better part,
And all those precious ornaments deface.
Sith to all other beasts of bloody race
A dreadful countenance she given hath;
That with their terror all the rest may chase,
And warn to shun the danger of their wrath.
But my proud one doth work the greater scath,
Through sweet allurement of her lovely hue;
That she the better may in bloody bath
Of such poor thralls her cruel hands imbrue.
   But, did she know how ill these two accord,
   Such cruelty she would have soon abhorred.

AMORETTI

XXXII

The painful smith, with force of fervent heat,
The hardest iron soon doth mollify;
That with his heavy sledge he can it beat,
And fashion to what he it list apply.
Yet cannot all these flames, in which I fry,
Her heart more hard than iron soft a whit:
Ne all the plaints and prayers, with which I
Do beat on th' anvil of her stubborn wit.
But still, the more she fervent sees my fit,
The more she freezeth in her wilful pride;
And harder grows, the harder she is smit
With all the plaints which to her be applied.
  What then remains but I to ashes burn,
  And she to stones at length all frozen turn!

XXXIII

Great wrong I do, I can it not deny,
To that most sacred empress, my dear dread,
Not finishing her *Queen of Faëry*,
That mote enlarge her living praises, dead.
But Lod'wick, this of grace to me arede:
Do ye not think th' accomplishment of it
Sufficient work for one man's simple head,
All were it, as the rest, but rudely writ?
How then should I, without another wit,
Think ever to endure so tedious toil!
Since that this one is tost with troublous fit
Of a proud love, that doth my spirit spoil.
  Cease then, till she vouchsafe to grant me rest;
  Or lend you me another living breast.

XXXIV

Like as a ship, that through the ocean wide,
By conduct of some star, doth make her way,
Whenas a storm hath dimmed her trusty guide,
Out of her course doth wander far astray:
So I, whose star, that wont with her bright ray
Me to direct, with clouds is overcast,
Do wander now, in darkness and dismay,
Through hidden perils round about me placed;
Yet hope I well that, when this storm is past,
My Helice, the loadstar of my life,

Will shine again, and look on me at last,
With lovely light to clear my cloudy grief.
   Till then I wander careful, comfortless,
   In secret sorrow, and sad pensiveness.

XXXV

My hungry eyes, through greedy covetise
Still to behold the object of their pain,
With no contentment can themselves suffice;
But, having, pine; and, having not, complain.
For, lacking it, they cannot life sustain;
And, having it, they gaze on it the more;
In their amazement like Narcissus vain,
Whose eyes him starved: so plenty makes me poor.
Yet are mine eyes so filléd with the store
Of that fair sight, that nothing else they brook,
But loathe the things which they did like before,
And can no more endure on them to look.
   All this world's glory seemeth vain to me,
   And all their shows but shadows, saving she.

XXXVI

Tell me, when shall these weary woes have end?
Or shall their ruthless torment never cease,
But all my days in pining languor spend,
Without hope of assuagement or release?
Is there no means for me to purchase peace,
Or make agreement with her thrilling eyes,
But that their cruelty doth still increase,
And daily more augment my miseries?
But, when ye have shewed all extremities,
Then think how little glory ye have gained
By slaying him, whose life, though ye despise,
Mote have your life in honour long maintained.
   But by his death, which some perhaps will moan,
   Ye shall condemnéd be of many a one.

XXXVII

What guile is this, that those her golden tresses
She doth attire under a net of gold;
And with sly skill so cunningly them dresses,
That which is gold, or hair, may scarce be told?

Is it that men's frail eyes, which gaze too bold,
She may entangle in that golden snare;
And, being caught, may craftily enfold
Their weaker hearts, which are not well aware?
Take heed, therefore, mine eyes, how ye do stare
Henceforth too rashly on that guileful net,
In which, if ever ye entrappéd are,
Out of her bands ye by no means shall get.
    Fondness it were for any, being free,
      To covet fetters, though they golden be!

XXXVIII

Arion, when, through tempest's cruel wrack,
He forth was thrown into the greedy seas;
Through the sweet music, which his harp did make,
Allured a dolphin him from death to ease.
But my rude music, which was wont to please
Some dainty ears, cannot, with any skill,
The dreadful tempest of her wrath appease,
Nor move the dolphin from her stubborn will,
But in her pride she doth persever still.
All careless how my life for her decays:
Yet with one word she can it save or spill.
To spill were pity, but to save were praise!
    Choose rather to be praised for doing good,
      Than to be blamed for spilling guiltless blood.

XXXIX

Sweet smile! the daughter of the Queen of Love,
Expressing all thy mother's powerful art,
With which she wonts to temper angry Jove,
When all the gods he threats with thund'ring dart:
Sweet is thy virtue, as thyself sweet art.
For, when on me thou shinedst late in sadness,
A melting pleasance ran through every part,
And me revivéd with heart-robbing gladness.
Whilst rapt with joy resembling heavenly madness,
My soul was ravisht quite as in a trance;
And feeling thence no more her sorrow's sadness,
Fed on the fullness of that cheerful glance,
    More sweet than nectar, or ambrosial meat,
      Seemed every bit which thenceforth I did eat.

XL

Mark when she smiles with amiable cheer,
And tell me whereto can ye liken it;
When on each eyelid sweetly do appear
An hundred graces as in shade to sit.
Likest it seemeth, in my simple wit,
Unto the fair sunshine in summer's day;
That, when a dreadful storm away is flit,
Through the broad world doth spread his goodly ray;
At sight whereof, each bird that sits on spray,
And every beast that to his den was fled,
Comes forth afresh out of their late dismay,
And to the light lift up their drooping head.
  So my storm-beaten heart likewise is cheered
    With that sunshine, when cloudy looks are cleared.

XLI

Is it her nature, or is it her will,
To be so cruel to an humbled foe?
If nature, then she may it mend with skill:
If will, then she at will may will forgo.
But if her nature and her will be so,
That she will plague the man that loves her most,
And take delight t' increase a wretch's woe;
Then all her nature's goodly gifts are lost:
And that same glorious beauty's idle boast
Is but a bait such wretches to beguile,
As, being long in her love's tempest tost,
She means at last to make her piteous spoil.
  O fairest fair! let never it be named,
    That so fair beauty was so foully shamed.

XLII

The love which me so cruelly tormenteth,
So pleasing is in my extremest pain,
That, all the more my sorrow it augmenteth,
The more I love and do embrace my bane.
Ne do I wish (for wishing were but vain)
To be acquit fro my continual smart;
But joy, her thrall for ever to remain,
And yield for pledge my poor captivéd heart;
The which, that it from her may never start,
Let her, if please her, bind with adamant chain:

And from all wand'ring loves, which mote pervart
His safe assurance, strongly it restrain.
   Only let her abstain from cruelty,
   And do me not before my time to die.

XLIII

Shall I then silent be, or shall I speak?
And, if I speak, her wrath renew I shall;
And, if I silent be, my heart will break,
Or chokéd be with overflowing gall.
What tyranny is this, both my heart to thrall,
And eke my tongue with proud restraint to tie;
That neither I may speak nor think at all,
But like a stupid stock in silence die!
Yet I my heart with silence secretly
Will teach to speak, and my just cause to plead;
And eke mine eyes, with meek humility,
Love-learned letters to her eyes to read;
   Which her deep wit, that true heart's thought can spell,
   Will soon conceive, and learn to construe well.

XLIV

When those renownéd noble peers of Greece,
Through stubborn pride, amongst themselves did jar,
Forgetful of the famous golden fleece;
Then Orpheus with his harp their strife did bar.
But this continual, cruel, civil war,
The which myself against myself do make;
Whilst my weak powers of passions warreyed are;
No skill can stint, nor reason can aslake.
But, when in hand my tuneless harp I take,
Then do I more augment my foes' despight;
And grief renew, and passions do awake
To battle, fresh against myself to fight,
   'Mongst whom the more I seek to settle peace,
   The more I find their malice to increase.

XLV

Leave, lady! in your glass of crystal clean,
Your goodly self for evermore to view:
And in myself, my inward self, I mean,
Most lively-like behold your semblant true.

Within my heart, though hardly it can shew
Thing so divine to view of earthly eye,
The fair Idea of your celestial hue,
And every part remains immortally:
And were it not that, through your cruelty,
With sorrow dimméd and deformed it were,
The goodly image of your visnomy,
Clearer than crystal, would therein appear.
   But, if yourself in me ye plain will see,
   Remove the cause by which your fair beams dark'ned be.

XLVI

When my abode's prefixéd time is spent,
My cruel fair straight bids me wend my way:
But then from heaven most hideous storms are sent,
As willing me against her will to stay.
Whom then shall I, or heaven or her, obey?
The heavens know best what is the best for me:
But as she will, whose will my life doth sway,
My lower heaven, so it perforce must be.
But ye high heavens, that all this sorrow see,
Sith all your tempests cannot hold me back,
Assuage your storms; or else both you, and she,
Will both together me too sorely wrack.
   Enough it is for one man to sustain
   The storms, which she alone on me doth rain.

XLVII

Trust not the treason of those smiling looks,
Until ye have their guileful trains well tried;
For they are like but unto golden hooks,
That from the foolish fish their baits do hide:
So she with flatt'ring smiles weak hearts doth guide
Unto her love, and tempt to their decay;
Whom, being caught, she kills with cruel pride,
And feeds at pleasure on the wretched prey:
Yet, even whilst her bloody hands them slay,
Her eyes look lovely, and upon them smile;
That they take pleasure in her cruel play,
And, dying, do themselves of pain beguile.
   O mighty charm! which makes men love their bane,
   And think they die with pleasure, live with pain.

AMORETTI

XLVIII

Innocent paper, whom too cruel hand
Did make the matter to avenge her ire:
And, ere she could thy cause well understand,
Did sacrifice unto the greedy fire.
Well worthy thou to have found better hire,
Than so bad end for heretics ordained;
Yet heresy nor treason didst conspire,
But plead thy master's cause, unjustly pained.
Whom she, all careless of his grief, constrained
To utter forth the anguish of his heart:
And would not hear, when he to her complained
The piteous passion of his dying smart.
    Yet live for ever, though against her will,
    And speak her good, though she requite it ill.

XLIX

Fair cruel! why are ye so fierce and cruel?
Is it because your eyes have power to kill?
Then know that mercy is the mighty's jewel:
And greater glory think, to save than spill.
But if it be your pleasure, and proud will,
To shew the power of your imperious eyes;
Then not on him that never thought you ill,
But bend your force against your enemies.
Let them feel the utmost of your cruelties;
And kill with looks as cockatrices do:
But him, that at your foot-stool humbled lies,
With merciful regard give mercy to.
    Such mercy shall you make admired to be;
    So shall you live, by giving life to me.

L

Long languishing in double malady
Of my heart's wound, and of my body's grief;
There came to me a leech, that would apply
Fit medicines for my body's best relief.
Vain man, quoth I, that hast but little prief
In deep discovery of the mind's disease;
Is not the heart of all the body chief,
And rules the members as itself doth please?
Then, with some cordials, seek first to appease
The inward languor of my wounded heart,

And then my body shall have shortly ease:
But such sweet cordials pass physician's art.
　Then, my life's leech! do your skill reveal;
　And, with one salve, both heart and body heal.

LI

Do I not see that fairest images
Of hardest marble are of purpose made,
For that they should endure through many ages,
Ne let their famous monuments to fade?
Why then do I, untrained in lover's trade,
Her hardness blame, which I should more commend?
Sith never aught was excellent assayed
Which was not hard t' achieve and bring to end.
Ne aught so hard, but he, that would attend,
Mote soften it and to his will allure:
So do I hope her stubborn heart to bend,
And that it then more steadfast will endure:
　Only my pains will be the more to get her,
　But having her, my joy will be the greater.

LII

So oft as homeward I from her depart,
I go like one that having lost the field,
Is prisoner led away with heavy heart,
Despoiled of warlike arms and knowen shield.
So do I now myself a prisoner yield
To sorrow and to solitary pain;
From presence of my dearest dear exiled,
Long-while alone in languor to remain.
There let no thought of joy, or pleasure vain,
Dare to approach, that may my solace breed;
But sudden dumps, and dreary sad disdain
Of all world's gladness, more my torment feed.
　So I her absence will my penance make,
　That of her presence I my meed may take.

LIII

The panther, knowing that his spotted hide
Doth please all beasts, but that his looks them fray;
Within a bush his dreadful head doth hide,
To let them gaze, whilst he on them may prey:

Right so my cruel fair with me doth play;
For, with the goodly semblant of her hue,
She doth allure me to mine own decay,
And then no mercy will unto me shew.
Great shame it is, thing so divine in view,
Made for to be the world's most ornament,
To make the bait her gazers to imbrue;
Good shames to be so ill an instrument!
  But mercy doth with beauty best agree,
  As in their Maker ye them best may see.

LIV

Of this world's theatre in which we stay,
My love, like the spectator, idly sits;
Beholding me, that all the pageants play,
Disguising diversly my troubled wits.
Sometimes I joy when glad occasion fits,
And mask in mirth like to a comedy:
Soon after, when my joy to sorrow flits,
I wail, and make my woes a tragedy.
Yet she, beholding me with constant eye,
Delights not in my mirth, nor rues my smart:
But when I laugh, she mocks; and when I cry,
She laughs, and hardens evermore her heart.
  What then can move her? if nor mirth nor moan,
  She is no woman, but a senseless stone.

LV

So oft as I her beauty do behold,
And therewith do her cruelty compare,
I marvel of what substance was the mould,
The which her made at once so cruel fair.
Not earth, for her high thoughts more heavenly are:
Not water, for her love doth burn like fire:
Not air, for she is not so light or rare:
Not fire, for she doth freeze with faint desire.
Then needs another element inquire
Whereof she mote be made; that is, the sky.
For to the heaven her haughty looks aspire:
And eke her mind is pure immortal high.
  Then, sith to heaven ye likened are the best,
  Be like in mercy as in all the rest.

LVI

Fair ye be sure, but cruel and unkind,
As is a tiger, that with greediness
Hunts after blood; when he by chance doth find
A feeble beast, doth felly him oppress.
Fair be ye sure, but proud and pitiless,
As is a storm, that all things doth prostrate;
Finding a tree alone all comfortless,
Beats on it strongly, it to ruinate.
Fair be ye sure, but hard and obstinate,
As is a rock amidst the raging floods:
'Gainst which, a ship, of succour desolate,
Doth suffer wreck both of herself and goods.
    That ship, that tree, and that same beast, am I,
    Whom ye do wreck, do ruin, and destroy.

LVII

Sweet warrior! when shall I have peace with you?
High time it is this war now ended were
Which I no longer can endure to sue,
Ne your incessant batt'ry more to bear:
So weak my powers, so sore my wounds appear,
That wonder is how I should live a jot,
Seeing my heart through-launchéd everywhere
With thousand arrows, which your eyes have shot:
Yet shoot ye sharply still, and spare me not,
But glory think to make these cruel stours.
Ye cruel one! what glory can be got,
In slaying him that would live gladly yours?
    Make peace therefore, and grant me timely grace,
    That all my wounds will heal in little space.

LVIII

By her that is most assured to herself

Weak is th' assurance that weak flesh reposeth
In her own power, and scorneth others' aid;
That soonest falls, whenas she most supposeth
Herself assured, and is of nought afraid.
All flesh is frail, and all her strength unstayed,
Like a vain bubble blowen up with air:
Devouring time and changeful chance have preyed,

Her glory's pride that none may it repair.
Ne none so rich or wise, so strong or fair,
But faileth, trusting on his own assurance;
And he, that standeth on the highest stair,
Falls lowest; for on earth nought hath endurance.
  Why then do ye, proud fair, misdeem so far,
  That to yourself ye most assuréd are!

LIX

Thrice happy she! that is so well assured
Unto herself, and settled so in heart,
That neither will for better be allured,
Ne feared with worse to any chance to start;
But, like a steady ship, doth strongly part
The raging waves, and keeps her course aright;
Ne aught for tempest doth from it depart,
Ne aught for fairer weather's false delight.
Such self-assurance need not fear the spite
Of grudging foes, ne favour seek of friends:
But, in the stay of her own steadfast might,
Neither to one herself nor other bends.
  Most happy she, that most assured doth rest;
  But he most happy, who such one loves best.

LX

They, that in course of heavenly spheres are skilled,
To every planet point his sundry year:
In which her circle's voyage is fulfilled,
As Mars in three-score years doth run his sphere.
So, since the wingéd god his planet clear
Began in me to move, one year is spent:
The which doth longer unto me appear
Then all those forty which my life out-went.
Than by that count, which lovers' books invent,
The sphere of Cupid forty years contains:
Which I have wasted in long languishment,
That seemed the longer for my greater pains.
  But let my love's fair planet short her ways,
  This year ensuing, or else short my days.

LXI

The glorious image of the Maker's beauty,
My sovereign saint, the idol of my thought,
Dare not henceforth, above the bounds of duty,

T' accuse of pride, or rashly blame for aught.
For being as she is, divinely wrought,
And of the brood of angels heavenly born;
And with the crew of blessed saints upbrought,
Each of which did her with their gifts adorn;
The bud of joy, the blossom of the morn,
The beam of light, whom mortal eyes admire;
What reason is it then but she should scorn
Base things, that to her love too bold aspire!
  Such heavenly forms ought rather worshipt be
  Than dare be loved by men of mean degree.

LXII

The weary year his race now having run,
The new begins his compassed course anew:
With shew of morning mild he hath begun,
Betokening peace and plenty to ensue.
So let us, which this change of weather view,
Change eke our minds, and former lives amend;
The old year's sins forepast let us eschew,
And fly the faults with which we did offend.
Then shall the new year's joy forth freshly send
Into the glooming world his gladsome ray:
And all these storms, which now his beauty blend,
Shall turn to calms, and timely clear away.
  So likewise, love! cheer you your heavy sprite,
  And change old year's annoy to new delight.

LXIII

After long storms and tempests' sad assay,
Which hardly I enduréd heretofore,
In dread of death, and dangerous dismay,
With which my silly bark was tosséd sore:
I do at length descry the happy shore,
In which I hope ere long for to arrive:
Fair soil it seems from far, and fraught with store
Of all that dear and dainty is alive.
Most happy he! that can at last achieve
The joyous safety of so sweet a rest;
Whose least delight sufficeth to deprive
Remembrance of all pains which him opprest.
  All pains are nothing in respect of this;
  All sorrows short that gain eternal bliss.

LXIV

Coming to kiss her lips, (such grace I found,)
Meseemed, I smelt a garden of sweet flowers,
That dainty odours from them threw around,
For damsels fit to deck their lovers' bowers.
Her lips did smell like unto gillyflowers;
Her ruddy cheeks like unto roses red;
Her snowy brows like budded bellamoures;
Her lovely eyes like pinks but newly spread;
Her goodly bosom like a strawberry bed;
Her neck like to a bunch of columbines;
Her breast like lilies, ere their leaves be shed;
Her nipples like young blossomed jessamines:
    Such fragrant flowers do give most odorous smell;
    But her sweet odour did them all excel.

LXV

The doubt which ye misdeem, fair love, is vain,
That fondly fear to lose your liberty;
When, losing one, two liberties ye gain,
And make him bond that bondage erst did fly.
Sweet be the bands, the which true love doth tie
Without constraint, or dread of any ill:
The gentle bird feels no captivity
Within her cage: but sings, and feeds her fill.
There pride dare not approach, nor discord spill
The league 'twixt them, that loyal love hath bound:
But simple truth, and mutual good-will,
Seeks with sweet peace to salve each other's wound:
    There faith doth fearless dwell in brazen tower,
    And spotless pleasure builds her sacred bower.

LXVI

To all those happy blessings, which ye have
With plenteous hand by heaven upon you thrown,
This one disparagement they to you gave,
That ye your love lent to so mean a one.
Ye, whose high worth's surpassing paragon
Could not on earth have found one fit for mate,
Ne but in heaven matchable to none,
Why did ye stoop unto so lowly state?
But ye thereby much greater glory gate,
Than had ye sorted with a prince's peer:

For now your light doth more itself dilate,
And in my darkness greater doth appear.
    Yet since your light hath once enlumined me,
    With my reflex yours shall increaséd be.

LXVII

Like as a huntsman after weary chase,
Seeing the game from him escaped away,
Sits down to rest him in some shady place,
With panting hounds beguiléd of their prey:
So, after long pursuit and vain assay,
When I all weary had the chase forsook,
The gentle deer returned the self-same way,
Thinking to quench her thirst at the next brook:
There she, beholding me with milder look,
Sought not to fly, but fearless still did bide;
Till I in hand her yet half trembling took,
And with her own good-will her firmly tied.
    Strange thing, meseemed, to see a beast so wild,
    So goodly won, with her own will beguiled.

LXVIII

Most glorious Lord of life! that, on this day,
Didst make Thy triumph over death and sin;
And, having harrowed hell, didst bring away
Captivity thence captive, us to win:
This joyous day, dear Lord, with joy begin;
And grant that we, for whom Thou diddest die,
Being with Thy dear blood clean washed from sin,
May live for ever in felicity!
And that Thy love we weighing worthily,
May likewise love Thee for the same again;
And for Thy sake, that all like dear didst buy,
With love may one another entertain!
    So let us love, dear love, like as we ought:
    Love is the lesson which the Lord us taught.

LXIX

The famous warriors of antique world
Used trophies to erect in stately wise;
In which they would the records have enrolled
Of their great deeds and valorous emprize.

AMORETTI

What trophy then shall I most fit devise,
In which I may record the memory
Of my love's conquest, peerless beauty's prize,
Adorned with honour, love, and chastity!
Even this verse, vowed to eternity,
Shall be thereof immortal monument;
And tell her praise to all posterity,
That may admire such world's rare wonderment;
   The happy purchase of my glorious spoil,
   Gotten at last with labour and long toil.

LXX

Fresh spring, the herald of love's mighty king,
In whose coat-armour richly are displayed
All sorts of flowers, the which on earth do spring,
In goodly colours gloriously arrayed;
Go to my love, where she is careless laid,
Yet in her winter's bower not well awake;
Tell her the joyous time will not be stayed,
Unless she do him by the forelock take;
Bid her therefore herself soon ready make,
To wait on Love amongst his lovely crew;
Where every one, that misseth then her make,
Shall be by him amerced with penance due.
   Make haste, therefore, sweet love, whilst it is prime;
   For none can call again the passéd time.

LXXI

I joy to see how, in your drawen work,
Yourself unto the bee ye do compare;
And me unto the spider, that doth lurk
In close await, to catch her unaware:
Right so yourself were caught in cunning snare
Of a dear foe, and thralléd to his love;
In whose strait bands ye now captivéd are
So firmly, that ye never may remove.
But as your work is woven all above
With woodbind flowers and fragrant eglantine,
So sweet your prison you in time shall prove,
With many dear delights bedeckéd fine.
   And all thenceforth eternal peace shall see
   Between the spider and the gentle bee.

LXXII

Oft, when my spirit doth spread her bolder wings,
In mind to mount up to the purest sky;
It down is weighed with thought of earthly things,
And clogged with burden of mortality;
Where, when that sovereign beauty it doth spy,
Resembling heaven's glory in her light,
Drawn with sweet pleasure's bait, it back doth fly,
And unto heaven forgets her former flight.
There my frail fancy, fed with full delight,
Doth bathe in bliss, and mantleth most at ease;
Ne thinks of other heaven, but how it might
Her heart's desire with most contentment please.
    Heart need not wish none other happiness,
    But here on earth to have such heaven's bliss.

LXXIII

Being myself captivéd here in care,
My heart, (whom none with servile bands can tie,
But the fair tresses of your golden hair,)
Breaking his prison, forth to you doth fly.
Like as a bird, that in one's hand doth spy
Desiréd food, to it doth make his flight:
Even so my heart, that wont on your fair eye
To feed his fill, flies back unto your sight.
Do you him take, and in your bosom bright
Gently encage, that he may be your thrall:
Perhaps he there may learn, with rare delight,
To sing your name and praises over-all:
    That it hereafter may you not repent,
    Him lodging in your bosom to have lent.

LXXIV

Most happy letters! framed by skilful trade,
With which that happy name was first designed,
The which three times thrice happy hath me made,
With gifts of body, fortune, and of mind.
The first my being to me gave by kind,
From mother's womb derived by due descent:
The second is my sovereign queen most kind,
That honour and large richesse to me lent:
The third, my love, my life's last ornament,
By whom my spirit out of dust was raised:

To speak her praise and glory excellent,
Of all alive most worthy to be praised.
  Ye three Elizabeths! for ever live,
  That three such graces did unto me give.

LXXV

One day I wrote her name upon the strand;
But came the waves, and washéd it away:
Again, I wrote it with a second hand;
But came the tide, and made my pains his prey.
Vain man, said she, that dost in vain assay
A mortal thing so to immortalize;
For I myself shall like to this decay,
And eke my name be wipéd out likewise.
Not so, quoth I; let baser things devise
To die in dust, but you shall live by fame:
My verse your virtues rare shall eternize,
And in the heavens write your glorious name.
  Where, whenas death shall all the world subdue,
  Our love shall live, and later life renew.

LXXVI

Fair bosom! fraught with virtue's richest treasure,
The nest of love, the lodging of delight,
The bower of bliss. the paradise of pleasure,
The sacred harbour of that heavenly sprite;
How was I ravisht with your lovely sight,
And my frail thoughts too rashly led astray!
Whiles diving deep through amorous insight,
On the sweet spoil of beauty they did prey;
And 'twixt her paps (like early fruit in May,
Whose harvest seemed to hasten now apace)
They loosely did their wanton wings display,
And there to rest themselves did boldly place.
  Sweet thoughts! I envy your so happy rest,
  Which oft I wished, yet never was so blest.

LXXVII

Was it a dream, or did I see it plain?
A goodly table of pure ivory,
All spread with junkets, fit to entertain
The greatest prince with pompous royalty:

'Mongst which, there in a silver dish did lie
Two golden apples of unvalued price;
Far passing those which Hercules came by,
Or those which Atalanta did entice.
Exceeding sweet, yet void of sinful vice;
That many sought, yet none could ever taste;
Sweet fruit of pleasure, brought from Paradise
By Love himself, and in his garden placed.
    Her breast that table was, so richly spread;
    My thoughts the guests, which would thereon have fed.

LXXVIII

Lacking my love, I go from place to place,
Like a young fawn, that late hath lost the hind;
And seek eachwhere, where last I saw her face,
Whose image yet I carry fresh in mind.
I seek the fields with her late footing signed;
I seek her bower with her late presence deckt,
Yet nor in field nor bower I her can find;
Yet field and bower are full of her aspéct:
But, when mine eyes I thereunto direct,
They idly back return to me again:
And, when I hope to see their true objéct,
I find myself but fed with fancies vain.
    Cease then, mine eyes, to seek herself to see;
    And let my thoughts behold herself in me.

LXXIX

Men call you fair, and you do credit it,
For that yourself ye daily such do see:
But the true fair, that is the gentle wit,
And virtuous mind, is much more praised of me:
For all the rest, however fair it be,
Shall turn to nought and lose that glorious hue;
But only that is permanent and free
From frail corruption, that doth flesh ensue.
That is true beauty: that doth argue you
To be divine, and born of heavenly seed;
Derived from that fair Spirit, from whom all true
And perfect beauty did at first proceed:
    He only fair, and what he fair hath made;
    All other fair, like flowers, untimely fade.

AMORETTI

LXXX

After so long a race as I have run
Through faeryland, which those six books compile,
Give leave to rest me being half fordone,
And gather to myself new breath awhile.
Then, as a steed refreshéd after toil,
Out of my prison I will break anew;
And stoutly will that second work assoil,
With strong endeavour and attention due.
Till then give leave to me, in pleasant mew
To sport my Muse, and sing my love's sweet praise;
The contemplation of whose heavenly hue,
My spirit to an higher pitch will raise.
  But let her praises yet be low and mean,
  Fit for the handmaid of the Faery Queen.

LXXXI

Fair is my love, when her fair golden hairs
With the loose wind ye waving chance to mark;
Fair, when the rose in her red cheeks appears;
Or in her eyes the fire of love does spark.
Fair, when her breast, like a rich-laden bark,
With precious merchandise she forth doth lay;
Fair, when that cloud of pride, which oft doth dark
Her goodly light, with smiles she drives away.
But fairest she, whenso she doth display
The gate with pearls and rubies richly dight,
Through which her words so wise do make their way
To bear the message of her gentle sprite.
  The rest be works of nature's wonderment:
  But this the work of heart's astonishment.

LXXXII

Joy of my life! full oft for loving you
I bless my lot, that was so lucky placed:
But then the more your own mishap I rue,
That are so much by so mean love embased.
For, had the equal heavens so much you graced
In this as in the rest, ye mote invent
Some heavenly wit, whose verse could have enchased
Your glorious name in golden monument.
But since ye deigned so goodly to relent
To me your thrall, in whom is little worth,

That little, that I am, shall all be spent
In setting your immortal praises forth:
   Whose lofty argument, uplifting me,
   Shall lift you up unto an high degree.

LXXXIII

Let not one spark of filthy lustful fire
Break out, that may her sacred peace molest;
Ne one light glance of sensual desire
Attempt to work her gentle mind's unrest:
But pure affections bred in spotless breast,
And modest thoughts breathed from well-temp'red sprites,
Go visit her in her chaste bower of rest
Accompanied with angelic delights.
There fill yourself with those most joyous sights,
The which myself could never yet attain;
But speak no word to her of these sad plights,
Which her too constant stiffness doth constrain.
   Only behold her rare perfection,
   And bless your fortune's fair election.

LXXXIV

The world that cannot deem of worthy things,
When I do praise her, say I do but flatter:
So does the cuckoo, when the mavis sings,
Begin his witless note apace to clatter.
But they that skill not of so heavenly matter,
All that they know not envy or admire;
Rather than envy, let them wonder at her,
But not to deem of her desert aspire.
Deep in the closet of my parts entire,
Her worth is written with a golden quill,
That me with heavenly fury doth inspire,
And my glad mouth with her sweet praises fill.
   Which whenas Fame in her shrill trump shall thunder,
   Let the world choose to envy or to wonder.

LXXXV

Venomous tongue, tipt with vile adder's sting,
Of that self kind with which the Furies fell
Their snaky heads do comb, from which a spring
Of poisoned words and spiteful speeches well;

Let all the plagues and horrid pains of hell
Upon thee fall for thine accursèd hire:
That with false forgéd lies, which thou didst tell,
In my true love did stir up coals of ire,
The sparks whereof let kindle thine own fire,
And, catching hold on thine own wicked head,
Consume thee quite, that didst with guile conspire
In my sweet peace such breaches to have bred!
   Shame be thy meed, and mischief thy reward,
   Due to thyself, that it for me prepared!

LXXXVI

Since I did leave the presence of my love,
Many long weary days I have outworn;
And many nights, that slowly seemed to move
Their sad protract from evening until morn.
For, whenas day the heaven doth adorn,
I wish that night the noyous day would end:
And, whenas night hath us of light forlorn,
I wish that day would shortly reascend.
Thus I the time with expectation spend,
And feign my grief with changes to beguile,
That further seems his term still to extend,
And maketh every minute seem a mile.
   So sorrow still doth seem too long to last;
   But joyous hours do fly away too fast.

LXXXVII

Since I have lackt the comfort of that light,
The which was wont to lead my thoughts astray;
I wander as in darkness of the night,
Afraid of every danger's least dismay.
Ne aught I see, though in the clearest day,
When others gaze upon their shadows vain,
But th' only image of that heavenly ray,
Whereof some glance doth in mine eye remain.
Of which beholding the Idea plain,
Through contemplation of my purest part,
With light thereof I do myself sustain,
And thereon feed my love-affamisht heart.
   But, with such brightness whilst I fill my mind,
   I starve my body, and mine eyes do blind.

AMORETTI

LXXXVIII

Like as the culver, on the baréd bough,
Sits mourning for the absence of her mate;
And, in her songs, sends many a wishful vow
For his return that seems to linger late:
So I alone, now left disconsolate,
Mourn to myself the absence of my love;
And, wand'ring here and there all desolate,
Seek with my plaints to match that mournful dove.
Ne joy of aught that under heaven doth hove
Can comfort me, but her own joyous sight:
Whose sweet aspect both God and man can move,
In her unspotted pleasance to delight.
    Dark is my day, whiles her fair light I miss,
    And dead my life that wants such lively bliss.

MADRIGALS

I

In youth, before I waxéd old,
The blind boy, Venus' baby,
For want of cunning made me bold,
In bitter hive to grope for honey:
But, when he saw me stung and cry,
He took his wings and away did fly.

II

As Dian hunted on a day,
She chanced to come where Cupid lay,
His quiver by his head:
One of his shafts she stole away,
And one of hers did close convey
Into the other's stead:
With that Love wounded my love's heart,
But Dian beasts with Cupid's dart.

III

I saw in secret to my dame
How little Cupid humbly came,
And said to her: "All hail, my mother!"
But, when he saw me laugh, for shame

His face with bashful blood did flame,
Not knowing Venus from the other.
"Then, never blush, Cupid," quoth I,
"For many have erred in this beauty."

IV

Upon a day, as Love lay sweetly slumb'ring
All in his mother's lap;
A gentle bee, with his loud trumpet murm'ring,
About him flew by hap.
Whereof when he was wakened with the noise,
And saw the beast so small;
"What's this" (quoth he) "that gives so great a voice
That wakens men withal?
In angry wise he flies about,
And threatens all with courage stout."

To whom his mother closely smiling said,
'Twixt earnest and 'twixt game:
"See! thou thyself likewise art little made,
If thou regard the same.
And yet thou suff'rest neither gods in sky,
Nor men in earth, to rest:
But, when thou art disposéd cruelly,
Their sleep thou dost molest.
Then either change thy cruelty,
Or give like leave unto the fly."

Natheless, the cruel boy, not so content,
Would needs the fly pursue;
And in his hand, with heedless hardiment,
Him caught for to subdue.
But, when on it he hasty hand did lay,
The bee him stung therefore:
"Now out alas," he cried, "and wellaway!
I wounded am full sore:
The fly, that I so much did scorn,
Hath hurt me with his little horn."

Unto his mother straight he weeping came,
And of his grief complained:
Who could not choose but laugh at his fond game,
Though sad to see him pained.

"Think now," (quoth she) "my son, how great the smart
Of those whom thou dost wound:
Full many thou hast prickéd to the heart,
That pity never found:
Therefore, henceforth some pity take,
When thou dost spoil of lovers make."

She took him straight full piteously lamenting,
And wrapt him in her smock:
She wrapt him softly, all the while repenting
That he the fly did mock.
She drest his wound, and it embalméd well
With salve of sovereign might:
And when she bathed him in a dainty well,
The well of dear delight.
Who would not oft be stung as this,
To be so bathed in Venus' bliss?

The wanton boy was shortly well recured
Of that his malady:
But he, soon after, fresh again inured
His former cruelty.
And since that time he wounded hath myself
With his sharp dart of love:
And now forgets, the cruel careless elf,
His mother's hest to prove.
So now I languish, till he please
My pining anguish to appease.

EPITHALAMION

YE learned sisters, which have oftentimes
Been to me aiding, others to adorn,
Whom ye thought worthy of your graceful rhymes,
That even the greatest did not greatly scorn
To hear their names sung in your simple lays,
But joyéd in their praise;
And when ye list your own mishaps to mourn,
Which death, or love, or fortune's wreck did raise,
Your string could soon to sadder tenor turn,
And teach the woods and waters to lament
Your doleful dreariment.
Now lay those sorrowful complaints aside;
And having all your heads with girlands crowned,
Help me mine own love's praises to resound;
Ne let the same of any be envide:
So Orpheus did for his own bride!
So I unto myself alone will sing;
The woods shall to me answer, and my echo ring.

Early, before the world's light-giving lamp
His golden beam upon the hills doth spread,
Having dispersed the night's uncheerful damp,
Do ye awake; and with fresh lustihead
Go to the bower of my belovéd love,
My truest turtle-dove,
Bid her awake; for Hymen is awake,
And long since ready forth his mask to move,
With his bright tead that flames with many a flake,
And many a bachelor to wait on him,
In their fresh garments trim.
Bid her awake therefore, and soon her dight,
For lo! the wishéd day is come at last,
That shall, for all the pains and sorrows past,
Pay to her usury of long delight:
And whilst she doth her dight,
Do ye to her of joy and solace sing,
That all the woods may answer, and your echo ring.

EPITHALAMION

Bring with you all the nymphs that you can hear
Both of the rivers and the forests green,
And of the sea that neighbours to her near:
All with gay girlands goodly well beseen.
And let them also with them bring in hand
Another gay girland,
For my fair love, of lilies and of roses,
Bound true-love wise, with a blue silk riband.
And let them make great store of bridal posies,
And let them eke bring store of other flowers,
To deck the bridal bowers.
And let the ground whereas her foot shall tread,
For fear the stones her tender foot should wrong,
Be strewed with fragrant flowers all along,
And diap'red like the discoloured mead.
Which done, do at her chamber door await,
For she will waken straight;
The whiles do ye this song unto her sing,
The woods shall to you answer, and your echo ring.

Ye nymphs of Mulla, which with careful heed
The silver scaly trouts do tend full well,
And greedy pikes which use therein to feed
(Those trouts and pikes all others do excel);
And ye likewise, which keep the rushy lake,
Where none do fishes take:
Bind up the locks the which hang scattered light,
And in his waters, which your mirror make,
Behold your faces as the crystal bright,
That when you come whereas my love doth lie,
No blemish she may spy.
And eke, ye lightfoot maids, which keep the deer,
That on the hoary mountain used to tower;
And the wild wolves, which seek them to devour,
With your steel darts do chase from coming near;
Be also present here,
To help to deck her, and to help to sing,
That all the woods may answer, and your echo ring.

Wake now, my love, awake! for it is time;
The rosy Morn long since left Tithone's bed,
All ready to her silver coach to climb;
And Phœbus gins to shew his glorious head.

EPITHALAMION

Hark! how the cheerful birds do chant their lays
And carol of Love's praise.
The merry lark her matins sings aloft;
The thrush replies; the mavis descant plays:
The ouzel shrills; the ruddock warbles soft;
So goodly all agree, with sweet consent,
To this day's merriment.
Ah! my dear love, why do ye sleep thus long,
When meeter were that ye should now awake,
T' await the coming of your joyous make,
And hearken to the birds' love-learnéd song,
The dewy leaves among!
For they of joy and pleasance to you sing,
That all the woods them answer, and their echo ring.

My love is now awake out of her dreams,
And her fair eyes, like stars that dimméd were
With darksome cloud, now shew their goodly beams
More bright than Hesperus his head doth rear.
Come now, ye damsels, daughters of delight,
Help quickly her to dight:
But first come, ye fair hours, which were begot
In Jove's sweet paradise of Day and Night;
Which do the seasons of the year allot,
And all, that ever in this world is fair,
Do make and still repair:
And ye three handmaids of the Cyprian Queen,
The which do still adorn her beauty's pride,
Help to adorn my beautifullest bride:
And, as ye her array, still throw between
Some graces to be seen;
And, as ye use to Venus, to her sing,
The whiles the woods shall answer, and your echo ring.

Now is my love all ready forth to come:
Let all the virgins therefore well await:
And ye fresh boys, that tend upon her groom,
Prepare yourselves, for he is coming straight.
Set all your things in seemly good array,
Fit for so joyful day:
The joyfull'st day that ever sun did see.
Fair sun! shew forth thy favourable ray,
And let thy lifeful heat not fervent be,

EPITHALAMION

For fear of burning her sunshiny face,
Her beauty to disgrace.
O fairest Phœbus! father of the Muse!
If ever I did honour thee aright,
Or sing the thing that mote thy mind delight,
Do not thy servant's simple boon refuse;
But let this day, let this one day, be mine;
Let all the rest be thine.
Then I thy sovereign praises loud will sing,
That all the woods shall answer, and their echo ring.

Hark: how the minstrels gin to shrill aloud
Their merry music that resounds from far,
The pipe, the tabor, and the trembling croud,
That well agree withouten breach or jar.
But, most of all, the damsels do delight
When they their timbrels smite,
And thereunto do dance and carol sweet,
That all the senses they do ravish quite;
The whiles the boys run up and down the street,
Crying aloud with strong confuséd noise,
As if it were one voice,
Hymen, iö Hymen, Hymen, they do shout;
That even to the heavens their shouting shrill
Doth reach, and all the firmament doth fill;
To which the people standing all about,
As in approvance, do thereto applaud,
And loud advance her laud;
And evermore they Hymen, Hymen sing,
That all the woods them answer, and their echo ring.

Lo! where she comes along with portly pace,
Like Phœbe, from her chamber of the east,
Arising forth to run her mighty race,
Clad all in white, that 'seems a virgin best.
So well it her beseems, that ye would ween
Some angel she had been.
Her long loose yellow locks like golden wire,
Sprinkled with pearl, and purling flowers atween,
Do like a golden mantle her attire;
And, being crownéd with a girland green,
Seem like some maiden queen.
Her modest eyes, abashéd to behold

EPITHALAMION

So many gazers as on her do stare,
Upon the lowly ground affixéd are;
Ne dare lift up her countenance too bold,
But blush to hear her praises sung so loud,
So far from being proud.
Nathless do ye still loud her praises sing,
That all the woods may answer, and your echo ring.

Tell me, ye merchants' daughters, did ye see
So fair a creature in your town before;
So sweet, so lovely, and so mild as she,
Adorned with beauty's grace and virtue's store?
Her goodly eyes like sapphires shining bright,
Her forehead ivory white,
Her cheeks like apples which the sun hath rudded,
Her lips like cherries charming men to bite,
Her breast like to a bowl of cream uncrudded,
Her paps like lilies budded,
Her snowy neck like to a marble tower;
And all her body like a palace fair,
Ascending up, with many a stately stair,
To honour's seat and chastity's sweet bower.
Why stand ye still, ye virgins, in amaze,
Upon her so to gaze,
Whiles ye forget your former lay to sing,
To which the woods did answer, and your echo ring?

But if ye saw that which no eyes can see,
The inward beauty of her lively sprite,
Garnisht with heavenly gifts of high degree,
Much more then would ye wonder at that sight,
And stand astonisht like to those which read
Medusa's mazeful head.
There dwells sweet love, and constant chastity,
Unspotted faith, and comely womanhood,
Regard of honour, and mild modesty;
There virtue reigns as queen in royal throne,
And giveth laws alone,
The which the base affections do obey,
And yield their services unto her will;
Ne thought of thing uncomely ever may
Thereto approach to tempt her mind to ill.
Had ye once seen these her celestial treasures.

And unrevealéd pleasures,
Then would ye wonder, and her praises sing,
That all the woods should answer, and your echo ring.

Open the temple gates unto my love,
Open them wide that she may enter in,
And all the posts adorn as doth behove,
And all the pillars deck with girlands trim,
For to receive this saint with honour due,
That cometh in to you.
With trembling steps, and humble reverence,
She cometh in, before th' Almighty's view;
Of her ye virgins learn obedience,
Whenso ye come into those holy places,
To humble your proud faces:
Bring her up to th' high altar, that she may
The sacred ceremonies there partake,
The which do endless matrimony make;
And let the roaring organs loudly play
The praises of the Lord in lively notes;
The whiles, with hollow throats,
The choristers the joyous anthem sing,
That all the woods may answer, and their echo ring.

Behold, whiles she before the altar stands,
Hearing the holy priest that to her speaks,
And blesseth her with his two happy hands,
How the red roses flush up in her cheeks,
And the pure snow, with goodly vermeil stain
Like crimson dyed in grain:
That even th' angels, which continually
About the sacred altar do remain,
Forget their service and about her fly,
Oft peeping in her face, that seems more fair
The more they on it stare.
But her sad eyes, still fastened on the ground,
Are governéd with goodly modesty,
That suffers not one look to glance awry,
Which may let in a little thought unsound.
Why blush ye, love, to give to me your hand,
The pledge of all our band!
Sing, ye sweet angels, Alleluia sing,
That all the woods may answer, and your echo ring.

EPITHALAMION

Now all is done: bring home the bride again;
Bring home the triumph of our victory:
Bring home with you the glory of her gain,
With joyance bring her and with jollity.
Never had man more joyful day than this,
Whom heaven would heap with bliss.
Make feast therefore now all this livelong day;
This day for ever to me holy is.
Pour out the wine without restraint or stay,
Pour not by cups, but by the bellyful.
Pour out to all that wull,
And sprinkle all the posts and walls with wine,
That they may sweat, and drunken be withal.
Crown ye God Bacchus with a coronal,
And Hymen also crown with wreaths of vine;
And let the Graces dance unto the rest.
For they can do it best:
The whiles the maidens do their carol sing,
To which the woods shall answer, and their echo ring.

Ring ye the bells, ye young men of the town,
And leave your wonted labours for this day:
This day is holy; do ye write it down,
That ye for ever it remember may.
This day the sun is in his chiefest height,
With Barnaby the bright,
From whence declining daily by degrees,
He somewhat loseth of his heat and light,
When once the Crab behind his back he sees.
But for this time it ill ordainéd was,
To choose the longest day in all the year,
And shortest night, when longest fitter were:
Yet never day so long, but late would pass.
Ring ye the bells, to make it wear away,
And bonfires make all day;
And dance about them, and about them sing,
That all the woods may answer, and your echo ring.

Ah! when will this long weary day have end,
And lend me leave to come unto my love?
How slowly do the hours their numbers spend!
How slowly does sad Time his feathers move!
Haste thee, O fairest planet, to thy home,

Within the western foam:
Thy tired steeds long since have need of rest.
Long though it be, at last I see it gloom,
And the bright evening-star with golden crest
Appear out of the east.
Fair child of beauty! glorious lamp of love!
That all the host of heaven in ranks dost lead,
And guidest lovers through the night's sad dread,
How cheerfully thou lookest from above,
And seem'st to laugh atween thy twinkling light,
As joying in the sight
Of these glad many, which for joy do sing,
That all the woods them answer, and their echo ring!

Now cease, ye damsels, your delights forepast;
Enough it is that all the day was yours:
Now day is done, and night is nighing fast,
Now bring the bride into the bridal bowers.
The night is come, now soon her disarray,
And in her bed her lay;
Lay her in lilies and in violets,
And silken curtains over her display,
And odoured sheets, and arras coverlets.
Behold how goodly my fair love does lie,
In proud humility!
Like unto Maia, whenas Jove her took
In Tempe, lying on the flow'ry grass,
'Twixt sleep and wake, after she weary was,
With bathing in the Acidalian brook.
Now it is night, ye damsels may be gone,
And leave my love alone,
And leave likewise your former lay to sing:
The woods no more shall answer, nor your echo ring.

Now welcome, night! thou night so long expected,
That long day's labour dost at last defray,
And all my cares, which cruel Love collected,
Hast summed in one, and cancelléd for aye:
Spread thy broad wing over my love and me,
That no man may us see;
And in thy sable mantle us enwrap,
From fear of peril and foul horror free.
Let no false treason seek us to entrap,

EPITHALAMION

Nor any dread disquiet once annoy
The safety of our joy;
But let the night be calm, and quietsome,
Without tempestuous storms or sad affray:
Like as when Jove with fair Alcmena lay,
When he begot the great Tirynthian groom:
Or like as when he with thyself did lie
And begot Majesty.
And let the maids and young men cease to sing,
Ne let the woods them answer, nor their echo ring.

Let no lamenting cries, nor doleful tears,
Be heard all night within, nor yet without:
Ne let false whispers, breeding hidden fears,
Break gentle sleep with misconceivéd doubt.
Let no deluding dreams, nor dreadful sights,
Make sudden sad affrights;
Ne let house-fires, nor lightning's helpless harms,
Ne let the Pouke, nor other evil sprites,
Ne let mischievous witches with their charms,
Ne let hobgoblins, names whose sense we see not,
Fray us with things that be not:
Let not the shriek-owl nor the stork be heard,
Nor the night-raven, that still deadly yells;
Nor damnéd ghosts, called up with mighty spells,
Nor grisly vultures, make us once afeard:
Ne let th' unpleasant quire of frogs still croaking
Make us to wish their choking.
Let none of these their dreary accents sing;
Ne let the woods them answer, nor their echo ring.

But let still silence true night-watches keep,
That sacred peace may in assurance reign,
And timely sleep, when it is time to sleep,
May pour his limbs forth on your pleasant plain;
The whiles an hundred little wingéd loves,
Like divers-feathered doves,
Shall fly and flutter round about your bed,
And in the secret dark, that none reproves,
Their pretty stealths shall work, and snares shall spread
To filch away sweet snatches of delight,
Concealed through covert night.

EPITHALAMION

Ye sons of Venus, play your sports at will!
For greedy pleasure, careless of your toys,
Thinks more upon her paradise of joys,
Than what ye do, albeit good or ill.
All night therefore attend your merry play,
For it will soon be day:
Now none doth hinder you, that say or sing;
Ne will the woods now answer, nor your echo ring.

Who is the same, which at my window peeps?
Or whose is that fair face that shines so bright?
Is it not Cynthia, she that never sleeps,
But walks about high heaven all the night?
O! fairest goddess, do thou not envý
My love with me to spy:
For thou likewise didst love, though now unthought,
And for a fleece of wool, which privily
The Latmian shepherd once unto thee brought,
His pleasures with thee wrought.
Therefore to us be favourable now;
And sith of women's labours thou hast charge,
And generation goodly dost enlarge,
Incline thy will t' effect our wishful vow,
And the chaste womb inform with timely seed,
That may our comfort breed:
Till which we cease our hopeful hap to sing;
Ne let the woods us answer, nor our echo ring.

And thou, great Juno! which with awful might
The laws of wedlock still dost patronize;
And the religion of the faith first plight
With sacred rites hast taught to solemnize;
And eke for comfort often callèd art
Of women in their smart;
Eternally bind thou this lovely band,
And all thy blessings unto us impart.
And thou, glad Genius! in whose gentle hand
The bridal bower and genial bed remain,
Without blemish or stain:
And the sweet pleasures of their love's delight
With secret aid dost succour and supply,
Till they bring forth the fruitful progeny;
Send us the timely fruit of this same night.

And thou, fair Hebe! and thou, Hymen free!
Grant that it may so be.
Till which we cease your further praise to sing;
Ne any woods shall answer, nor your echo ring.

And ye high heavens, the temple of the gods,
In which a thousand torches flaming bright
Do burn, that to us wretched earthly clods
In dreadful darkness lend desiréd light;
And all ye powers which in the same remain,
More than we men can feign,
Pour out your blessing on us plenteously,
And happy influence upon us rain,
That we may raise a large posterity,
Which from the earth, which they may long possess
With lasting happiness,
Up to your haughty palaces may mount;
And, for the guerdon of their glorious merit,
May heavenly tabernacles there inherit,
Of blessed saints for to increase the count.
So let us rest, sweet love, in hope of this,
And cease till then our timely joys to sing;
The woods no more us answer, nor our echo ring!

Song! made in lieu of many ornaments,
With which my love should duly have been deckt,
Which cutting off through hasty accidents,
Ye would not stay your due time to expect,
But promised both to recompense;
Be unto her a goodly ornament,
And for short time an endless monument.

FOUR HYMNS

MADE BY

EDM. SPENSER

TO THE RIGHT HONOURABLE AND MOST VIRTUOUS LADIES

THE LADY MARGARET

COUNTESS OF CUMBERLAND, AND

THE LADY MARY

COUNTESS OF WARWICK

HAVING in the greener times of my youth composed these former two Hymns in the praise of Love and Beauty, and finding that the same too much pleased those of like age and disposition, which being too vehemently carried with that kind of affection, do rather suck out poison to their strong passion than honey to their honest delight, I was moved by the one of you two most excellent ladies, to call in the same. But, being unable so to do, by reason that many copies thereof were formerly scattered abroad, I resolved at least to amend, and, by way of retractation, to reform them, making, instead of those two Hymns of earthly or natural love and beauty, two others of heavenly and celestial. The which I do dedicate jointly unto you two honourable sisters, as to the most excellent and rare ornaments of all true love and beauty, both in the one and the other kind; humbly beseeching you to vouchsafe the patronage of them, and to accept this my humble service, in lieu of the great graces and honourable favours which ye daily shew unto me, until such time as I may, by better means, yield you some more notable testimony of my thankful mind and dutiful devotion. And even so I pray for your happiness. Greenwich this first of September, 1596. Your Honours' most bounden ever,

in all humble service,

ED. SP.

AN HYMN IN HONOUR OF LOVE

    Love, that long since hast to thy mighty power
Perforce subdued my poor captivéd heart,
And raging now therein with restless stour,
Dost tyrannize in every weaker part;
Fain would I seek to ease my bitter smart
    By any service I might do to thee,
    Or aught that else might to thee pleasing be.

And now t' assuage the force of this new flame,
And make thee more propitious in my need,
I mean to sing the praises of thy name,
And thy victorious conquests to arede,
By which thou madest many hearts to bleed
Of mighty victors, with wide wounds imbrued,
And by thy cruel darts to thee subdued.

Only I fear my wits enfeebled late,
Through the sharp sorrows which thou hast me bred,
Should faint, and words should fail me to relate
The wondrous triumphs of thy great god-head:
But, if thou wouldst vouchsafe to overspread
Me with the shadow of thy gentle wing,
I should enabled be thy acts to sing.

Come, then, O come, thou mighty God of Love,
Out of thy silver bowers and secret bliss,
Where thou dost sit in Venus' lap above,
Bathing thy wings in her ambrosial kiss,
That sweeter far than any nectar is;
Come softly, and my feeble breast inspire
With gentle fury, kindled of thy fire.

And ye, sweet Muses! which have often proved
The piercing points of his avengeful darts;
And ye, fair nymphs! which oftentimes have loved
The cruel worker of your kindly smarts,
Prepare yourselves, and open wide your hearts
For to receive the triumph of your glory,
That made you merry oft when ye were sorry.

And ye, fair blossoms of youth's wanton breed,
Which in the conquests of your beauty boast,
Wherewith your lovers' feeble eyes you feed,
But starve their hearts that needeth nurture most,
Prepare yourselves to march amongst his host,
And all the way this sacred hymn do sing,
Made in the honour of your sovereign king.

  Great God of Might, that reignest in the mind
And all the body to thy 'hest dost frame,
Victor of gods, subduer of mankind,

That dost the lions and fell tigers tame,
Making their cruel rage thy scornful game,
And in their roaring taking great delight;
Who can express the glory of thy might?

Or who alive can perfectly declare
The wondrous cradle of thine infancy,
When thy great mother Venus first thee bare,
Begot of Plenty and of Penury,
Though elder than thine own nativity,
And yet a child, renewing still thy years,
And yet the eldest of the heavenly peers?

For ere this world's still moving mighty mass
Out of great Chaos' ugly prison crept,
In which his goodly face long hidden was
From heaven's view, and in deep darkness kept,
Love, that had now long time securely slept
In Venus' lap, unarmèd then and naked,
Gan rear his head, by Clotho being wakèd:

And, taking to him wings of his own heat,
Kindled at first from heaven's life-giving fire,
He gan to move out of his idle seat;
Weakly at first, but after with desire
Lifted aloft, he gan to mount up higher,
And, like fresh eagle, make his hardy flight
Through all that great wide waste, yet wanting light.

Yet wanting light to guide his wand'ring way,
His own fair mother, for all creatures' sake,
Did lend him light from her own goodly ray:
Then through the world his way he gan to take,
The world, that was not till he did it make,
Whose sundry parts he from themselves did sever,
The which before had lain confusèd ever.

The earth, the air, the water, and the fire,
Then gan to range themselves in huge array,
And with contráry forces to conspire
Each against other by all means they may,
Threat'ning their own confusion and decay:
Air hated earth, and water hated fire,
Till Love relented their rebellious ire.

He then them took, and, tempering goodly well
Their contrary dislikes with lovéd means,
Did place them all in order, and compel
To keep themselves within their sundry reigns,
Together linkt with adamantine chains;
Yet so, as that in every living wight
They mix themselves, and shew their kindly might.

So ever since they firmly have remained,
And duly well observéd his behest;
Through which now all these things that are contained
Within this goodly cope, both most and least,
Their being have, and daily are increased
Through secret sparks of his infuséd fire,
Which in the barren cold he doth inspire.

Thereby they all do live, and movéd are
To multiply the likeness of their kind,
Whilst they seek only, without further care,
To quench the flame which they in burning find;
But man, that breathes a more immortal mind,
Not for lust's sake, but for eternity,
Seeks to enlarge his lasting progeny:

For having yet in his deducted sprite
Some sparks remaining of that heavenly fire,
He is enlumined with that goodly light,
Unto like goodly semblant to aspire;
Therefore in choice of love he doth desire
That seems on earth most heavenly to embrace,
That same is Beauty, born of heavenly race.

For sure of all that in this mortal frame
Containéd is, nought more divine doth seem,
Or that resembleth more th' immortal flame
Of heavenly light, than Beauty's glorious beam.
What wonder then, if with such rage extreme
Frail men, whose eyes seek heavenly things to see,
At sight thereof so much enravished be?

Which well perceiving, that imperious boy
Doth therewith tip his sharp empois'ned darts,
Which glancing through the eyes with countenance coy

Rest not till they have pierced the trembling hearts,
And kindled flame in all their inner parts,
Which sucks the blood, and drinketh up the life
Of careful wretches with consuming grief.

Thenceforth they plain, and make full piteous moan
Unto the author of their baleful bane:
The days they waste, the nights they grieve and groan,
Their lives they loathe, and heaven's light disdain;
No light but that, whose lamp doth yet remain
Fresh burning in the image of their eye,
They deign to see, and seeing it still die.

That whilst thou tyrant Love dost laugh and scorn
At their complaints, making their pain thy play,
Whilst they lie languishing like thralls forlorn,
The whiles thou dost triumph in their decay;
And otherwise, their dying to delay,
Thou dost emmarble the proud heart of her
Whose love before their life they do prefer.

So hast thou often done (ay me, the more!)
To me thy vassal, whose yet bleeding heart
With thousand wounds thou mangled hast so sore
That whole remains scarce any little part;
Yet, to augment the anguish of my smart,
Thou hast enfrozen her disdainful breast,
That no one drop of pity there doth rest.

Why then do I this honour unto thee,
Thus to ennoble thy victorious name,
Since thou dost shew no favour unto me,
Ne once move ruth in that rebellious dame,
Somewhat to slack the rigour of my flame?
Certes small glory dost thou win hereby,
To let her live thus free, and me to die.

But if thou be indeed, as men thee call,
The world's great parent, the most kind preserver
Of living wights, the sovereign lord of all,
How falls it then, that with thy furious fervour,
Thou dost afflict as well the not-deserver,
As him that doth thy lovely hests despise,
And on thy subjects most dost tyrannize?

HYMN IN HONOUR OF LOVE

Yet herein eke thy glory seemeth more,
By so hard handling those which best thee serve,
That, ere thou dost them unto grace restore,
Thou may'st well try if they will ever swerve,
And may'st them make it better to deserve;
And, having got it, may it more esteem,
For things hard gotten men more dearly deem.

So hard those heavenly beauties be enfired,
As things divine, least passions do impress,
The more of steadfast minds to be admired,
The more they stayéd be on steadfastness;
But baseborn minds such lamps regard the less,
Which at first blowing take not hasty fire;
Such fancies feel no love, but loose desire.

For Love is lord of truth and loyalty,
Lifting himself out of the lowly dust
On golden plumes up to the purest sky,
Above the reach of loathly sinful Lust,
Whose base affect through cowardly distrust
Of his weak wings dare not to heaven fly,
But like a moldwarp in the earth doth lie.

His dunghill thoughts, which do themselves inure
To dirty dross, no higher dare aspire,
Ne can his feeble earthly eyes endure
The flaming light of that celestial fire
Which kindleth love in generous desire,
And makes him mount above the native might
Of heavy earth, up to the heavens' height.

Such is the power of that sweet passíon,
That it all sordid baseness doth expel,
And the refinéd mind doth newly fashion
Unto a fairer form, which now doth dwell
In his high thought, that would itself excel;
Which he beholding still with constant sight,
Admires the mirror of so heavenly light.

Whose image printing in his deepest wit,
He thereon feeds his hungry fantasy,
Still full, yet never satisfied with it;

Like Tantale, that in store doth starvéd lie,
So doth he pine in most satiety;
For nought may quench his infinite desire,
Once kindled through that first conceivéd fire.

Thereon his mind affixed wholly is,
Ne thinks on aught but how it to attain;
His care, his joy, his hope, is all on this,
That seems in it all blisses to contain,
In sight whereof all other bliss seems vain;
Thrice happy man! might he the same possess,
He feigns himself, and doth his fortune bless.

And though he do not win his wish to end,
Yet thus far happy he himself doth ween,
That heavens such happy grace did to him lend,
As thing on earth so heavenly to have seen
His heart's enshrinéd saint, his heaven's queen,
Fairer than fairest, in his feigning eye,
Whose sole aspéct he count felicity.

Then forth he casts in his unquiet thought,
What he may do, her favour to obtain;
What brave exploit, what peril hardly wrought,
What puissant conquest, what adventurous pain,
May please her best, and grace unto him gain;
He dreads no danger, nor misfortune fears,
His faith, his fortune, in his breast he bears.

Thou art his god, thou art his mighty guide,
Thou, being blind, lett'st him not see his fears,
But carriest him to that which he hath eyed,
Through seas, through flames, through thousand swords
  and spears;
Ne aught so strong that may his force withstand,
With which thou armest his resistless hand.

Witness Leander in the Euxine waves,
And stout Æneas in the Trojan fire,
Achilles pressing through the Phrygian glaives,
And Orpheus, daring to provoke the ire
Of damnéd fiends, to get his love retire;
For both through heaven and hell thou makest way
To win them worship which to thee obey.

And if, by all these perils and these pains,
He may but purchase liking in her eye,
What heavens of joy then to himself he feigns!
Eftsoons he wipes quite out of memory
Whatever ill before he did aby:
Had it been death, yet would he die again,
To live thus happy as her grace to gain.

Yet, when he hath found favour to his will,
He nathëmore can so contented rest,
But forceth further on, and striveth still
T' approach more near, till in her inmost breast
He may embosomed be and lovéd best;
And yet not best, but to be loved alone:
For love can not endure a paragon.

The fear whereof, O how doth it torment
His troubled mind with more then hellish pain!
And to his feigning fancy represent
Sights never seen, and thousand shadows vain,
To break his sleep, and waste his idle brain:
Thou that hast never loved canst not believe
Least part of th' evils which poor lovers grieve.

The gnawing envy, the heart-fretting fear,
The vain surmises, the distrustful shows,
The false reports that flying tales do bear,
The doubts, the dangers, the delays, the woes,
The feignéd friends, the unassuréd foes,
With thousands more than any tongue can tell,
Do make a lover's life a wretch's hell.

Yet is there one more curséd than they all,
That canker-worm, that monster, jealousy,
Which eats the heart and feeds upon the gall,
Turning all love's delight to misery,
Through fear of losing his felicity.
Ah, gods! that ever ye that monster placed
In gentle love, that all his joy 's defaced!

By these, O Love! thou dost thy entrance make
Unto thy heaven, and dost the more endear
Thy pleasures unto those which them partake,

As after storms, when clouds begin to clear,
The sun more bright and glorious doth appear;
So thou thy folk, through pains of purgatory
Dost bear unto thy bliss, and heaven's glory.

There thou them placest in a paradise
Of all delight and joyous happy rest,
Where they do feed on nectar heavenly-wise,
With Hercules and Hebe, and the rest
Of Venus' darlings, through her bounty blest;
And lie like gods in ivory beds arrayed,
With rose and lilies over them displayed.

There with thy daughter Pleasure they do play
Their hurtless sports, without rebuke or blame,
And in her snowy bosom boldly lay
Their quiet heads, devoid of guilty shame,
After full joyance of their gentle game;
Then her they crown their goddess and their queen,
And deck with flowers thy altars well beseen.

Ay me! dear lord! that ever I might hope,
For all the pains and woes that I endure,
To come at length unto the wishéd scope
Of my desire, or might myself assure
That happy port for ever to recure!
Then would I think these pains no pains at all,
And all my woes to be but penance small.

Then would I sing of thine immortal praise
An heavenly hymn, such as the angels sing,
And thy triumphant name then would I raise
'Bove all the gods, thee only honouring,
My guide, my god, my victor, and my king:
Till then, dread lord! vouchsafe to take of me
This simple song, thus framed in praise of the

AN HYMN IN HONOUR OF BEAUTY

Ah! whither, Love! wilt thou now carry me?
What wontless fury dost thou now inspire
Into my feeble breast, too full of thee?
Whilst seeking to aslake thy raging fire,
Thou in me kindlest much more great desire,
And up aloft above my strength dost raise
The wondrous matter of my fire to praise.

That as I erst, in praise of thine own name,
So now in honour of thy mother dear,
An honourable hymn I eke should frame,
And, with the brightness of her beauty clear,
The ravisht hearts of gazeful men might rear
To admiration of that heavenly light,
From whence proceeds such soul-enchanting might.

Thereto do thou, great goddess! Queen of Beauty,
Mother of love, and of all world's delight,
Without whose sovereign grace and kindly duty
Nothing on earth seems fair to fleshly sight,
Do thou vouchsafe with thy love-kindling light
T' illuminate my dim and dullèd eyne,
And beautify this sacred hymn of thine:

That both to thee, to whom I mean it most,
And eke to her, whose fair immortal beam
Hath darted fire into my feeble ghost,
That now it wasted is with woes extreme,
It may so please, that she at length will stream
Some dew of grace into my withered heart,
After long sorrow and consuming smart.

What time this world's great Workmaster did cast
To make all things such as we now behold,
It seems that he before his eyes had placed
A goodly pattern, to whose perfect mould
He fashioned them as comely as he could;
That now so fair and seemly they appear,
As nought may be amended anywhere.

That wondrous pattern, wheresoe'er it be,
Whether in earth laid up in secret store,
Or else in heaven, that no man may it see
With sinful eyes, for fear it to deflore,
Is perfect Beauty, which all men adore;
Whose face and feature doth so much excel
All mortal sense, that none the same may tell.

Thereof as every earthly thing partakes
Or more or less, by influence divine,
So it more fair accordingly it makes,
And the gross matter of this earthly mine,
Which clotheth it, thereafter doth refine,
Doing away the dross which dims the light
Of that fair beam which therein is empight.

For, through infusion of celestial power,
The duller earth it quick'neth with delight,
And lifeful spirits privily doth pour
Through all the parts, that to the looker's sight
They seem to please. That is thy sovereign might,
O Cyprian Queen! which flowing from the beam
Of thy bright star, thou into them dost stream.

That is the thing which giveth pleasant grace
To all things fair, that kindleth lively fire,
Light of thy lamp, which, shining in the face,
Thence to the soul darts amorous desire,
And robs the hearts of those which it admire;
Therewith thou pointest thy son's pois'ned arrow,
That wounds the life, and wastes the inmost marrow.

How vainly then do idle wits invent,
That beauty is nought else but mixture made
Of colours fair, and goodly temp'rament
Of pure complexions, that shall quickly fade
And pass away, like to a summer's shade;
Or that it is but comely composition
Of parts well measured, with meet disposition!

Hath white and red in it such wondrous power,
That it can pierce through th' eyes unto the heart,
And therein stir such rage and restless stour,

As nought but death can stint his dolour's smart?
Or can proportion of the outward part
Move such affection in the inward mind,
That it can rob both sense and reason blind?

Why do not then the blossoms of the field,
Which are arrayed with much more orient hue,
And to the sense most dainty odours yield,
Work like impression in the looker's view?
Or why do not fair pictures like power shew,
In which oft-times we nature see of art
Excelled, in perfect limning every part?

But ah! believe me there is more than so,
That works such wonders in the minds of men;
I, that have often proved, too well it know,
And whoso list the like assays to ken,
Shall find by trial, and confess it then,
That Beauty is not, as fond men misdeem,
An outward shew of things that only seem.

For that same goodly hue of white and red,
With which the cheeks are sprinkled, shall decay,
And those sweet rosy leaves, so fairly spread
Upon the lips, shall fade and fall away
To that they were, even to corrupted clay;
That golden wire, those sparkling stars so bright,
Shall turn to dust, and lose their goodly light.

But that fair lamp, from whose celestial ray
That light proceeds, which kindleth lovers' fire,
Shall never be extinguished nor decay;
But, when the vital spirits do expire,
Unto her native planet shall retire;
For it is heavenly born and cannot die,
Being a parcel of the purest sky.

For when the soul, the which derivéd was,
At first, out of that great immortal Sprite,
By whom all live to love, whilom did pass
Down from the top of purest heaven's height
To be embodied here, it then took light
And lively spirits from that fairest star,
Which lights the world forth from his fiery car.

Which power retaining still or more or less,
When she in fleshly seed is eft enraced,
Through every part she doth the same impress,
According as the heavens have her graced,
And frames her house, in which she will be placed,
Fit for herself, adorning it with spoil
Of th' heavenly riches which she robbed erewhile.

Thereof it comes that these fair souls, which have
The most resemblance of that heavenly light,
Frame to themselves most beautiful and brave
Their fleshly bower, most fit for their delight,
And the gross matter by a sovereign might
Tempers so trim, that it may well be seen
A palace fit for such a Virgin Queen.

So every spirit, as it is most pure,
And hath in it the more of heavenly light,
So it the fairer body doth procure
To habit in, and it more fairly dight
With cheerful grace and amiable sight.
For of the soul the body form doth take:
For soul is form, and doth the body make.

Therefore wherever that thou dost behold
A comely corpse, with beauty fair endued,
Know this for certain, that the same doth hold
A beauteous soul, with fair conditions thewed,
Fit to receive the seed of virtue strewed.
For all that fair is, is by nature good;
That is a sign to know the gentle blood.

Yet oft it falls that many a gentle mind
Dwells in deforméd tabernacle drowned,
Either by chance, against the course of kind,
Or through unaptness in the substance found,
Which it assuméd of some stubborn ground,
That will not yield unto her form's direction,
But is deformed with some foul imperfection.

And oft it falls, (ay me, the more to rue!)
That goodly beauty, albe heavenly born,
Is foul abused, and that celestial hue,

Which doth the world with her delight adorn,
Made but the bait of sin, and sinners' scorn,
Whilst every one doth seek and sue to have it,
But every one doth seek but to deprave it.

Yet nathëmore is that fair beauty's blame,
But theirs that do abuse it unto ill:
Nothing so good, but that through guilty shame
May be corrupt, and wrested unto will:
Natheless the soul is fair and beauteous still,
However flesh's fault it filthy make;
For things immortal no corruption take.

But ye, fair dames! the world's dear ornaments
And lively images of heaven's light,
Let not your beams with such disparagements
Be dimmed, and your bright glory dark'ned quite;
But mindful still of your first country's sight,
Do still preserve your first informéd grace,
Whose shadow yet shines in your beauteous face.

Loathe that foul blot, that hellish firebrand,
Disloyal lust, fair beauty's foulest blame,
That base affections, which your ears would bland,
Commend to you by love's abuséd name,
But is indeed the bondslave of defame;
Which will the garland of your glory mar,
And quench the light of your bright shining star.

But gentle love, that loyal is and true,
Will more illumine your resplendent ray,
And add more brightness to your goodly hue,
From light of his pure fire; which, by like way
Kindled of yours, your likeness doth display;
Like as two mirrors, by opposed reflection,
Do both express the face's first impression.

Therefore, to make your beauty more appear,
It you behoves to love, and forth to lay
That heavenly riches which in you ye bear,
That men the more admire their fountain may;
For else what booteth that celestial ray,
If it in darkness be enshrinéd ever,
That it of loving eyes be viewéd never?

But, in your choice of loves, this well advise,
That likest to yourselves ye them select,
The which your forms' first source may sympathize,
And with like beauties' parts be inly decked;
For, if you loosely love without respect,
It is no love, but a discordant war,
Whose unlike parts amongst themselves do jar.

For love is a celestial harmony
Of likely hearts composed of stars' concent,
Which join together in sweet sympathy,
To work each other's joy and true content,
Which they have harboured since their first descent
Out of their heavenly bowers, where they did see
And know each other here beloved to be.

Then wrong it were that any other twain
Should in love's gentle band combinéd be
But those whom Heaven did at first ordain,
And made out of one mould the more t' agree;
For all, that like the beauty which they see,
Straight do not love; for love is not so light
As straight to burn at first beholder's sight.

But they, which love indeed, look otherwise,
With pure regard and spotless true intent,
Drawing out of the object of their eyes
A more refinéd form, which they present
Unto their mind, void of all blemishment;
Which it reducing to her first perfection,
Beholdeth free from flesh's frail infection.

And then conforming it unto the light,
Which in itself it hath remaining still,
Of that first Sun, yet sparkling in his sight,
Thereof he fashions in his higher skill
An heavenly beauty to his fancy's will;
And, it embracing in his mind entire,
The mirror of his own thought doth admire.

Which seeing now so inly fair to be,
As outward it appeareth to the eye,
And with his spirit's proportion to agree,

He thereon fixeth all his fantasy,
And fully setteth his felicity;
Counting it fairer than it is indeed,
And yet indeed her fairness doth exceed.

For lovers' eyes more sharply sighted be
Than other men's, and in dear love's delight
See more than any other eyes can see,
Through mutual receipt of beamës bright,
Which carry privy message to the sprite,
And to their eyes that inmost fair display,
As plain as light discovers dawning day.

Therein they see, through amorous eye-glances,
Armies of loves still flying to and fro,
Which dart at them their little fiery lances;
Whom having wounded, back again they go,
Carrying compassion to their lovely foe;
Who, seeing her fair eyes' so sharp effect,
Cures all their sorrows with one sweet aspéct.

In which how many wonders do they rede
To their conceit, that others never see!
Now of her smiles, with which their souls they feed,
Like gods with nectar in their banquets free;
Now of her looks, which like to cordials be;
But when her words' embássade forth she sends,
Lord, how sweet music that unto them lends!

Sometimes upon her forehead they behold
A thousand graces masking in delight;
Sometimes within her eyelids they unfold
Ten thousand sweet belgards, which to their sight
Do seem like twinkling stars in frosty night;
But on her lips, like rosy buds in May,
So many millions of chaste pleasures play.

All those, O Cytherea! and thousands more
Thy handmaids be, which do on thee attend,
To deck thy beauty with their dainties' store,
That may it more to mortal eyes commend,
And make it more admired of foe and friend:
That in men's hearts thou may'st thy throne install,
And spread thy lovely kingdom over-all.

Then Iō, triumph! O great Beauty's Queen,
Advance the banner of thy conquest high,
That all this world, the which thy vassals bene,
May draw to thee, and with due fealty
Adore the power of thy great majesty,
Singing this hymn in honour of thy name,
Compiled by me, which thy poor liegeman am!

In lieu whereof grant, O great sovereign!
That she, whose conquering beauty doth captíve
My trembling heart in her eternal chain,
One drop of grace at length will to me give,
That I her bounden thrall by her may live,
And this same life, which first fro me she reaved,
May owe to her, of whom I it received.

And you, fair Venus' darling, my dear dread!
Fresh flower of grace, great goddess of my life,
When your fair eyes these fearful lines shall read,
Deign to let fall one drop of due relief,
That may recure my heart's long pining grief,
And shew what wondrous power your beauty hath,
That can restore a damnéd wight from death.

AN HYMN OF HEAVENLY LOVE

Love, lift me up upon thy golden wings,
From this base world unto thy heaven's height,
Where I may see those admirable things
Which there thou workest by thy sovereign might,
Far above feeble reach of earthly sight,
That I thereof an heavenly hymn may sing
Unto the God of Love, high heaven's king.

Many lewd lays (ah! woe is me the more!)
In praise of that mad fit which fools call love,
I have in th' heat of youth made heretofore,
That in light wits did loose affection move;
But all those follies now I do reprove,
And turnéd have the tenor of my string,
The heavenly praises of true love to sing.

HYMN OF HEAVENLY LOVE

And ye that wont with greedy vain desire
To rede my fault, and, wond'ring at my flame,
To warm yourselves at my wide sparkling fire,
Sith now that heat is quenchéd, quench my blame,
And in her ashes shroud my dying shame;
For who my passéd follies now pursues,
Begins his own, and my old fault renews.

BEFORE this world's great frame, in which all things
Are now contained, found any being-place,
Ere flitting Time could wag his eyas wings
About that mighty bound which doth embrace
The rolling spheres, and parts their hours by space,
That High Eternal Power, which now doth move
In all these things, moved in itself by love.

It loved itself, because itself was fair;
(For fair is loved) and of itself begot,
Like to itself his eldest son and heir,
Eternal, pure, and void of sinful blot,
The firstling of his joy, in whom no jot
Of love's dislike or pride was to be found,
Whom he therefore with equal honour crowned.

With him he reigned, before all time prescribed,
In endless glory and immortal might,
Together with that third from them derived,
Most wise, most holy, most almighty Sprite!
Whose kingdom's throne no thought of earthly wight
Can comprehend, much less my trembling verse
With equal words can hope it to rehearse.

Yet, O most blessed Spirit! pure lamp of light,
Eternal spring of grace and wisdom true,
Vouchsafe to shed into my barren sprite
Some little drop of thy celestial dew,
That may my rhymes with sweet infuse imbrue,
And give me words equal unto my thought,
To tell the marvels by thy mercy wrought.

Yet being pregnant still with powerful grace,
And full of fruitful love, that loves to get
Things like himself, and to enlarge his race,

His second brood, though not in power so great,
Yet full of beauty, next he did beget
An infinite increase of angels bright,
All glist'ring glorious in their Maker's light.

To them the heavens' illimitable height
(Not this round heaven, which we from hence behold,
Adorned with thousand lamps of burning light,
And with ten thousand gems of shining gold,)
He gave as their inheritance to hold,
That they might serve him in eternal bliss,
And be partakers of those joys of his.

There they in their trinal triplicities
About him wait, and on his will depend,
Either with nimble wings to cut the skies,
When he them on his messages doth send,
Or on his own dread presence to attend,
Where they behold the glory of his light,
And carol hymns of love both day and night.

Both day and night is unto them all one;
For he his beams doth still to them extend,
That darkness there appeareth never none;
Ne hath their day, ne hath their bliss, an end,
But there their termless time in pleasure spend;
Ne ever should their happiness decay,
Had not they dared their Lord to disobey.

But pride, impatient of long-resting peace,
Did puff them up with greedy bold ambition,
That they gan cast their state how to increase
Above the fortune of their first condition,
And sit in God's own seat without commission;
The brightest angel, even the Child of Light,
Drew millions more against their God to fight.

Th' Almighty, seeing their so bold assay,
Kindled the flame of his consuming ire,
And with his only breath them blew away
From heaven's height, to which they did aspire,
To deepest hell, and lake of damnéd fire,
Where they in darkness and dread horror dwell,
Hating the happy light from which they fell.

HYMN OF HEAVENLY LOVE

So that next offspring of the Maker's love,
Next to himself in glorious degree,
Degendering to hate, fell from above
Through pride, (for pride and love may ill agree)
And now of sin to all ensample be:
How then can sinful flesh itself assure,
Sith purest angels fell to be impure?

But that Eternal Fount of love and grace,
Still flowing forth his goodness unto all,
Now seeing left a waste and empty place
In his wide palace, through those angels' fall,
Cast to supply the same, and to install
A new unknowen colony therein,
Whose root from earth's base groundwork should begin.

Therefore of clay, base, vile, and next to nought,
Yet formed by wondrous skill, and by his might,
According to an heavenly pattern wrought,
Which he had fashioned in his wise foresight,
He man did make, and breathed a living sprite
Into his face most beautiful and fair,
Endued with wisdom's riches, heavenly, rare.

Such he him made, that he resemble might
Himself, as mortal thing immortal could;
Him to be lord of every living wight
He made by love out of his own like mould,
In whom he might his mighty self behold;
For Love doth love the thing beloved to see,
That like itself in lovely shape may be.

But man, forgetful of his Maker's grace
No less than angels whom he did ensue,
Fell from the hope of promised heavenly place,
Into the mouth of death, to sinners due,
And all his offspring into thraldom threw,
Where they for ever should in bonds remain
Of never-dead yet ever-dying pain;

Till that great Lord of Love, which him at first
Made of mere love, and after likéd well,
Seeing him lie like creature long accurst

In that deep horror of despairéd hell,
Him, wretch, in dole would let no longer dwell,
But cast out of that bondage to redeem,
And pay the price, all were his debt extreme.

Out of the bosom of eternal bliss,
In which he reignéd with his glorious Sire,
He down descended, like a most demiss
And abject thrall, in flesh's frail attire,
That he for him might pay sin's deadly hire,
And him restore unto that happy state
In which he stood before his hapless fate.

In flesh at first the guilt committed was,
Therefore in flesh it must be satisfied;
Nor spirit, nor angel, though they man surpass,
Could make amends to God for man's misguide,
But only man himself, who self did slide:
So, taking flesh of sacred virgin's womb,
For man's dear sake he did a man become.

And that most blessed body, which was born
Without all blemish or reproachful blame,
He freely gave to be both rent and torn
Of cruel hands, who with despightful shame
Reviling him, that them most vile became,
At length him nailéd on a gallow-tree,
And slew the Just by most unjust decree.

O huge and most unspeakable impression
Of love's deep wound, that pierced the piteous heart
Of that dear Lord with so entire affection,
And sharply launching every inner part,
Dolours of death into his soul did dart,
Doing him die that never it deserved,
To free his foes, that from his 'hest had swerved!

What heart can feel least touch of so sore launch,
Or thought can think the depth of so dear wound?
Whose bleeding source their streams yet never staunch
But still do flow, and freshly still redound,
To heal the sores of sinful souls unsound,
And cleanse the guilt of that infected crime
Which was enrooted in all fleshly slime.

O blessed Well of Love! O Flower of Grace!
O glorious Morning-Star! O Lamp of Light!
Most lively image of thy Father's face,
Eternal King of Glory, Lord of Might,
Meek Lamb of God, before all worlds behight,
How can we thee requite for all this good?
Or what can prize that thy most precious blood?

Yet nought thou ask'st in lieu of all this love,
But love of us, for guerdon of thy pain:
Ay me! what can us less than that behove?
Had he required life of us again,
Had it been wrong to ask his own with gain?
He gave us life, he it restoréd lost;
Then life were least, that us so little cost.

But he our life hath left unto us free,
Free that was thrall, and blessed that was banned;
Ne aught demands but that we loving be,
As he himself hath loved us afore-hand,
And bound thereto with an eternal band,
Him first to love that us so dearly bought,
And next our brethren, to his image wrought.

Him first to love great right and reason is,
Who first to us our life and being gave,
And after, when we faréd had amiss,
Us wretches from the second death did save;
And last, the food of life, which now we have,
Even he himself, in his dear sacrament,
To feed our hungry souls, unto us lent.

Then next, to love our brethren, that were made
Of that self mould, and that self Maker's hand,
That we, and to the same again shall fade,
Where they shall have like heritage of land,
However here on higher steps we stand,
Which also were with selfsame price redeemed
That we, however of us light esteemed.

And were they not, yet since that loving Lord
Commanded us to love them for his sake,
Even for his sake, and for his sacred word,

Which in his last bequest he to us spake,
We should them love, and with their needs partake;
Knowing that, whatsoe'er to them we give,
We give to him by whom we all do live.

Such mercy he by his most holy rede
Unto us taught, and to approve it true,
Ensampled it by his most righteous deed,
Shewing us mercy (miserable crew!)
That we the like should to the wretches shew,
And love our brethren; thereby to approve
How much, himself that lovéd us, we love.

Then rouse thyself, O Earth! out of thy soil,
In which thou wallowest like to filthy swine,
And dost thy mind in dirty pleasures moil,
Unmindful of that dearest Lord of thine;
Lift up to him thy heavy clouded eyne,
That thou his sovereign bounty may'st behold,
And read, through love, his mercies manifold.

Begin from first, where he encradled was
In simple cratch, wrapt in a wad of hay,
Between the toilful ox and humble ass,
And in what rags, and in how base array,
The glory of our heavenly riches lay,
When him the silly shepherds came to see,
Whom greatest princes sought on lowest knee.

From thence read on the story of his life,
His humble carriage, his unfaulty ways,
His cank'red foes, his fights, his toil, his strife,
His pains, his poverty, his sharp assays,
Through which he passed his miserable days,
Offending none, and doing good to all,
Yet being maliced both of great and small.

And look at last, how of most wretched wights
He taken was, betrayed, and false accused;
How with most scornful taunts, and fell despights,
He was reviled, disgraced, and foul abused;
How scourged, how crowned, how buffeted, how bruised;

And lastly, how 'twixt robbers crucified,
With bitter wounds through hands, through feet, and
    side!

Then let thy flinty heart, that feels no pain,
Empiercéd be with pitiful remorse,
And let thy bowels bleed in every vein,
At sight of his most sacred heavenly corse,
So torn and mangled with malicious force;
And let thy soul, whose sins his sorrows wrought,
Melt into tears, and groan in grievéd thought.

With sense whereof, whilst so thy softened spirit
Is inly toucht, and humbled with meek zeal
Through meditation of his endless merit,
Lift up thy mind to th' Author of thy weal,
And to his sovereign mercy do appeal;
Learn him to love that lovéd thee so dear,
And in thy breast his blesséd image bear.

With all thy heart, with all thy soul and mind,
Thou must him love, and his behests embrace;
All other loves, with which the world doth blind
Weak fancies, and stir up affections base,
Thou must renounce and utterly displace,
And give thyself unto him full and free,
That full and freely gave himself to thee.

Then shalt thou feel thy spirit so possest,
And ravisht with devouring great desire
Of his dear self, that shall thy feeble breast
Inflame with love, and set thee all on fire
With burning zeal, through every part entire,
That in no earthly thing thou shalt delight,
But in his sweet and amiable sight.

Thenceforth all world's desire will in thee die,
And all earth's glory, on which men do gaze,
Seem dirt and dross in thy pure-sighted eye,
Compared to that celestial beauty's blaze,
Whose glorious beams all fleshly sense doth daze
With admiration of their passing light,
Blinding the eyes, and lumining the sprite.

Then shall thy ravisht soul inspiréd be
With heavenly thoughts far above human skill,
And thy bright radiant eyes shall plainly see
Th' Idea of his pure glory present still
Before thy face, that all thy spirits shall fill
With sweet enragement of celestial love,
Kindled through sight of those fair things above.

AN HYMN OF HEAVENLY BEAUTY

RAPT with the rage of mine own ravisht thought,
Through contemplation of those goodly sights,
And glorious images in heaven wrought,
Whose wondrous beauty, breathing sweet delights
Do kindle love in high-conceited sprites;
I fain to tell the things that I behold,
But feel my wits to fail, and tongue to fold.

Vouchsafe then, O thou most Almighty Sprite!
From whom all gifts of wit and knowledge flow,
To shed into my breast some sparkling light
Of thine eternal Truth, that I may show
Some little beams to mortal eyes below
Of that immortal beauty, there with thee,
Which in my weak distraughted mind I see;

That with the glory of so goodly sight
The hearts of men, which fondly here admire
Fair seeming shews, and feed on vain delight,
Transported with celestial desire
Of those fair forms, may lift themselves up higher,
And learn to love, with zealous humble duty,
Th' eternal fountain of that heavenly beauty.

Beginning then below, with th' easy view
Of this base world, subject to fleshly eye,
From thence to mount aloft, by order due,
To contemplation of th' immortal sky;
Of the sore falcon so I learn to fly,
That flags awhile her fluttering wings beneath,
Till she herself for stronger flight can breathe.

Then look, who list thy gazeful eyes to feed
With sight of that is fair, look on the frame
Of this wide universe, and therein rede
The endless kinds of creatures which by name
Thou canst not count, much less their natures aim;
All which are made with wondrous wise respect,
And all with admirable beauty deckt.

First, th' earth, on adamantine pillars founded
Amid the sea, engirt with brazen bands;
Then th' air still flitting, but yet firmly bounded
On every side, with piles of flaming brands,
Never consumed, nor quencht with mortal hands;
And, last, that mighty shining crystal wall,
Wherewith he hath encompasséd this All.

By view whereof it plainly may appear,
That still as everything doth upward tend,
And further is from earth, so still more clear
And fair it grows, till to his perfect end
Of purest beauty it at last ascend;
Air more than water, fire much more than air,
And heaven than fire, appears more pure and fair.

Look thou no further, but affix thine eye
On that bright, shiny, round, still moving mass,
The house of blessed God, which men call sky,
All sowed with glist'ring stars more thick than grass,
Whereof each other doth in brightness pass,
But those two most, which, ruling night and day,
As king and queen, the heavens' empire sway;

And tell me then, what hast thou ever seen
That to their beauty may comparéd be,
Or can the sight that is most sharp and keen
Endure their Captain's flaming head to see?
How much less those, much higher in degree,
And so much fairer, and much more than these,
As these are fairer than the land and seas?

For far above these heavens, which here we see
Be others far exceeding these in light,
Not bounded, not corrupt, as these same be,

But infinite in largeness and in height,
Unmoving, uncorrupt, and spotless bright,
That need no sun t' illuminate their spheres,
But their own native light far passing theirs.

And as these heavens still by degrees arise,
Until they come to their first Mover's bound,
That in his mighty compass doth comprise,
And carry all the rest with him around;
So those likewise do by degrees redound,
And rise more fair; till they at last arrive
To the most fair, whereto they all do strive.

Fair is the heaven where happy souls have place,
In full enjoyment of felicity,
Whence they do still behold the glorious face
Of the Divine Eternal Majesty;
More fair is that, where those Ideas on high
Enrangéd be, which Plato so admired,
And pure Intelligences from God inspired.

Yet fairer is that heaven, in which do reign
The sovereign Powers and mighty Potentates,
Which in their high protections do contain
All mortal princes and imperial states;
And fairer yet, whereas the royal Seats
And heavenly Dominations are set,
From whom all earthly governance is fet.

Yet far more fair be those bright Cherubins,
Which all with golden wings are overdight,
And those eternal burning Seraphins,
Which from their faces dart out fiery light;
Yet fairer than they both, and much more bright,
Be th' Angels and Archangels, which attend
On God's own person, without rest or end.

These thus in fair each other far excelling,
As to the Highest they approach more near,
Yet is that Highest far beyond all telling,
Fairer than all the rest which there appear,
Though all their beauties joined together were;
How then can mortal tongue hope to express
The image of such endless perfectness?

HYMN OF HEAVENLY BEAUTY

Cease then, my tongue! and lend unto my mind
Leave to bethink how great that beauty is,
Whose utmost parts so beautiful I find;
How much more those essential parts of his,
His truth, his love, his wisdom, and his bliss,
His grace, his doom, his mercy, and his might,
By which he lends us of himself a sight!

Those unto all he daily doth display,
And shew himself in th' image of his grace,
As in a looking-glass, through which he may
Be seen of all his creatures vile and base,
That are unable else to see his face,
His glorious face! which glistereth else so bright,
That th' Angels selves cannot endure his sight.

But we, frail wights! whose sight cannot sustain
The sun's bright beams when he on us doth shine,
But that their points rebutted back again
Are dulled, how can we see with feeble eyne
The glory of that Majesty Divine,
In sight of whom both sun and moon are dark,
Comparéd to his least resplendent spark?

The means, therefore, which unto us is lent
Him to behold, is on his works to look,
Which he hath made in beauty excellent,
And in the same, as in a brazen book,
To read enregist'red in every nook
His goodness, which his beauty doth declare;
For all that's good is beautiful and fair.

Thence gathering plumes of perfect speculation,
To imp the wings of thy high-flying mind,
Mount up aloft through heavenly contemplation,
From this dark world, whose damps the soul do blind,
And, like the native brood of eagles' kind,
On that bright Sun of Glory fix thine eyes,
Cleared from gross mists of frail infirmities.

Humbled with fear and awful reverence,
Before the footstool of his majesty
Throw thyself down, with trembling innocence,

Ne dare look up with córruptible eye
On the dread face of that great Deity,
For fear, lest if he chance to look on thee,
Thou turn to nought, and quite confounded be.

But lowly fall before his mercy seat,
Close covered with the Lamb's integrity
From the just wrath of his avengeful threat
That sits upon the righteous throne on high;
His throne is built upon Eternity,
More firm and durable than steel or brass,
Or the hard diamond, which them both doth pass.

His sceptre is the rod of Righteousness,
With which he bruiseth all his foes to dust,
And the great Dragon strongly doth repress,
Under the rigour of his judgement just;
His seat is Truth, to which the faithful trust,
From whence proceed her beams so pure and bright
That all about him sheddeth glorious light:

Light, far exceeding that bright blazing spark
Which darted is from Titan's flaming head,
That with his beams enlumineth the dark
And dampish air, whereby all things are read;
Whose nature yet so much is marvelléd
Of mortal wits, that it doth much amaze
The greatest wizards which thereon do gaze.

But that immortal light, which there doth shine,
Is many thousand times more bright, more clear,
More excellent, more glorious, more divine,
Through which to God all mortal actions here,
And even the thoughts of men, do plain appear;
For from th' Eternal Truth it doth proceed,
Through heavenly virtue which her beams do breed.

With the great glory of that wondrous light
His throne is all encompasséd around,
And hid in his own brightness from the sight
Of all that look thereon with eyes unsound;
And underneath his feet are to be found
Thunder and lightning and tempestuous fire,
The instruments of his avenging ire.

There in his bosom Sapience doth sit,
The sovereign darling of the Deity,
Clad like a queen in royal robes, most fit
For so great power and peerless majesty,
And all with gems and jewels gorgeously
Adorned, that brighter than the stars appear,
And make her native brightness seem more clear.

And on her head a crown of purest gold
Is set, in sign of highest sovereignty;
And in her hand a sceptre she doth hold,
With which she rules the house of God on high,
And manageth the ever-moving sky,
And in the same these lower creatures all
Subjected to her power imperial.

Both heaven and earth obey unto her will,
And all the creatures which they both contain;
For of her fullness which the world doth fill
They all partake, and do in state remain
As their great Maker did at first ordain,
Through observation of her high behest,
By which they first were made, and still increast

The fairness of her face no tongue can tell;
For she the daughters of all women's race,
And angels eke, in beauty doth excel,
Sparkled on her from God's own glorious face,
And more increast by her own goodly grace,
That it doth far exceed all human thought,
Ne can on earth comparéd be to aught.

Ne could that painter (had he livéd yet)
Which pictured Venus with so curious quill,
That all posterity admiréd it,
Have portrayed this, for all his mast'ring skill;
Ne she herself, had she remainéd still,
And were as fair as fabling wits do feign,
Could once come near this beauty sovereign.

But had those wits, the wonders of their days,
Or that sweet Teian poet, which did spend
His plenteous vein in setting forth her praise,

Seen but a glimpse of this which I pretend,
How wondrously would he her face commend,
Above that idol of his feigning thought,
That all the world should with his rhymes be fraught!

How then dare I, the novice of his art,
Presume to picture so divine a wight,
Or hope t' express her least perfection's part,
Whose beauty fills the heavens with her light,
And darks the earth with shadow of her sight?
Ah, gentle Muse! thou art too weak and faint
The portrait of so heavenly hue to paint.

Let angels, which her goodly face behold
And see at will, her sovereign praises sing,
And those most sacred mysteries unfold
Of that fair love of mighty heaven's King;
Enough is me t' admire so heavenly thing,
And being thus with her huge love possest,
In th' only wonder of herself to rest.

But whoso may, thrice happy man him hold,
Of all on earth whom God so much doth grace
And lets his own Belovéd to behold;
For in the view of her celestial face
All joy, all bliss, all happiness, have place;
Ne aught on earth can want unto the wight
Who of herself can win the wishful sight.

For she, out of her secret treasury
Plenty of riches forth on him will pour,
Even heavenly riches, which there hidden lie
Within the closet of her chastest bower,
Th' eternal portion of her precious dower,
Which mighty God hath given to her free,
And to all those which thereof worthy be.

None thereof worthy be, but those whom she
Vouchsafeth to her presence to receive,
And letteth them her lovely face to see,
Whereof such wondrous pleasures they conceive,
And sweet contentment, that it doth bereave

Their soul of sense, through infinite delight,
And them transport from flesh into the sprite.

In which they see such admirable things,
As carries them into an ecstasy,
And hear such heavenly notes and carollings,
Of God's high praise, that fills the brazen sky;
And feel such joy and pleasure inwardly,
That maketh them all worldly cares forget,
And only think on that before them set.

Ne from thenceforth doth any fleshly sense,
Or idle thought of earthly things, remain;
But all that erst seemed sweet seems now offence,
And all that pleasèd erst now seems to pain;
Their joy, their comfort, their desire, their gain,
Is fixèd all on that which now they see;
All other sights but feignèd shadows be.

And that fair lamp, which useth to inflame
The hearts of men with self-consuming fire
Thenceforth seems foul, and full of sinful blame;
And all that pomp to which proud minds aspire
By name of honour, and so much desire,
Seems to them baseness, and all riches dross,
And all mirth sadness, and all lucre loss.

So full their eyes are of that glorious sight,
And senses fraught with such satiety,
That in nought else on earth they can delight,
But in th' aspect of that felicity,
Which they have written in their inward eye;
On which they feed, and in their fastened mind
All happy joy and full contentment find.

Ah, then, my hungry soul! which long hast fed
On idle fancies of thy foolish thought,
And, with false beauty's flatt'ring bait misled,
Hast after vain deceitful shadows sought,
Which all are fled, and now have left thee nought
But late repentance through thy follies brief;
Ah! cease to gaze on matter of thy grief:

And look at last up to that Sovereign Light,
From whose pure beams all perfect beauty springs,
That kindleth love in every godly sprite,
Even the love of God; which loathing brings
Of this vile world and these gay-seeming things;
With whose sweet pleasures being so possest,
Thy straying thoughts henceforth for ever rest.

PROTHALAMION

OR

A SPOUSAL VERSE

MADE BY
EDM. SPENSER

IN HONOUR OF THE DOUBLE MARRIAGE OF THE TWO HONOURABLE AND VIRTUOUS LADIES, THE LADY ELIZABETH AND THE LADY KATHERINE SOMERSET, DAUGHTERS TO THE RIGHT HONOURABLE THE EARL OF WORCESTER, AND ESPOUSED TO THE TWO WORTHY GENTLEMEN, M. HENRY GILFORD AND M. WILLIAM PETER, ESQUIRES

CALM was the day, and through the trembling air
Sweet-breathing Zephyrus did softly play
A gentle spirit, that lightly did delay
Hot Titan's beams, which then did glister fair;
When I (whom sullen care,
Through discontent of my long fruitless stay
In prince's court, and expectation vain
Of idle hopes, which still do fly away,
Like empty shadows, did afflict my brain),
Walked forth to ease my pain
Along the shore of silver-streaming Thames;
Whose rutty bank, the which his river hems,
Was painted all with variable flowers,
And all the meads adorned with dainty gems
Fit to deck maidens' bowers,
And crown their paramours
Against the bridal day, which is not long:
  Sweet Thames! run softly, till I end my song.

There, in a meadow, by the river's side,
A flock of nymphs I chancéd to espy,
All lovely daughters of the flood thereby,
With goodly greenish locks, all loose untied,
As each had been a bride;

And each one had a little wicker basket,
Made of fine twigs, entrailéd curiously,
In which they gathered flowers to fill their flasket,
And with fine fingers cropt full feateously
The tender stalks on high.
Of every sort, which in that meadow grew,
They gathered some; the violet, pallid blue,
The little daisy, that at evening closes,
The virgin lily, and the primrose true,
With store of vermeil roses,
To deck their bridegrooms' posies
Against the bridal day, which was not long:
   Sweet Thames! run softly, till I end my song.

With that I saw two swans of goodly hue
Come softly swimming down along the lee;
Two fairer birds I yet did never see;
The snow, which doth the top of Pindus strew,
Did never whiter shew,
Nor Jove himself, when he a swan would be,
For love of Leda, whiter did appear;
Yet Leda was (they say) as white as he,
Yet not so white as these, nor nothing near;
So purely white they were,
That even the gentle stream, the which them bare,
Seemed foul to them, and bad his billows spare
To wet their silken feathers, lest they might
Soil their fair plumes with water not so fair,
And mar their beauties bright,
That shone as heaven's light,
Against their bridal day, which was not long:
   Sweet Thames! run softly, till I end my song.

Eftsoons the nymphs, which now had flowers their fill,
Ran all in haste to see that silver brood,
As they came floating on the crystal flood;
Whom when they saw, they stood amazéd still,
Their wond'ring eyes to fill;
Them seemed they never saw a sight so fair,
Of fowls so lovely, that they sure did deem
Them heavenly born, or to be that same pair
Which through the sky draw Venus' silver team;
For sure they did not seem

PROTHALAMION

To be begot of any earthly seed,
But rather angels, or of angels' breed;
Yet were they bred of summer's-heat, they say,
In sweetest season, when each flower and weed
The earth did fresh array;
So fresh they seemed as day,
Even as their bridal day, which was not long:
    Sweet Thames! run softly, till I end my song.

Then forth they all out of their baskets drew
Great store of flowers, the honour of the field,
That to the sense did fragrant odours yield,
All which upon those goodly birds they threw
And all the waves did strew,
That like old Peneus' waters they did seem,
When down along by pleasant Tempe's shore,
Scatt'red with flowers, through Thessaly they stream,
That they appear through lilies' plenteous store,
Like a bride's chamber floor.
Two of those nymphs, meanwhile, two garlands bound
Of freshest flowers which in that mead they found,
The which presenting all in trim array,
Their snowy foreheads therewithal they crowned,
Whilst one did sing this lay,
Prepared against that day,
Against their bridal day, which was not long:
    Sweet Thames! run softly, till I end my song.

"Ye gentle birds! the world's fair ornament,
And heaven's glory, whom this happy hour
Doth lead unto your lovers' blissful bower,
Joy may you have, and gentle heart's content
Of your love's complement;
And let fair Venus, that is Queen of Love,
With her heart-quelling son upon you smile,
Whose smile, they say, hath virtue to remove
All love's dislike, and friendship's faulty guile
For ever to assoil.
Let endless peace your steadfast hearts accord,
And blessèd plenty wait upon your board:
And let your bed with pleasures chaste abound,
That fruitful issue may to you afford,

Which may your foes confound,
And make your joys redound
Upon your bridal day, which is not long:
    Sweet Thames! run softly, till I end my song."

So ended she; and all the rest around
To her redoubled that her undersong,
Which said their bridal day should not be long:
And gentle Echo from the neighbour ground
Their accents did resound.
So forth those joyous birds did pass along,
Adown the lee, that to them murmured low,
As he would speak, but that he lackt a tongue,
Yet did by signs his glad affection show,
Making his stream run slow.
And all the fowl which in his flood did dwell
Gan flock about these twain, that did excel
The rest, so far as Cynthia doth shend
The lesser stars. So they, enrangéd well,
Did on those two attend,
And their best service lend
Against their wedding day, which was not long:
    Sweet Thames! run softly, till I end my song.

At length they all to merry London came,
To merry London, my most kindly nurse,
That to me gave this life's first native source,
Though from another place I take my name,
An house of ancient fame:
There when they came, whereas those bricky towers
The which on Thames' broad agéd back do ride,
Where now the studious lawyers have their bowers,
There whilom wont the Templar Knights to bide,
Till they decayed through pride:
Next whereunto there stands a stately place,
Where oft I gainéd gifts and goodly grace
Of that great lord, which therein wont to dwell,
Whose want too well now feels my friendless case:
But ah! here fits not well
Old woes, but joys, to tell
Against the bridal day, which is not long:
    Sweet Thames! run softly, till I end my song.

PROTHALAMION

Yet therein now doth lodge a noble peer,
Great England's glory, and the world's wide wonder,
Whose dreadful name late through all Spain did thunder,
And Hercules' two pillars standing near
Did make to quake and fear:
Fair branch of honour, flower of chivalry!
That fillest England with thy triumph's fame,
Joy have thou of thy noble victory,
And endless happiness of thine own name
That promiseth the same;
That through thy prowess, and victorious arms,
Thy country may be freed from foreign harms;
And great Eliza's glorious name may ring
Through all the world, filled with thy wide alarms,
Which some brave Muse may sing
To ages following,
Upon the bridal day, which is not long:
  Sweet Thames! run softly, till I end my song.

From those high towers this noble lord issuing,
Like radiant Hesper, when his golden hair
In th' ocean billows he hath bathéd fair,
Descended to the river's open viewing,
With a great train ensuing.
Above the rest were goodly to be seen
Two gentle knights of lovely face and feature,
Beseeming well the bower of any queen,
With gifts of wit, and ornaments of nature,
Fit for so goodly stature,
That like the twins of Jove they seemed in sight,
Which deck the baldric of the heavens bright;
They two, forth pacing to the river's side,
Received those two fair brides, their love's delight;
Which, at th' appointed tide,
Each one did make his bride
Against their bridal day, which is not long:
  Sweet Thames! run softly, till I end my song.

SONNETS

WRITTEN BY SPENSER

COLLECTED FROM THE ORIGINAL PUBLICATIONS IN WHICH THEY APPEARED

I

To the right worshipful my singular good friend, M. Gabriel Harvey, Doctor of the Laws.

HARVEY, thee happy above happiest men
I rede; that, sitting like a looker-on
Of this world's stage, dost note with critic pen
The sharp dislikes of each condition:
And, as one careless of suspicion,
Ne fawnest for the favour of the great;
Ne fearest foolish reprehension
Of faulty men, which danger to thee threat:
But freely dost, of what thee list, entreat,
Like a great lord of peerless liberty;
Lifting the Good up to high honour's seat,
And the Evil damning evermore to die:
   For Life, and Death, is in thy doomful writing!
   So thy renown lives ever by inditing.

Dublin, this 18th of July, 1586.

        Your devoted friend, during life.

II

(Prefixed to "Nennio, or A Treatise of Nobility," &c.)

Whoso will seek, by right deserts, t' attain,
Unto the type of true nobility;
And not by painted shews, and titles vain,
Derivéd far from famous ancestry:
Behold them both in their right visnomy
Here truly portrayed, as they ought to be,

And striving both for terms of dignity,
To be advancéd highest in degree.
And, when thou dost with equal insight see
The odds 'twixt both, of both them deem aright,
And choose the better of them both to thee.
But thanks to him, that it deserves, behight;
  To Nenna first, that first this work created,
  And next to Jones, that truly it translated.

III

Upon the History of George Castriot, alias Scanderbeg, King of the Epirots, translated into English

Wherefore doth vain antiquity so vaunt
Her ancient monuments of mighty peers,
And old heröes, which their world did daunt
With their great deeds, and filled their children's ears?

Who, rapt with wonder of their famous praise,
Admire their statues, their colossi great,
Their rich triumphal arcs which they did raise,
Their huge pyrámids, which do heaven threat.

Lo! one, whom later age hath brought to light,
Matchable to the greatest of those great;
Great both by name, and great in power and might,
And meriting a mere triumphant seat.

  The scourge of Turks, and plague of infidels,
  Thy acts, O Scanderbeg, this volume tells.

IV

(Prefixed to "The Commonwealth and Government of Venice")

The antique Babel, Empress of the East,
Upreared her buildings to the threat'ned sky:
And second Babel, tyrant of the West,
Her airy towers upraiséd much more high.
But, with the weight of their own surquedry,

They both are fallen, that all the earth did fear,
And buried now in their own ashes lie;
Yet shewing, by their heaps, how great they were.
But in their place doth now a third appear,
Fair Venice, flower of the last world's delight;
And next to them in beauty draweth near,
But far exceeds in policy of right.
　Yet not so fair her buildings to behold
　As Lewkenor's style that hath her beauty told.

GLOSSARY

Abie, aby, to pay the penalty for, suffer for, abide by, endure
Abord, from the bank, astray, at a loss
Abusion, deception, disgrace
Accoy, to subdue, daunt, tame
Accloy, to clog, choke, encumber
Adaw, to daunt, tame, moderate
Adays, daily
Address, to prepare, adjust, direct, clothe, arm; *addrest*, ready
Adrad, afraid, terrified
Adventure, to attempt, venture
Advise, to consider, perceive, take thought of
Advisement, counsel, advice
Aetion, pseudonym for Drayton
Affect, disposition
Afflicted, low, humble
Aflot, afloat, awash, flooded
Afterclaps, unexpected strokes or events
Aggrate, to please, delight
Aguise, to deck, adorn
Albe, although, in spite of
Alegge, to lessen, allay
Algate, algates, altogether, always, by all means; nevertheless
All, although; *all as*, as if
Als, also
Alsoon, as soon
Amenance, carriage, behaviour
Apay, to please, satisfy
Arc, arch
Arede (p.p. *ared*), to tell, teach, interpret; to appoint, detect
As, as if
Assay, to try, assail; *ill assayed*, ill affected
Assize, measure, estimate
Assoil, to absolve, discharge, renew
Assoil, to assail

Assot, besotted
Assure, to assert confidently, have confidence in
Astert, to befall, come upon suddenly
Astonied, astonished, stunned
Attone, together, agreed, at one
Attones, at once
Avail, to sink, descend, lower
Avail, value, profit, benefit
Avise, to perceive, consider
Awhape, to terrify

Babe, doll
Baldric, belt
Bail, release
Bandog, mastiff
Base, the game of prisoner's base; *bidding base*, challenging at that game
Bat, stick
Bate, attacked, baited
Battailant, embattled, fortified
Behight, to speak, name, address, ordain
Behold, to hold, retain, capture
Behote, called
Belay, to beset, encompass
Belgards, fair (or kind) looks
Belive, forthwith, quickly
Bellibone, a fair maid, bonny lass
Bene, are
Bent, obedient
Beseen, "well-beseen," of good appearance, comely
Besprent, besprint, besprinkled
Bestad, bested, situated, disposed, ordered
Bet, did beat
Betight, to betide
Biggen, cap
Bilbo, Bilbao, noted for its swords

GLOSSARY

Bland, to soothe, flatter, cajole
Bloncket liveries, grey coats
Blont, blunt, unpolished, rough
Bode, dwelt; *bootless bode*, lived uselessly, without profit
Bloosme, blossom, flower
Bloosming, blossoming
Bolt, arrow
Bood, abode
Bord, to accost, talk with; *at bord*, alongside
Bordrags, border raids
Borrel, rustic
Borrow, pledge, security
Bought, fold, coil, knot
Brace, to encompass
Breach, violation
Breme, boisterous, rough, chill
Breve, briar
Brigandine, kind of light vessel
Brize, gadfly
Brocage, pimping
Bugle, glass bead
Burganet, steel cap used by pikemen
Buskets, bushes
But-if, unless
Buxom, obedient, yielding
By-and-by, one by one, immediately
Bynempt, named, bequeathed, uttered (on oath), declared
Byze, Byzantium

Cabinet, little cabin, arbour
Cærule, azure
Can, knows
Cantion, song
Careful, full of care, sorrowful
Cark, care, sorrow, grief
Case, condition, plight
Cast, to resolve, attempt
Chamfred, wrinkled, furrowed
Chanceful, risky, hazardous
Chapter, capital of a column
Charm, to tune; a tune, song
Cheer, countenance, favour, mood, food
Cherishment, tenderness
Chevisance, enterprise, undertaking
Chevisaunce, a flower

Chief, "wrought with a chief," worked with a head (like a nosegay)
Cleanly, skilfully
Clepe, to call
Clink, clicket, latch
Closely, secretly
Clouted, bandaged with a clout or rag
Cocked, in cocks or heaps
Colour, pretence
Colourable, specious, plausible
Colourably, with a hidden meaning
Coloured, deceitful, crafty
Colewort, cabbage-plant
Complement, perfection, union
Compline, evensong
Con, to know
Conceit, idea, opinion
Concent, harmony
Conditions, qualities
Conspire, to agree
Conteck, dispute
Contempt, contemned, despised
Conveyance, underhand dealing
Cope, to chop, bargain with
Copesmate, companion
Corage, nature, mind
Corbe, crooked
Corpse, (living) body
Cosset, a hand-reared lamb
Cost, to approach
Costmary, an aromatic plant, used in flavouring
Couet, to covet
Counterfeasance, counterfeiting, mimicry
Counterpoint, counterstroke; plot, trick
Cour, to cover, protect
Couth, could; knew, knew how
Crag, neck
Crank, boldly, lustily
Cratch, manger
Crazy, cracked
Crew ("priestës *crew*"), cruet, cruse
Croud, fiddle
Cruddle, to curdle
Crumenall, purse
Culver, dove

GLOSSARY

Dearnly, sorrowfully, mournfully
Deface, to abash, destroy
Defame, dishonour, disgrace
Delay, to temper
Demiss, submissive, base
Despight, anger, malice, injury, defiance
Devise, to purpose; to describe, recount
Dight, to order, arrange, dress
Diriges, dirges
Dirk, to darken; dark; darkly
Discoloured, many-coloured
Discure, to discover
Disease, to distress
Dispace (oneself), to wander to and fro
Distain, to sully, defile
Distraughted, distracted
Divide, to allocate, give forth in various directions
Divined, deified
Dole, doole, sorrow, grief
Doom, judgement, censure
'Doubted, redoubtable
Drearihead, dreariness, affliction
Dreed, dread
Drent, drowned
Droil, drudge, toil
Duest, most deserved, appropriate

Eath, easy
Edified, built
Eft, afterwards, also
Eftsoons, soon after, forthwith
Eke, to eke out, protract; also
Eld, old age
Embase, to humble, lower; *embased*, degraded
Embassade, embassy
Embay, to bathe, bask
Empale, to encircle, border
Emperish, to enfeeble
Empight, fixed
Emule, to emulate, rival
Enaunter, lest
Encheason, reason, cause, occasion
Endeavourment, endeavour, labour
Endoss, to inscribe
Engine, wile, deceit, contrivance
Engross, to write in large letters
Enrace, to implant

Enragement, rapture
Ensue, to pursue
Entertain, reception, welcome
Estranged, removed abroad
Eyas, newly fledged hawk

Fain, glad, eager; gladly
Faitour, cheat, deceiver, vagabond
Falser, a deceiver
Featously, neatly
Fee, wealth, property, service
Feign, to imagine, pretend
Fet, to fetch, derive; fetched
Fiant, warrant
Fine, to refine
Flasket, basket
Flaw, gust of wind
Fleet, to float
Fon, a fool
Fondly, fonly, foolishly
Fondness, folly
Fone, foes
For, for fear of
Forego, to go before, precede
Fore-red, foretold
Foresay, to renounce
Forhail, to distract
Forlore, forlorn, lost, deserted
Forpass, to pass by
Forswat, spent with heat
Forswonk, tired with over-work
Fren, stranger, enemy
Frorn, frozen
Frowy, musty, stale
Fume, to pass away like smoke
Funeral, death, destruction

Galage (galoche), a wooden shoe
Galingale, sweet cyperus
Gang, to go
Gar, to cause, make
Gastful, fearful, dreary
Gate, way
Gate, goat
Geason, rare, uncommon
Gelt, gold
Gelt, gelded (fig.)
Ghost, vision
Gin (pret. *gan*), to begin
Gipsen, gipsy
Girland, girlond, garland
Giust, tournament, tilt

GLOSSARY

Glade, to gladden
Glitterand, glittering
Glose, to comment on, interpret
Goodlihead, goodness, goodly appearance
Goolds, marigolds
Gossip, kinsman
Grail, gravel
Grase, to grow, be prevalent
Grate, to fret, harass
Gree, rank, station, degree
Greet, to weep; weeping, lamentation
Gride, to pierce
Gulf, throat, maw
Gulfing, flowing (like a gulf)

Had-I-wist (=had I known), a vain regret or pursuit
Hale, health, welfare
Han, have
Happely, haply, by chance
Hask, a wicker basket for fish
Heame, home
Heartless, timid
Heben, ebony
Heeling, heel-piece of a stocking
Hem, them
Hent, took, seized
Her, their
Herse, the solemn obsequy in a funeral
Hery, to praise, worship, honour
Hest, behest, command
Heydeguies, lively dances
Hidder, young male sheep
Hight, is called; called, summoned
Host, to entertain, lodge; *to host*, to be guests
Hote (cf. *hight*), was called; mentioned
Hove, to abide, wait, linger
Hugger-mugger, in secret, secretly
Husband, husbandman, farmer

Imp, scion, child, offspring
Impacable, unappeasable
Indignify, to disparage
Infest, to attack, assail; to make hostile
Infuse, infusion
Ingate, entrance

Inly, inwardly, thoroughly
Inn, dwelling, lodging
Intendiment, knowledge, understanding
Interdeal, negotiation
Inure, to use, practise, accustom

Jacob staff, a pilgrim's staff
Jasp, jasper
Javel, a worthless wretch
Jolly, handsome, gallant, cheerful, big
Jouissance, merriment, mirth

Keep, to take heed, take care of; that which is kept, charge; heed, care
Ken, to know, try, ascertain, recognize
Kerns, rustics, peasants
Kesar, emperor
Kidst, knewest
Kind, nature, sex, respect, manner

Layd, faint, reduced, subdued
Larded, fattened
Latched, seized, caught
Launch, to lance, pierce
Lay, laity
Lay, lea, field
Leaps, baskets in which to catch or keep fish
Leasing, lying, falsehood
Ledden, dialect, speech
Lee, river, current
Leese, to loose
Lepped, did leap
Lere, to learn; lesson, lore
Levin, lightning
Lewd, ignorant, wicked, foolish
Lief, dear, beloved; willing
Lig, ligge, to lie
Light, quickly
Likely, similar
Lin, to cease
Line, linen
List, to desire, like; (impers.) to please
Livelode, livelihood
Loast, loosened, loose
Lope, leapt
Lore, lorn, left, deserted

GLOSSARY

Lorrel, rogue, blackguard
Losed, loosed
Lout, to bow, do obeisance
Lust, pleasure, desire; to wish for
Lustihead, pleasure, lustfulness, vigour, lustiness
Lymiter, a friar licensed to beg within a certain district

Macerate, to harass
Madding, frenzied
Maidenhead, first-fruits
Maintenance, behaviour
Make, to write poetry
Make, companion, mate
Malefice, evil deed
Maliced, regarded with malice
Mantle, to stretch the wings (as a hawk on its perch)
Martyrize, to devote as a martyr
Mavis, song-thrush
May, maiden
Mazer, a bowl or drinking-cup made of maple-wood
Meanly, moderately
Meare, boundary
Medle, to mix
Meint, ment, meynt, mingled, united
Melampode, black hellebore
Melling, meddling
Memories, services for the dead
Mew, to imprison; den, prison
Misgone, gone astray
Misguide, trespass
Missay, to speak ill
Mister, sort of, manner of
Mo, moe, more
Mochell, much
Moil, to defile
Moldwarp, mole
Moorish, marshy
Morion, helmet
Most-what, generally, for the most part
Mote, may, must, might
Mott, measured
Mought, might, could
Mystery, profession, trade

Nar, near, nearer
Nas, has not
Natheless, nathless, netheless, none the less, nevertheless
Ne, nor
Needments, necessaries
Newel, new thing
Nigh, to draw near
Nill, will not
Nip, to slander
Nis, is not
Not, know not
Nould, would not
Nourice, nurse
Novels, news
Noyous, disagreeable
Nurtred, trained, skilled

Orichalc, a kind of brass
Ought, owned, owed
Ouzel, blackbird
Over-all, everywhere
Overcraw, to crow over
Overdight, covered over, overspread
Overgive, to give over
Overgo, to surpass, overcome
Overgrast, grown over with grass
Overhail, to draw over
Overkest, overcast
Owe (*her fall*), be bound (to fall)

Paddock, toad
Painful, painstaking, hard-working
Pall, a cloak of rich material
Paragon, companion, equal, match
Paravant, pre-eminently
Parget, plaster
Passionate, that moves to compassion, pitiful
Paunce, pansy
Peize, to weigh down
Perdie (=*par dieu*), truly, certainly, indeed
Peregal, equal
Perseline, parsley
Pieced, imperfect
Pight, fixed, placed, fastened
Pill, to spoil, plunder
Pine, sorrow, grief
Plain, to complain, lament
Port, portance, demeanour, bearing

Pouke, the goblin known as Puck or Robin Goodfellow
Pouldred, powdered, spotted
Pousse, pease, pulse
Prick, bull's-eye of target
Pricket, a buck in its second year
Prief, proof, experience
Prime, spring-time, morning (6 a.m.)
Primitias, first-fruits
Primrose (fig.), the chief, the most excellent
Principals, the two principal feathers in each wing (falconry)
Purchase, to obtain, get, win
Pursuivant, pursuer, officer with warrant

Quail, to fade, wither
Queme, to please
Quire, company
Quit, quite (p.p. *quight*), to set free, requite, repay
Quook, quaked

Rabblement, rabble, confusion, tumult
Rackt, extorted
Rail, to flow, pour down
Rakehell, worthless, rascally
Rathe, early, quickly, soon
Rather, early-born
Raught, reached, granted
Raunch, to wrench
Ray, to defile, soil
Reave (pret. *reft, raft*), to bereave, take away (forcibly)
Recure, to cure; to recover, regain
Red, made ready
Rede, to know, declare, explain or advise, discover, perceive; advice, counsel
Reek, to care, reck
Regiment, government, domain
Revoked, called back
Rew, row; *in rew*, in order
Ronts, runts, young bullocks
Roundle, roundelay
Rout, crowd, troop
Rove, to shoot at a chance mark (archery)
Ruddock, redbreast
Rueless, ruthless
Rutty, rooty

Sale, a wicker net (made of sallows or willows)
Sample, example
Say, a fine cloth
Scarabee, a beetle
Scath, hurt, damage, ruin
Scope, aim
Sdeign, to disdain; disdain
Sdeignful, disdainful
Seem, to beseem
Self, selfsame
Setuale, valerian
Shend, to disgrace, put to shame, surpass
Shidder, young female sheep
Shield, "God shield," God forbid
Shrifts, confessions
Sib, akin, related
Sicker, surely, certainly
Sike, such
Silly, simple, innocent
Singults, sobs
Sith, since
Sithe, time
Sithens, since, since that time
Sits, is becoming
Skill, to signify, to be a matter of importance
Slipper, slippery
Smirk, neat, trim
Sneb, snib, to reprove, snub
Solein, sad
Somedeal, somewhat
Soot, sweetly
Sooth, augury, truth
Sops in wine, a pink, the clove-pink
Sore falcon, a falcon of the first year
Sort, company; to associate with
Sovenance, remembrance
Speculation, seeing, vision
Speed, to succeed
Sperre, to bolt, shut
Spight, injury, disgrace
Spill, to ravage, destroy
Spired forth, shot forth
Spring, springal, youth
Squib, a paltry trifling fellow

GLOSSARY

Stain, to eclipse, excel
Stalled, rescued, released
Stank, weary
Startup, rustic half-boot or buskin
State, stately
Stay, duration
Stead, station, place
Steven, voice, cry
Stie, to ascend
Stomach, courage, spirit
Stonied, astonished, alarmed
Sound, a moment of time
Stound, astonishment, amazement, trouble, sorrow
Stour, tumult, disturbance, battle, passion, fit
Strain, to constrain, force; to put into verse
Strake, struck
Stud, trunk, stock; shrub, bush
Sue, to follow, solicit
Suffisance, abundance
Surquedry, pride, insolence, presumption
Surview, to overlook, survey
Swain, labourer, youth
Swerd, sword
Swink, labour, toil
Swound, swoon

Tabrere, player on a tabor or drum
Taking, plight, condition
Tambourins, small drums
Tapet, tapestry, figured work
Tawdry lace, a lace (girdle) such as was bought at the fair of St. Audrey (Etheldreda)
Tead, torch
Teen, grief, sorrow, pain
Temperature, commixture
Termless, unlimited
Thereto, besides
Thewed, trained, instructed, endued
Thilk, that same, this
Tho, then
Throughly, thoroughly
Tickle, uncertain, insecure
Tide, time, season, opportunity
Timeless, untimely
Timely, seasonable, early
Tinct, tinged

Tine, affliction, pain, sorrow
Tined, kindled
Tire, to attire, adorn
Tod, a thick bush
Too, very; *too very*, exceedingly
Tooting, spying out, peeping
Trace, to walk, pursue one's way
Tract, track, trace, course (of time)
Train, wile, deceit, snare
Treachour, traitor
Trentals, services of thirty masses for the dead
Trode, path, footstep; trodden
Try, to experience, contend, prove; *a daw try*, prove a jackdaw or fool
Tyranne, tyrant

Uncase, to strip
Uncrudded, uncurdled
Underfong, to ensnare, entrap; to undertake
Underlay, to surpass
Undersay, to affirm in contra- to any one
Undersong, burden (of a song)
Uneath, scarcely, with difficulty, uneasily; difficult
Unhappy, unfortunate
Unkent, unknown
Unkind, unnatural
Unsoot, unsweet
Until, unto, towards
Unweeting, not knowing, unconscious
Unwont, unaccustomed
Usurped, used, affected
Utter, to put out or forth

Vade, to go, vanish
Vainesse, vanity
Villain, vile
Virelays, light songs
Visnomy, physiognomy, visage
Void, to go, depart

Wailful, lamentable
War, worse
War, knob or protuberance on a tree
Warreyed, made war on
Wayment, to lament; lamentation

GLOSSARY

Weanel, a weanling, lamb or kid
Weet, to know
Weetless, unconscious, ignorant, thoughtless
Weld, to wield, govern, influence
Welk, to wane, fade
Wex, to wax, grow, become
What for a, what sort of a
Whelky, shelly
Whenas, when
Whereas, where
Whether, whither, which of two
Whilom, formerly, once
Wight, person, being
Wight, active
Wightly, quickly
Wimble, nimble
Witch, reed
Wite, blame; *witen*, to blame
Witeless, blameless
Womanhead, womanhood, womankind, womanliness
Won (*wonning*), dwelling-place, abode
Won, *woon*, to dwell
Wonned, were wont
Wood, mad, frantic, furious
Wot, know, knows
Wox, *woxen*, become, grown
Wrack, wreck, destruction
Wroken, avenged
Wry, awry, crooked
Wull, will

Yate, gate
Yblent, blinded, dazzled
Yclepe, to call
Yconned, learnt
Ydrad, afraid
Yede, to go
Yeven, given
Yfere, together, in company with
Ylk, same
Yode, went
Youngth, youth
Youngthly, youthful
Younker, a youth
Ythundered, struck by a thunderbolt
Ytost, harassed
Ywis, certainly, truly
Ywroken, avenged

EVERYMAN'S LIBRARY AND EVERYMAN PAPERBACKS: A Selection

indicates the volumes also in paperback: for their series numbers in Everyman Paperbacks add 1000 to the EML numbers given.

BIOGRAPHY

Brontë, Charlotte. *Life* by Mrs Gaskell	318
Byron, Lord. *Letters*	931
Cellini, Benvenuto. *The Life of Benvenuto Cellini*	51
Dickens, Charles. *Life* by John Forster	781, 782
Evelyn, John. *Diary*	220, 221
Hudson, W. H. *Far Away and Long Ago*	956
Hutchinson, Mrs Lucy. *Memoirs of the Life of Colonel Hutchinson*	317
Johnson, Dr Samuel. *Boswell's Life of Dr Johnson,*	1, 2
Keats, John. *Life and Letters* by Lord Houghton	801
Lives of the English Poets by Dr Samuel Johnson	770, 771
Napoleon Buonaparte. *Letters*	995
Nelson. *Letters*	244
Pepys, Samuel. *Diary*	53, 54, 55
Scott, Sir Walter. Lockhart's *Life of Scott*	39
Sévigné, Mme de. *Selected Letters*	98
Vasari, Giorgio. *Lives of the Painters, Sculptors and Architects*	784, 785, 786, 787

ESSAYS AND CRITICISM

Bacon, Francis. *Essays*	10
Chesterton, G. K. *Stories, Essays and Poems*	913
Coleridge, Samuel Taylor. *Shakespearean Criticism*	162, 183
De Quincey, Thomas. *Confessions of an English Opium-Eater*	223
The English Mail Coach and Other Writings	609
Eckermann. *Conversations with Goethe*	851
Emerson, R. Waldo. *Essays*	12
An Everyman Anthology	663
Hazlitt, William. *Lectures on the English Comic Writers*	411
Huxley, Aldous. *Stories, Essays and Poems*	935
Johnson, Dr Samuel. *The Rambler*	994
Lamb, Charles. *Essays of Elia* and *Last Essays of Elia*	14
Lawrence, D. H. *Stories, Essays and Poems*	958
Macaulay, Thomas B.	
Critical and Historical Essays	225, 226
Miscellaneous Essays; Lays of Ancient Rome; Miscellaneous Poems	439
Machiavelli, Niccolo. *The Prince*	280
Milton, John. *Prose Writings*	795

Mitford, Mary. *Our Village*	927
Newman, Cardinal. *On the Scope and Nature of University Education;* and *Christianity and Scientific Investigation*	723
*Paine, Thomas. *The Rights of Man*	718
Rousseau, J.-J. *Émile*	518
Steele, Richard. *The Tatler*	993
Writing of the 'Nineties. From Wilde to Beerbohm	773

FICTION

*American Short Stories	840
Austen, Jane. The principal novels including:	
Emma	24
Mansfield Park	23
Northanger Abbey and *Persuasion*	25
Pride and Prejudice	22
Sense and Sensibility	21
Balzac, Honoré de	
The Country Doctor	530
Eugénie Grandet	169
Old Goriot	170
Bennett, Arnold. *The Old Wives' Tale*	919
*Boccaccio, Giovanni. *Decameron*	845, 846
*Borrow, George. *The Romany Rye*	120
Brontë, Anne. *The Tenant of Wildfell Hall* and *Agnes Grey*	685
Brontë, Charlotte	
Jane Eyre	287
The Professor	417
Shirley	288
Villette	351
*Brontë, Emily. *Wuthering Heights* and *Poems*	243
*Bunyan, John. *Pilgrim's Progress,* Parts I and II	204
Butler, Samuel. *Erewhon* and *Erewhon Revisited*	881
*Carroll, Lewis. *Alice in Wonderland; Through the Looking Glass*	836
Cervantes, Miguel de. *Don Quixote de la Mancha*	385, 386
Collins, Wilkie	
The Moonstone	979
The Woman in White	464
Conrad, Joseph	
Lord Jim	925
The Nigger of the 'Narcissus'; Typhoon; The Shadow Line	980
Nostromo	38
The Secret Agent	282
Defoe, Daniel	
The Fortunes and Misfortunes of Moll Flanders	837
The Life, Adventures and Piracies of the Famous Captain Singleton	74
Robinson Crusoe and *The Farther Adventures of Robinson Crusoe.* Parts I and II complete	59

Dickens, Charles. The principal novels including:
*Barnaby Rudge	76
Bleak House	236
*A Christmas Carol and other Christmas Books	239
David Copperfield	242
*Great Expectations	234
*Hard Times	292
*Little Dorrit	293
Martin Chuzzlewit	241
Nicholas Nickleby	238
The Old Curiosity Shop	173
*Oliver Twist	233
*The Pickwick Papers	235
*A Tale of Two Cities	102

Dostoyevsky, Fyodor. The principal novels including:
The Brothers Karamazov	802, 803
*Crime and Punishment	501
*The House of the Dead	533
*The Idiot	682
*Letters from the Underworld and Other Tales	654

Dumas, Alexandre. The principal novels including:
*The Black Tulip	174
The Count of Monte Cristo	393, 394
*The Three Musketeers	81
Twenty Years After	175

Eliot, George. The principal novels including:
*Adam Bede	27
Daniel Deronda	539, 540
Middlemarch	854, 855
*The Mill on the Floss	325
*Silas Marner, the Weaver of Raveloe	121

Fielding, Henry
Amelia	852, 853
*Joseph Andrews	467
*Tom Jones	355, 356

Flaubert, Gustave
Madame Bovary	808
*Salammbô	869
*Sentimental Education	969

Forster, E. M.
A Passage to India	972

France, Anatole. At the Sign of the Reine Pédauque and The Revolt of the Angels — 967

French Short Stories of the 19th and 20th Centuries — 896

Gaskell, Mrs Elizabeth. The principal novels including:
*Cranford	83
*Mary Barton	598
North and South	680
Sylvia's Lovers	524
Wives and Daughters	110

Gogol, Nikolay. *Dead Souls*	72
*Goldsmith, Oliver. *The Vicar of Wakefield*	29
*Goncharov, Ivan. *Oblomov*	87
*Gorky, Maxim. *Through Russia*	74
*Grossmith, George. *The Diary of a Nobody*	96
*Hardy, Thomas. *Stories and Poems*	70
Hawthorne, Nathaniel	
The House of the Seven Gables	17
The Scarlet Letter	12
Hugo, Victor	
The Hunchback of Notre Dame	42
Les Misérables	363, 36
Toilers of the Sea	50
James, Henry	
The Ambassadors	98
The Turn of the Screw and The Aspern Papers	91
*Jerome, Jerome K. *Three Men in a Boat* and *Three Men on the Bummel*	11
Kingsley, Charles. *Westward Ho!*	2
*Kipling, Rudyard. *Stories and Poems*	69
*Lytton, Lord. *The Last Days of Pompeii*	8
Maugham, Somerset. *Cakes and Ale*	93
*Maupassant, Guy de. *Short Stories*	90
*Melville, Herman. *Moby Dick; or the White Whale*; *Typee* and *Billy Budd*	18
*Meredith, George. *The Ordeal of Richard Feverel*	91
Priestley, J. B.	
Angel Pavement	93
Bright Day	67
*Pushkin, Alexander. *The Captain's Daughter and Other Stories*	89
Rabelais, François. *The Heroic Deeds of Gargantua and Pantagruel*	826, 82
Reade, Charles. *The Cloister and the Hearth*	2
Richardson, Samuel. *Clarissa*	882–
*Russian Short Stories	758
Scott, Sir Walter. The principal novels including:	
The Bride of Lammermoor	12
Guy Mannering	13
The Heart of Mid-Lothian	134
Ivanhoe	1
Quentin Durward	14
Waverley	7
*Shelley, Mary. *Frankenstein*	616
Shorter Novels, Elizabethan	824
*Sienkiewicz, Henryk. *Quo Vadis?*	970
Smollett, Tobias	
The Expedition of Humphry Clinker	97
Peregrine Pickle	838, 839
Roderick Random	790

*Somerville and Ross. *Some Experiences of an Irish R.M.*	978
Stendhal. *Scarlet and Black*	945, 946
*Sterne, Laurence. *Tristram Shandy*	617
Stevenson, R. L.	
Dr Jekyll and Mr Hyde; The Merry Men; Will o' the Mill; Markheim; Thrawn Janet; Olalla; The Treasure of Franchard	767
The Master of Ballantrae; Weir of Hermiston	764
Treasure Island and *New Arabian Nights*	763
Strindberg, Johann August. *The Red Room*	348
Surtees, Robert. *Jorrocks' Jaunts and Jollities*	817
Tales of Detection	928
Thackeray, W. M.	
Henry Esmond	73
The Newcomes	465, 466
Vanity Fair	298
The Virginians	507, 508
Tolstoy, Count Leo	
Anna Karenina	612, 613
Master and Man	469
War and Peace	525, 526, 527
Trollope, Anthony. The principal novels including:	
The Warden	182
Barchester Towers	30
Framley Parsonage	181
The Small House at Allington	361
The Last Chronicle of Barset	391, 392
Turgenev, Ivan	
Fathers and Children	742
Smoke	988
Virgin Soil	528
*Twain, Mark. *Tom Sawyer* and *Huckleberry Finn*	976
*Verne, Jules. *Five Weeks in a Balloon; Around the World in Eighty Days*	779
Voltaire	
Candide, and Other Tales	936
Wells, H. G.	
Ann Veronica	977
The Wheels of Chance; The Time Machine	915
*(Paperback) The Time Machine only	
*Woolf, Virginia. *To the Lighthouse*	949

HISTORY

Anglo-Saxon Chronicle	624
Bede, The Venerable. *The Ecclesiastical History of the English Nation*	479
*Creasy, Sir Edward. *Fifteen Decisive Battles of the World, from Marathon to Waterloo*	300

Gibbon, Edward. *The Decline and Fall of the Roman Empire*	434, 435, 436, 474, 475, 476
Green, J. R. *A Short History of the English People*	727, 728
Macaulay, Thomas B. *The History of England*	34, 35, 36, 37
Prescott, W. H.	
History of the Conquest of Mexico	397, 398
*History of the Conquest of Peru	301
Thucydides. *History of the Peloponnesian War*	455

LEGENDS AND SAGAS

Chrétien de Troyes. *Arthurian Romances*	698
Kalevala, or the Land of Heroes	259, 260
Layamon and Wace. *Arthurian Chronicles*	578
The Mabinogion	97
Malory, Sir Thomas. *Le Morte D'Arthur*	45, 46
The Nibelungenlied	312
*The Story of Burnt Njal	558

POETRY AND DRAMA

Anglo-Saxon Poetry	794
*Barrie, J. M. *Plays and Stories*	184
Beaumont and Fletcher. *Select Plays*	506
*Blake, William. *Poems and Prophecies*	792
A Book of British Ballads	572
Browning, Robert. *Poems and Plays*	41, 42, 502, 965, 966
*Burns, Robert. *Poems and Songs*	94
Chaucer, Geoffrey	
Canterbury Tales	307
Troilus and Criseyde	992
Clare, John. *Selected Poems*	563
Cowper, William. *Poems*	872
*Dante, Alighieri. *The Divine Comedy*	308
Donne, John. *Complete Poems*	867
Dryden, John. *Poems*	910
*Eighteenth-Century Plays (Paperback under title 'The Beggar's Opera')	818
Everyman and Medieval Miracle Plays	381
Goldsmith, Oliver. *Poems and Plays*	415
Homer	
Iliad	453
Odyssey	454
Horace. *The Collected Works*	515
Ibsen, Henrik	
A Doll's House; The Wild Duck; The Lady from the Sea	494

*Ghosts; The Warriors at Helgeland; An Enemy of the People	552
Peer Gynt	747
*International Modern Plays	989
Jonson, Ben. Plays	489, 490
*Keats, John. Poems	101
Langland, William. Piers Plowman	571
Marlowe, Christopher. Plays and Poems	383
Milton, John. Poems	384
Molière, Jean Baptiste Poquelin de. Comedies	830, 831
*Poe, Edgar Allan. Poems and Essays	791
*Poems of Our Time, 1900–60	981
*Restoration Plays	604
Shakespeare, William. Plays	153, 154, 155
Shaw, George Bernard. The Devil's Disciple; Major Barbara; Saint Joan	109
Spenser, Edmund. The Faerie Queene	443, 444
*Synge, J. M. Plays, Poems and Prose	968
*Tchekhov, Anton. Plays and Stories	941
*Thomas, Dylan. Collected Poems: 1934–1952 (Aldine Paperback 87)	581
*Twenty-four One-Act Plays	947
*Webster, John, and Ford, John. Selected Plays	899
Whitman, Walt. Leaves of Grass	573
*Wilde, Oscar. Plays, Prose Writings and Poems	858
Wordsworth, William, Poems	203, 311, 998

RELIGION AND PHILOSOPHY

Aristotle. Metaphysics	1000
Augustine, Saint. Confessions	200
Berkeley, George. A New Theory of Vision, and Other Writings	483
*Browne, Sir Thomas. Religio Medici, and Other writings	92
Burton, Robert. The Anatomy of Melancholy	886, 887, 889
Chinese Philosophy in Classical Times	973
Descartes, René. A Discourse on Method; Meditations on the First Philosophy; Principles of Philosophy	570
Hindu Scriptures	944
*Kant, Immanuel. Critique of Pure Reason	909
The Koran	380
Law, William. A Serious Call to a Devout and Holy Life	91
Leibniz, Gottfried. Philosophical Writings	905
Locke, John. An Essay Concerning Human Understanding	332, 984
Marcus Aurelius Antoninus. The Meditations of Marcus Aurelius	9
More, Sir Thomas. Utopia	461

Pascal, Blaise. *Pensées*	874
Plato	
The Laws	275
The Republic	64
The Trial and Death of Socrates	457
Prayer Books of Edward VI	448
Spinoza, Benedictus de. *Ethics; On the Correction of the Understanding*	481

SCIENCES: POLITICAL AND GENERAL

Aristotle. *Ethics*	547
Boyle, Robert. *The Sceptical Chymist*	559
Darwin, Charles. *The Origin of Species*	811
Euclid. *The Elements of Euclid*	891
Hobbes, Thomas. *Leviathan*	691
Locke, John. *Two Treatises of Civil Government*	751
Marx, Karl. *Capital*	848, 849
Mill, John Stuart. *Utilitarianism; Liberty; Representative Government*	482
Owen, Robert. *A New View of Society* and *Other Writings*	799
Ricardo, David. *The Principles of Political Economy and Taxation*	590
Smith, Adam. *The Wealth of Nations*	412, 413
Wollstonecraft, Mary. *The Rights of Women*	825

TRAVEL AND TOPOGRAPHY

Bates, H. W. *The Naturalist on the River Amazons*	446
Borrow, George. *The Bible in Spain*	151
Boswell, James. *Journal of a Tour to the Hebrides with Samuel Johnson*	387
Calderón de la Barca, Frances. *Life in Mexico*	664
Cobbett, William. *Rural Rides*	638, 639
Cook, Captain James. *Voyages of Discovery*	99
Darwin, Charles. *The Voyage of the 'Beagle'*	104
Defoe, Daniel. *A Tour Through the Whole Island of Great Britain*	820, 821
Kinglake, A. W. *Eothen*	337
*****Park, Mungo,** *Travels*	205
*****Polo, Marco.** *Travels*	306
Portuguese Voyages	986
Speke, John Hanning. *Journal of the Discovery of the Source of ths Nile*	50
Stevenson, R. L. *An Inland Voyage; Travels with a Donkey; The Silverado Squatters*	766
*****Stow, John.** *The Survey of London*	589
*****White, Gilbert.** *A Natural History of Selborne*	48